"So how do **in front of my**

Mohab took Jala's hands to his lips. "I intend to show everyone how proud I am to be your intended, that this was a hope I had since I first saw you."

She withdrew her hands. "No need to go overboard or you'll only make them suspicious."

She didn't believe him. He hadn't thought of marriage in the years he'd craved her from afar, since he'd never thought marriage was in the cards for him at all.

But now, with the turn his life had taken, everything was different. He'd come here still not clear about what he wanted beyond that he wanted her for as long as he could have her. Now he wanted everything. "So your original agreement stands as is?"

He held his breath. Hoping against hope…

Then she breathed, "Yes."

* * *

Seducing His Princess is part of the
Married By Royal Decree series:
When the king commands, they say "I do!"

SEDUCING HIS PRINCESS

BY
OLIVIA GATES

Published in Great Britain 2014
by Mills & Boon, an imprint of Harlequin (UK) Limited,
Eton House, 18-24 Paradise Road, Richmond, Surrey, TW9 1SR

© 2014 Olivia Gates

ISBN: 978 0 263 91460 3

51-0314

Harlequin (UK) Limited's policy is to use papers that are natural, renewable and recyclable products and made from wood grown in sustainable forests. The logging and manufacturing processes conform to the legal environmental regulations of the country of origin.

Olivia Gates has always pursued creative passions such as singing and handicrafts. She still does, but only one of her passions grew gratifying enough, consuming enough, to become an ongoing career—writing.

She is most fulfilled when she is creating worlds and conflicts for her characters, then exploring and untangling them bit by bit, sharing her protagonists' every heart-wrenching heartache and hope, their every heart-pounding doubt and trial, until she leads them to an indisputably earned and gloriously satisfying happy ending.

When she's not writing, she is a doctor, a wife to her own alpha male and a mother to one brilliant girl and one demanding Angora cat. Visit Olivia at www.oliviagates.com.

To my endlessly loving and supportive mother.
Thank you for being there for me always.
Love you, always.

Prologue

Six years ago...

A fist of foreboding squeezed Mohab Aal Ghaanem's heart.

Najeeb was back. And Jala had gone to see him.

Although he had contrived to keep her from seeing Najeeb for months now as part of his original mission to keep them apart, when Najeeb had returned in spite of all his machinations, there'd been nothing further Mohab could do. Nothing but demand Jala not see Najeeb.

And what reason could he have given for asking her not to see his cousin and crown prince? That he was jealous?

She would have been shocked by the notion. At best, this would have made her think he didn't trust her, or that he wasn't the progressive man she thought him to be. Personal freedom and boundaries were very touchy subjects with her, and she had serious issues with the "repressive male dinosaurs" prevalent in their culture.

At worst, she might have suspected that he had other motives for wanting to prevent that meeting with her "best friend," motives that went beyond simple possessiveness. As he did.

So he'd stood back and watched her leave for that dreaded yet inevitable rendezvous. And she hadn't returned.

Not that she'd said she would. Having an early business meeting the next day close to her house in Long Beach, it made sense for her to spend the night at her home. He wished he could have waited for her there, but though she'd given him keys, the gesture had been only as a token of trust. She'd been adamant about not making their relationship public knowledge before she was ready to do so. He was probably working himself up for nothing but…

B'Ellahi… What was he *thinking?* It *was* for nothing. Jala had agreed to marry him. She was his, body and heart. He'd been her first, and he'd always be her only. He should have stopped worrying about how their relationship had started long ago, shouldn't have tried to keep Najeeb away once his…purpose had been achieved—even if the way it had been had taken him by surprise. He'd already been attracted to Jala, but he surely hadn't imagined when he'd first approached her that he'd fall for her that hard, that totally.

Emptying his lungs, he strode away from the window. He could barely make out anything from sixty floors up anyway.

Though he was sure he would have seen her.

Since he'd first laid eyes on her, she'd been the only one he ever truly saw, even when others should have been in his focus. As on the day of the hostage crisis, when he'd been sent to save Najeeb and had saved Jala, too.

Najeeb. Again. Everything always came back to him.

Mohab had kept his cousin away from New York, away

from Jala, for as long as possible. Any more contrivances would have made Najeeb suspect he was being manipulated. And since there were only a handful of people who had enough power to keep the crown prince of Saraya jumping—his father, King Hassan, his brothers and Mohab himself—Najeeb would have eventually drawn the proper conclusions.

By elimination, only Mohab, as the kingdom's top secret-service agent, had the skills and resources to invade Najeeb's privacy, to rearrange his plans, to nudge him wherever he wanted. The next step would have been finding out *why*.

So Mohab had been forced to let his cousin come back. To let Jala go to him. At nine o'clock this morning. That had been eleven hours ago.

What could be taking her so long?

Kaffa. Enough. Why not just call her instead of having a full-blown obsessive episode?

So he did. And it went straight to voice mail. Time and again.

When another hour passed and she hadn't called back, he tore out of his penthouse, numb with dread.

By the time he arrived at her house his nerves had snapped, one at a time. What if she was lying unconscious or unable to reach her phone? What if she'd been mugged… or worse? She was so beautiful, and he'd seen how men looked at her. What if someone had followed her home?

He barged inside and was hit at once with the certainty. She was there. Her presence permeated the place.

He ran upstairs, homing in on her. As he approached her bedroom, he heard sounds. To his distraught ears, they sounded like distress. Coming from the bathroom.

He tore inside. And there she was. In the shower cubicle. Facing the door. She saw him as soon as he saw her.

At his explosive entry, she lurched, her steam-obscured

face contorting, her lips parting. He assumed she'd gasped or even cried out. He could hear nothing now above the cacophony of his own turmoil and the spray of water. All he knew was that she was here. She was safe.

And he was tearing off his clothes, his only need to prove to himself both facts.

Then he was inside the cubicle, dragging her into his arms, groaning as he felt her warm resilience slamming against his aching flesh, her cry shuddering through him as he drove trembling hands into her soaked tresses, his feverish gaze roaming her water-streaked face. That face, that body, that essence, had taken control of his fantasies from the instant he'd seen her, from the very moment he'd claimed her. And she'd claimed him right back. Throughout these past five months, with each caress, with each passion-filled encounter, he found himself craving her more and more. His hunger for her knew no bounds.

"Mohab…"

He swallowed her gasp, drove his tongue inside her fragrant, delicious depths and she started squirming, building his fire higher. He needed to be inside her, possessing her, pleasuring her. Reassuring himself she was whole and all his.

His hand glided between her smooth thighs, sought her core. His fingers slid between her slick folds, and his head almost burst with the sledgehammer of arousal. Knowing she would love his urgency, that the edge of discomfort his ferocity would cause would amplify her pleasure, he cupped her perfect buttocks and opened her silky thighs around his hips. Capturing her lips again and again in ravaging kisses, he sought her entrance, flexed then sheathed himself in her molten tightness in one long, forceful thrust.

The sharpness of her cry, a testament to the intensity of her enjoyment, heightened his frenzy, her hot gust of passion expanding in his own lungs. Then he withdrew and pistoned back, needing to merge with her, dissolve in her, knowing it would send her berserk. It was unraveling him, too—acute sensations layering with every plunge, ratcheting with each withdrawal. The carnal groans torn from their depths rode him higher and higher. He felt his climax hurtling from his very essence, felt her shuddering uncontrollably, heard the sound of her tortured squeals telling him she'd explode in ecstasy if he gave her the cadence and force she needed.

Unable to prolong this torment a second more, he gave it to her, his full force behind his jackhammering thrusts, until she convulsed in his arms and her shrieks of pleasure snapped his own tension. He all but felt himself detonate in a violent release, the most intense he'd ever felt, his seed burning through his length, jetting into her depths to mingle with her own gushing climax.

At last, the severity of sensations leveled, leaving him so satiated, so depleted, he could barely stand. She collapsed in his arms as she always did. Taking her down to the floor, he soothed her, and she surrendered to his ministrations, letting him fondle and suckle her, pour wonder and worship all over her.

Then he carried her out of the shower and dried them both off. As he bent to take her to bed, she pushed out of his arms, unsteadily waddling away to fetch her bathrobe.

He winced. How insensitive could he be? He'd scared her witless bursting in here, made her limp with satiation for hours and could only think of continuing their intimacies?

He put on his pants as she turned to him, wrapped in the stark white bathrobe, her golden flesh glowing in contrast. The need to ravish her again almost overpowered him.

"What was *that* all about?"

He saw the hardness in her eyes before he heard it in her tone. Something he'd never been exposed to before.

Suddenly wary, he shrugged. "Wasn't it self-evident?"

"Not to me. What brought you here in the first place?"

Disturbed by her coldness, especially after the inferno they'd just shared, he told her what he could. At the tail end of his account, he released a breath he hadn't realized he'd been holding. "And then I found you in there and all I could think was that you're safe. And I was, as always, starving for you." He tried a coaxing smile. "Finding you already unwrapped was most opportune."

"So you thought it was okay to barge in here and just have your way with me?"

The harsh accusation hit him between the eyes. She'd never been angry with him before. And to be so for the first time today, of all days, jarred him.

He found his own voice hardening. "You loved every second. You came so hard you blew my brains out."

She shrugged, not contesting that truth, those molten-gold eyes growing harder. "The point is, you disregarded my choice. Your overriding tactics have become a pattern."

"What 'overriding tactics'?"

"All your manipulation, ending with trying to keep me from seeing Najeeb. You think I'm so oblivious I didn't notice? Oh, I noticed, all right…every time you nudged and cajoled. Every time you artfully overruled me. You're almost undetectable, but I've had enough time and proximity to decipher your methods."

So she'd caught on.

Either he'd underestimated her astuteness…or he couldn't keep a cool enough head around her to maintain the seamless subterfuge he normally employed in his professional life.

Coming clean wasn't an option, though. He couldn't let her know why he'd originally approached her, or how he'd kept Najeeb away, or why. He couldn't risk that she might suspect the genuineness of his current involvement. They already had too much working against their relationship to introduce internal strife. The feud that had long raged between their families was enough of an obstacle on its own. He had to deny any culpability. There was just too much at stake.

"Why would I want to stop you from seeing Najeeb?"

She glared up at him, then turned and walked out.

Unable to believe she'd turned her back on him, he watched her, that fist of foreboding squeezing his insides again.

Mohab finished dressing, then followed her into her bedroom. His mind churning, he approached her where she stood across the room in jeans and a T-shirt, raven hair starting to dry into a waterfall of gloss, looking heart-breakingly perfect.

"I'm sorry I got carried away in there," he started. "I didn't think you'd mind…didn't think at all. I've never been so frightened in my life, and I overreacted…."

"I could have said stop. I didn't. So let's drop it."

"Let's not. If you're angry with me, don't just freeze me out." He stopped before her, ran a finger down her velvet cheek. "I beg your forgiveness, *ya habibati,* if you felt I was disregarding your choices. I didn't mean to, and I—"

"Don't." Her interruption was exasperated this time. "It doesn't matter. I actually think it's a good opportunity to finally tell you what I've been putting off for too long."

"Tell me what?"

"That I wasn't in any condition to make a rational decision when I accepted your marriage proposal."

His heart faltered. "What do you mean?"

"I was experiencing a postsex high for the first time, which was heightened by the fact that I was already indebted to you for saving my life during the hostage crisis. So when you hit me with your proposal, I found myself saying yes. I've tried to take it back ever since, but you wouldn't let me."

"You did no such thing." Denial rasped out of him. He shook his head, as if to snap out of the nightmare. "Is this why you kept putting off telling anyone about us? Not because you were afraid our families' feud would impact our relationship, but because you were having second thoughts?"

"I'm not just having second thoughts. I'm *certain* I don't want to get married."

That was it? A case of commitment phobia? That was something he could deal with.

He drew a breath of relief into his tight chest. "I can understand your wariness. You struggled for your independence. You might think you'd lose it with marriage. But I'll never encroach on your freedoms…." At her baleful glance, he insisted, "Whatever my transgressions, they were unintended. Guide me in navigating your comfort zones and I'll always abide by them. If I pushed you into a commitment too soon, I'll wait until you're ready."

"I'll never be ready to marry *you*."

He stared at her, beyond shocked, the ferocity of her rejection an ax cleaving into his heart.

Just yesterday, he'd thought everything was perfect between them. And she'd had all this resentment seething inside her? How had he been so oblivious?

This led him to the only possible explanation. A dreadful one. "Have you received a better offer?"

At his rough whisper, she turned away again. He wanted to pounce on her, to roar that she couldn't do this to him, to them. He remained paralyzed, sick electricity arcing in his clenched fists, jumbling his heart's rhythm.

He forced more mutilating deductions from numb lips. "Since this is coming right after you visited Najeeb, I assume he finally popped the question."

She bent to pick up her laptop, as if she'd already dismissed him from her life. Heartache morphed into fury, all his early, long-forgotten suspicions about the nature of her relationship with Najeeb crashed into his mind.

"That's why you wheedled into his life, isn't it? But then he left, and you thought he wouldn't come through, and you were…what? Keeping me as plan B in case he didn't propose? And now you got the offer you were after all along, the one where you become a future queen, and I'm suddenly redundant?"

She turned the eyes of a total stranger to him. "I'd hoped we could part on civil terms."

"Civil?" His growl sounded like a wounded beast's. "You expect me to stand aside and let you marry my cousin?"

"I expect you to know you have no say in what I do."

And he went mad with pain and rage. "You can't just toss me aside and hook up with him. In fact, you can forget it. Najeeb will withdraw his offer as soon as I tell him how I made you…ineligible to be his princess. Regularly, hard and long, for five months. That I even took you after you said yes to him."

Her eyes filled with something he'd never dreamed he'd see in them. Loathing. "And I expected you to take my decision like a gentleman. But I'm glad you showed me how vicious and dishonorable you can be when you're thwarted. Now I know beyond a shadow of a doubt that I was right to end this."

His blood congealed as she turned away. "You really think you *can* end it…just like that?"

Hearing his butchered growl, she turned at the door. "Yes. And I hope you won't make it uglier than it has already become."

His feet dragged under the weight of his heart as he ap-

proached her. "*B'Ellahi*...you loved me.... You said so....
I *felt* it."

"Whatever I said, whatever you think you felt, it's over.
I never want to see you again."

He caught her, the feel of her intensifying his desperation. "You might think you mean it now, but you're mine,
Jala. And no matter how long it takes, I swear to you, I
will reclaim you. I will make you beg to be mine again."

"I was never yours. If you think you have a claim on
me, I *will* repay you for saving my life one day. But not
with my life."

His fingers sank into her shoulders, as if it would stop
her from vanishing. "I don't care who Najeeb is. I'll destroy him before I let him have you. I'll destroy anyone
who comes near you."

The disdain in her eyes rose. Everything he said sent
her another step beyond retrieval.

"So now I know why you're called *Al Moddammer*."
The Destroyer. The label he'd earned when he'd decimated
conspiracies and terrorist organizations. "You annihilate
anyone who becomes an obstacle to your objectives. Not
to mention anyone who comes close to *you*."

His heart seized painfully. He'd never thought she'd
ever use *that* knowledge against him. What else had he
been wrong about?

Her disgust as she severed his convulsive grip told
him this was it. It was over. Worse still, it might never
have been real. Everything they'd shared, everything he'd
thought they'd meant to each other might have all been in
his mind.

Before she receded out of his life, she murmured, "Find
yourself someone else who might have a death wish. Because I don't."

One

"Do you have a death wish?"

Mohab almost laughed out loud. A bitterly amused huff did escape him as he rose to his feet to meet the king of Judar.

What were the odds? That these exact words would be the first thing Kamal Aal Masood said to him when they'd been the last thing the man's kid sister had flung at Mohab?

Guess it *was* true what was said about Kamal and Jala. That the two youngest in the Aal Masood sibling quartet could have been identical twins—if they hadn't been born male and female and twelve years apart. Their resemblance *was* uncanny.

With the historical enmity between their kingdoms, Mohab had only seen Kamal from afar. He'd last beheld him at the time of his *joloos*—as he'd sat on the throne, five and a half years ago. Not that Mohab had manipulated his way into Judar that night to see him. Jala had been his only objective. But *she* hadn't attended her own brother's wedding. Yet another thing he'd failed to predict where she was concerned.

Something else he'd failed to predict was how it would feel seeing this guy up close. Kamal looked so much like Jala, it...ached deep in his chest.

It was as if someone had taken Jala and turned her into an older, intimidating male version of herself. They shared the same wealth of raven hair, the same whiskey-colored eyes and the same bone structure. The only differences were those of gender. Kamal's bronze complexion was shades darker than Jala's golden flawlessness, and at six foot six, the king of Judar would tower over his sister's statuesque five-nine, just as *he* once had. Her big brother was also more than double her size, but they shared the same feline grace and perfect proportions. While all that made her the embodiment of a fairy-tale princess, Kamal was the epitome of a hardened desert raider, exuding limitless power. And exercising it, too.

At forty, Kamal was one of the most influential individuals in the world, and had been so even before his two older brothers had abdicated the throne of Judar to him in a chain reaction of court drama and royal family scandals that still rocked the region and changed its course forever.

Now Kamal's lupine eyes simmered with the trademark menace famous for intimidating anyone he seared with his gaze. "Anything you find particularly amusing, Aal Ghaanem?"

"Your opening remark revived a memory of another... person mentioning death wishes." At Kamal's fierce glower, Mohab's smile spread. "What? You think I find you, or being escorted here like a prisoner of war, amusing?"

He'd expected worse arriving in Judar, with tensions

between Saraya and Judar at a historic high. In fact, just yesterday, his king had all but declared war on Judar during a global broadcast from a UN summit. For Mohab, a prince of Saraya second in rank only to the king and his heirs, to land uninvited on Judarian soil in these fraught times was cause for extreme concern. Especially when said prince also happened to be the former head of Saraya's secret service. He'd expected to be put on the first flight out of Judar. Or even to be taken into custody.

In a preemptive bluff, he'd asserted he had time-sensitive business with King Kamal and the king would punish whoever detained him. That sent border security officials at the airport scrambling for orders from the royal palace. Mohab had half expected his gamble to fall through, that Kamal would have him kicked out of the kingdom. But within minutes, a dozen of Judar's finest secret-service men had descended on Mohab, breathing down his neck all the way here.

Apparently they considered him that dangerous. He was flattered, really.

"So you find death wishes a source of amusement? A daredevil by nature, not only by trade, eh? Figures. But aren't you also supposed to be meticulous and prudent? I thought that's why you're still in one piece after all the crazy stunts you've pulled. Isn't it the first thing you're taught when you're hatched in Saraya—that Judar doesn't sustain life for your species?"

His species. The Aal Ghaanems. The Aal Masoods' mortal enemies. *Aih*. There was *that* stumbling block, too.

"So again…*do* you have a death wish? Don't you know that, now more than ever, a high-profile Sarayan like you at large in Judar could have been targeted for any level of retribution?"

Mohab flattened a palm over his heart. "I'm touched you're concerned about keeping me in one piece. But I assure you, I behaved in an exemplary fashion, antagonizing no one."

"No one but me. Arriving unannounced, terrorizing my subjects, forcing me to drop everything to investigate your incursion. Is this your king's last hope now that he's put his foot in his mouth on global feed? Is he afraid I'll finally knock him off his throne, as I should have long ago? Has he sent his wild card to deal with the crisis...at the root?"

"You think I'm here to...what? Assassinate you?" A huff of incredulity burst from Mohab. "I may be into impossible missions, but I'm not fond of suicidal ones. And I was almost strip-searched for anything that could even make you sneeze."

Kamal's laserlike gaze contemplated Mohab's mocking grin. "From my reports, you can probably take out my royal guard stripped and with both hands tied behind your back."

"Ah, you flatter me, King Kamal. I'd need one hand to go through them all."

The other man's steady gaze told him Kamal believed Mohab was capable of just that—and more—and wasn't the least bit fooled by his joking tone. "I have records of some true mission-impossible scenarios that you've pulled off. If anyone can enter a maximum-security palace with only the clothes on his back and manage to blow it up and walk away without a scratch, it's you."

Mohab's lips twitched. "If you believe I can get away with your murder, why did you agree to see me?"

"Because I'm intrigued."

"Enough to risk letting such a lethal entity within reach? You must be bored out of your mind being king."

Kamal exhaled. "You don't know the half of it—or how good *you* have it. A prince who is in no danger of finding himself on a throne, a black-ops professional who had the luxury of switching to a freelance career...emphasis on the 'free' part."

"While *you're* the king of a minor kingdom you've made into a major one, and a revered leader who has limitless power at his fingertips and the most amazing family a man can dream of having."

"Apart from my incomparable wife and children, I'd switch places with you in a heartbeat."

Mohab laughed out loud. "The last thing I expected coming here is that I'd be standing with you, in the heart of Aal Masood territory, with us envying each other."

"In a better world, I would have offered you anything to have your skills at my disposal and you at my side. Too bad we're on opposite sides with no way to bridge the divide."

Mohab pounced on the opening. "That's why I'm here. To offer not only to bridge that divide, but to obliterate it."

Kamal frowned. "You deal in extractions, containments and cleanups. Why send you to offer political solutions?"

"I'm here on my own initiative because *I'm* the solution."

His declaration was met by an empty stare.

Then Kamal drawled, "Strange. You seem quite solid." Mohab chuckled at Kamal's unexpected dry-as-tinder wit, drawing a rumble from Kamal. "I have zero tolerance for wastes of time. If you prove to be one, you will spend a few nights as an honored guest in my personal dungeon."

"Is this a way to talk to the man who can give you Jareer?"

Kamal clamped his arm. "*Kaffa monawaraat wa ghomood*...enough evasions and ambiguity. Explain, and fast, or..."

"Put down your threats. I *am* here to mend our kingdoms' relations, and there's nothing I want more than to accomplish that as fast as possible."

"*Zain*. You have ten minutes."

"Twenty." Before Kamal blasted him, Mohab preempted him. "*Don't* say fifteen."

Kamal's gaze lengthened. "As an only child you missed out on having an older sibling kick your ass in your formative years. I'm close to rectifying your deficiency."

Mohab grinned. "Think you can take me on, King Kamal?"

"Definitely."

And Mohab believed it. Kamal wasn't a pampered royal depending on others' service and protection. This man was a warrior first and foremost. That he'd chosen to fight in the boardroom and now in the world's political arenas didn't mean he wouldn't be as effective on an actual battlefield.

Before Mohab made a rejoinder, the king turned and crossed his expansive stateroom to the sitting area. Mohab suspected it was to hide a smile so as not to acknowledge this affinity that had sprung up between them.

Kamal resumed speaking as soon as Mohab took a seat across from him. "So why do you think *you* can give me Jareer...when I already have it, Sheikh Prince Solution?"

A laugh burst out of Mohab's depths. That clinched it. He didn't care that other people thought Kamal scary or boorish. To him, the guy was just plain rocking fun.

Kamal's lips twisted in response, but didn't lift.

"There is no law prohibiting an Aal Masood from smiling at an Aal Ghaanem, you know."

Kamal's lips pursed instead. "I may issue one prohibiting just that. The way you're going, you might end up making the dispute between Judar and Saraya even more... insoluble."

Mohab sighed. "So...Jareer, euphemistically referred to as our kingdoms' *contested region*..."

"*And* currently known as our kingdoms' *future war zone,*" Kamal finished.

Not if Mohab managed to resolve this.

Jareer used to be under Saraya's rule. But the past few Sarayan monarchs had had no foresight. They'd centralized everything, neglecting then abandoning outlying regions. Jareer, on the border with Judar, had always been considered useless, because it lacked resources, and traitorous, because its citizens were akin to "enemy sympathizers." So when Judar had laid claim to Jareer, with its people's welcome, Mohab's grandfather, King Othman, had considered it good riddance.

But when Mohab's uncle, King Hassan, sat on Saraya's throne, he'd reignited old conflicts with Judar. His favorite crusade had been reclaiming Jareer. Not because he'd suspected its future importance, but to spite the region's inhabitants—and because he wanted more reasons to fight the Aal Masoods.

Then, two months ago, oil had been discovered in Jareer. Now the situation had evolved from an idle conflict between two monarchs to a struggle over limitless wealth and power. In a war between the two kingdoms, Saraya would be decimated for generations to come.

Only Mohab had the power to stop this catastrophe. Theoretically. There was still the possibility that Kamal would hear his proposition and reward his audacity by throwing him in that personal dungeon before wiping Saraya off the face of the earth.

One thing made Mohab hope this wouldn't happen. Kamal himself. He was convinced that, though Kamal had every reason to crush Saraya, he would rather not. He hadn't become one of the greatest kings by being reactionary—or by achieving prosperity for his kingdom at the cost of another kingdom's destruction.

At least, Mohab hoped he was right. He *had* read Kamal's "twin" all wrong once before after all....

"I will be disappointed if, after all this staring at me, you can't draw me from memory."

Jarred out of his thoughts by Kamal's drawl, Mohab blinked at him. "You just remind me of someone so much, it keeps sidetracking me."

"The same someone who made the death wish comment, eh?"

Not only brilliant, but intuitive, too. Mohab nodded.

"And there I was under the impression I was unique."

Mohab sighed. "You are…both of you. Two of a kind."

Kamal sat forward, ire barely contained. "As charmed as I am by all this…*nostalgia* of yours, I have a date with my wife in an hour, and I'd rather be late for my own funeral than for her. I might make you early for yours if you don't talk. Fast."

"All right. I am the rightful heir to Jareer."

Kamal's eyebrows shot up. He hadn't seen this coming. No one could have.

Mohab explained. "For centuries, Jareer was an independent land, and my mother's tribe, the Aal Kussaimis, ruled it up till a hundred and fifty years ago. But with my great-great-grandmother marrying an Aal Ghaanem, a treaty was struck with Saraya to annex the region, with terms for autonomy while under Sarayan rule and with provisions for secession if those terms weren't observed.

"When Jareer found itself on its own again under my grandfather's rule, it saw no reason to enforce the secession rules, as it was effectively separated from Saraya anyway. Then Judar offered its protection. But in truth, Jareer belongs to neither Judar nor Saraya. It belongs to my maternal tribe. I would have brought you the records of our claim for as far back as a thousand years, but after yesterday's fiasco, I had to rush to intervene before I could get everything ready. However, rest assured, the claim is heavily documented by the tribe's elders and historians."

Kamal blinked as if emerging from a trance. "That's your solution? Inserting the Aal Kussaimis as preceding claimants? Widening the dispute and adding more fuel to the fire?"

"Actually, I am ending the dispute. The Aal Kussaimis' claim trumps both the Aal Ghaanems' and the Aal Masoods'. Any regional or international court would sanction that claim."

Kamal's eyes burned with contemplation. "If all this is true, shouldn't I be talking to the tribe's elder? Who can't be you since you're…how old? Thirty?"

"Thirty-eight. But while it's true I'm not the tribe's elder, I am the highest-ranking tribe member by merit. I was elected the tribe's leader years ago. Which effectively makes me the king of Jareer."

Kamal's lashes lowered. A testament to his surprise.

When his gaze rose again, it was tranquil. That didn't fool Mohab for a second. He could almost hear the gears of Kamal's formidable mind screeching.

"Interesting. So you're claiming to be *King* Solution. Even if you prove to be the first, how do you propose to be the second?"

"Proving my claim is a foregone conclusion. The second should be self-evident."

"Not to me."

Jala's exact words that fateful night. Said in the same tone. Kamal's likeness to her had suddenly ceased to be reminiscent and had become only grating.

Mohab gritted his teeth. "My uncle assumed I would never invoke my claim, that I would always let him speak for me concerning Jareer's fate. And he was right—I didn't have time to be more than an honorary leader and had no desire to upset a status quo my people were perfectly content with under Judar's protection. But now things have changed."

Kamal huffed. "Tell me about it. Just two months ago, you were the 'rightful heir' to a stretch of desert with three towns and seven villages whose people lived on date and Arabian coffee production, souvenir manufacturing and desert tourism. Now you're the king of a land sitting on top of one of the biggest oil reservoirs ever discovered."

"I have no personal stake in Jareer's newfound wealth. I'm not interested in being richer, and I never wanted to be king. However, my people are demanding I declare Jareer an independent state and that I become their full-fledged ruler. But business and politics aren't my forte. So while I will do my people's bidding, I think it's in their best interests to leave their new oil-based prosperity to the experts."

"By experts, I assume you mean oil moguls."

"With you in charge of every step they take into Jareer."

Kamal raised one eyebrow. "You want me to run the show?"

"Yes."

Kamal digested this. "So that's Judar and Jareer and the oil companies. What about Saraya?"

"As a Sarayan, too, and because I admit the treaties with Saraya were never properly resolved before entering into the new ones with Judar, I will recognize its claim."

"So you claim Jareer, and split the cake between us all. Why do you assume I'll consider it? If I can have the whole cake?"

He sat forward, holding Kamal's gaze. "I do because you're an honorable man and a just king. Because I believe you'll do everything in your power to avoid escalating hostilities between our kingdoms. Before, it was about family feuds and pride. Now we're talking staggering wealth and power. If you decimate my claim and take all of Jareer, those who stand to lose that much would cause unspeakable damage. I regularly deal with situations that rage over way less, and believe me, nothing is worth the price of such conflicts."

"So how do you propose we split the cake?"

"For its historical role and ties to Jareer, and because both Judar and Jareer will need its cooperation, Saraya will get twenty percent of Jareer's oil. In recognition of Judar's more recent claim and its much bigger role in Jareer till this day, Judar gets forty percent. Jareer gets the other forty percent. Plus, its inhabitants would be first in line for all benefits and job opportunities that arise, and you will also be responsible to provide training for them."

"You've got it all worked out, don't you?"

"I have been working on my pitch since the oil's discovery. I was far from ready, but my uncle's theatrics at the UN yesterday forced my hand prematurely."

"What if I don't like your percentages or terms?"

"I would grant you whatever you wish."

"Even if you wanted to, as kings, we're not omnipotent. Why would your people agree to let you be so generous with their resources?"

Here it was. Moment of truth. The point of all this.

He took the plunge. "They would because it would be the *mahr* of your sister, Princess Jala."

Kamal rose to his feet in perfect calmness. It screamed instantaneous rejection more than anything openly indignant would have.

"No."

The cold, final word fell on Mohab like a lash. As Jala's rejection once had.

He resisted the urge to flinch at the sting. "Just no?"

"Consider yourself honored I deemed to articulate it. That you dared to voice this boggles the mind."

"Why?"

Kamal glared down at him. "I'll have my secretary of state draw you up an inventory of the reasons."

"Give me the broad lines."

"How about just one? Your bloodline."

"You'd condemn a man by others' transgressions?"

"We do inherit others' mistakes and enmities."

"And we can resolve them, not insist on regurgitating hatreds and spawning warring generations."

"The Aal Masoods aren't angels, but there is good reason why we abhor you, why all attempts at peacemaking fell through for centuries. Surely you remember the last marriage between our kingdoms and what your great-grandfather did to my great-aunt. I'm not letting my sister marry a man who comes from a family where the men mistreat their women."

"My great-grandfather and uncle don't represent the rest of us. *I* am nothing like them. You can investigate me further. And then consider the merits of my proposal. Once I claim Jareer, my uncle can retreat from his warpath. We'd appease his pride while going over his head in forging peaceful relations between all sides, to the benefit of all our people." Mohab rose to his feet to face him. "What I'm proposing is the best solution for all concerned, now and into the far future. And you know it."

After a protracted stare, Kamal finally exhaled. "We can forge peace with other kinds of treaties. Why bring marriage into this? And more important, why Jala? If you want to solidify the new alliance in the oldest way in the book, and the most enduring in our region, the Aal Masoods have other princesses who would definitely be more acceptable to your stick-in-the-mud family."

"My family has nothing to do with it. Jala is *my* choice." Kamal's astonishment made Mohab decide to come clean, as much as it was prudent to. "I had a…thing for Jala years ago, and I thought she reciprocated. It didn't end as I hoped. Now, years later, with both of us still unattached, I thought it might be fate's way of telling me I had to make another attempt at claiming the one woman who captured my fancy…and wouldn't let go. So while resolving our kingdoms' long-standing conflicts would certainly be a bonus, she's always been my main objective."

Expecting Kamal, as Jala's brother, to be offended—or at least to grill him about the nature of the "thing" he'd had for Jala—Kamal surprised him again, a hint of a smile dawning. "You mean discovering oil in Jareer and the crisis that ensued just presented you with the best bargaining chip to propose? And you didn't propose before because you never had enough leverage?"

Mohab shrugged, tension killing him. "Do I have enough now?"

Kamal's smile became definite. "If I disregard the stench of your paternal lineage and consider you based on your own merits, this might be a good idea. A perfect one, even. Knowing Jala, she'd never marry of her own accord and I hate to think she'll end up alone. And you, apart from the despicable flaw of having the Aal Ghaanem blood and name, seem like a…reasonably good match for her."

"So you're saying yes?"

"A yes isn't mine to say. I can't force her to marry you and wouldn't even if I could. Clearly this marriage quest of yours is hardly a done deal, since you require my intervention to even reach her. I won't ask what earned you a place on Jala's viciously strict no-approach list. *Ullah* knows I'm the last man to go all holier-than-thou on you for whatever transgression you committed to deserve this kind of treatment."

What would Kamal say if Mohab told him he didn't know exactly why he'd deserved that till this day?

Kamal gazed into the distance as if peering into a distasteful past. "I once did unforgivable things to the one woman who'd captured *my* fancy and wouldn't let go, and it took the intervention of others to give me that second chance with her."

"So you're paying it forward."

Kamal's eyes returned to his, the crooked smile back. "I am. *But* if she agrees to marry you, I'll take *sixty* per cent as her *mahr*. If she refuses, the whole deal is off—and we'll draw up another treaty that saves your king's face so he can go sit in his throne and stop throwing war-agitating tantrums."

Mohab's first impulse was to kiss Kamal on both cheeks. This was beyond anything he'd come here expecting.

He extended his hand to Kamal instead, his smile the widest it had been in...six years. "Deal. You won't regret this."

Kamal shook his hand slowly. "You were wrong when you said you don't know much about business. You know nothing. You could have gotten me to agree to thirty per cent. You're holding all the cards after all."

Mohab's smiled widened more. "I'm not so oblivious that I don't know the power I wield. But I would never haggle over Jala's *mahr*. If my decision didn't affect millions of people in both Saraya and Jareer, I would have given you the whole thing."

"You got it that bad?" Kamal drilled him with an incredulous gaze. "Do you *love* her?"

Love? He once had...or thought he had. But now he knew it hadn't been real. Because nothing real could ever exist for a man like him. He only knew he couldn't move on. And that she hadn't moved on, either. He was still obsessed with their every touch, had starved for her every pleasure. Love didn't enter into the equation. Not only was it an illusion, it was one he couldn't afford.

But the pact he'd struck with Kamal was real. As was

his hunger for Jala. That was more than enough. In fact, that was everything.

Kamal waved his hand. "Don't answer that. I don't think you *can* answer. If you haven't seen her in years, whatever you felt for her back then might be totally moot once you come face-to-face with each other again. So I won't hold you to this proposal for now. But since Jala is the most intractable entity I have the misfortune to know and love…" At Mohab's raised eyebrow, Kamal sighed. "*Aih,* she takes after her older brother, as Aliyah tells me."

Mohab did a double take. It was amazing, the change that came over Kamal's face as he mentioned his wife and queen. It was as if he glowed inside just thinking of her.

Kamal went on. "But for this to have a prayer of working, I need to give you much more of a helping hand than putting you in the same room with her. I need to give *her* a shove. I'll make it sound as if refusal isn't an option. Of course, if she *really* wants to refuse, she will, no matter what." His lips spread into a smile again. "All I can hope is that if I make things sound drastic enough, it'll give you that chance to make your approach. The rest… is up to you."

Two

"You…*what?*"

Jala stared at Kamal, her shrill cry ringing in her own ears.

Staggering, she collapsed on the nearest horizontal surface, gaping up at Kamal who came to stand over her.

"I lied."

Ya Ullah. She *had* heard right the first time.

Another cry of sheer incredulity scratched her throat raw. "How could you do this to me? Are you *insane?*"

Kamal shrugged, not looking in the least repentant. "I had to get you here. Sorry."

"*Sorry?* You let me have a thousand panic attacks during the hours it took me to get here, thinking that Farooq was lying in hospital, critically injured, and you say… sorry?"

Even now that she knew Farooq was safe, the horror still reverberated in her bones. She'd never known such desperation, not even when she'd been held hostage and thought she'd die a violent death.

Fury seethed inside of her. "Don't you know what you did to me? As I thought of beautiful, vital Farooq lying broken, struggling for his life, how I wept as I thought how much he had to live for, as I thought of Carmen losing her soul mate, of Mennah growing up without her father.... You're a monstrous *pig,* Kamal!"

Kamal winced. "I said he was injured but that he was stable. I wanted you here, but didn't want to scare you more than necessary. How am I responsible for your exaggerations?"

"How? *How?*" She threw her hands up in the air in frustration. "How does Aliyah *bear* you?"

Kamal had the temerity to flash her that wolfish grin of his. "I never ask. I just wallow in the miracle of her, and that she thinks I'm the best thing that ever walked the earth."

"Then Aliyah, although she *looks* sane, is clearly deranged. Or under a spell...."

"It's called love." Kamal raised his hands before she exploded again. "I *am* sorry. But you said you'd never set foot here again, and I knew you wouldn't come unless you thought one of us was dying."

"I know you're ruthless and manipulative and a dozen other inhuman adjectives but...argh! Whatever you needed to drag me here for, you could have tried telling me the truth first!"

Kamal smirked. "*Aih,* and when that didn't work, I would have tried the lie next. I *would* have ordered you to come, but knowing you, you would have probably renounced your Judarian citizenship just so I'd stop being your king. If you weren't that intractable I wouldn't have had to lie, and you wouldn't have had those harrowing sixteen hours."

"So it's now my fault? You—you humongous, malignant rat! What could possibly be enough reason for you to drag me back here with this terrible lie?"

"Just that Judar is about to go to war."

She shot back up to her feet. "*Kaffa*, Kamal...enough. I'm already here. So stop *lying*."

His face was suddenly grim. "No lie this time." He put his hand on her shoulder, gently pressed her down to the couch, coming down beside her this time. "It's a long story."

She gaped at him as he recounted it, plunging deeper into a surreal scape with every word.

But wars did erupt over far less, especially in their region. This was real.

When he was done, she exhaled. "You can't even consider war over oil rights, no matter how massive. Aren't you the wizard of diplomacy who peacefully resolves conflicts to every side's benefit?"

"Seems you're not familiar with King Hassan." A scoff almost escaped her. Oh, she was *so* very familiar with King Hassan. "Some people are immune to diplomacy."

"And *you're* not posturing and allowing your council to egg you on with hand-me-down rivalries and vendettas?"

It was Kamal's turn to scoff. "Give me some credit, Jala. I care nothing about any of this bull. *I* don't have an inflamed ego and don't borrow others' enmities."

"Yet you're letting someone who has and does drag you down to his level, when you should contain him and his petty aggressions." She exhaled her exasperation. "No wonder I did everything I could to get out of this godforsaken region and had to be told my oldest brother was dying to set foot here again. All this feudal backwardness is just...nauseating. You'd think nothing ever changed since the eleventh century!"

"War over oil rights is *very* twenty-first century."

"Congratulations to all of you, then, for your leap into modern warfare. I hope you'll enjoy deploying long-range missiles and playing high-tech war games." She muttered something about monkeys under her breath. "I still don't get why you conned me back here. You want me to have a front row seat with you lunkheads when the war begins?"

He reached for her hand, his eyes cajoling. Uh-oh.

"You actually play the lead role in averting this catastrophe."

"What could I possibly have to do with resolving your political conflicts?"

"Everything really. Only you can stop the war now, by marrying an Aal Ghaanem prince."

"What?"

"Only a blood-mixing union will end hostilities and forge a long-lasting alliance."

She snatched her hand from his grasp, erupting to her feet. "Did I say you were stuck in the eleventh century? You've just stumbled five more centuries backward. *Not* so good seeing you, Kamal. And don't expect to lay eyes on me for a long while. Certainly never in Judar again."

Kamal gave her that unfazed glance that made her want to shriek at the top of her lungs. "It's this or war. The war you know full well would come at an unthinkable price to everyone in Judar—and in Saraya and Jareer, too."

Wincing at the terrible images his words smeared across her imagination, she gritted out, "Let's say for argument's sake that I don't think you're all insane to be still dabbling in marriages of state to settle political disputes. The Aal Masoods have many princesses who're just right for the role of political bride. In fact, some have been born and bred for the role. So how are any of you foolish enough to consider *me*—aka the Prodigal Princess?"

Lethal steel came into Kamal's eyes. "Others' opinions are irrelevant. You're *the* princess of Judar. Only your blood could end centuries of enmity and forge an unbreakable alliance. So it's not a choice. You are getting married to the Aal Ghaanem prince."

"Wow. If you wore a crown, I'd think it got too tight on your swelling head and gave you brain damage. Anyway, if you think you can sacrifice me at the altar of your tribal reconciliations, you're suffering from serious delusions."

"We all offer sacrifices when our kingdom needs us."

"What sacrifices?" She coughed a furious chuckle. "To remain married to Carmen, Farooq tossed his crown-prince rank to Shehab when our kingdom needed him. Shehab did the same with you, to marry Farah. You grabbed the rank and *sacrifice* only because it got you Aliyah in the bargain. You're all living in ecstatic-ever-afters because you did exactly what you wanted and never sacrificed a thing for 'our kingdom.'"

"Farooq and Shehab had the option of passing on their duty. I didn't, like you don't now. And I thought it *was* a sacrifice when I accepted my duty."

"No, you didn't. You knew nothing less than another threat of war would get Aliyah to say good-morning to you again. You pounced on the 'duty' that would make her your queen and pretended to hate your 'fate.'" At his raised eyebrows, she smirked. "I can figure things out pretty good, *ya akhi al azeez*. So spare me the sacrifice speech, brother dear. You're out of your mind if you think you can sway me into this by appealing to my patriotism."

"Then it will be your steep humanitarian inclinations. You've been in war zones. You know that once war starts, there's no stopping the chain reaction that harvests lives in its path. As a woman who lives to alleviate the suffering of others, and who can stop this nightmarish scenario, you'll do anything to abort it, even if you abhor Judar and the whole region. And the very idea of marriage."

The terrible knowledge that he was right, if there was

no other choice, seeped into her marrow. "So now what? You'll line up Aal Ghaanem princes and I'll pick the least offensive one? And the one I pick would just accept being sacrificed for his kingdom's peace and prosperity?"

"If a man considers marrying you a sacrifice, he must be devoid of even a drop of testosterone."

"You won't appeal to my feminine ego, either. Any man in the region would rather jump out of a ten-story window than marry a woman like me, *the* princess of Judar or not."

"A woman like you would be an irreplaceable treasure to any man in any region."

"Blatant brotherly hyperbole aside, no, *a woman like me* wouldn't. A woman living alone in the West since she was eighteen is the stuff of region-wide dishonor around here. It had to be something as dire as the threat of war and the promise of unending oil to sweeten my scandalous pill for one of those stuck-in-the-dark-ages princes."

"The new generation of princes are nowhere as bad as that."

"The only one I know who isn't is Najeeb. But I bet *he* won't be joining the lineup." Her lips twisted with remembered bitterness. "King Hassan would never sacrifice his heir to such a fate as me, no matter the incentives."

Kamal waved his hand. "You won't suffer the discomfort of a lineup. The Aal Ghaanem prince has already been chosen."

She almost had to pick her jaw off the floor this time. "How can I express my gratitude that you've gone the extra mile and abolished whatever choice I had in this antiquated process?"

Kamal's lips twitched. "Let me rephrase my extremely misleading statement. The Aal Ghaanem prince volunteered. And he is already here. But he had the consideration to let me prepare you before he came in. So shall I send him in…or do you need some more time before you meet your groom-to-be?"

She sank back onto the couch, objections and insults swarming so violently it was impossible to pick one to voice.

Calmly disregarding her apoplectic state, Kamal bent and kissed her cheek. "Give this a chance, and it'll all work out for the best. You have me as the best example for *assa ann takraho shai'an wa hwa khairon lakkom.*"

You may hate something and it's for your best.

Before she could do something drastic, like poke him in the eye, he straightened, turned on his heel and walked away.

She watched him disappear, all her mental functions on the fritz.

What had just happened?

Was she really back in Judar? Only to find herself being pushed into a far worse cage than anything her previous life here had been? Could it be true that refusal wasn't an option?

Suddenly a suspicion cleaved into her brain.

The logical progression to this nightmare.

The identity of this "volunteer."

The man who was the reason she'd sworn never to return to this region. He *was* an Aal Ghaanem prince, even if the world forgot that most of the time.

But he would never volunteer to…to…

You're mine, Jala. And no matter how long it takes, I swear to you, I will reclaim you. I will make you beg to be mine again.

The promise…the *threat*…that had circulated in her being for six long years, burning her to the core with its malicious arrogance and possessiveness, reverberated in her bones.

No. He'd just said that out of spite, to poison whatever

reprieve walking away would grant her. He hadn't really wanted to reclaim her. Not when he'd only claimed her as a means to an end. An end he must believe he'd long achieved....

Her heart kicked, had her pitching forward to the edge of her seat. The door of the reception room was opening.

The next moment, her heart battered her ribs. Time ceased. Reality fell away. Everything converged on one thing. The shadow separating from the darkness. A shape she remembered all too well.

Him.

No. *No.* Not when she'd finally managed to purge his malignant memory. She must stop this confrontation from coming to pass, flee...*now.*

She didn't move. Couldn't. Could only sit there, her every nerve unraveling as soundless steps brought him into the circle of light where she sat exposed, besieged.

His eyes were the first things that emerged out of the gloom. Those fire pits had haunted her dreams and tormented her waking hours since she'd last seen them.

But the tremors arcing through her weren't from what she saw in them, or the blow of his presence or its implications. It was the awareness that had swept her from the first moment she'd ever encountered him. Even amidst the terror of the hostage crisis, it had yanked her out of reality, plunged her into a stunned free fall where only he existed. For that same feeling to mushroom again now, after all that had happened...

He blinked, and the vice garroting her snapped, propelling her to her feet and to the French windows.

Her steps picked up speed as her exit to the palace gardens neared...then it disappeared. Behind a wall of muscle and maleness. It was as if he'd materialized in her path.

He didn't try to detain her, didn't need to. His very aura snared her. And that was before her gaze streaked up, found him looking at her with that trance-inducing intensity.

Finding him so near, after all these years, after what he'd cost her....

Her grip on consciousness softened. The world swirled as she stared up at him, a prisoner to her own enervation. And again the sheer injustice of it all hit her.

No one should be endowed with all this. He was too... everything. And even in the subdued lighting and through the veil of her own wavering senses she could see he was even more than she remembered. Six years had taken him from the epitome of manhood to godlike levels.

He towered over her, even though she was six feet in her heels, his physique that of an Olympian, his face that of an avenging angel, every inch of him composed of planes and hollows and slashes of power and perfection. Adding to his lethal assets, his wealth of sun-gilded mahogany hair was now long enough to be gathered at his nape, the severe scrape emphasizing the ruggedness of his leonine forehead and the vigor of his hairline. A trim new beard and mustache accentuated the jut of his cheekbones and the dominance of his jawline and completed the ruthless desert raider image. Maturity had added more of everything to that supreme being of bronze and steel who'd taken her breath away and had held it out of reach for as long as he'd had her under his spell. Something she'd thought she'd broken.

But if, after all she'd been through, all the maturation she'd thought she'd undergone, he could still look at her and take control of her senses, then the spell couldn't *be* broken.

But this unadulterated coveting in his eyes... She couldn't be reading it right.

Still, when he took a step closer, he vibrated with something that simulated barely checked hunger. Which would be unleashed at the slightest provocation—a word, a gasp....

But she was incapable of even those. She'd expended all her power in her escape effort. Now she was caught in stasis, waiting for his next move to reanimate her.

None came. He stared down at her, as if her nearness affected him just as acutely. When *he'd* been the one who'd planned this ambush, who'd been lying in wait for her.

The barricades around her resentment melted, shattering her inertia, imbuing her limbs with the steadiness of outrage as she put the distance he'd obliterated back between them.

"Guess your memory must be patchy from all the head blows I hear is an occupational hazard in your line of work. Your presence can only be explained by partial to total amnesia."

Another blink lowered his thick, gold-tipped lashes, eclipsing the infernos of his eyes and his reaction. Then they swept up, exposing her to a different kind of heat. Surprise? Challenge? Humor?

Just the idea that it could be the latter poured acid on her inflamed nerves. "Let me fill one paramount hole in your recollections. What I last said to you remains in full force now. I never want to see you again. So you can take whatever game you think you're playing and go straight to hell."

She swept around then, desperation to get away from him fueling her steps...and her arm was snagged in a hard, warm grip.

Before she could fully register the bolt that zapped her, a tug swirled her around smoothly, as if in a choreographed dance, and brought her slamming against him from breast to calf.

Before she could draw another breath, one of his hands slipped into the hair at her nape, immobilizing her head and tilting her face upward. The other hand trailed a heavy path of possession down to her buttocks. Then, as he held her prisoner, exerting no force but that of his will, he let her see it. The very thing she'd once reveled in experiencing—the lethal beast he kept hidden under the civilized veneer. Its cunning savagery had assured his survival in the dangerous existence he'd chosen, his triumph over the most deadly enemies. That beast appeared to be starving—and she was what would sate its cravings.

Holding her stunned gaze, his own crackling with a dizzying mixture of calculation and lust, he lowered his head.

Feeling she'd disintegrate at the touch of his lips, she averted her face at the last moment.

His lips landed at the corner of her mouth, plucking convulsively at her flesh. The familiarity of his lips, the unfamiliarity of his facial hair, sparked each nerve ending individually. The gusts of his breath filled her with his scent, burying her under an avalanche of memory. Of how it used to feel to lose herself to the ecstasy of his powerful possession.

The hand on her buttocks pressed her closer, letting her feel his arousal, wringing hers from her depths. Before she could deal with this blow, the hand holding her head combed through her hair. Each stroke sent delight cascading from every hair root, spilled moans from her depths in answer to the unintelligible bass murmurings from him. Then his other hand caressed its way beneath her jacket, freeing her blouse from her skirt…and delving below.

A gasp tore out of her as those calloused fingers splayed against her sizzling flesh, imprinting it like a brand, making her instinctively press closer. And then he took his onslaught to the next level.

Yanking up her skirt, he slipped below her panties to cup her buttocks, kneading her taut flesh hungrily before hauling her against him. Weightless, in his power, she keened as the long-craved steel of his erection ground against her core. A scalding growl rolled in his gut as he tugged one thigh, opening her around his hips, spreading her for his domination, while the hand at her back plastered her heaving chest against his. Her breasts swelled with each rub against his hard power, the abrasion of their clothes turning her nipples to pinpoints of agony.

She writhed in his hold as he singed kisses down her neck, ravaged her in suckles that would mark her skin, sending vicious pleasure hurtling through her blood, lodging into her womb with each savage pull.

All existence converged on him, became him—his body and breath, his taste and feel, his hands and mouth—as he strummed her flesh, reclaimed her every inch and response. With just a touch, she'd ceased to be herself, becoming a mass of need wrapped around him, open to him, his to exploit and plunder…to pleasure and possess.

She could no longer hear anything but her thundering heart and their strident breathing as he raised her up and slid her down his body in leisurely excursions. He had her riding his erection through their clothes. He dipped his head to capture her nipple through her bra in massaging nips, sending never-forgotten ecstasy corkscrewing through her every nerve ending.

Her moans droned, interrupted only by sharp intakes of breath. The flowing throb between her thighs escalated into pounding, tipping from discomfort into pain until she cried out. At her distressed if unmistakable demand, he shuddered beneath her, snapping his head up. Then, eyes glazed with ferocity, he crashed his lips onto her wide-open mouth and thrust deep.

She plunged into his taste, fierce wonder spreading in her flickering awareness. How did she remember it so accurately, crave it so acutely still?

Then everything ceased as his tongue invaded her, commanded hers to tangle and duel and drink deeper from the well of passion she'd once drowned in.

Then something stirred in her, shutting down her mind; something cold and ugly tore through the delirium. A realization.

This had happened before. This had been what he'd done to her that last time. He'd taken over her senses, exploited her responses, inundated her with physical satisfaction... and almost decimated her soul and psyche in the process.

Now he'd taken her over again, as if a mountain of pain and resentment didn't exist between them. She was letting him pull her strings again when he only ever saw her as a means to an end. Having an even bigger end this time, he'd decided to go into all-out invasion mode from the get-go. And she was letting him. *No.*

Anger and humiliation shattered the spell, had her struggling in his arms as if fighting for her life.

Stiffening for a long moment, as if unable to make up his mind whether that was an attempt to get away or to press closer, he finally tore his lips from hers and slid her down his body and back to the ground.

Every muscle burning from the slow poison of need with which he'd reinfected her, she staggered, groping for equilibrium. She'd taken barely a step away when his hands descended on her shoulders and pulled her back against him.

She couldn't even tremble, the control she'd long struggled for shattered, leaving her drained. She could only lean back against him limply, her head rolling on his shoulder.

Taking this as consent, he cupped her breasts, pressing against her as he groaned in her ear. "I didn't intend to do this. I still have no control over what I'm doing right this second. I walked in here and it was as if time hit Rewind, as if we'd never been apart. And just like you always do, you overrode my every rational thought and impulse with

a look, a word. Then I touched you and you responded…
like you're responding still…."

This zapped her with just enough energy to push out of
his arms. "Sure. It's my fault."

He let her put distance between them this time. "There's
no fault here. Just the phenomenon that exists between us,
this absolute physical affinity we share. But I really didn't
intend to kiss you."

"*Kiss* me? That's what you call a kiss?"

A rough huff of self-deprecation escaped him. "So I
almost took you standing up, probably would have, not
giving a second thought that we're in the middle of your
brother's stateroom, if you hadn't stopped me. You have
that effect on me. I see you and I can only think of pleasuring you."

Once she'd believed his every word. She'd been certain
that what they did share *was* a phenomenon, as undeniable
and unstoppable as a force of nature. Then she'd found out
the truth. It was clear he thought she didn't know, that he
didn't need to invent a new deception.

He approached her again, one of those hands stroking
a gossamer touch down her cheek. "But you're wrong.
About the last thing you said to me. No matter how many
blows to the head I sustain, nothing could make me forget
it. You said, *Find yourself someone else who might have
a death wish. Because I don't.*"

He remembered. Word for word.

Figured. He was said to possess a computerlike mind,
always archiving, networking, extrapolating. On top of
his fighting prowess and weapons mastery, it was what
made him the ultimate modern warrior and strategist in
this information age.

She pulled away from the debilitation of his touch. "And
that statement has been solidified by the passage of time
and reinforced by this new stunt. So, since you have a flaw-

less memory, what else is wrong with you? Haven't I already turned down your marriage proposal once before?"

Perfect teeth sank into his lip, making her feel they'd sunk into hers again. "I prefer to dwell on when you said yes."

She ignored the tingling of her lips. "Only to follow it with a resounding no, when I came to my senses. Now you're using an impending war to reintroduce the subject? Since it's not faulty memory, I assume these are your new orders?"

Something blipped in his gaze. It was gone before she could fathom it. But even that much from him was telling. He was taken aback and clearly had no idea that she was onto him.

Infusing her tone with all the cool derision she could, she cocked her head at him. "This surprises you? Hmm, maybe I must reconsider all I heard about your reputation as a know-it-all spymaster. Anyway, if you're still not sure what I mean… Yes, I do know. Everything."

Three

She knew. Everything.

For stunned moments that was all that filled Mohab's mind. Then alarm diminished and questions crowded in its place.

What was "everything" according to her? Whatever she thought that was, could that be the reason behind her sudden rejection six years ago?

He stared at her as she stood safe feet away, tall and majestic in a cream skirt suit that made her skin glow, still the most magnificent thing he'd ever seen. Even more than he'd remembered. And he'd thought he remembered everything about this woman whose memory had refused to relinquish its hold over him, whose feel still seethed beneath his skin, whose taste still lingered on his tongue.

But he'd come here today hoping what he remembered had been exaggerated, that his many sightings of her during the past years had perpetuated the delusion, that one up close look would dissipate it.

Then he'd walked into Kamal's stateroom, and one look at her had dashed any hopes he'd ever entertained of finally purging her from his system. Everything he'd remembered about her had been diluted. Or maturity had only intensified her effect on him. He *hadn't* meant to drown in her. But the years of separation, instead of dampening his responses, had only made it impossible for him to ration them.

His gaze swept her ripe curves. His every inch ached, remembering how they'd fit against his angles, how her supple softness had filled his hands, cushioned his hardness, accommodated his demand. His fingers buzzed as they relived skimming her warm, velvet skin, overflowing with her resilient flesh, winding in her silky, raven tresses. His lips and tongue stung with the phantom sensations of feeling hers again, hot and moist and fragrant, surrendering to his invasion, demanding his dominance.

He'd almost taken her, in a near-literal reenactment of their last time together, before saying one word to her. And how she'd responded. He'd felt her every inch vibrate to his frequency, every nerve resonate with his urgency. Even now, after she'd collected herself and retreated behind a barricade of cold contempt, he could still feel it seething. Her mind was another matter, though. If outrage could flay, he'd be minus skin now. He certainly felt as raw as if he was.

So was her rage a reaction to his incursion, or did the developing situation only pile on top of the "everything" she claimed to know?

He could ask, since she seemed to be forthcoming all of a sudden. But he wasn't here to dredge up the past. And if he could still just touch her and they'd both go up in flames, that was all he needed to know.

All he needed, period.

But she was waiting for him to make some kind of response to her revelation. He'd give her one, all right. Just not what she might expect.

He walked back to where she'd retreated. "So you know everything?" At her curt nod, he shoved his hands into his pockets so they wouldn't reach for her again. "Let's test this claim, shall we?"

That twist surprised her. *Zain.* Good. He shouldn't be the only one not knowing if he was coming or going here.

He cocked his head at her. "Do you know that I committed a cardinal sin during that hostage crisis?"

The tangent seemed to confuse her.

When she answered, the modulated voice that had sung its siren song in his ear for years was lower, huskier. "If you mean killing, I know all too well. Those moments, when you stormed the conference hall with your black-ops team and took out our captors, is forever branded in my memory. I watched you...terminate six of our captors single-handedly, with a precision I only thought happened in movies." Those slanting, dense eyebrows he'd loved to trace and lips drew together. "But I didn't think you considered killing a sin. Not in your line of work."

"Killing *is* my line of work. At least, it's part of the job description. Though 'killing' isn't what I call it. I prefer 'eliminating lethal threats to innocents.'"

Her eyes turned a somber cognac as she nodded. She didn't contest that he spoke the simple truth, that people like him were a necessity to control the monsters who roamed the earth. She'd obviously seen enough in *her* line of work to know that his extreme measures were indispensable at times. Just as they had been that day when she'd been taken hostage with five hundred others at that conference in Bidalya.

But she could have contradicted him to score a point. That she didn't, that she remained objective even to the detriment of her own attack, thrilled him.

He sighed. "But the sin I committed had nothing to do with the violence I perpetrated. I committed the cardinal sin of my line of work."

"How so?"

"I deviated from the plan, improvised. I could have gotten so many killed."

Again, counter to his expectations, her eyes grew impassioned as she contradicted him, in *his* defense. "But you saved hundreds, all of us who remained. And you didn't seem to be improvising. You acted with such certainty, such efficiency, it was as if everything had been rehearsed. To the point that it felt as if the captors themselves were playing an exact role in the sequence you designed."

"If it seemed like that to you, it was because of my men's outstanding skills, and because I managed to compensate on the fly. But that doesn't mean I didn't make a huge mistake." Her eyes were puzzled but engrossed. He could tell that she couldn't wait to see where he was taking this. "Do you remember what I did when we stormed in?"

She nodded stiffly, as if it still pained her to think of that harrowing time. And who could blame her? She'd watched three people get killed in cold blood as proof of their captors' resoluteness. She'd once told him that knowing the true meaning of helplessness, failing to protect those people, had damaged her more than her fear of meeting the same fate.

"What do you remember?"

Her exquisite features contorted with the reluctance to conjure up the memories. Still, she answered, "It was so explosive, but I remember it frame for frame. You burst in while one of them was threatening Najeeb that he'd start blowing parts off him. Then I met your eyes across the distance and…and…"

"Go on."

She swallowed. "You streaked toward me, blowing

away those men left and right, and then you were in front of me—shielding me—as you and your team finished off the rest."

"And that was my sin. *Najeeb* was my mission. And I took one look at you across that hall and made the instantaneous decision to save you first."

Her eyes widened; her lips opened on a soundless exclamation. She'd evidently never thought to question what he'd done.

When she finally talked, her whisper was impeded. "But you blasted away the one who was threatening him as you ran to me. You gave no one a chance to use him as shield or to harm him."

"I should have run *to* him, should have shielded *him*. As my crown prince, he should have been my only priority. Instead, I made that you."

"But you managed to save him and everyone else."

"Only because I managed to compensate, as I said. Najeeb could have gotten shot before I ended the threat to him. And knowing full well the widespread damage his injury or death would have caused, retaliations that would have reaped far more than five hundred lives, I still risked that."

Time seemed to stretch as bewilderment glimmered in her gemlike eyes.

She let out a shaky breath. "So what are you saying? That you took one look at me and were so bowled over you decided to risk everyone's lives—including your own—for *me*?"

"No. That's not what I'm saying. I was...bowled over a bit before that."

He watched her mouth drop open. This was news to her. He'd never intimated that he'd seen her before that day. But he'd seen her over two years earlier, had searched her out many times afterward.

"But it was the first time I'd seen you!"

"I saw no upside in letting you see me, or in acting on my interest. You were, as you pointed out so many times when we were together, an Aal Masood…and I was an Aal Ghaanem. The Montagues and Capulets didn't have a thing on our moronically feuding houses. I also didn't think it would be wise or fair to ever involve a woman in my crazy existence." He exhaled. "Then I saw you in danger and every rational thought flew out the window."

Her eyes filled with so much; he struggled not to drag her to him and kiss them closed.

Then they emptied of everything, leaving only hardness. "Why are you telling me this now?"

He shrugged. "I am testing your claim that you know everything. I just proved that you don't."

"You proved only that you spin a good yarn. As I already knew you did. Is this one supposed to appeal to my ego?"

A mirthless huff escaped him. "You think I'm making this up? Why? To butter you up for my current purposes? I wish. As someone who knows what a bullet feels like ripping through my flesh, I would have preferred one to admitting how fallible I am, how unprofessional I was, how I risked everyone's lives to protect a woman who didn't know me…whom I believed could never be mine."

Steel mixed with gold in her gaze, clearly not buying his admissions. Funny. If he'd ever thought he'd confess this to her, he wouldn't have dreamed this would be her reaction.

Might as well confess the rest, let her make whatever she wished of it. "When I burst in and I met your eyes, saw that mixture of terror and courage and fury…I couldn't imagine I wouldn't be able to look in those eyes again, to get the chance to know you. My instincts took over…and I let them."

She averted those eyes, depriving him of their touch.

"Yet after you went to such lengths to save me, you didn't follow up on your wish to 'know' me. Not for over a year."

He exhaled heavily. "I might have saved the day, for you and for everyone else, but *I* knew how badly I messed up. I guess I was punishing myself for failing to fulfill my duty and couldn't reward my failure by giving myself the gift of knowing you, the one behind my lapse."

She raised her eyes, that derision back in full force. "So was it guilt that stopped you from giving yourself the 'gift' of knowing me, or was it that you didn't think it 'wise or fair' to involve a woman in your crazy existence?"

"Both. And the family feud. Everything."

"Then, a year later, you just decided to disregard all those overpowering reasons you had not to approach me. Once you made that first contact, you relentlessly courted me all the way to your bed. Then, before I could catch my breath, you pushed for marriage. And when I tried to slow things down, you pushed harder. And when I decided to put a stop to it, you threatened you'd slander me and destroy any man who came near me."

He gritted his teeth on the memory of his despair, when he'd felt her slipping through his fingers. "These were my most indefensible moments. Trying to hang on to you, then going almost berserk when I couldn't."

"Yeah, sure," she scoffed. "You lost control out of sheer emotion. That coming from the ice-cold man they sent after the Mata Haris of the world, to seduce, entrap and destroy them."

It was his turn to blink in surprise. She knew that? How?

She elaborated on just how much she knew. "I've been told how you are the man to rely on when a woman is involved, the incomparable undercover agent no female can resist. You're not only known as *Al Moddammer,* but *Qatel an-Nesaa*—the lady-killer. And you're claiming you took one look at the twenty-year-old nobody I was, an obscure member of your family's hereditary enemies, and couldn't think straight on account of my irresistibility?"

He exhaled. "That does about sum it up."

"Tut."

That click of her tongue shot straight to his loins. Any second now he was going to ravish her again, come what may.

Unaware of his state, she went on, "I expected better from the ultimate secret-service weapon that you are. Some airtight premise, at least something more plausible. Seems I have to revise many things I believed about you. You do remember I prefaced this unfortunate encounter, before you took that detour into badly scripted drama, by mentioning that I know everything, don't you?"

"Again I say I wish it was anything but the pathetic truth. So, against all my intentions, I find myself forced to ask, according to you, what *is* everything?"

Her eyes became icy embers. "Everything from the moment I went to meet Najeeb and found you waiting for me instead."

Jala watched those eyes of his blaze at her declaration.

She'd never been able to decide when they were most hypnotic: when they glowed with a constant flame or when they fluctuated—as they'd been doing throughout this confrontation—their pupils expanding and constricting, giving the intense tawny irises the illusion of burning coals.

She'd dreamed of those fiery eyes, his voice, his touch, for over a year after the hostage crisis. And it had had nothing to do with his saving her life. He'd just…overwhelmed her. He'd melted her just by looking at her, just by being near. When feeling that way had been totally out of character for her. She'd been too mature for her age, as her brothers had always told her. Cerebral, almost jaded.

But Mohab…he *had* bowled her over. For over a year, she'd relived every single second of being pressed against the body he'd fearlessly offered as her shield. She'd suffocated with remembered terror that a bullet could tear through his perfection. Then she'd relived every second as he'd sheltered her away from the scene of carnage. But before she could have even a word with him, the Bidalyan government had bundled all the hostages, sending them back to their countries to close that case as quickly as possible.

For months afterward, she'd gone crazy trying to find out who he was. Until Najeeb, her fellow hostage, had sought her out.

Najeeb had been magnificent during the crisis. Levelheaded, fearless, shrewd, he'd managed their captors like a veteran used to being under fire. It was certain more people would have died if not for his intervention. He'd recognized her as the only one he could depend on and they'd forged an instantaneous bond, as if they'd always worked together, minimizing damages for two agonizing days.

Then one of their captors had cracked, started shrieking he'd blow bits off Najeeb, as the highest-ranking royal, so his father would pressure the Bidalyans to meet their demands faster. But just as the situation had escalated, Mohab had exploded onto the scene.

It had surprised her to find out from Najeeb that their savior had been the head of Saraya's special forces, not Bidalya's. Turned out Bidalya had ceded control of the hostage retrieval to Mohab so he'd be responsible for his crown prince's fate, and because he was the best at what he did.

But finding out he was also Najeeb's older paternal cousin had dashed even her fantasies. Najeeb could be her friend in spite of their families' enmity. But friendship wasn't what she'd wanted from Mohab. Not that she'd thought she'd see him again.

Then, one day, he'd just appeared, instead of Najeeb, to escort her to her first award ceremony. She'd been so delirious with this windfall she hadn't questioned how or why. Even when Najeeb had called, explaining the emergency that would keep him away for months and hadn't mentioned sending Mohab, she hadn't thought it odd. She'd taken everything Mohab had said as uncontestable truth.

That first evening had been magical, and he'd been the perfect companion. He'd suggested lunch the next day and she'd jumped at his invitation, had continued to grab every opportunity to be with him for the next two months, with Mohab showing her more facets of himself, each impossible to resist.

Not that resisting had been a consideration. Then, as if he'd known just when she'd become ready for more, he'd taken her to his penthouse, and then he'd taken her....

"Will you answer my question, or will you keep the 'everything' you know a mystery?"

His taunt pulled her out of the plunge into the past, which appeared to have been only a moment in real time.

She was loath to dredge up the sordid past, but she'd cornered herself into doing just that.

What the hell.

She leveled her best denigrating gaze on him. "How is it a mystery when we both know you only entered my life to eliminate me from Najeeb's? That I was just another mission to *Qatel an-Nesaa?*"

Four

Jala watched his pupils expand until it looked as if his eyes were being engulfed by black holes.

He finally inhaled. "What's the source of your info?"

"What do you think?"

"Najeeb." It was a statement. "What did he tell you?"

"The truth."

A long exhalation, then Mohab moved, brushing past her on his way to the couch. He sat down in one of those movements of pure power and grace. "I injured my knee in my last mission, so standing isn't a favorite activity at the moment." When she only stared down at him, he sighed. "I also pulled a muscle in my neck."

His perfectly formed hand caressed the space beside him, enticing her to fill it, making her feel it over her back, below her panties, kneading and owning all over again.

She gritted her teeth against the resurgence of lust. "And I should care about your discomfort? The man who's responsible for dragging me back to this godforsaken region and behind this farce that's causing me nothing but discomfort?"

"Point taken. But this will take longer than I expected and it would alleviate at least your physical discomfort if you sit for the duration."

"Actually, this won't take *any* longer. I already told you to go to hell. I'm sure you chest-thumping males will find another way to settle your war once you give up on me as a convenient chess piece in your backward power games."

She thought she was safely out of his range, but when she turned away it was her hand he snagged this time. Her balance was so compromised she needed only a coaxing tug to tumble over him.

Breath burst from her lungs as her body impacted his, even when it did so softly. His effortless power supported most of her weight in midplummet, arranging her to land across his body, one arm cushioning her back, the other gathering her thighs over his lap.

Before she could even recoil, he flattened her breasts to the expanse of his chest, swamping her in the intoxication of his scent and heat. "I'm a breath away from picking up where we left off, Jala. This time, neither of us will be able to stop. So if you don't want me to make love to you right here on your brother's couch, distract me."

She hated him, but herself more, for knowing he'd only spoken the truth. All her pleasure centers were revving, her body readying itself for him. Craving *had* been seething beneath her skin all this time. She had to end this before he exploited that weakness. More than he already had.

"Would a poke in the eye be distracting enough for you? Or do you prefer something bitten off?"

"I'd take any voluntary touch from you, but—" he released her thighs and scooped her hands into his palms "—I'd prefer not to add to my injuries right now. There's another thing that would dampen my arousal. Having this out at last. Talk to me."

"I already said all I had to say, then and now."

"All right. I'll do the talking. So Najeeb told you 'the truth.'" She nodded, hoping to lull him enough so she'd be able to squirm away with as little indignity as possible. He sighed, pressing his chest harder into her. "Truths are overrated, points of view and perspectives at best. So tell me his version, what you sanctioned as the only one there is."

"I'll play your aggravating game on one condition."

"Let you go?" Her glare said that didn't deserve the oxygen it would take to say yes. He sighed deeper. "I doubt anything you say can be worth not holding you like this."

A growl rolled in her gut. "I would have preferred to end this with your dignity and appendages intact, but at this point, I'm not against screaming bloody murder to get rid of you. The royal guard won't care who you are. By the time I pull them off you, you'll have more than a creaking knee and neck."

The smile playing across his cruelly sensuous lips became a full-fledged grin, as if she'd just made him a delightful promise. "I had this discussion with your brother a few days ago, about who'd win in such a confrontation— his royal guard or me with my hands tied behind my back."

And the worst part? She could believe the odds *would* be in his favor. Damn him.

"But since I can't risk your brother's current goodwill if I damage his soldiers, I'll pass on a demonstration."

He released her, oh, so slowly, and she felt nerves spooling inside every inch that separated from him. Even withdrawing his touch was as exquisite as bestowing it.

Ya Ullah...why was she so afflicted? Why was he the only man who'd ever accessed her controls and so... uncontrollably? How was her mental and emotional aversion so divorced from her sensual response? Why was it so absolute?

And he knew exactly what he was doing to her; he was playing her responses like a virtuoso. A ruthless expert in manipulating the female body and psyche.

Najeeb had told her Mohab had played many women before her. As, no doubt, he had countless others after her. Probably during. Not ones like the inexperienced and already infatuated young woman she'd been, but cunning, jaded women who'd seen and done it all, even hardened criminals and spies. Yet he'd still taken them in with his overwhelming sexuality and perfectly simulated charm and chivalry. She hadn't had a chance.

A new wave of mortification poured strength into her limbs as she pushed away from him. He didn't help her this time, forcing her to dip with all her weight into his unyielding power for support. The way he threw his head back against the back of the couch, his rumble of enjoyment as her fingers sank into his muscles, the way his heavy lids lowered, turning his eyes to burning slits as he watched her struggle up, assailed her with the memory of all the times he'd looked and sounded like that as she'd ridden him to oblivion....

Severing contact, she thought she'd managed to escape his compulsion when he ensnared her again.

Holding her head in the cradle of his hands, striking her immobile with his very gentleness, he exhaled softly. "Just one more."

Then he took her lips in a kiss that all but extracted her soul.

She took it all, helpless to do anything but let him invade her with pleasure, her body singing in delight, weeping with need. After a series of conquering plunges, he slowed to clinging plucks that had her almost keeling over him again. He finally relinquished her lips with a last groan of regret.

Feeling her legs had turned to jelly, she barely reached the facing armchair before collapsing on it.

"I hope you've had your fun."

At her rasp, his eyes simmered like some supernatural beast's. "You know I didn't. You know exactly how I have fun. Hard, protracted, borderline-fatal-with-pleasure fun."

She managed not to shudder. Yeah. She knew. Every cell in her body seemed to know nothing else. They'd had mega doses of "fun" in the five months they'd been intimate. Whenever she'd thought it couldn't get better, it had, like a force picking up momentum. Familiarity had only kept shifting the addiction to higher gears. It had been so intense, had felt so pure, it had been a devastating blow when she'd learned the truth.

Exhaling the remembered misery, she made her decision. Letting your enemy find out how much you knew wasn't wise, but maybe getting it all out would help purge it—and him—from her system once and for all.

"Let's start with when Najeeb left New York. Or shall we say when you set up the emergencies he'd been called back to Saraya to handle, with his father allegedly sick and unable to deal with them."

His eyes lost that languid sensuality, but there was no other sign of response.

She went on. "For months everything seemed to thwart him, and he grew suspicious, decided to go to the source of all info—his mother. After making him swear he'd never confront his father, Queen Safaa admitted that King Hassan believed Najeeb would end up marrying me, a daughter of the hated Aal Masoods, and it would cost him his position as his heir, as Saraya's tribes wouldn't abide the introduction of Aal Masood blood into the royal family.

He even feared the Aal Ghaanems might lose the throne altogether to an uprising."

Mohab still had no reaction. But then again, why should he react? He already knew all this.

She exhaled. "To stop this calamity, King Hassan had one hope of breaking up our relationship. You. The kingdom's most lethal secret weapon. I was a homeland security threat of the highest order after all. As someone who was raised to despise the Aal Masoods, the idea that your crown prince might sully your line with the blood of your hated enemies was probably as unthinkable to you.

"Najeeb's mother related how you shared your king's opinion of me—the then-minor princess who flaunted her region's values and disgraced her brothers by living a degenerate life in the West. You agreed that I was manipulating the honorable Najeeb, using our shared ordeal to ride him to the status of a future queen. When the king authorized you to get rid of me, he knew how you'd do it. The same way you rid the kingdom of every black widow who tried to compromise the royal family or the integrity of the kingdom."

His gaze remained unchanged, betraying nothing.

Figured. He'd betrayed nothing through their five-month relationship. Not one action or glance or word had given her a clue that it had all been an act. The reverse had been true. Everything from him had been fierce, consistent, unequivocal, had felt more real than anything she'd ever experienced. Discovering the truth had hit so out of the blue, it had crushed her.

Her world had warped, every emotion and passion she'd felt for him becoming shame, humiliation.

She went on, emptying her voice of any remembered anguish. "You seduced me only to make me ineligible for Najeeb, then asked me to marry you to perfect your act, no doubt to drop me like a used napkin the moment you were sure your crown prince was safe."

Najeeb had been livid at his father, but more at Mohab, if only for the interference, the duplicity. His outrage had been mitigated by his belief that he'd saved her in time. She had never exposed the depths of her fall and folly to her friend. Only wanting the mess over with, she'd made Najeeb promise he'd never confront Mohab. She'd just wanted to walk away.

Numb and feeling used, she'd stumbled home, had stood in that shower for what might have been hours. Then Mohab had come. His urgency and passion, which her senses still hadn't been able to recognize as fake, had had her body detonating with a fireball of lust and her mind spiraling in blankness.

Afterward everything had spilled over, razing her with the devastation of fury and mortification.

After Mohab had finally gone, she'd collapsed. Not in any dramatic way, just a gradual descent into depression, her misery deepening with time and repercussions. It had taken her years to climb out.

Now, just as she was finally over her ordeal and firmly on stable footing, the man responsible for it all had come back to destroy the peace she'd struggled so long and hard for.

"So that's why you decided you didn't want to marry me after all, and so abruptly."

His deep statement roused her from her musings.

She gave him the only answer he'd get from her. "It just gave me the reason to bail, as I'd been wanting to, without caring how I did it."

"That's why you didn't confront me, no matter how much I pushed? You weren't interested in hearing my defense, since you'd already decided to walk out on me?"

At her nod, he shook his head, as if deprecating himself for wanting to hear her discoveries *had* been the only reason behind her rejection. No doubt out of pride, as that would make her the only woman who had walked away from him. Buying her claim didn't make things better, but it *was* something, since she'd rather crawl back to the airport in today's heat wave rather than give him the triumph of knowing how fully he'd taken her in.

"So craving me was one thing, marrying me was another."

"Who said I craved you?"

His mock reproving look sent blood surging to her loins. "Let's not dispute the indisputable, *ya jameelati*. You did, and I just proved you still do."

Her insides clenched at his taunt, his calling her his beauty. "I'm just a hot-blooded woman."

"That's why you were a virgin when I first took you?"

The way he said *took you* reverberated in her being.

For there was no other way to describe what he'd done to her that first night. Or any other time after that. He'd shown her what her body and being had always been capable of, but would have lain untapped if not for his unlocking their potential. Her wildest dreams before him hadn't known to venture into the realms where he'd taken her.

But she'd still woken up in his arms that first time feeling anxious. Though she'd believed him to be progressive, Saraya was even more ultraconservative than Judar, and she'd feared he might despise her for surrendering to him outside the marriage bed. She feared that because it would have meant he wasn't the man she'd fallen in love with. And if he did, she would have considered him worth nothing but good riddance, but it would still have wounded her terribly.

But he'd assuaged her fears as soon as he'd opened his eyes. He'd seamlessly played his part, had been euphoric, indulgent, even poetic about how proud he'd been that she'd bestowed her innocence on him, given him the honor of initiating her into intimacy. Then he'd asked her to marry him.

Even though she'd never thought of marriage, except to reject it, she'd found herself saying yes....

"Well?"

His challenge reminded her she hadn't answered his taunt. "Oh, you're harping on my being a virgin at the advanced age of twenty-one? A young woman still struggling to leave her stiflingly conservative upbringing behind? You expected me to go to the States and hop into bed with every man I fancied?"

"You'd been there for three years. Enough time to change your outlook and behavior, especially at that age, if you'd wanted to. But you fancied no one. I was your first. In every way. I know."

"You mean as the infallible intelligence god you are?"

"No. As the man who awakened you."

Damn him. He saw too much, knew everything.

"And once I *awakened,* thanks to your expert... rousing..."

"Nothing happened. You didn't replace me in your bed."

She gaped at him. How did he...? Did that mean...?

Before she could blow a valve, he went on calmly, "*This* I know as the incomparable intelligence god that I am."

If people could explode, Jala would have, Mohab thought.

He'd tripped the one wire that could set her off. One of *two* wires. The first was passion, which he was gratified he could still trigger with a touch. The second was privacy.

It had always been her biggest hang-up. She'd been near obsessive about it. Her insistence on never meeting him where anyone might recognize her had at first made him think it was a cunning effort to have his cake and eat Najeeb's, too. But as his preconceptions had melted, and she'd opened up with details of her life in Judar, he'd understood how hard-won her autonomy had been. After a lifetime of having her breaths counted and steps monitored, she'd sworn...*no more.*

He watched her rise, every inch aching to have her in his arms again. But that wouldn't move anything forward. And he was afraid that if she surrendered again, he wouldn't be able to stop.

"You had me under surveillance?" she seethed.

He sighed. Not his favorite topic, discussing his obsession with her. "I'm not good at letting go."

"Sure. Do you have a bridge to sell me with that? So what was it, really? You forgot to call off my surveillance detail and reports kept hitting your desk?"

At his raised eyebrow, she took a furious step toward him. "We're in full-disclosure mode, aren't we? So how about you not pretend you didn't have my every move documented before you approached me? It's evident you formulated a plan to entrap me in the most time-efficient manner based on my character analysis. But after you ended my supposed threat to your crown prince, what purpose did keeping tabs on me serve? Was it to make sure I didn't go after another of your kingdom's princes after you made sure Najeeb found me 'ineligible' to be his future queen?"

Wincing at the words that had haunted him with shame, he shook his head. "I didn't tell Najeeb anything."

"I don't believe you."

Her instantaneous rejection was what he deserved. Not only had he threatened to do just that, Najeeb *had* cut off all relations with her, proving to her that Mohab had carried out his threat.

But he hadn't. He'd lived dreading news of her impending marriage to Najeeb. When that had never come to pass, he'd found out why. His uncle had told Najeeb that Mohab *had* fulfilled his mission in proving that Jala was dissolute, but if Najeeb desired her, he could enjoy her, as Mohab once had.

Even though he'd been hurt and jealous, believed she'd chosen Najeeb over him, he'd also come to admit that she'd had every right to change her mind about marrying him. And he'd been *furious* that Najeeb had ended what he'd professed to be a strong friendship based on hearsay, or even the truth of their relationship. If that made her dissolute in Najeeb's eyes, when the man hadn't staked a prior claim, it made him despicable.

He'd been unable to abide his uncle's defamation and his cousin's desertion of her. In a gesture of ultimate contempt, he'd resigned his job and left their and Saraya's service.

He exhaled. "Ask Najeeb. He'll tell you I haven't talked to him since that night. You had every right to leave me, and I'll be forever ashamed I threatened to slander you for it."

Her glare wavered only to harden again. "Even if I believe that, you have other transgressions waiting in line. How dare you have me followed?"

Savoring the bewitching sight she made in her fury, he said, "As long as I'm already damned, and I have no hope of having the extenuating circumstances sanctioned, I might as well tell you that I've been keeping tabs on you far longer than you think. I started right after I first saw you attending a conference with your oldest brother Farooq in Washington."

Her eyes rounded. "That was ten years ago!"

"*Aih.* You were only eighteen and the most incredible thing I'd ever seen. I felt the chemistry that sizzles between us singe me even then, even when you didn't see me."

Her disbelief was almost palpable. "It's not *possible* I didn't see you."

"You do remember what I do for a living, don't you? If I want to stay out of sight, that's where I remain."

But he'd been unable to stop following her after that first sighting. He'd known he'd never approach her, but she'd become his fantasy when he'd never had one before.

Then that hostage crisis had happened. Her name had been the only thing he'd seen on that hostage list before he'd stormed in, and he'd made the decision to save her first right then. Facing that had made him more enraged at himself, his anger mounting the more he found himself struggling not to go after her, and to hell with all the reasons to stay away.

"And you expect me to believe you were enthralled at first sight? A sight I didn't even reciprocate?"

"Seems you never looked in the mirror."

"C'mon…you have tons of gorgeous women littering your path, and I'm not even that. I'm too…androgynous."

An incredulous laugh burst out of him. "Then I don't know what that says about me, since you define femininity to me." Before she ricocheted with another rebuttal, he cut her off. "Aren't you going to hear my version of what happened?"

"Will you tell me Najeeb or I jumped to conclusions, or some other lameness like that? Don't bother. I already told you I don't care. It was just a welcome bit of news that made breaking up with you much easier."

He had to accept that. It seemed he hadn't realized how controlling his kind of life had made him, how severely allergic she had been, and still was, to any infringement on her free will. Her distress *had* been acute every time he'd pushed to announce their engagement. She'd kept saying she wanted more private time before their families and their feud infringed on their relationship. It seemed the more he tried to push for moving forward, the more she'd resented his attempts to herd her toward his objective. She would probably have ended it on that account alone. Her discoveries about his subterfuge had just rushed everything to its conclusion.

He patted the space beside him again. "You still need to know my side, just so you know 'everything' for real."

She only flung a dismissing hand at him. "Suit yourself."

"Thank you, Your Ungraciousness." He bowed his head mockingly. "So…when my uncle assigned me the mission of sabotaging you and Najeeb, I pounced on it, but only as a pretext to finally approaching you. That alone made me wonder if you might be as dangerous as my uncle believed. After all, how could you be the sweet innocent I thought you to be if you affected *me* this way, when the world's most lethal seductresses didn't turn a hair in me? If I was so enthralled from afar, what chance did Najeeb have?"

He *had* approached her, hoping she'd turn out to be nothing like his fantasies and he could end her hold over him. Saving Najeeb would have been incidental.

But from that first night, he'd lost sight of the whole world in her company, then of his own reality in her arms. He'd forgotten who he was and what kind of life he led to the point he'd asked her to marry him.

"But you changed your mind once you were with me, right?"

"When I was with you I *had* no mind. But if anyone gets your reservations back then, it's me. You had your reasons for shunning marriage, and I had mine."

Not that his dread had stopped him from wanting to go through with it, from becoming progressively more impatient with her postponements, even when he hadn't realized they'd been signs of trouble. This obliviousness had been why he'd been so shocked when she'd ended it. Then, after he'd found out why she hadn't hooked up with Najeeb, she'd disappeared.

He'd turned the world upside down searching for her, to no avail. He'd only found her when she'd resurfaced on her own, following a yearlong humanitarian trek in uncharted areas in South America. He hadn't let her out of his sight since.

And all the while, he'd been seeking a pretext to go after her again. Now that he'd finally found it, he would get her. She just didn't know it yet.

He swept her in an aching glance. "But my proposal, as ill-advised as it was, *was* real." At her disbelieving huff, his lips twisted. "Whatever you think I thought or felt, not even I can feign that much hunger, for that long or at all."

"But men don't have to feign anything. Put a willing woman in their bed and that's all she wrote."

"Your inexperience with anyone else but me is showing." He rose, savoring every nuance of her chagrin at being unable to contest his exclusive ownership of her body. "Those indiscriminate men you describe are aroused by the novelty, the challenge. They are notorious for losing…steam quickly when with a familiar body, no matter how tempting. But the more I had you, the more my hunger for you raged. I craved you enough that I would have jumped into an inferno—or even into marriage—to keep you."

"Then it's fortunate Najeeb's revelations pushed me to make the decision I'd been circling for a while, saving us both from a fate worse than hell."

"I'm just telling you my side. And now that you've told me yours, I understand why you walked away. A combination of commitment phobia, resentment and outrage is pretty potent. You were doing what you believed was right for yourself. But that's your mind. What about your body? How long did it ache in demand for mine? How severe were the withdrawal pangs?"

Something dark and enormous expanded in her eyes.

His heart hammered. *Ya Ullah,* was that…anguish?

The disturbing expression was gone before he could be sure he'd seen it. "I can tell you for a fact that for the next year there was no aching or withdrawal."

That didn't sound like a spiteful denial. She meant this.

Could it be she'd walked away at no cost to herself? There'd been no emptiness in her gut and loins, no burning in her senses and skin, needing his assuagement, his completion? Could the love she'd sobbed out loud in pleasure-drenched nights have evaporated so absolutely that not even a remnant of the physical yearning remained?

No. He wouldn't buy that. She'd melted again at his touch. Her body still proclaimed him its mate and master.

As if to contradict his conviction, she said, "I haven't had other men since because I was too busy with work, and I'm not the kind for one-night stands. It wasn't because I was pining for you."

"If you'd found the intensity of attraction and totality of arousal you had with me, you would have made time. But you wanted that or nothing at all. Sometimes hunger is so vast, nothing but what you crave would fulfill it." Giving her no chance to back away, he took her in his arms. "I know, because nothing could fulfill my craving but you."

"Yeah, sure." She squirmed, only inflaming him more.

He hauled her tighter against him. "Fact is sometimes stranger than fiction. It was as unreal to me as it sounds to you now. This chemistry we share wasn't only an aphrodisiac, but a mind-altering substance."

"Sounds like something you wouldn't want to abuse. So why are you doing this? Or are you just making the best of your 'mission' this time, too?'

"This time, it's all me. How much has Kamal told you?"

Sullenly, she told him. Kamal had only told her the general situation, hadn't even mentioned him by name. So he now filled in his part of the story, leaving out only that he could abort the hostilities without her marrying him.

She digested everything, inert in his arms, eyes somber. "So you're going to be king. That's unexpected. But it also enables you to resolve this without little Aal Masood me."

Her analytical powers were unerring. As he well knew.

But he couldn't corroborate her analysis or this was over before it began. "The peace through marriage is what my uncle would agree to."

"How ironic. I was the only woman he couldn't abide for his heir, now I'm the only one to serve his purposes." She pushed away, hard. "He can go to hell, right along with you."

He hated to play this card, but he'd run out of options. "You once said you would repay me one day."

That made her go rock still, a world of reproach filling her cognac eyes. "I also said I won't do that with my life."

"I'm not asking for your life. Just your hand in marriage. Just your body in my bed."

A scoff burst from her. "My choice, my future and my body. That just about wraps up what makes up my life."

He shrugged. "Not really."

"Oh? What else is there that you're not laying claim to?"

"Plenty. Your heart, your mind, your soul." At her immovable glare, he found no recourse but to push. "I *am* collecting my debt now, Jala. It is that imperative." For him.

Apprehension gradually replaced ire on her exquisite face.

Then she finally exclaimed, "You're all really going to do something insane if we don't get married?"

And he seized that first wavering in her resolve, drove his advantage home. "We have to get married. Nobody said we have to *stay* married."

Five

Jala couldn't believe it.

That gargantuan weasel had made her say yes.

He'd used his every weapon, from seduction to logic to cajoling, playing havoc with her vulnerabilities and convictions, making her revoke her edict consigning him to hell.

But then, the situation *was* dire.

From her work in regions festering with conflict, she was too familiar with how wars ignited over much less than the current stakes. In places like their region, where pride and tribalism and other inherited, obsolete conventions still ruled to a great degree beneath the modernized veneer, once blood was spilled, enmities could—and did—rage for centuries.

Kamal and Mohab, damn them both to hell, had pegged her accurately. They'd both counted on her inability to stand by and let something like this happen if she could help it. They'd known that after her first shock and outrage, once she realized it was true only she could help, she would.

But she drew the line at marrying Mohab to do it. The best she'd do was agree to a fake engagement.

Yeah, another one. But one she *knew* was fake. She'd go through the motions for the sake of peace.

And that was *huge* of her. Engagements around here were excruciating, rife with maddening customs and obscene intrusions. Wedding preparations made some of the war zones she'd been to look peaceful.

But she'd use those torturous rituals to draw out this charade until treaties were signed. Then she'd bail out.

One thing still had her red-alert sensors clanging, though. The ease with which Mohab had agreed to her terms.

At first, he'd insisted only an actual marriage would appease King Hassan, that they'd have to dispense with an engagement to give him the quick union that would force him from his warpath. He'd suggested a six-month period before separating. According to him, that was enough time to settle all treaties and resolve all disputes.

But when she'd countered with the most she'd agree to, and that he'd have to convince King Hassan to sign the treaties *during* their pseudoengagement, he'd consented with disturbing equanimity.

Suddenly she felt as though a rocket had gone off inside her head. She knew *why* his acquiescence had disturbed her. Because it must have been what that insidious rat had been after all the time!

He must have anticipated her first point-blank refusal. So he'd let her get this out of her system. Being ruthlessly results oriented, he must have known an agreement wouldn't be a possibility. The best he could expect from this first encounter was to stall her, stop her from leaving Judar and secure any level of cooperation.

So he'd kept applying pressure here so she'd sidestep there, pushed and pulled, kissed and caressed, laid bare secrets, exhumed heartaches, appealed to her ego and seared her senses in a steady barrage. When he'd felt her waver, he'd hit her with a solution that had too high a cost. At this point, he must have projected two outcomes. Since she'd already entered the cooperative zone, either she'd buckle and accept outright, or she'd counter with her own offer, bargaining a lower price. Either way, he'd achieve his objective. Her, here, playing along.

That it was only for now and not for real didn't bother him. This was only round one to him. Being Machiavellian and a long-term thinker, he most certainly wouldn't abide by the limits of what she'd granted. And as a master strategist, he had every reason to expect he wouldn't have to. If he'd gotten her to concede that much in under two hours, he'd probably estimated he'd have her dancing to his tune in two days.

She was now certain he would keep on giving her as much rope as she asked for…and use it to lasso and truss her up.

Consternation bubbled on a stifled shriek. She even stomped her foot. It landed with a damp thud on the sand, not the satisfying bang she'd needed.

Groaning in frustration, her gaze jerked around the four-mile shore. Still alone. At least, apparently so.

But of course she wasn't alone. Kamal must have given his guards orders to keep out of her sight. He wouldn't want to infringe on her personal space, aggravating her more than he'd already had.

But there was no doubt dozens of eyes were watching *the* princess of Judar taking a stroll along the shore surrounding the royal palace. She wondered why they'd even bother. No one came within ten miles of the palace or its extensive grounds, by land or by sea. It wasn't even one of those days when the palace and satellite buildings were open for tourists. The only way someone could target her would be by satellite or long-range missile.

Oh, well. She had known what kind of intrusions she'd signed on for the moment she'd agreed to stay in Judar and play Mohab's game. The kind that had once had her running to the States and hiding in blessed anonymity and heavenly aloneness.

The first eighteen years of her life here had surely taken their toll. Though she loved her brothers fiercely, her experience in Judar had been the opposite of theirs in every respect. Even if, at the time, they'd just been three of the former king's multitude of nephews, they'd been everything the region and the royal family valued. Male, magnificent, with personal assets running out of their ears. They'd had every freedom, along with privilege and power, to counter all the responsibilities, expectations and pressures.

While she, the unplanned child her parents had had twelve years after they thought they were done having children, had been a mistake—and a female one at that. To compound her problems, when she'd been only three her mother had been diagnosed with cancer. After a long struggle, when she'd been forced to relinquish Jala's upbringing to others, she'd died when Jala was ten. Less than a year later, her father, totally destroyed by his wife's long illness and death, had died, too, leaving Jala to the care of her older brothers, relatives and hired help.

The next years had been a nightmare. Her brothers, while they'd doted on her, had been too busy forging their success to have much time for her. As one who hated to ask for help or attention, she'd never let them know of her dismal state of mind. She'd felt isolated from the royal family, and from her culture, where she'd never felt she fit in.

But as she'd grown older, she'd been progressively more besieged by the restrictions that being female in Judar entailed, compounded by the fact that she had no mother to fend for her. And while she had enough royal status to suffer its downsides, she had enjoyed none of its advantages. Her situation had been further complicated when she'd refused the privileges offered women here, which she considered condescending and sexist, making her an outcast among her peers. By the time she was finished high school, she'd felt she'd do something drastic if she didn't get away.

Then her maternal aunt's husband was appointed the ambassador of Judar to the United States. Frantic to make use of this possible ticket out, she'd hounded her brothers until they'd agreed to let her go with their aunt to continue her education there. She'd arrived in the States four months before her eighteenth birthday and had left her aunt's custody the day after her birthday party.

Seizing on her freedom of choice at once, she'd started fulfilling her lifelong ambition to follow Farooq in his humanitarian relief efforts.

It had been while attending that ill-fated conference in Bidalya that she'd first set eyes on Mohab. And it had been during the ceremony where she'd received her first work-related award that he'd effectively entered her life.

Now he'd reentered it. And she was back in Judar.

And it was all because of him.

Mohab. Even his name aggravated her right now. His parents had to give him such a lofty one, didn't they? And he had to be an exasperating bastard and live up to it, didn't he? Awe-inspiring. Feared. Even frightening. And he'd gone on to be far more. Spellbinding. Overwhelming. Devastating.

Okay. It wasn't all because of him. This impending war wasn't of his orchestration. And the cruel twist of fate that made her the king of Judar's sister, and Mohab the imminent king of Jareer, was also beyond him.

But now she thought of it, another thing was his fault. Their whole confrontation last evening.

After that preemptive opening seduction scene, he'd proceeded to scramble her entrenched belief that she'd just been another body and mission to him, asserting that he'd wanted her for far longer than she'd even thought. He'd claimed he'd monitored her for years, compromised his duty and disregarded his orders for her, craved her so much that he'd proposed for real. And all along, he'd kept pulling her back into mindlessness, as if he'd been unable to keep his passion in check.

Then she'd agreed to play her part and he'd just… stopped. He'd stood by calmly and just let her leave.

Did that mean everything he'd told her had been more manipulation designed to shove her into the slot where he needed her? Then, once he had, he'd just retracted his tentacles and settled back into neutral mode?

That made the most sense. She *had* long ago become reconciled to the fact that a man who'd chosen Mohab's line of work must be made of a different material than other human beings. To deal with the atrocities he was required to face head-on, he must have long since shut down his basic human emotions. And to fulfill his stealth missions, he must have become an expert at simulating those emotions at will.

But even knowing that, he'd managed to fool her again. He'd anesthetized her judgment and nullified her instincts. She'd actually begun believing his claims and had all but drowned in his passion. His nonexistent passion.

And that was the worst of it all. That after everything that had happened, her senses and responses would forever remain dependent on a mirage. Like Tantalus, she was destined to shrivel up with thirst for an illusion.

What kind of fate was it that always made her his target, his chess piece? Why had fate infected her with this unremitting hunger that nothing had ever eradicated, when he felt none for her, for real, in return? Why, after she'd suppressed it for years until she'd thought she'd been cured, had it taken only his reappearance to drag it out of her depths? And now that the fever had spiked again, how could she subdue it, at least enough to keep on functioning?

A wave of too-familiar dejection crashed over her as she slit her eyes against the brilliant setting sun, suddenly cold to her marrow in the balmy March breeze.

Legs heavy and numb, she started back to the palace. And, in spite of everything, it took her breath all over again.

Anyone looking at it would think it was a historical monument, but she'd attended its inauguration as the new seat of power in Judar just eleven years ago during her late uncle's rule. It had since become a monument as important as the Taj Mahal, and sure gave that legendary edifice a run for its money. It was still as mind-boggling to her as it had been the first time she'd seen it.

Nestled in an extensively landscaped park and surrounded by silver beaches and emerald waters, it crouched in the middle of the peninsula, its grounds almost covered like a massive starship from beyond the stars. Now in the golden drape of a breathtaking sunset, it felt as if it had been conjured by magic from another realm.

That wasn't too far from the truth. Thousands of unique talents, all masters of art and architecture, had put this place together. And from what she'd seen of its interior, modern magicians of technology had imbued it with the ultimate in luxury and functionality, too.

Approaching the palace from its shore-facing side took her through street-wide paths paved in earth-colored cobblestones and lined by soaring palm trees and flower beds. She strode through gates, courtyards, pavilions, everything bearing the intricacies and influences of the cultures that had melded together to form Judar. If she'd been in anything approaching a normal frame of mind, she would have savored the magnificence of this place. But now the majesty that surrounded her—and what it signified of her royal connections and their current implications for her life—oppressed her.

Scaling the convex stone steps that converged like a fan from a hundred feet at the bottom to thirty at the top, she gazed up at the massive palace that soared on four levels, echoing every hue of the desert, topped by a complex system of domes covered in mosaics and gold finials.

As she approached the entrance, two footmen in ornate uniforms seemed to materialize out of nowhere to open the twenty-foot mahogany double doors inlaid with gold and silver.

Smiling at them or offering thanks was useless, since they looked firmly ahead, avoiding eye contact. She crossed into the circular columned hall that had to be at least two hundred feet in diameter with a ceiling dome at least half that.

Her gaze swam around the superbly lit sweeping spaces, getting only impressions of neutral color schemes and sumptuous decor and furnishings. Again it felt deserted. Or everyone was giving her space. Which was very welcome. She didn't want to meet anyone right now, even in passing.

At the end of the hall, she entered an elevator that transported her in seconds to her fourth-floor quarters.

As she entered the expansive three-chambered wing and crossed to the bedroom, the sensory overload of sweet incense and opulence hit her. Yearning for her simple, cozy, two-room American abode twisted inside her like a tornado.

"Oh, you're here!"

The bright exclamation had her swinging around, almost severing her already compromised balance.

Aliyah. Kamal's wife and her queen. And a more fitting queen she'd never seen. As a former model, Aliyah was even taller than Jala, but now boasted the lush curves of a woman who'd ripened with the passion of a virile man, and with bearing his son and daughter. Her mahogany hair was in a thick braid over her shoulder, and she was swathed in a floor-length dress the color of her chocolate eyes.

She had Carmen with her. As Farooq's wife, Carmen was the crown prince's consort and yet another specimen of feminine gorgeousness, looking like a statuesque Rita Hayworth in her garnet-haired period but with turquoise eyes. Farah, the wife of her second-oldest brother, Shehab, was the only one missing. Shehab called her his Emerald Fairy for her eyes, and in Jala's opinion he was right all around, and Farah was the most ethereally stunning of the three.

If she'd cared about her looks, Jala would have suffered serious insecurity in the presence of those three visions. As it was, she was delighted her brothers had found women who were as beautiful on the outside as they were on the inside and who adored them. It was always such a pleasure to see them. Even though their relationship consisted mostly of video chatting, since the three couples seldom left Judar due to their growing families and responsibilities.

"We did knock." Carmen grinned at her apologetically as she beckoned the four women who accompanied her and Aliyah, no doubt their ladies-in-waiting. All were laden with packages. "We assumed you weren't here when you didn't answer, and thought to leave you the stuff with a note."

"We brought you everything we could think of to see what you need and what fits," Aliyah explained.

Carmen smiled at the women who'd piled the "stuff" in the sitting area, then gestured for them to leave. "Kamal said you need everything since you left New York without packing a thing."

"Yeah, because he told me your husband was lying in hospital battling the grim reaper."

Carmen blanched, the very idea of that evidently making her sick to her stomach. "He *what?*"

"*Exactly* what I said to him when he revealed that it was only a ruse to get me here."

"*Ya Ullah!*" Aliyah groaned, looking mortified. "I'll brain him for you. If you haven't already."

"I only let him live for you and the kids," Jala mumbled.

Aliyah hugged her, contrite on her husband's behalf. "I'm *so* sorry. He's a colossal pain but..." She sighed, eyes becoming dreamy. "I let him live because he's so utterly irresistible."

Jala knew exactly what she meant. *She* was caught, again, in the web of such an inexorable force. Just not happily so.

"You're talking to the world's second foremost expert on Kamal, regrettably my so-called twin and now horrifically my king, too. I am thinking of surrendering my Judarian nationality so I'd deprive him of wielding that kind of power over me."

"As if anyone can make you do anything you don't want." Carmen's scoff was certainty itself.

Farooq's wife had once told Jala she thought her the strongest, most courageous and independent person she knew. If only Carmen knew that there was someone who'd always made Jala do whatever *he* wanted. Was still making her do it....

"Listen, we know you must be dying for an early night, so we won't keep you." Carmen linked her arm in Jala's.

"Let's open everything, and we'll see what suits you, what you need changed and what we forgot."

Aliyah followed them. "When Kamal said we should leave you alone all day, since you had a big day yesterday, I had no idea how big it was. No thanks to him. Giving you the scare, then the surprise of your life in succession."

"He told you, huh?" Jala huffed. "What am I *saying?* I think he tells you stuff before he tells it to himself."

Aliyah's exquisite face lit up with that expression of a woman secure in her power over her man, of his total love, which she reciprocated to her last breath. "He does think aloud with me. But not this time. I was told after the fact."

"After he settled the pact to sign me over in marriage to the future king of Jareer, you mean? To stop a war that old goat king of Saraya wouldn't think twice about instigating?"

Aliyah whooped. "Kamal calls him 'old goat,' too. You two really are twins!"

Carmen chuckled. "We heard you met said future king of Jareer last night. With how things are between Judar and Saraya, we never had the pleasure, but we've been hearing all sorts of things about him…like he's materialized right out of *Arabian Nights.* I've even heard women here make blasphemous comments about him—that he's even more impressive than *our* men."

Even loving her brothers as she did, Jala had to agree. Regretfully. She didn't know if it was better or worse to get more confirmation that he affected all women the same way.

Suddenly she jumped.

Carmen started. "What is it?"

Groaning, Jala got her phone out of her pocket. "Just my phone. It never vibrated that hard." Or she had surplus electricity coursing through her system. "Just a sec."

She cast a look at the number as she answered. A

blocked one. Probably one of her colleagues that the service provider here was unable to show on caller ID due to the international number.

"I am here."

She lurched harder this time. *Mohab.*

Here? Where? In her wing? Outside in the sitting room…?

"In the palace."

Oh.

"Are you in your quarters?"

She snatched a look at Carmen and Aliyah, who'd turned their backs, giving her privacy. "Yes."

"Where is it?"

"Why?"

"I plan on visiting you."

"And I plan on not receiving you."

"*Zain.* Turn on your laptop."

"Huh?"

"I'll have to improvise. Making love to you across cyberspace isn't ideal, but it might be a good idea to keep my distance until I take the edge off…the first few times."

Her knees almost buckled. "Why don't you go ahead on your own? Cyberspace is full of…material you can help yourself to."

She saw Carmen's back stiffen. It was imperceptible, but she'd heard her. And no doubt understood.

And that royal bastard continued to pour more dark magic into her inflamed brain. "I'm very fastidious about the…material…I help myself to. I have a specific movie that I have…helped myself to, times beyond count. I've long memorized every frame, had remastered it for better image and sound quality so I can help myself to it… into infinity."

A movie. Of her. As he'd massaged her, pampered her,

owned her every inch, brought her to ecstasy over and over again before he'd mounted her and thrust her to oblivion.

It had been one of her deepest scars, knowing that she'd trusted him so much she'd allowed this, that he had that evidence of her stupidity and self-destructiveness, a weapon to wield against her to serve his purposes.

"I would do anything for new material." His voice dropped an octave into the darkest reaches of temptation. "*Anything,* Jala." He let out a ragged breath that all but fried her synapses. "Turn on your laptop and we'll proceed."

She ground her teeth, refusing to press her legs together. He wasn't doing this to her, and over the phone, too, with her sisters-in-law feet away. "So I turn my laptop on and you magically see me from yours?"

"You keep forgetting who I am."

"You can tap into my computer?" she snapped.

"Of course. But I don't need to now. I just need to know your chat login. Which I do. Now hurry. The longer you make me wait, the longer before I'm appeased. I'm already half out of my mind with keeping my hands off you last night."

"You did no such thing!"

Her exclamation made both Aliyah and Carmen fidget. They must now be formulating a very good idea of what was going on.

Ya Ullah...she hated him!

"You know I did." He did that thing again with his voice that strummed the chords in the core of her being. "You know what I do with my hands when I don't keep them off you. But I kept something on. Your clothes. I almost had a heart attack needing to peel them off you. Take them off for me now, Jala. I want to see you now, want to imagine my hands on you. Show me yourself, *ya jameelati.*"

Ya Ullah—even now, he had her spontaneously combusting from a distance. Her body was readying itself, the clothes he'd asked her to remove were suddenly suffocating shackles, abrading aching flesh.

"I have company."

"Get rid of them." His command was terse, tense, uncompromising.

"I can't," she choked, smiling wanly at the two ladies who'd finished unpacking and were fidgeting, not knowing what to do. "I'm hanging up now."

"Do that, and I'll come over."

"You don't know where I am!"

"I can pinpoint your location via GPS. I was only asking as a courtesy, so you'd volunteer it willingly."

"What do you think I can do now, huh?"

"Would you have done what I asked had you been alone?"

Carmen strode by her to usher in the ladies, who brought in more packages, looking relieved to stop pretending to be talking to Aliyah and not hearing everything Jala said.

Jala cast her a brittle smile, trying to sound neutral as she almost choked on her answer. "I would have considered it."

"Liar." This was crooned in the darkest, deepest tone he'd ever hit her with. "You would have made a protracted feast of tormenting me."

That coming from the master of torment. Oh, the irony.

"*Zain.* If you can't open your laptop, we'll use the phone. I'll show you myself, instead."

Her legs gave out. She groped for the nearest chair, gesturing weakly at the ladies that she was okay, hoping they'd just leave. They didn't. They continued to work until she almost screamed she wanted to be alone to deal with this nerve-racking man without having them witness her being seduced out of her mind by him.

Mohab droned on until she felt her brain sizzling. "Remember how you used to revel in exposing me? Taking each shred of clothes off me with fingers that shook with urgency, with teeth that chattered with arousal?"

"Mohab..."

As soon as his name moaned out of her, begging mercy, she could almost see Aliyah's and Carmen's ears pricking up. Now they knew for sure who'd been tormenting her all this time.

"But I'll leave you to your visitors on one condition."

"What?" she croaked.

"The moment they're gone, you'll come to me."

To their credit, after Mohab released her from his long-distance torture, Aliyah and Carmen behaved as if they'd heard nothing as they concluded their business, which it turned out they *had* needed to stay to conclude. Before they disappeared, she thought she saw them exchanging furtive smiles.

Yeah. They were probably putting two and two together. And coming up with a thousand.

She took her time, showering, drying her hair, dressing in fresh clothes. Then she headed to the wing Mohab had been given. Aliyah had backhandedly provided its location.

At his door, she knocked, then stood back.

The door opened almost instantaneously. Across the threshold, there he was, looking fall-to-your-knees gorgeous—*Mohab*.

In a black-on-black suit and shirt, his skin simmered and his eyes glowed in the soft ambient light. Only the top section of his hair was held back now; the rest flowed like thick sheets of silk to sigh over his collar.

A wave of fierce hunger rolled over her. She bore its impact without any outward sign, looking up at him across the threshold. He only stepped aside. Knowing there'd be eyes documenting her entry into his chambers, she walked inside.

The wing looked much like the one she occupied, but it smelled different. His scent had already permeated the place. It coated her lungs, tingled on her tongue. His unique brand of virility and vigor, of scorching desert sun and flaying wind, of ruthless terrain and cleansing rain. Of cold-blooded termination and boiling-over passion.

His appreciation sizzled over her as his eyes swept her white-cotton-clad body, sensuality playing on his sculpted lips, humming from him like electricity from a high-voltage cable.

She bore the brunt of his silent, sensual onslaught, then, in utmost tranquillity and premeditation, she swung her arm and socked him in the jaw.

Six

Pain exploded in Jala's hand.

She'd thrown punches before, but nothing had ever hurt that bad. Figured. Mortal beings' jaws weren't made of some indestructible amalgam like *Arabian Nights* refugee here.

She might have broken her hand. And wrist. And elbow.

But she wouldn't obey the need to shake the agony out and howl. The unmovable bastard hadn't even rocked under what she'd thought a very good punch. Only his smile had vanished, his expression becoming that of a predator who'd just encountered an unexpected opponent, exhilarated by the discovery, raring for an all-out tumble.

Then, oh, so slowly, he raised his hand and rubbed his jaw, softly scratching against his beard. It sent a frisson of stimulation through her, as if those fingers had scraped against her most sensitive spots. She managed not to shudder.

"Was that so hard?"

Huh? What?

"Giving me that first voluntary touch." He rubbed his jaw again, this time moving it from side to side, as if making sure everything was still slotted in place and functioning. "Not bad at all, as first voluntary touches go."

Wishing she could generate heat vision, she glared at him. "If only you'd told me you expected a first voluntary *punch,* I would have obliged you much faster."

His grin turned into a wince and back to a grin. "Good thing I'm sporting a beard. I would have had a hard time explaining the bruise. That *was* a perfect jab. Or should I say, sucker punch?"

"*Please.* You saw it coming a light-year away. You could have blocked it if you wanted."

"If you think I saw anything but you glowing like a golden goddess in that torture device of a dress, you give me too much credit. You reduce me to my basic beast and the most simpleminded and oblivious of men."

Why was he *doing* this? Reengaging his seduction program? Was there something he still needed from her? Was he making sure she was hot enough for the required malleability?

"At least believe that if I'd seen this punch coming, I would have ducked so you wouldn't hurt your hand."

"Oh, sure. You care about the hand that just socked you."

"I care about nothing *but* your every bone and pore and inch. All I want is to show you how much…I care. But wait…"

He suddenly turned and strode away, disappeared into the kitchenette. In moments, he came back with a bag of ice. Stopping before her, he took her hand, ran gentle fingers over the knuckles that throbbed with a dull ache, his eyebrows knotting as he examined the forming bruise.

Placing the ice on her knuckles, he gritted his teeth, as if her gasp hurt him.

"Next time, use a heavy, blunt object."

A shudder rattled through her, at his dark mutter more than at the icy numbing. She'd known she'd pay the price for her recklessness in pain and limited mobility for a while. But she'd thought it a small price for venting her frustration in the one way she hadn't tried yet. Physically.

She only felt worse now—stupid on top of out-of-control and futile. And his solicitude had turned the tables on her. She'd known he wouldn't retaliate, but she'd hoped it would surprise him into baring his fangs, or at least dropping his mask. He'd done that once, that night six years ago.

She'd always conjured those moments when he'd snarled at her like a wounded beast, when unstoppable longing for him had almost snuffed her will to go on. But even then, he'd exposed her to the full range of his faces. Passionate, anxious, shocked, angry, possessive, bewildered and betrayed. Thinking none of those had been real had only made her unable to trust her judgment again. Just as she couldn't now.

Carefully removing the ice, he lifted her hand to his lips. Holding her eyes as if he wanted her to let him into her soul, he feathered each knuckle with a kiss that was tender, almost reverent. And something in the center of her being buckled.

For him to be kissing the hand that had just inflicted an act of aggression and affront on him was too much. Unsteadily, she withdrew her hand.

He exhaled, flexed his hand as if it hurt, too, before it went up to the side of his neck.

Then he suddenly grinned at her. "What do you know… you fixed my neck!"

The spontaneity of his grin, the ease, the *warmth,* how real this all felt—her longing for the man she'd once loved with every fiber of her being—suddenly overwhelmed her. The yearning that had writhed inside her like a burning serpent lurched so hard that her nails dug into her good hand's palm until they almost broke her skin.

"Okay. You achieved your purpose, made sure my sisters-in-law heard the kind of conversation you forced on me…."

His hand rose in protest. "How could I have known they were with you?"

"Because you apparently keep me under surveillance every second I'm awake, maybe even when I'm asleep."

"I told you I didn't know where you were."

"Even if I believe this, I told you I had company. In fact, having anyone else present would have been even more damaging. But you established what you wanted. That our relationship goes far beyond last night, and its past nature is also implicit if you could talk to me with such… audacity."

"How could they have known I was being…audacious?"

"Because your phone seduction session made my responses clear to anyone who knows anything about sexual innuendo. So—you've established my 'impurity' and your role in it. Now, even if I want to back down, it will be at the cost of disgracing my family, now that my 'shame' is out. While you will keep the high moral ground, even if you're the once defiler of my honor, since you're here now doing the honorable thing."

He coughed an incredulous laugh. "Where are you getting all this? If you believe your sisters-in-law suspect anything, and it disturbs you, I'll take care of it. I started my 'phone seduction' before I knew you weren't alone, and I didn't continue it because of any of the motives you assign me. You're crediting me with a premeditation I already told you I'm incapable of around you."

Feeling her head would burst with frustration, she began

to turn away when a cabled arm slipped around her waist, clasping her to his formidable length. "I was up all night, Jala, every inch of me *roaring* for you. I let you go last night because I thought I must give you some breathing room. But my resolutions vanished the moment I got here. All I could think was that you were near, and all I planned was having you, and this time not letting you walk away. As you did last night. As you did six years ago."

She pushed out of his arms. "You can stop doing this."

"I can't. I can never stop wanting you."

"I mean it, Mohab. Stop it. I already told you I'm going through with this charade. Now drop the seduction act."

The arms reaching for her stopped in midmotion, dropping to his sides. "What reason do you assign me for acting this time, if, according to you, I've already fulfilled my purpose?"

She shrugged, shoulders knotted, throat closing. "I never know anything where you're concerned."

"Didn't you say you know everything about my motivations and methods?" He shook his head. "Does this mean you didn't believe anything I said last night?"

She didn't know anymore. The dejection in his eyes, the intensity she felt from him, all added to the verdict of her senses. Even if she couldn't trust those, she couldn't disregard her observations.

His reaction to her punch had been seamless. If he'd been acting, he would have been resenting it—and her. It would have manifested in even momentary fury, in an instinctive spark of retaliation, before he curbed it. He'd only been astonished, and the instant hue of his surprise had been acceptance, indulgence, even elation. As if he'd meant it when he'd said he'd take anything from her, as if he welcomed any punishment she inflicted if it would vent her anger toward him.

She *could* be seeing what she wanted to see all over again, but she…

All her hairs stood on end. Something had slithered in the background, at ground level….

Her tension deflated on a squeaked exclamation. "A cat!"

She blinked at the magnificent creature. A robust white Turkish Angora, clearly just woken up from a sound catnap with the way it stopped to stretch and arch. Then it slunk toward them, languidly weaving its way around furniture.

"I wonder whose it is!" She turned incredulous eyes to Mohab. "Did you know it was here?"

Her eyes almost popped at the change that came over Mohab's expression as he looked at the cat. It was the tender delight she'd only seen on people's faces when they beheld their babies.

"I should hope so, since she's mine. Or should I say, I'm hers?" He bent as the cat approached him, tail straight up and trembling in the cat-tail-language equivalent of "I'm crazy about you," before rearing up on her hind legs like a baby asking to be picked up. Mohab obliged at once, scooping her up, cradling her expertly against his massive chest…and getting white fur all over his pristine black clothes.

Purring so loudly the sound vibrated in Jala's ears, the cat surrendered to Mohab's pampering as he cooed to her. "Who's awake? Who's had a good nap?"

She gaped at the incongruent scene. Mohab, that lethal juggernaut, all but melting over a cat.

Mohab had a cat.

As the knowledge hit bottom in her mind, another movement made her snap her gaze to the same direction where Whitey had come from, only to find more felines advancing.

He had *cats. Four* of them.

Or maybe there were more still napping in there. At this point, she would believe just about anything.

One of the cats, a miniature glossy-black panther, broke into a lope and threw himself at Mohab's feet. Then, butting his head against Mohab's legs, he made him widen his stance so he could weave between them in excited figure eights. The other two cats, a tabby Scottish Fold and a Russian Blue, soon joined in, purring the place down.

Mohab looked over at her when he had two cats in his arms, his expression that of a proud dad.

The tightness in her throat grew thorns. "Is this your… pride?"

"They are my pride and joy. They're my family."

The word *family* penetrated her heart, a shard that had never stopped driving deep.

He'd once told her his life story. He was an only child and, like her, both his parents were dead. But he hadn't lost them to illness or to heartbreak. He'd lost them—twelve years ago, now—in a terrorist attack. One meant for him.

Whenever she remembered that she'd used that knowledge to take a stab at him, she still choked with shame. It hadn't mattered that she'd been mad with agony—it had still been unforgivable. Some things should never be used as a weapon, no matter what. Should never be used at all. It had been dishonorable of her to use such an intimate and painful injury against him.

It never ceased to torment her that she owed him that much. Her life, and an apology for that cruel transgression. But since she'd thought she'd never settle those debts with him, she'd added them to her forward payment to the world.

But he'd invoked her debt last night. Then there'd been everything else. And just when she thought she was confused enough about him, she discovered he had cats!

She found herself asking, "You travel with them?"

He bent down, gently letting both cats jump lithely from his embrace. "People travel with their kids, don't they?"

The way he said that tightened her throat more. "You never told me you liked cats. Or that you had any."

Straightening, he approached her with a stealthy grace, like a huge version of the felines, his eyes radiating this new warmth that seeped to her core. "I didn't then. I've always loved cats, all animals for that matter, but my life-style made me unable to adopt any. In my previous post, I had no control over my schedule. After I resigned—and after I settled a...personal project that took me all over the world five years ago—I set up my own business. Then I got my beauties, here—all rescue kitties, each with a story of her or his own." Suddenly his expression changed, as if something disturbing had just occurred to him. "You don't like cats?"

Her heart thudded at the alarm in his eyes. "I'm *crazy* about them. I had three cats when I lived in Judar, but I lost them all before I left. I fostered only in the States, since my globe-trotting lifestyle wouldn't accommodate a cat. Unlike you, I don't have my own private jet to haul them along with me."

His smile broke out again. "Let's test this claim, shall we? My darlings are cat-lover detectors. We'll let them scan you, but be advised...their verdict is final and in-contestable."

He might be joking, but she was anxious they might snub her. Why, she didn't know. She was doing her best to alienate him, so why did she wish to appeal to his "kids"?

She swallowed the contrary lump of nervousness. "How will you know they approve of me?"

"How do cats show approval?"

"Each cat has his or her own way of showing it."

"Exactly." He flashed her a sizzling smile as he prowled to the sitting area, took off his jacket, dropped it to the ground and let his cats walk over it. "I should have changed into something light colored as soon as I let them out of the carriers. Only Rigel goes with this outfit."

His shoulders seemed to widen as he slowly started to unbutton his black shirt. Her heart stuttered. He was stripping.

She could swear the silk slithered off his skin with an aching sigh, as if it hated to separate from his flesh. She knew just how it felt, remembered how her hands used to ache for the time when they could glide all over him.

As his formidable back was exposed, symmetry and perfection made into a symphony of muscle and sinew, her salivary glands gushed. She was literally drooling over him.

At the damask burgundy couch in the center of the sitting area he turned to her, giving her a full frontal assault.

He was even more magnificent than she remembered. His chest had broadened, his abdomen had become more defined, every bulge and slope harder, packing more power, every line chiseled by endless stamina and determination. Her breasts swelled, reliving nights of abandon writhing beneath that chest, her stomach clenched with the memory of that ridged abdomen bearing down on her, working her into a frenzy. Her core throbbed with the moist heat that had been simmering since he'd walked into that stateroom.

Then in one of those movements that made her want to devour every glorious inch of him, he sank down on the couch.

Spreading his bulk over the cushions, he braced his legs wide apart and caressed the couch on both sides. The invitation was for his cats this time, who zoomed to obey, climbing all over him, butting their heads against every part of him, jumping on the back of the couch so they could reach his face and rub and kiss and lick him all over it. He surrendered to their love with a look of bliss, his eyes fixing her in a steady barrage of seduction.

Before this, he was the most overwhelming man to her, just by existing. Now this was…cruel. This had to be the most mind-bending thing he'd ever exposed her to. The sight of him, surrounded by cats, letting them plumb the depths of his love, roaming all over him in total trust and affection.

Did that man want to blow her ovaries?

He caught the ginger Scottish Fold who was crossing his lap and deposited a kiss on his head. "This is Mizar… as you can see why." She certainly could. The tomcat was a magnificent tabby with the cutest white apron in history. Mohab put him down to answer the impatience of the Russian Blue as she asked for her turn. "And this is Nihal. She is addicted to water taps, so I have to leave her a trickle on all the time. Always a challenge on flights." Nihal meant thirst quenching, so very appropriate, too. After she took her turn in her "daddy's" embrace she moved on and Mohab turned to the little panther. "And this is Rigel. I bet you know why I called him that."

She sure did. *Rigel* meant foot, and Rigel was definitely a foot cat, the one who'd hurled himself at Mohab's feet. Actually Rigel, the star, meant The Foot of the Great One, which was very apt for both cat and owner….

Hey…wait! "These are all star names, ones discovered by ancient astronomers from the region."

Surprise flared in his eyes. "They *are* my little stars. Very observant…and knowledgeable of you."

Pleasure revved inside her stomach. She'd once craved his praise, praise he'd lavished on her, that had made her feel like the most special person in the world. So even in that regard, nothing had changed.

"And this is Sette—my mistress and queen of my household." The white cat jumped on his lap, curled up and rested her head on his thigh, eyes focused in the distance. Mohab swept her in strokes, making Jala feel his hand running down *her* back. "But *you* can be my human mistress and queen."

Queen. She still couldn't get her head around the fact that Mohab wasn't just a prince anymore. Or just a major force in the world of extragovernmental crisis management. He would have his own throne. And if she married him, she'd be his queen.

Which couldn't happen. He would have to look for someone else to…

The thought lodged into her brain like a red-hot ax.

How dog in the manger was that? She wouldn't be his, and she couldn't bear completing a thought where another woman was?

But that wasn't new. She'd spent years shying away from any thoughts along these lines, always keeping her mind in a fever of preoccupation so she'd never focus on images of Mohab with other women, when he must have had scores.…

"Won't you proceed with our test?"

His soft question severed her oppressive musings. Feeling any sudden movement would collapse her to the ground, she started toward him. The moment she moved, all four cats seemed to suddenly take notice of her, ears pricking, bodies in attention mode, eyes fixing her with the same intensity as their daddy's.

She came down on the far end of the couch, taking care not to touch any of the cats. Mizar was the first one who approached, sniffing her tentatively. She'd missed having a cat so much, all she wanted was to grab his robust body and bury her face in his thick fur.

Reeling back the urge, she gave Mizar her hand to sniff, cooing to him, "*Ma ujmalak ya sugheeri*...do you know how beautiful you are, my little one?" Mizar answered by bonking her hand with his head. Her heart trembled with this affection it only reserved for animals. "Oh, you do know exactly how delightful you are, you compact package of joy, you!"

The cat made his decision and climbed onto her lap, reaching up to bump his head into her chin.

She giggled, everything emptying from her mind but the delight cats always engendered in her. "*Ya Ullah*...you magical creature. I had a ginger boy like you once, but without your apron. He was as sweet as you and I miss him so very much...."

Hot needles pricked behind her eyes, dissolved in moist pain that she'd thought she'd expended so many years ago.

Needing to hide it from Mohab, she picked up Mizar and buried her face in his nape. A prod on her shoulder came from her side. It was Nihal, asking to be introduced. She turned to the cat, offering her hand. But Nihal, having seen Mizar already on her, dispensed with preliminaries and climbed down Jala's arm to arch and rub against her side and then settle down against her thigh, a front leg draped over it. Rigel jumped from the couch, sniffed her feet first, then jumped up and joined the lap-warming party. At last, Sette rose regally from Mohab's lap and sashayed over, pushing Mizar out of the way in the center of Jala's lap and making the spot hers.

Distributing strokes, delighting in their softness and trust, heart dancing to the frequency of their purrs, Jala looked at Mohab, her smile unfettered for the first time since...her days with him. "This is the best way to die, drowning in cats!"

He didn't smile back. Before her smile faltered, Mohab rose quietly, came to stand before her, his legs brushing hers as she sat covered in his cats. Then he came down on his knees before her.

Her breath left her in a choking gasp as he leaned forward, his hands brushing her heavy, aching breasts as his arms slid behind her. "You didn't only pass, *ya jameelati*, you broke my cat's fastidiousness and suspiciousness barrier in record time. They didn't even take to me that fast. It's official, they have marked you as a bona fide cat slave."

Her smile broke out again, wavering this time. He bore down on her, this time making his cats vacate her lap and rearrange themselves around her. He pressed himself between her legs, making her open them for him, bringing him fully against her, the hard flesh of his bare chest burning through her dress, his harder arousal pressing into the junction of her thighs. She watched his face approaching hers with the same fatalism one would give an approaching train.

"How about *living* drowning in cats?" His lips landed on her jaw, nuzzled its way up to her ear. "I and my family are all yours for the taking, *ya jameelati*. So take us."

This was so…incredible an offer it would have been everything she'd want from life if it had been real and only for her. If it had been in another life where the past and its losses hadn't taken place. This way, it was just more pain.

Her useless arms pushed against him. "I said I will *say* I'll marry you, not that I will."

He gathered her closer again. "And I will take anything you're willing to give. If you won't marry me, even temporarily, you can still be with me. You can still have me."

"You expect me to sweep everything under the rug and just fall into your arms again?"

"Under the rug is where all the irrelevant crap of the past belongs. And in my arms is where you do."

Her senses leaped so hard she felt as if they'd tear out of the confines of her body. All they'd ever wanted was to smother themselves in his nearness, his pleasures. Damn them. And damn him. Pulling her strings, dangling himself, reminding her how it had felt to be mingled with his flesh, riding his need, drenched in pleasure, inundated with satisfaction.

"You and *Al Shaitaan* are closely related, aren't you?" She exhaled. "Forget that. The devil must come to you for conniving lessons." And temptation and seduction ones. "You must be his chief consultant."

He just smiled. And why not? He felt her buckling.

She'd be damned if she did again, when he'd already condemned her to six years of misery. She wasn't letting hormones run amok again, wouldn't let them suppress her self-preservation.

"Why are you *doing* this?"

"Because it's the only thing I *can* do, *ya ameerati al jameelah*. I've starved for you and I'll do anything so I can sate myself with you again."

She stared into his eyes and again could only *feel* his sincerity. As if whatever else hadn't been right, this was the one thing that had always been real...his desire for her.

Years of damaged self-worth and disbelief in her judgment trembled one last time...then everything shattered.

As if feeling the second it did, his arms tightened, bringing her colliding with his steely mass, his lips taking hers and swallowing her moan of surrender.

Then she found herself being plucked up by his momentum as he pitched backward on the lush Persian carpet, sprawled over it and stretched her on top of him. She vaguely felt the cats jumping after them, felt them prodding, as if to make sure they were okay.

Cradling her head in his large palms, Mohab turned his to his cats. "I'm going to make love to Jala now, so go eat or bathe or something. We won't have time for you for a while."

As if they understood him, the cats slunk away.

Turning his attention back to her, he pulled her down, had her lips sinking into his and her core on his erection. He rocked against her, promising her, deluging her in readiness. Coherence dissolved on his invading tongue, drowned in his taste, her senses igniting like firecrackers with every plunge, sweep and groan....

Remember what he cost you. The havoc he'd still wreak if you surrender. And you still *didn't contest your main gripe.*

Feeling as if she'd left a layer of skin stuck to his hot lips and hands, she scrambled off him, getting to her feet clumsily before plopping on the couch again.

Brooding with hunger, radiating it, he rose to his elbows, stretching before her half-naked like a god of abandon.

Before she crawled back over him, she bit her tingling lips. "So I got this part. You want me. Fine. How about we discuss another concern? Your transgressions?"

He was on his feet in what should have been an impossible movement. She was in good shape herself, but this was a level of fitness and strength that was almost scary.

His lips twisted. *"Ma gatalnahom bahthann baad?"*

Haven't we already killed them with investigation? The regional expression for draining a topic of life.

She nodded, still shaky. "The old ones. But with you, there's always new ones." She sucked in a burning stream of aggravation. "You spied on me. You evidently still do."

"I tried to stop. I couldn't."

So simple. So stymieing. Why couldn't she do herself the life-saving favor of not wanting him anymore?

He threw himself down beside her, grimacing. "That's not true. I *didn't* try. I knew I couldn't stop watching over you." Head resting on the couch, he turned his face toward her, inches from her own. "Jala, we both try to save the world in our own ways. But I'm the one who's versed in its dangers, who can take measures to eradicate them. I won't apologize for keeping tabs on you. You lead a very dangerous life."

"I do social and humanitarian work!"

"In the world's most dangerous places. Apart from the damages that could befall anyone just being there, you're a temptation to even the most harmless of men."

She gaped at him.

"It's bigger than me, Jala, the need to know you're safe. And since I'm the one best equipped to keep you safe, I do."

Incredulity burst out of her. "*I* keep me safe."

For a split second, his eyes said she knew nothing.

This brought her sitting up. "Are you telling me you saved me from a danger I was unaware of?"

Another blip said he'd saved her from far more than *a* danger. But he just shook his head. "Just leave it. I wasn't 'spying' on you. I was reassuring myself of your safety and making sure you were safe. There's a big difference."

The lump that now inhabited her throat again grew harder.

Believing this would change so much. Mean too much. And she couldn't handle more changes of perspective right now. The foundations of her existence, as miserable as they'd been, had constituted her stability. Losing them all, having to erect so many new ones so suddenly, was too...overwhelming. And he was already enough on his own.

In defense, she groped for one of her established suspicions. "Or you were afraid I'd go after Najeeb again?"

He huffed a mirthless laugh. "And what would I have done if you did? I believed you'd gone to him when you left me, and there was nothing I could do about it." At her glower, he ground out, "I *didn't* tell him anything."

She had no idea why, but this time, she believed him.

Yet another pillar knocked over.

After a moment in which he seemed to debate the wisdom of divulging another piece of the puzzle, he said, "I only found out later why Najeeb cut all ties with you."

And he told her why. At least what he believed to be true. *She* knew the real reason why Najeeb hadn't contacted her again. Because she wouldn't let him. But Mohab believed King Hassan's slandering had ended her relationship with Najeeb.

After discovering King Hassan had been behind her ordeal in the past, and knowing he was now the reason behind this current crisis, she didn't feel bad about not exonerating him from *that* specific crime. It hadn't been for lack of trying that he wasn't guilty of it after all.

Mohab was continuing, "Then you disappeared, and I couldn't find you for months. When you resurfaced, there was no way I was going to let you out of my sight again."

She let out her bated breath. "If I say I believe you, you have to promise to stop."

He must have gauged they'd entered the negotiation zone as he bore down on her again, deluging her in a fresh wave of temptation. "Why? Who wouldn't want a guardian angel like me? I'm very handy, you know. People pay me tens of millions to keep them safe. I am offering you a free ride for life."

His arms were halfway around her when she pushed out of them again and stood up, teetering with the urge to throw herself back into them, come what may. But this was just too soon, too fast…too much. She needed to slow down, take a look at where she was jumping, before she plunged into the deep end…again.

Groaning, he stood up as well, his eyes suddenly totally serious for the first time since she'd seen him again. "I've told you the truth about everything so far. All but one thing."

Her breath deserted her as she turned fully toward him.

Looking as if he was dragging shrapnel from his own flesh, he rasped, "You don't have to marry me…or even say you would. You can leave right now, and there'd be no war."

Seven

Mohab met his own eyes in the steamed-up mirror and reached a conclusion. He was insane.

He'd gotten Jala to agree to a fake engagement, then progressed to alleviate her every doubt about the sincerity of his desire. Her surrender to his lovemaking, her mind-blowing response, had admitted her equal need. Her capitulation had only been a matter of time. If he'd just kept his mouth shut, he might have had her in his bed again by now.

But he hadn't kept his mouth shut.

Mizar and Sette rubbed against his legs, distracting him from wanting to bash himself over the head.

Sighing, he picked them up and headed out of the bathroom with Nihal and Rigel weaving between his legs. Even they couldn't make him feel better now. They actually made him feel worse. All they did was remind him of his pleasure at Jala's delight in them, of how it had felt to share them with her.

Topping up their treats in the kitchenette, he told them

he needed to be alone. As usual, they understood him and gave him space, not following him to the wing's reception chamber.

He stood in the middle of the magnificent space Kamal had bestowed on him and could still barely believe he was actually here. An Aal Ghaanem treated as an honored guest in the Aal Masood stronghold. A week ago, that would have been the material of a ridiculous joke. But Kamal had been given a second chance with his queen and was making a real effort to pay it forward.

And what had *he* done with all of Kamal's support and all the ground he'd managed to gain with Jala? He'd voluntarily blown it all to hell.

He could still see Jala standing across from him, her face a frozen mask after he'd divulged that last bit of truth. Then she'd said one word.

"Explain."

He had. He'd told her everything, hadn't left out one single detail this time. After he'd finished, she'd just turned and walked out of his quarters.

That had been three days ago. She'd left the palace that same night. He'd thought she'd head straight to the airport and fly out of Judar, never to return. But her security detail had called to report that she'd checked into a hotel on the other side of Durgham. Moving all the way across the capital had been a clear message that she'd wanted to distance herself from the palace. And him. Trying to call her had yielded no results. She wasn't answering anyone's phone calls. Then she'd turned her phone off. And it was all his fault.

Exhaling forcibly, he moved to the French doors, stared sightlessly at the palace grounds. He had to face the fact that he couldn't have done anything else.

He'd lied to her too much during their relationship, hidden too much. At first believing he had to, then fearing the consequences of exposure. Then he'd seen her again, and she'd given him the full disclosure he'd long craved. And he'd realized that, apart from her own hang-ups about intimacy and commitment, the real reason he'd lost her all those years ago was because he hadn't been honest with her. After realizing that, he could hide nothing anymore. He'd wanted her to want him based on full disclosure, too, needed to have her this time in total honesty.

But after he'd confessed everything about the past, about his feelings, only one thing had remained. Her total freedom of choice about whether to be with him or not. So he'd given it to her.

And she'd chosen not to be with him.

The only reason he'd stayed in Judar till now was because she had. According to Farooq and Shehab, the ones she'd let near, having ostracized Kamal as well, she'd stayed only to see their kids a few times before she left. But she wouldn't remain in the palace where both the perpetrators of this latest deception resided. It was probably a matter of a couple days before she left. It would be over then.

Who was he kidding? It was *already* over. It had been over the minute she'd realized she didn't have to put up with seeing him again. And it didn't matter if he still wanted him. To Jala, freedom and autonomy and honesty had always mattered far more than her desires, no matter how ferocious those were.

A growl of exasperation burst from his depths. Enough. He'd set up an elaborate gamble to resolve this need for her that continued to eat at him, and he'd lost. Everything had depended on being able to win her, and he'd done so fleetingly, before he'd lost her again…big-time.

But he hadn't lost her because he'd told her the full truth—it was because he'd started this whole thing with another charade. He'd catastrophically miscalculated all over again. Seemed it was hopeless. Whenever it involved her, he, the master strategist, had once more been reduced to a bumbling idiot.

Growling again, unable to stay where she wasn't, he strode out of the wing.

He had to see Kamal before he left, tell him they'd have to plan another way to contain his uncle's wrath. As for Jala, he'd have to get her out of his system some other way....

"You're better than I gave you credit for. *Way* better."

Mohab squeezed his eyes shut as the deep, amused voice hit him between the shoulder blades.

His condition was much worse than he'd thought. He hadn't even felt Kamal approach.

What the hell. Get this over with.

He turned to Kamal...and almost winced. That was it. He no longer considered Kamal his new favorite person. This guy was just too happy. And it swamped Mohab with such...futility. A hopelessness that he'd ever feel anything like that.

"I was coming to see you...." he began.

Kamal took his arm. "I could have just called you, but I had to see you again and picture you in your future capacity, now that it has emerged from the realm of speculation to fact."

Mohab's frown deepened. He didn't get one word of what Kamal had just said.

Kamal went on, spouting more gibberish. "I really thought the next I heard from Jala would be with a proposal on how to avert the war without her involvement. And the worst part? Even if we'd been dealing with the original, critical situation, I had no doubt she'd present me with a real solution."

Kamal huffed a laugh at the word *solution,* which had evidently become an inside joke between them. However,

Mohab wasn't in any laughing mood over it, or over anything else, anymore.

Kamal continued, "She's been known to formulate workable solutions for some seemingly impossible situations to the satisfaction of all sides in some of the world's most volatile regions."

Mohab knew that. He'd followed her work closely, with the utmost interest and admiration. And more than a little humility and self-deprecation. For she'd been able, with far fewer resources and powers, to peacefully do what he'd thought could only be resolved through his extreme measures. And while he'd discreetly helped her wherever he could, he'd been honing his methods on her example.

But why was Kamal telling him all this now? Or was he the one who couldn't make sense of anything anymore?

Kamal, who'd taken him back to his quarters, was going on as they entered. "Then she leaves, and I think the next time I want to see her I'll have to chase after her on one of her jaunts around the world. But I should have known better than to predict Jala the Unpredictable. She left the palace only to go stay in a three-star hotel."

"I know that."

Kamal's fond expression deepened. "She was never one for luxury, but her work seems to have made her allergic to it. Not to mention her chronic independence issues. The eyes around here must have had her climbing walls. *Ya Ullah!*" His exclamation made Mohab blink. "I was told you brought cats, but I thought they mistook some other containers for carriers."

His cats were scurrying to welcome him back, slowing down to a curious, cautious prowl when they found he had company.

Grinning widely, Kamal bent to offer them his hands to sniff. "Four cats! There's no end to your surprises, Mohab, is there? Wait till my kids find out you have these beauties. You'll be their favorite uncle."

The word *uncle* stabbed him. He was destined not to be anyone's uncle. Anyone's anything. Seemed Kamal was still under the misapprehension that he might marry Jala.

Gritting his teeth, he watched his cats show Kamal the same level of instant trust and acceptance they'd shown Jala. Kamal probably *felt* the same as her to them, too.

Which was another reason he couldn't be around her brother any longer. "Listen, Kamal…"

Kamal straightened with Mizar in his arms, grinning. "I *do* want to listen—to just how you did it. I knew you were effective, but this borders on magic."

And Mohab had enough of all the ambiguity. "What the hell are you talking about?"

"I'm talking about Jala, of course. She just called me and told me to start the wedding preparations."

For the first time in his life, Mohab was totally in the dark.

Jala had told Kamal she would marry him.

Then, after Kamal had left, she'd called, making him certain he hadn't been hallucinating. She'd informed him that their "engagement" would be celebrated tomorrow over a family dinner.

He'd demanded to see her before said dinner, but she'd hung up without even a goodbye. He still wondered if he'd only listened to a prerecorded announcement.

Yet he couldn't care. This was his third, and probably final, chance—and he was not going to squander it this time.

To that end, he'd better get that wild-eyed look under control. Though the tuxedo-clad man who was reflected back at him in the ornate full-length mirror looked suave and polished, his expression was that of a starving wolf.

"I see why you didn't hear me knock. You're lost in admiring your own grandeur."

The soft mockery lashed him, had him swinging around. *Jala.*

She'd always been his ideal of femininity, the sum total of his fantasies, but tonight, she'd taken her sorcery to a new level. In an old-gold dress made of ethereal materials that wrapped her every curve to distressing advantage, she was overpowering...even otherworldly.

She headed for the open French doors and stopped with her back to him, contemplating the gardens at night. He approached her as if afraid she'd disappear if he made any sudden moves, and she looked at him over her shoulder with eyes as mysterious as Judar's night. Her hair sifted in the jasmine-laden night breeze with swishes that strummed his every nerve.

"You said you wanted to talk."

"Since you hung up on me, I didn't think you registered my request, or thought it not worth consideration."

"I reconsidered. We need to touch base before we face the combined forces of our families for the first time together."

He slid his arms around her, crisscrossed them beneath her breasts and pulled her back against his body. This was probably a damaging move right now. But he was beyond holding back. These past three days had been three days beyond the limits of his endurance.

Even though he felt her tense as he bent to breathe her in, she didn't resist. He went dizzy as the feel and scent and heat of her vitality and femininity eddied in his arteries.

"I thought I'd never see you again. Jala, *habibati...*"

He turned her in his arms and captured her lips with all his pent-up hunger and frustration.

Feeling her luscious mouth open beneath his, having his lungs fill with intoxication as she gasped a scorching gust of passion, tore aside any semblance of moderation. Bypassing all preliminaries, he plunged into her depths, his tongue dueling with hers as he squeezed her against him, his hands kneading down her body to bunch up the chiffon layers of her skirt and seek the sizzling velvet of her flesh. He dipped beneath the lace, cupping the perfection of her buttocks.

She tore her lips from his. "This isn't why I'm here…"

Gritting his teeth, he reluctantly let her go. If their engagement dinner wasn't less than half an hour away, he would have convinced her otherwise.

It was still with utmost satisfaction that he watched her hands tremble as she smoothed out the disarray created by his passion. "I'm here to explain why I'm doing this."

"As long as you've reconsidered, I don't care why."

"You should, because I think you miscalculated."

Hah. Tell him about it. But she was probably referring to some other miscalculation he was as yet unaware of.

"You think you can curb your uncle and dictate your terms, resolving the crisis without my…participation. And though I commend you for deciding to be forthright at last, even when it was counterproductive to your other purposes, I believe you're wrong in thinking I'm not necessary to achieve your goal. You'd be right if we were talking about someone other than your uncle. But with his track record of paranoia and volatile pride he could still escalate the situation if Saraya's percentage doesn't appeal to him, or if he feels slighted, even if it means going to war against you, too."

"So what are you saying, exactly?" he asked carefully.

"That the marriage solution remains what he'd be most likely to accept, the one that would save him face. If you give him the added deference of being the one who puts his hand in Kamal's, with both acting as our proxies, his pride would bind him to peace from then on."

Kamal had been right. She was totally unpredictable. This was the last thing he'd expected her to do.

But there she was, doing exactly what Kamal had said she would. Coming up with a levelheaded and thorough analysis of the situation, based on her knowledge of all the players, and formulating the most workable solution. It again showed him he shouldn't have tried to manipulate her to seal the deal, should have come clean and hoped she'd make this offer on her own.

He inhaled. "That's extremely astute. And exceptionally thoughtful of you, to go to the effort of thinking this through so thoroughly and then agree to help, even after I tried to maneuver you into doing so under false pretenses."

Her strong shoulders jerked dismissively, causing her breasts to jiggle slightly and sending another rush of hormones roaring through him.

"Seems the first time is the worst. Then you get used to it." Before he could swear there'd be no more manipulation, she went on, "So anyway, I am your best bet, as you've already figured out, so I've decided to pitch in."

He pulled her back into his arms, meshing their gazes. *"Ashkorek, ya jameelati."*

She again pushed out of the circle of his arms. Story of his life from now on, it seemed.

"Don't thank me yet. I said this is what's most likely to get your uncle to cooperate, not that it's certain it will."

He shoved his hands into his pockets. "I don't care about the outcome. I only care about your intention."

She slanted him an unfathomable glance. "You seem to be in an uncaring mood today. Or is this your usual state? Probably." Another shoulder jerk. Another surge of lust. "You should start practicing caring. Being a king is quite a bit different from being a terminator."

"If anyone can teach me to care, it's you. As my queen."

Her gaze wavered. Was that...vulnerability?

Next split second it was gone, making him wonder if he'd even seen it.

"So about tonight…" she began.

No comment? Since she didn't intend to be his queen? "What about it?"

"My sisters-in-law must have told my brothers their deductions about our relationship, based on your famous phone striptease session. Or, if by some miracle they managed some discretion, everyone must know by now that we're not strangers to each other. So how do you intend to play this in front of my family and yours?"

He raised her hands to his lips. "I intend to show everyone how proud I am to be your intended, that this was a hope I had harbored since I first saw you."

She withdrew her hands. "No need to go overboard, or you'll only make them suspicious."

She didn't believe him. Maybe because his statement was untrue. He *hadn't* thought of marriage in the years he'd craved her from afar, since he'd never thought marriage was in the cards for him at all. Even when he'd proposed, he had no picture of how marriage would fit into his existence.

But now, with the turn his life had taken, everything was different. Although he'd initially come here unclear about what he wanted, beyond the fact that he wanted her with a hunger that continued to consume him, he now wanted everything he could possibly have with her.

Her own stance seemed to be unchanged, though.

He had to hear her spell it out. "So your original agreement stands, as is?"

He held his breath. Hoping against hope…

Then she breathed, "Yes."

Eight

As soon as Mohab entered the expansive dining room in the king's quarters with Jala, the nine people seated at one end of the gigantic table stood up and clapped.

Mohab saw only one person. *Najeeb.*

Heat shot to his head. What was *he* doing here?

As per Jala's mandate, only the people necessary to the peace efforts should have been present. That had meant Kamal and his queen, Mohab's uncle and his queen and him and Jala.

He'd wholeheartedly welcomed that, had been enormously relieved when his uncle had begged off attending on account of illness. But to support Mohab's bid for the "incomparable Jala's" hand, King Hassan had promised to send her a priceless set of jewelry from Saraya's royal treasury.

It had been the ultimate irony to hear his uncle speaking in such glowing terms of the woman he'd once gone to dishonorable lengths to ensure didn't sully his royal family. Now that she was *the* princess of Judar, Hassan was embarrassingly eager to have her blood mingle with that of his family.

But Mohab had relaxed prematurely about tonight. King Hassan had sent Najeeb in his stead. Najeeb had also brought Jawad and Haroon, his second-oldest brothers among nine full and half siblings. But it was Najeeb's presence alone that disturbed Mohab. He'd avoided Najeeb for years, for every reason there was. A face-to-face with him, now of all times, topped the list of his least-favorite surprises ever. And he'd had some doozies in his time.

"Fi seh'hut al aroosain." Kamal raised a crystal glass filled with burgundy liquid, no doubt Judar's famous date wine, toasting the health of the bride- and groom-to-be.

Everybody raised their glasses and voices in salute, smiles of pleasure coating all faces. All faces but Najeeb's.

He didn't approve of this.

"So I had to do something as drastic as get engaged to end the Aal Masoods' and Aal Ghaanems' centuries-old theatrics, you testosterone-overdosed cavemen?"

General laughter rose in answer to Jala's humorous admonition as she smoothly unspooled from his loose embrace and entered the circle of welcome that opened for her. She was at once enfolded into the love and delight of her brothers and their wives. He envied them her readiness to go into their arms, to receive and return their kisses, to exchange smiles with them that were unmarred by the past.

Then she turned to his cousins, and his envy became resentment. Watching her bestow ease and humor on them actually hurt when he'd gotten nothing that approached either from her. When it brought back how it had felt to be inundated in both. It didn't help that those two hulking buffoons were totally enthralled as this magical creature welcomed them as friends and future family members.

Then it was Najeeb's turn.

He watched them approach each other with all the trepidation of someone watching a collision, one that would pulverize him. The hesitation of the long absence and the uncertainty of the other's reception evaporated with every step until they met halfway. Then she reached out both hands to him and he clasped them in his with just as much eagerness. But it was the tenderness on both their faces as their tentative smiles blossomed that had jealousy surging through him like a geyser. He felt that if he opened his mouth right now, he'd scorch the whole room.

He had no idea what he said to Jala's family as they gathered around to congratulate him. All he could see was Najeeb's head bent close to Jala's, making his blood boil.

"Take it easy, Mohab, or the guy might drop dead."

That was Shehab. Mohab curbed an imprecation as he tore his gaze away from Najeeb to look at Shehab. The man's black eyes were dancing with mischief, having evidently documented Mohab's reaction to Najeeb and Jala's reunion.

Another surge of savagery coursed in his blood. "Right now, I'm not sure that would be a bad thing."

Shehab chuckled, looking very pleased with Mohab's response. "If Najeeb drops dead, Jawad won't be far behind. He'd jump out of his fighter jet without a parachute if he found himself the crown prince of Saraya. Only Najeeb, in his endless wisdom and stamina, can deal with your uncle."

Mohab almost bared his teeth at Shehab. Hearing about Najeeb's endless wisdom—and stamina—was more fuel to his fire.

"And don't be too hard on Najeeb. It's only expected that any man would turn into a slobbering fool around Jala."

Mohab forced a smile to his taut face. "You trying to make me go rearrange my little cousin's face, and spend the rest of my engagement night in *your* little brother's dungeon?"

Shehab guffawed this time, definitely delighted with Mohab's vehemence, which he no doubt considered revealed the depth of his involvement with his sister. "Wouldn't *that* be a far more memorable engagement night than this inane dinner you and your fiancée imposed on us?"

Farah, Shehab's wife, turned to her husband, emerald eyes gleaming with curiosity. "What am I missing?"

Shehab scooped her to his side, his smile so bedeviling Mohab considered manually wiping it off his face. "Mohab here is so head over heels with Jala, he's having a male aggression crisis just watching her greet an old friend."

Farah waved her hand dismissingly. "Najeeb is a *really* old friend." Then she started recounting the story of Jala's and Najeeb's friendship.

Mohab suffered all he could before interjecting, "I already know all that. I was there the first time they met." When she looked confused, he explained further. "I was the one who led the extraction team and ended the hostage crisis."

Delight surged on Farah's face. "Oh, you're her knight in black-ops armor! How unbelievably romantic that after saving her life all these years ago, you'd reenter it as her prince charming!"

"That even tops the way we met, *ya rohi.*" Shehab gazed down at her with such indulgence, Mohab made a mental note to check his blood sugar as soon as he left their company.

Farah poked Shehab in equal adoration. "You mean when you set me up?" Mohab wanted to scoff "you, too?" as Farah turned to him with a mock-stern expression. "This perfect husband you see now first approached me swathed in Tuareg garb and masqueraded as someone else to seduce me into marrying him, thinking I was the former king of Zohayd's illegitimate daughter, all in the name of keeping Judar's peace."

Mohab couldn't hold back his scoff this time. It seemed seducing a woman for their kingdom's sake, then falling for her was an epidemic among the princes in this region.

"Let's get this engagement party under way, people," Kamal called out. "We're all experts at talking while eating."

As voices rose in approval and everyone moved back to the splendidly laid-out table, Mohab found himself surrounded by Jala's family while she was assimilated into his.

For the next hour a superb dinner was served, but he could taste none of it. Being separated from Jala and watching her with his cousins, with Najeeb, killed any appetite and any ability to enjoy her family's company.

At one point, as he stared at the grinning faces of the loving couples around the table, he reached a final conclusion. The Aal Masood family all suffered from toxic levels of happiness, and exposure to them was detrimental to his health. And sanity.

But he could see something besides sickening bliss on their faces. It was the shrewd realization that all was not as it should be with him and Jala. He waited with bated breath for someone to allude to this, but as if to stop their suspicion from becoming conviction, Jala left his cousins and came to stand behind Farooq.

Leaning over her oldest brother, she draped supple arms over his shoulders and kissed his cheek. "Can I have my fiancé back now? Cross-examined him to your heart's content?"

Her arm brushed against him and her hair swished forward, deluging him in her scent. Everything inside him clamored, almost drowning Farooq's guffaw.

"As if. You've got yourself one tight-lipped groom-to-be here. Figures, though, with what he does for a living. But the poor guy barely touched his dinner since he was busy eating you up. I don't think he even heard most of what we said to him."

Kamal chuckled. "I bet Mohab's ideal engagement dinner would have been having you alone somewhere secluded by the sea. I think we only managed to torture him with this dinner."

"Which is as it should be," Shehab said, winking at her. "In another age, we would have made him roam the desert in search of mythical treasures, then return to jump through hoops of fire for the privilege of your hand."

Mohab twisted his lips at her brothers. "Braving the desert unarmed and on foot, and then ending my trek by battling hungry hyenas over a fire pit *would* have been preferable to sitting across this ridiculously wide table from Jala throughout our so-called engagement party." He swept the three men a challenging look. "You *should* test me. The honor and privilege of her hand demands every proof that I actually deserve it. So prepare your trials. The more impossible, the better."

And he meant every word. He'd do anything for Jala. For this wasn't a matter of wanting to get her out of his system anymore. This was about winning her. Properly this time. And forever. He finally faced what he'd avoided acknowledging for years: what she was to him. This woman he'd wanted from the first moment, who he had pined for through the years of alienation, who he had watched over and learned from.

He'd never stopped loving her. And with everything she'd done and still did, every breath she took, she kept proving to him that he'd always been destined to love her.

He loved her now more than he ever had or even believed possible.

Feeling her eyes on him after his impassioned pledge,

he turned the force of his conviction on her, told her, wordlessly, but with everything in him, what he felt.

Meeting her eyes, he felt her spirit touch his, as it had from the very beginning. Now, even through the barrier she'd erected between them since that fateful night, it jolted through him again, how kindred it felt, how deep her hold over him was, how absolute. And he no longer wanted to sever it. He only wanted to cherish and revel in it. He only wanted to convince her to let him in again, to let him love her with everything he had, as he'd failed to in the past.

But something in her eyes sent his heart hammering. That vulnerability. And something else. Pain. Bottomless pain.

It disturbed him so much it had him on his feet, just as Farooq stood to vacate his place for her.

Heart ramming his rib cage, he held her seat as she sat, trying to catch her gaze again, to confirm what he'd seen. But there was nothing but a bright, neutral smile as she murmured thanks and looked away as her brothers continued poking and prodding him.

"No surprises here, Mission Impossible Man," Shehab said. "Wrestling impossible odds and facing lethal dangers must be easier for you than sitting still through a social function."

Kamal sighed. "Wait till you're king. You'll suffer through those till you want to *cause* mayhem to escape them."

Taking Jala's place between his cousins, Farooq chimed in, "Hmm, I can make use of your willingness to do anything for Jala. I have some chronic…problems I need taken care of."

Reaching for the hand Jala rested on the table, he enveloped it, a thrill going through him when she relinquished it to him. "Make me a list and consider them resolved."

Farooq grinned at Jala. "I'm sold. I like your fiancé. It's very handy to have a cleanup expert in the family."

"How about you ask him for a thousand red camels in the bargain?" Carmen ribbed her husband.

Everyone laughed at Carmen's allusion to one of the most famous folklore stories in the region, the immortal love story of Antarah and Ablah. Antarah, a slave who won his freedom through heroic feats, asked for his beloved's hand, only for her father to get rid of his nuisance by sending Antarah on an impossible mission to acquire rare camels from far-flung enemy territory, alone, unarmed and having nothing to bargain with. Antarah, of course, accomplished all this, and in the end won his Ablah.

If only everyone knew *his* mission impossible—winning back what he'd lost of Jala's heart and then reaching the parts he'd never been able to touch—was far harder than any overwhelming odds they could throw at him.

After an interval of gaiety as they exchanged anecdotes and tales from the past about more men in his situation, dessert was served.

Jawad, who'd been the most outspoken of his cousins during the evening, grinned at him so widely he wanted to hurl a plate between his perfect teeth. "When Najeeb told us Mohab was getting hitched, we just had to see the impossibility of who'd made him consider this suicidal move."

"Then we see Jala…and the rest of you ladies—" Haroon made a theatrical gesture around the table "—and now we know. Judar is the ultimate babe producer…and magnet."

Najeeb glared at his younger brothers. "I knew it was the biggest mistake I've made in recent memory letting you two tag along. Now I know how the enmity between our families started. It must have been instigated by men with big mouths and bigger eyes, like you."

"Chill, bro." Jawad grinned unrepentantly. "Those guys

know for a fact they have rare jewels that anyone with a heartbeat would admire." He flashed the ladies another killer smile. "I bet they'd be offended if we pretended we didn't notice."

"Yeah." Haroon smirked at Najeeb. "So maybe it was a tight ass like you, one who couldn't take a joke or wholesome admiration, who started the enmities."

Najeeb looked heavenward, then over at the Aal Masoods, focusing on Kamal. "See what I have to put up with? Now that you've seen my spare heirs, I hope you really appreciate yours."

"Oh, our baby brother, Kamal, appreciates the hell out of us." Farooq chuckled, eliciting an exasperated growl from Kamal. "You on the other hand, Najeeb, are to be pitied…"

Having had enough and still holding Jala's hand, Mohab rose. "And here I want to thank you all for celebrating this momentous occasion with me and Jala." He panned his gaze among Jala's family. "But though I truly appreciate the welcome you've shown me, and *forood walaa'ee wa ta'ahtee,* my pledge of allegiance and obedience stands. Kamal was right. There's nothing I want more than to have Jala to myself, at least for part of the evening, to make its memory a perfect one. So please, continue to celebrate, and excuse us as we go have our own personal celebration."

As he pulled back the chair for Jala and she stood up lithely, his heart again convulsed when he noticed the glance she exchanged with Najeeb. Shehab and Farooq ribbed him some more, while Kamal said nothing, the gaze encompassing him and Jala still…unconvinced.

Kamal must realize Jala's lack of interaction with him wasn't a matter of shyness in front of her brothers, or on account of the suddenness of their resumed relationship and its rapid development. After all, Kamal was a man versed in both his sister's nature and in matters of the heart. He must realize something was wrong.

But still giving him all the support he could, Kamal waved his hand in mock imperiousness. "You may be excused, but only because we now have said pledge of allegiance and obedience, and can do anything at all with you."

As everyone laughed again, Jala said, "It's only fair to warn you that while you'll have the allegiance, you'll be out of luck where the obedience is concerned. From personal experience you know where *that* will be expended." She turned and winked at her sisters-in-law. "Right, ladies?"

As her family all laughed, and Jawad and Haroon begged to hear some obedience examples—to fortify their resolve *never* to marry—she waved a final goodbye. Then she turned and headed out of the dining room, with him a step behind her.

Once they were away from the royal quarters, he opened the first door he found and pulled her into the chamber's darkness, lifting her off the ground, already kissing her.

Her gasp filled him as her lips opened beneath his. Tasting the tart sweetness of berry sauce on her tongue, he groaned, plunging deeper, seeking more of her taste, demanding her surrender. For long minutes, she gave it to him as he pressed her against the door, opening her thighs around his hips and grinding at her core through their clothes, simulating the possession he was going insane for.

"Jala, *habibati*..."

She suddenly lurched and pushed at him.

Putting her back on her feet, he twisted a hand in the luxury of her hair, able to see her now that his sight had adapted to the faint lights coming from the windows. "Let me love you, *ya jalati*. Stop pushing me away. Let me close again. I know you want me as much as I want you."

Her breasts still heaved against his chest, her body

arched involuntarily into his even when her words rejected him. "I don't care what I want. This isn't what I agreed to."

"Then agree to this now. To giving us another chance."

"*No.* I don't want another chance. I want to play my part until we're sure your uncle will sign the treaties, then I want to leave. This is what I want to do. What I *need* to do."

The desperation in her voice struck him in his vitals, made him stagger away.

And because he had admitted to himself that he loved her, only wanted her to be happy whatever the cost to him, he couldn't pursue his seduction anymore. Not if, for some reason he couldn't fathom, it distressed her that much. It might kill him to let her go, but he'd rather die than hurt her.

His shoulders slumped with defeat. "My uncle is sending you a set from the royal treasury. It's his way of saying the peace treaty is as good as signed."

After a long moment of staring at him, she whispered, "That's great. I mean, that you think he'd sign, not about the jewels."

He waved her qualification away. He knew she cared nothing about material things, and not because she had plenty of them. She made no use of her status in any way, not for herself. She used all her privileges to serve the world.

"I have the drafts of the treaties ready, and after Kamal approves them, I'll present my uncle with them. My package for Saraya is very generous, but as you believe, he wouldn't have felt secure enough or irreversibly connected to Judar without a union of blood. Which he now believes he'll have, thanks to your cooperation. I don't expect he'll pose any further threat to peace."

Her eyes wavered. This had clearly come out of left field for her. She'd expected him to continue his pursuit, his seduction. And here he was telling her there was no longer any reason for her to play along at all.

He exhaled roughly. "I had my chance with you, and I blew it. Or maybe there was never a chance to be had with you, then or now. I will take part in all the wedding preparations, so both my uncle and Kamal believe everything is in order and on schedule. I'll push for an early signing of the treaties, which, now that my uncle is so amenable, I expect will be soon. Once he signs, I'll reveal the truth and absorb whatever fallout ensues, away from you. Until then, I'll give Kamal some convincing reason for leaving the palace. I'll go in the morning, so you don't have to put up with seeing me again."

Nine

Something tore Mohab from the tentacles of fitful sleep.

The heart that no exertion or danger managed to send thundering, thundered now, past the comfort zone and into distress.

It only ever beat that way for Jala.

Jala. Had something happened to…?

He shot up in bed, alarm swamping him.

"Sorry I startled you."

Mohab felt as if he'd been hit by lightning.

Jala. Here. On his bed.

Leaning across him, body draped in white silk, silvered by the moon's cool illumination, hair raining in sheets of solid darkness across the thighs twisted in his sheets, she looked like a night goddess, his every fantasy made flesh.

This had been the dream he'd been having. That she'd come to him. He'd felt her entering his room and…

He was still asleep!

But he felt awake. She felt real. But she couldn't be real. She'd said no. Such an impassioned, desperate no.

So had he gone over the deep end? He'd been building up to a breakdown for years now. Was this it? He'd start wish-fulfilling wide-awake? Having delusions?

"I couldn't stay away anymore. I couldn't let you leave without telling you I still want you. Now more than ever."

He *was* hearing those words. She was saying them. He knew because even he couldn't imagine the way she made them sound, wouldn't be that ambitious, that delusional as to make them such a throb of passion, such a scald of longing.

She was here. And she had said those words. Not the ones he needed, but still far more than he deserved.

I still want you. Now more than ever.

On their thousandth rotation inside of a single second, he reached out a hand to her face, still half expecting to find nothing but emptiness, for her image to dissipate.

His fingers touched the hot velvet of her cheek.

Groaning at the confirmation, he swung around to his bedside lamp. He had to see her better than the crescent moon through his open windows allowed.

With the chamber flooded in golden light, he turned to her and saw that the lace and satin nightgown and matching robe were cream, not white, the color offsetting the rich gold of her polished flesh.

Then he saw her eyes. Unlocked for him at last, letting him see inside her, see the full measure of her hunger.

Already hard beyond pain, heart trembling with disbelief still, he reached back to her, careful not to make any sudden moves, still afraid this dream might come to an end as every tortured one had in the past six years.

When he was an inch from touching her again, she did something that stopped his heart. What she'd done that night he'd first taken her to his penthouse.

She melted back on the bed, as if she couldn't support herself anymore, threw her arms above her head, arched in surrender, a sultry moan spilling from deep rose lips.

"I *want* you, Mohab."

Surging with her demand, he came over her, straddled her hips, cupping her face in trembling hands. "*Aih,* want me, *ya habibati, atawassal elaiki*—I beg you. I'm yours to want."

"Mohab…kiss my lips, give me yours…"

She reached up and grabbed his hair. This was why he'd let it grow, because she'd once told him she wanted it longer to pull him by, to tether him closer to her on their wild rides. Now she dragged his head with it, surging up to crash her mouth against his. Her tongue delved inside him, tangling in abandon with his.

He let her storm him, let her show him the measure of her pent-up craving and impatience. Then he took over.

He'd show her six years' worth of hunger. Then he'd give her satiation well worth the wait.

He bit into her lower lip, showing her the power of his own craving, before he suckled it inside his mouth in long, smooth pulls, drawing more plumpness into her succulent flesh, then plunging his tongue inside her.

Her whimpers became incessant, her hands clenched in his hair as she wrestled with him for deeper surrender, the pain of her urgency excruciating pleasure. She crushed her breasts into his chest, cushioning him, one leg escaping his prison to wind around his hip in abandon. She was showing him she wanted anything he'd do to her. Anything at all.

Then she moaned into his mouth, "Touch me, Mohab, all over. Do everything to me, don't be gentle…I can't bear for you to be gentle…. I want your full force. I want you inside me, hard and long and now…*now,* Mohab. I can't wait anymore…I can't wait…."

Elation sizzled in his blood. She'd never been this vocal, never told him what she wanted or how she wanted it.

"*Aih, gulili aish betridi*—tell me what you want, *ya galbi.*" His voice shook as he pushed the robe off her shoulders, then raised her arms over her head once more and, in a luxurious upward sweep, freed her from her nightgown. She only had bikini panties beneath, which he took off, as well. Then he pulled back to fill his eyes with her. *"Ma ajmalek, ya habibati, ajmal men zekrayati, men ahlami."*

"*You* are." She pressed kisses onto any part of him she reached, his chest, arms, hands. "So much more beautiful than my memories and my dreams."

Arousal hammering in his blood, pounding in his loins, he sculpted her in a frenzy of memory and rediscovery, owned each remembered inch of her silken skin, kneading new curves, digging into strength and soft femininity. Her flesh hummed beneath his fingers, electrifying him.

Her teeth sank into his hand. "Touch my breasts...."

A chuckle revved in his chest, resonating his delight that she was so aggressively demanding his pleasuring. He loved it.

"*Amrek ya hayati,* command me." He took their weight in his palms and stared at their ripened perfection, stroking their turgid flesh in wonder, squeezing their incredible resilience, circling the buds he'd tasted during so many rides to ecstasy. They were thicker now, darker, more mouthwatering.

With a long whimper, she attacked his pajama bottoms. He let her push them down his hips, growling as she released an erection that had long hardened to steel. Rising to release himself fully, he watched her fling herself up at him, then rumbled as she bunched her hands in his back muscles and latched her teeth into the muscles of his abdomen and torso, writhing against him as if she'd mingle their flesh.

He subdued her back to the bed and she wound herself around him, her voice a thread about to snap. "Come inside me, Mohab…don't make me wait anymore…please… *please*…"

He devoured her pleas, unleashed now that he knew only the savagery of his need would satisfy her.

His lips relinquishing hers, he sowed a path of kisses and suckles lower, until he possessed her breasts, raining bites over their engorged beauty until she crushed his head to her, mashing her flesh into his mouth. He latched on to one nipple, then the other, alternating heavy pulls and sharp nips, each rewarded by a lurch and a shriek.

When he felt her stimulation becoming distress, his hands dragged over her soft, satiny flesh to her core. Spreading her, he slid between her feminine lips, growling with the extent of her readiness. He was coming apart needing to be inside her, but he had to prepare her. For he *wouldn't* be gentle when he took her. As she'd commanded. Clamping his lips on hers, he probed her, plunged two, then three fingers inside her hot channel.

Her thighs clamped his hand, her fingers dug into his scalp as her body convulsed, sharp, spasmodic squeals gusting into his lungs. She was climaxing. With but a touch. He'd aroused her that much.

He allowed himself a moment to watch her in the throes of satisfaction, the sight he'd starved for for six bleak years. Then he took her mouth again, doing to it what his fingers still did to her core, feeding her frenzy, loving every jerk, drinking every last whimper until she slumped in his arms, all precious, satisfied woman.

Or so he thought. In a minute, her lips found his chest again, her leg rubbing against his hardness. Imprisoning it in both of his, he clamped the hand that greedily caressed his shaft.

"I want to touch you, Mohab, taste you…."

The memory alone of her head bowed at his loins, her hair spread on his thighs, the sweep of her back, the flare of her hips as she rubbed herself against his legs like a feline in heat, moaning her pleasure as she worshipped him with trembling hands and swollen lips, almost made him come.

"Later, Jala. Own me later. *Areed aklek, akhullusek*—I want to devour you, finish you."

"No…just come inside me…." She wrapped her legs around his hips, ground her moist heat over his erection.

He savored the torture for a moment, absorbing her need, then opened her folds with the head of his erection, and she mewled and spread herself wider for him, the sound and sight almost making his skull burst. He circled the engorged bud of her arousal, drawing more keens, more prodding twists in his hair. Then he slid from her grasp and moved between her thighs.

Before she could protest again, he took her feminine lips in a voracious kiss, his tongue lapping her in long sweeps. Her protests fractured only when he suckled her bud until he had her thrashing, begging. When he knew she couldn't stand anymore, he bit down on her.

The force of her release razed through his body, almost triggering his. He again pushed three fingers inside her, sharpening her pleasure, lapping up its flood until her voice broke and her body slumped.

Still lapping at her, soothing now, he rested his head over her trembling thigh, tenderness a rising tide through the sustained agony. How he'd missed pleasuring her.

Her shaking hands wound in his hair again, dragging him up by it as he'd dreamed she'd do for so long. He obeyed her, swept up over her, sank languorously into her kiss. Reveling in her hands roaming his body, he could feel her extracting his soul, reclaiming him with her raging need.

She suckled his earlobe, bit it, sending a million arrows lodging into his erection, whispered in a voice roughened by abandon and satisfaction, "*Now* will you come inside me?"

"*Enti to'morini*...you only have to command me."

"I did nothing but command you...to no avail."

A guffaw ripped out of him. The fact that she was teasing him now was so unexpected, so delightful.

His hands dug into the buttocks undulating against him. "You call this 'no avail'?"

In answer, she pressed her body and lips to his. "I call anything that doesn't end with you inside me that."

"I spent six years planning all the ways I'd pleasure you when I finally got my hands and lips on you again, *ya rohi*."

She pulled him back over her, eyes feverish. "I only want one way. You. Inside me. *Now,* Mohab."

His heart boomed with gratitude and pride. She didn't want just any pleasure, no matter how fierce. She wanted the pleasure of union, with him.

It was humbling that she desired him as much as before and more. But his passion had intensified through the forging of denial and disappointment, frustration and separation, though mostly by total, unconditional love. Why had hers strengthened? He couldn't tell, could only give thanks.

For one last moment before he joined them, he held her eyes as he loomed over her, and they swallowed him whole.

"Take me."

Obeying her desperate demand, he thrust into her in one savage plunge, sheathing himself inside her tight heat to the hilt, hurtling home, his only home. Her scream felt as if it tore from her lungs, pure, excruciating pleasure, as his bellow had been. She arched up in a steep bow, seeking his possession, needing his urgency and ferocity, and he gave it to her. He withdrew all the way, then forged back even deeper, harder, the near impossible fit driving him out of his mind, until he'd built to a jackhammering rhythm with his full force behind it.

Too soon, her screams merged as she bucked beneath him...then shattered in convulsions that clamped her around him, wrenching at his length in a fit of release. He rode the breakers of her orgasm, withdrawing and plunging in a fury, feeding her frenzy until her screeches stifled and her heart accelerated beyond the danger zone, her tears pouring thickly.

"Come with me...."

Her sob broke him. He let go, buried himself to her womb, wished he could bury all of himself inside her, and surrendered to the most ferocious orgasm he'd ever known, jetting his essence into her depths in gush after agonizing gush, roaring his love, his worship.

"Ahebbek ya hayati, ya rohi...Jala, aabodek..."

Pleasure stormed through him, held him in a merciless vice for long minutes, then it suddenly unleashed its grip, let him breathe, unlocked his muscles. He collapsed over her, driving deeper into their merging.

When he had control over his body again, he withdrew to look down at her, and his heart swelled at the sight of the goddess she'd become. A soundly slumbering one right now. His lips shook on a smile of satisfaction. So he could still pleasure her into oblivion.

Gratitude swamped him again as he made his pledge to the fates. If he couldn't have her love, he'd wallow in her desire, fulfill her every need, lavish all his love and trust and honor on her. He'd keep her hungrier for more still, do anything to keep her beside him.

Until he made her love him. For real. And forever.

Jala jerked out of a place of total darkness and bliss to the sight of Mohab over her, the feel of him inside her.

His weight felt like the gravity holding her universe together. The universe that had spun out of control when he'd told her he'd leave and she wouldn't be seeing him again.

The eruption of despair had overwhelmed her. She'd pushed him away, thinking she'd been defending herself, saving her sanity. But the idea of losing him again and forever had torn aside inhibitions, rationality, even survival. She'd had to have him again, even if the cost was eternal misery. Nothing had changed, or would ever change. She would always need him beyond self-preservation. And she'd thrown herself into the heaven and hell of his arms again.

The conflagration that had followed, what he'd done to her, proved she'd only forgotten how it had felt to be with him. Or that this ecstasy was new.

It *was* new. And far more potentially destructive for it.

"Jala, *habibati*..." Mohab's voice cascaded like warm midnight waters over her as he turned them around, draping her over him, maintaining their union. "Are you all right?"

No. You exist and I'll never be all right.

Forcing herself to keep it light, she rubbed her face into his pectorals, response gushing again in the core he occupied as the glistening sprinkle of his chest hair tickled her lips. "You really need to ask?"

He smoothed large, calloused hands over her back. "You were moaning. I thought I was too heavy so I took most of my weight off you, changed positions, but you're still tense. You're uncomfortable with me inside you?"

He *was* too big, too thick, and it seemed as if he hadn't subsided at all. He did stretch her into an edge of pain that was addictive, overwhelming, and as he'd driven all that power inside her, it had been beyond exhilarating. The idea of all that he was, focused in one act of sheer desperation, as much at her mercy as she was at his, filled her, body and soul. She'd thought her younger self had experienced the height of shattering emotions, and that was why she'd felt so empty and bereft when she'd lost him. Turned out, she'd known nothing.

When her answer was delayed, he started raising her off him. She panicked, squeezed him with all her strength, kept him inside her.

He threw his head back on a bass groan, his mane fanning on the rumpled sheets, his hands digging into her buttocks, thrusting his own buttocks up to grind himself farther inside her.

She collapsed on him, a cry of shocked pleasure opening her lips on his corded neck as he nudged her womb. *"Mohab..."*

Rising to a sitting position with her straddling his hips, he leaned against the headboard, held her hips in his palms and raised her until the head of his erection emerged from her entrance, then he let her sink over the girth slicked in their pleasure.

"Ride me, *ya rohi*. Take me and take your pleasure of me."

Feeling faint with sensation, she braced herself against the worked wood, thighs trembling as she tried to scale his length. She'd managed only half when his mouth engulfed one nipple, his fingers twisting the other.

She crashed down on him, felt him push into her cervix. *"Mohab...please..."*

He took her arms from their slump, placed them on his shoulders, then held her hips and moved her up and down, traveling the length of his erection in leisurely journeys to the rhythm of his long, deep suckles of her nipples until the pressure in her core threatened to implode. "Before you, I never dreamed pleasure like that existed. I never want to stop pleasuring you, *ya hayat galbi*."

Life of my heart. One of the extravagant endearments that he'd lavished on her in the past.

Hearing it now nearly tipped her over into the abyss, made her wail, "Mohab...I can't... Too much..."

Again he understood. Easing her onto her back, he rose above her, spreading her wider around his bulk as he lunged forward, letting her feel the rawness of the strength that could and had pulverized men twice her size, now leashed to become carnality and cherishing instead. He stretched her around his invasion and stilled, throbbing in her depths, his fiery eyes holding her streaming ones, until she was one exposed nerve ending.

"*You* are too much. Everything you are. Take me, Jala, all of me." He withdrew as he talked, then rammed back into her.

As if this was his first thrust all over again, she shredded her larynx on a shriek. She dug her fingernails into his buttocks, wanting him to stab her to the heart, destroy her once and for all.

And he did.

She convulsed, stilled into a whiteout before everything detonated, wave after wave radiating from his driving manhood to raze her, reform her for the next sweep.

Then it shot beyond her ability to withstand. He'd joined her in this darkest ecstasy, roaring his completion, his orgasm boosting hers as surge after surge of his seed splashed into her womb, finishing her with delight...and desolation.

From the depths of satiation, Jala opened eyes that felt glued shut. Her breath hitched, and her body heated instantaneously as she found herself enveloped in him.

Mohab. As in all her dreams, as in those five months they'd been lovers. Curved around her, his legs encompassing her, his head propped on one hand, the other sweeping her in caresses, his eyes and lips radiating pure male satisfaction.

She reached out, ran numb fingertips down his beard. It was amazingly soft, just the right length to lose any stubbly feel. Just remembering how it had felt against her lips, against every inch of her, was enough to have her squirming with arousal again. Not to mention the feel of his hair as she'd binged on the freedom of twisting her hands in it and pulling on it.

"How long have I been out?" Her voice was thick and raspy. The voice of a woman who'd been savagely pleasured. She did feel gloriously sore, every cell shrieking with life.

"An hour or so," he teased. "Watching you tumble into unconsciousness in the aftermath of my possession, then documenting your abandon to slumber, every inch flushed and drained with satiation…" He sighed deeply, rubbed his beard against her shoulder as he plastered her more securely to his length. "It remains the most fantastic sight I've ever seen. It *is* the most gratifying thing in the world, knowing that I can still knock you out with pleasure."

"Anything I can do for your male ego," she croaked.

He hugged her exuberantly before pulling back, his eyes turning serious. "Mine is all tied up in my ability to satisfy you, Jala. And now that I know for certain that this is something only I can do, I won't let you fight our need anymore. We must and will be together."

She closed her eyes, warding off the intensity in his.

It did nothing to reduce the brutality of temptation. She couldn't resist him or her need for him. But she had to lay down limits before he swallowed her whole.

She opened her eyes. "As I just proved, I want you beyond my ability to resist. So I will be with you."

He sat up, his eyes intent. "What do you mean…with me?"

"I'll marry you. For those six months you proposed."

Ten

It had been a torturous whirlwind since that night she'd surrendered to her need for Mohab and told him she'd take his original offer of a six-month marriage.

When she had, he'd brooded down at her for a long moment…then he'd proceeded to plunder her throughout the rest of the night…and morning.

That had been three weeks ago. Time had never passed so slowly. Or so fast.

And tonight was their wedding night.

Once Mohab had secured her agreement, he'd pushed for cutting short the intended three-month engagement. Now he knew he'd have a sure response from his uncle after their wedding, he wanted it as soon as possible. Especially since it was clear, after their one night together, that they'd have no more until they were officially married.

After their explosive reunion, they'd suddenly found themselves surrounded at all times. She suspected Kamal's eyes in the palace had reported her nocturnal visit to

Mohab, and to curtail the scandal that would surely ensue if it became known the princess of Judar was entering her intended's bed prematurely, he'd conspired to keep them apart. Since Kamal *had* alluded to the fact that the anticipation before the ceremony invariably made the wedding night all the more…special, she was positive that her constant state of deprivation was her dastardly brother's doing.

But maybe she shouldn't be so impatient to start the marriage that would have her in Mohab's bed again. Because once it did start, she'd start counting down the minutes to its end.

But knowing there would be nothing permanent between them, she'd already decided to take what she could of him, with him, hoard memories for the future. A future she'd always known would be empty, but would now be bleak.

Emptying a chest tight with futility, she forced burning eyes to take in the vista from her window. She wouldn't let heartache dissolve into tears and face tonight with eyes that told its story. She had to play her part tonight, had to honor Mohab in front of his people, fill her temporary position as his bride and queen as best she could.

But even the land that felt untouched by time, being exposed to its ambiance of purity and the serenity that permeated it, failed to imbue her with any measure of calm.

Though this land had touched her on her most fundamental level from the moment she'd laid eyes on it, just like its most influential son had, she still regretted that she'd agreed when Mohab had insisted their wedding take place here.

Jareer. His ancestral land. Where he would become king tonight. And she'd become his queen. Temporarily.

Once she'd lost the right to be here, the memory of experiencing this place with him would be one more injury and loss to live with.

At Mohab's insistence, Kamal had relinquished the right to have his sister's wedding in Judar. He'd thoroughly approved of Mohab wanting to make her his—and Jareer's—queen on the same night of his *joloos,* when he claimed the newly forged throne.

Since being this accommodating was so unlike Kamal, she'd teasingly accused him of letting Mohab walk all over him just so he'd end her long-lamented spinsterhood. Kamal had only teased back, "Of course, why else?"

And here she was, in Zahara, what passed for Jareer's capital.

They'd come two weeks ago to prepare for the dual celebration. By *they,* she meant *everyone.* Her getting hitched was such a big deal that her family had left Judar unattended to make sure her wedding went, well, without a hitch.

Not that Mohab was letting anyone do anything. Apart from Carmen, who was a master event planner, and Aliyah, a world-renowned artist who had eagerly taken charge of dressing everyone, he had adamantly refused to let anyone lift a finger in anything but recreation. As such, he spent his every waking hour being the perfect host to everyone.

While acting as their tour guide, he'd been a mine of information. According to him, this area had been settled since prehistoric times, and to prove it he'd taken them to see the local caves with their ancient rock paintings. He'd showed them the monuments of every culture that had left their mark on the region, with the most influential being Ottoman, Persian and Indian, but all wrapped up in an Arabian feel.

Apart from the many tourist spots the region boasted, it had surprised her how much there was to do around here. There was a vast array of outdoor activities—from hiking to dune skating to horseback riding, to swimming in and lazing around sparkling springs, to bonfire banquets at night.

It had been bittersweet watching Mohab dote on her sisters-in-law and nephews and nieces and bond with her brothers. They had all taken to him—especially Kamal—which caused her extra delight…and dejection, when she knew that this would all end on a prearranged date.

As it had to.

But through it all, she'd done everything she could not to dwell on that inevitable end before they even began. And in those moments that she managed to forget, she'd reveled in his spoiling. For *how* he'd spoiled her.

Though nothing he did could make up for being unable to have him again. Since they'd come here, he hadn't even had a chance to kiss her. Well, he did, constantly, but only her hands, shoulders and cheeks. And then there were the scorching caresses, the devouring, brooding glances, the laden-with-promise smiles and the lavish words of praise. Everything had kept her on the verge of spontaneous combustion.

Sighing, she focused on the scene in the distance, with Zahara's houses arranged in graduated compositions of whitewashed adobe and red and yellow-ocher stone. At night, before the full moon rose, they were only shades of gray, but in the daylight they looked like an explosion of flowers atop the sandstone hills.

Mohab had insisted on coming here by land, saying the scenery on the way was worth the six-hour drive from Durgham. And it had been. She'd never seen such variations to the desert, the terrain flowing from undulating dunes to hilly pastures to mountainous heights to combinations of everything.

Then this castle had materialized in the horizon, reigning over Zahara, and it had taken her breath away.

Nestled in the containment of the craggy mountain

that overlooked the vista of Zahara, against an ocean of dunes, it crouched behind soaring ancient walls shielded by battlements that summoned to mind Saladin and the Crusades. That night it had loomed against an impossibly starry night, with torchlight fluctuating from the inside and the guard posts shedding their firelight on the outside, drenching it in a deeper, supernatural tinge.

It had been the Aal Kussaimis' stronghold until the time of Sheikh Numair, Mohab's maternal great-grandfather. But after Jareer had signed the treaty with Saraya, and no one inhabited it anymore, this place had fallen into decay.

But Mohab had had it restored in order to boost Jareer's tourist business. He'd succeeded, since the citadel had become one of the region's most frequented historical sites. Like her, tourists found it a once-in-a-lifetime experience, as they wandered through its maze of passages, extensive grounds and interconnected structures, feeling as if they were taking a stroll in the past. Tonight the place would rise against a full moon, and be bathed in the lights of the extensive tent set just outside its walls for the wedding celebration.

She'd expected the guests to include world movers and shakers, but to hear that two presidents and one king from the Western world were attending had made her feel the gravity of the whole situation. This wasn't just a royal wedding, but a major political event. Mohab was claiming more than a bride tonight—he was claiming the throne of a land that would feature heavily in global power from now on.

Standing up, she looked around the chamber Mohab had assigned her till their wedding. He'd restored every inch to its original condition with painstaking authenticity, but had outfitted it with every modern luxury and amenity. She could see herself living here, going away only for work, but always coming back home here.

Home. She'd never felt she had a home. But this majestic place—which was permeated with Mohab's unique, indomitable essence—felt like home.

Not that it mattered how it felt. Her stay here was only a transient one. Now, even the hour she'd managed to negotiate alone before everyone swarmed around her to prepare her for the most momentous night of her life was almost up.

"You hour is up, sweetie."

Groaning, she turned to her sisters-in-law, who were striding through the chamber's ancient oak door. "You must have a stopwatch in your lineage, Aliyah."

The ladies laughed at her lament as Aliyah ushered in her ladies-in-waiting with everything Jala would be wearing. Jala's only input had been picking a color scheme. Living in jeans or utilitarian dresses, she hadn't been about to trust herself with an opinion beyond that. Needing to look the part of Mohab's bride and queen, she'd left it all to Aliyah's artistry and experience as a queen, and to the other two ladies who were far better versed than she was in fulfilling the demands of their titles.

Carmen clapped impatiently. "Hop to it! Your hour of meditation crunched the time to get you ready to a measly thirty minutes!"

Jala bowed. "Yes, O Mistress of Magnificent Events."

Farah chuckled as she fanned her hands in excitement. "You don't know the half of it. Everything you think you saw, or thought the preparations would amount to, is *nothing* to the end result. And I thought Carmen made *my* wedding rival a fable from *One Thousand and One Nights!*"

Carmen chuckled. "I actually didn't do much this time. Your Mohab is so ultraefficient, not to mention head over heels in love with you, he's the one who's done most of the work to give you the best wedding in modern times."

Jala was an old hand by now in maintaining a bright smile when everyone kept stating how much Mohab was in love with her. They had no idea how it actually was between them. But how could they? To them, it must seem like a fairy tale, and they must believe that everything Mohab lavished on her was based on what they all defined as love. None of them could imagine that her relationship was nothing like theirs, that his involvement was fueled by pure passion and garnished by convenience, and that the whole thing had an expiration date.

Putting down a jewelry box with Saraya's royal insignia that contained the heirloom pieces King Hassan had bestowed on Jala, insisting she wear them for her wedding, Carmen grinned. "And this magnificent place worked on its own. Any touch I put was multiplied tenfold by its magic."

Jala could well believe it. Not that this diminished Carmen's and Mohab's efforts in any way.

Farah nodded. "And the people of Jareer themselves. I've never seen a collective so ready for entertainment and versed in preparing celebrations."

"Yeah, and I thought the people in Judar were like that in comparison to the States," Carmen said. "But being here showed me how modern life had taken root in Judar, too, preoccupying everyone. Here every birth and wedding, cultural or religious occasion is a feast *everyone* attends and takes part in."

Farah grinned her pleasure. "And we've been the lucky recipients of their enthusiasm and expertise through our stay. It's going to be such a downer going back to indoor court life and our relatively isolated family lives now." She winked. "Good thing we have our men to keep us… intensely entertained."

Chuckling in corroboration, Aliyah appeared from behind the screen that doubled as the dressing room. "We're ready for you, Jala. As Carmen said, hop to it."

Jala did hop to it. She wanted this over with.

In under ten minutes, she was looking at herself in

amazement in the full-length gilded mirror. It was a good thing she'd left herself in Aliyah's hands. That image reflected at her *was* a princess. And a future queen.

Still not believing how the parts she'd had fitted on her had come together, she ran her hands down the incredible deep gold Persian/Indian creation that accentuated her curves and offset her coloring. It had a deep off-shoulder décolletage, a nipped waistline and a layered skirt with a tapering trail. It was heavily embellished in breathtakingly intricate floral designs of silver and bronze thread and was worked with sequins, beads, pearls, crystals and appliqué in every shade of burnt orange, crimson and garnet. The *lehenga*-like skirt was organza over silk taffeta, embroidery sweeping down its lines in arcs. Everything was topped off by a lace and chiffon *dupatta* veil, perched on her swept-up hair, in gradations of gold and crimson with scalloped, heavily embellished edges.

She stood gazing at herself as the ladies adorned her in the priceless pieces of Sarayan treasure, which they thought were part of her *shabkah,* but in reality would only be on loan. The centerpiece of the collection was a twenty-four-karat gold necklace that spread over her collarbones and cascaded to fill most of the generous décolletage tapering just above her barely visible cleavage. It was the most amazing and delicate lacy pattern she'd ever seen in a piece of jewelry, inlaid with diamonds and citrines, with a gigantic bloodred ruby in the center of the design.

The other pieces matched the necklace's delicacy and intricacy, from the shoulder-length earrings to the *tikka* headpiece, to the armband, web ring and anklet. By the time she was adorned in everything, she looked like a walking exhibition, but had to admit—she looked *fantastic.* If no one noticed the shadows in her eyes, that was.

But even those were obscured by the makeup Aliyah

applied. When Aliyah stood back and said, "Voila!" Jala could barely recognize herself.

"*Ya Ullah,* Aliyah," she groaned as she stood up. "Mohab will probably ask you what happened to his intended bride!"

Laughter rang around the chamber as Aliyah revolved around her one last time to ensure everything was in order. "You're just not used to putting any makeup on. You look exactly as you always do, but with a little emphasis."

"A little? I look like a makeup ad!"

"We women need something extra to face cameras, not like those men of ours who look fantastic in any conditions. But since you're the most beautiful woman ever, all you needed was a brush of mascara, a line of kohl and a smear of lipstick."

"The most beautiful woman ever, my foot!" Jala snorted.

Aliyah chuckled. "Being Kamal's female edition makes you incontestably that to me. But then Mohab thinks so, too, and certainly not because you look like Kamal."

"Are you ladies done making me and Mohab choke?"

Kamal. He was here to take her to her groom. And he was teasing them with the common belief that people choked when others talked about them.

He approached her, his eyes so loving, so proud, she was the one who choked and threw herself into his arms.

He hugged her off the ground, kissing her forehead. "My little, beloved sister—I am so happy you finally have someone to love you as you should be loved."

There was no stopping the tears from gushing this time. All she wanted to do was burrow into his powerful, protective arms and sob her heartache to him. If only...

Aliyah pounced to separate them before Jala smothered her face in Kamal's chest and spoiled all her efforts. "Postpone tear-inducing declarations to *el sabaheyah,* will you?"

Stepping away from Kamal, she feigned a smile. "If

you think you'll ambush me and Mohab tomorrow morning, pretending to congratulate us but really checking on the satisfactoriness of the consummation, you have another think coming."

"I don't care how old you are," Kamal growled. "Or that you're getting married. You're my baby sister and I'd rather not hear about you and consummation in the same sentence."

She poked him teasingly. "So you're okay with knowing it's happening, just don't want to *hear* about it?"

Kamal shuddered. "One more word and I take you back to Judar and put you where no man can get his paws on you."

Aliyah hooted. "My husband, the hopelessly overprotective brother."

Jala smirked. "Hope he's not as hopelessly old-fashioned a lover."

Kamal mock growled and lunged at her.

Everyone continued to laugh as they left her chambers and proceeded to where both the wedding and *joloos* rituals were taking place, picking up her bridal procession on the way. Jala was relieved no one had thought her overwrought moments had been anything more than the prewedding jitters of a woman about to enter into a union that would change her life forever.

As it would. Just not the way everyone thought it would.

Then everything stalled in her mind as she entered the massive hall in the heart of the citadel. Farah had been right. She'd seen the preparations, but couldn't have imagined how it would all come together.

Wrapped in the mist of musky incense, under the firelight of a thousand torches perched high on the stone walls in polished brass holders, the whole scene was a plunge into the most lavish eras of bygone empires, or even *One Thousand and One Nights*.

As her dazed glance swept the space, the details were almost too much to take in. Cascading satin banners with Jareer's tribal insignias. Acres of tulle and voile wrapping around columns, raining from the hundred-foot-high ceiling and spanning the elaborate Arabesque framework. And the hall that Mohab had installed exploding with flower arrangements. The hundreds of people present looked like sparkling gems themselves in all kinds of finery, from lavish modern evening gowns and tuxedos, to costumes that belonged in a masquerade.

Then everything ceased to exist. In the depths of the hall, on top of a maroon-satin covered platform, with two elaborately carved and gilded ceremonial chairs at his back, there he stood. Mohab.

His hair is loose. It was the first thing that burst into her mind. He'd never worn it down in public before. But now it brushed the top of his massive shoulders, its thick luxury and vitality gleaming with sun strands in the firelight.

The second thing that impinged on her hazy awareness was that he was dressed like he *had* stepped out of the Arabian Nights. Like everyone in her bridal procession, his clothes had the same color scheme, if in much darker tones. A burgundy *abaya* cascaded from his shoulders to his feet over a gold-beige top embroidered in his tribal motifs. Dark maroon pants clung to his muscled thighs before disappearing into darker leather boots.

He looked like the embodiment of the might of the desert, the implacability of the fates. And he glowed. She swore he did. From the inside. With power and distinction. And she loved him with everything in her. Despite the harsh lessons of the past and the permanent injuries lying in the future.

An eruption of thuds made her lurch, even though she'd known it was coming. The matrons of the tribe began her bridal procession with a boisterous percussive *zaffah* that was a variation of what she was used to in Judar.

She snatched a look behind her at the older women with their chins and temples tattooed. One of them was two feet to her side, whacking away at a *mihbaj* wooden grinder.

Then others joined on all the local percussive instruments—the tambourine-like *reg,* the bigger jangle-free *duff* and the vase-shaped hand drum called a *darabukkah.* After that rousing introduction, melody players joined in, an evocative droning emanating from the string *rababah,* and the squealing of reedlike *mizmar.* Then voices rose, from all around, singing congratulations to the bridegroom for his incomparable bride.

She found herself rushing beside Kamal, powered by Mohab's hunger that demanded her at his side. Once they were on top of the platform, her eyes clung to her most beloved people, Kamal and Mohab, locked in a firm embrace that exchanged pledge and trust, before withdrawing to grip each other by one hand, while their other exchanged her from brother to husband.

Then she was clasped tight to Mohab's side, drowning in him, in the hyperreality of it all.

Putting his lips to her ears as the song continued, he whispered, "Do you know I play the *darabukkah?*"

The totally unexpected comment had her gasping, "Can I have a demonstration later?"

"Only if you promise to dance for me."

She lurched as if he'd scalded her. And he had. He'd injected a whole scene of abandoned sensuality into her imagination. Of her, in an explicitly revealing belly-dancing costume, undulating in a fever to the carnal rhythm, getting hotter with every move before he pulled her on top of him, thrust up into her and rode her into oblivion....

The music stopped, bringing her runaway imaginings to

a grinding halt. Then the *ma'zoon* came forward to begin the marriage ritual. *It was really happening.*

Mohab took her hand in his and the cleric covered their clasped fingers in a pristine white cloth, placing his palm atop them and intoning the marriage declarations. They repeated only the last parts after him, each accepting the other as a spouse. As the cleric stepped away, she thought that was it and she'd managed to survive the ritual without further upheavals. But before she could move, Mohab took her other hand in his.

Looking soulfully into her eyes, his voice rang out to fill the hall, deep and reverent. "That was what any man pledges to any woman he marries. But *my* pledge to you is that you have all of me, have always had all of me and will always have all of me. All that I own, all that I do and all that I am."

She stared up at him, nothing in her bursting heart and chaotic mind translating into words, let alone anything as evocative as what he'd just said. It was all she could do to remain on her feet as the crowd roared with applause again.

In a tumult over what he'd just said, wondering if it had been for show or if it could possibly be true, she watched the Aal Kussaimi tribe elder climb up onto the platform.

He announced that by the unanimous vote of all tribes of Jareer, Mohab was appointed as king of their land, with his heirs after him inheriting the title.

After that, she could barely register anything as the cacophony rose to deafening levels while every tribe elder came up to kiss Mohab's shoulder and offer him the symbol of their tribe, pledging their allegiance and obedience.

Then only she and Mohab remained, and he was talking.

"By the responsibility you granted me, and the privilege you bestowed on me, as your king, I pledge I will rule with justice and mercy, doing everything in my power to fulfill your aspirations and achieve your prosperity." He led her to the edge of the platform. "As my first decree as king of Jareer, I give you my one treasure to rule beside me, in her wisdom and compassion, your queen…Jala Aal Masood."

Cheers rocked the hall, rising to thundering levels as Mohab smashed the region's every ban on displays of public affection and devoured her in a deeply explicit kiss.

Without hesitation, she sank into the rough demand, the ecstasy of his taste and feel. She *would* take it all with him, every second, every breath, every spark of his desire, and make a reservoir of memories for the life ahead devoid of all of that, of him.

Amid a storm of cheering led by her family, he finally relinquished her lips. Then, grinning down at her, eyes blazing with exhilaration, he shouted to her over the din, "Shall we give them the *joloos* they're after?"

Nodding, his enthusiasm infecting her, she rushed after him to their thrones. After he'd seated her in hers, he came down before her on one knee, his eyes roiling with hunger as he kissed her hand. Then he whispered something she couldn't hear. But she read it on his lips. *"Maleekati."*

My queen.

Somehow she didn't burst into tears. But she knew the memory of this moment would fuel weeping jags far into her future, probably till the day she died.

With one last kiss on her hand, he rose to his feet and a hush descended, as if everyone held their breath. She knew just how they felt. Her breath clogged in her lungs as she watched him glide to his throne with the regality of a king born. Then, sweeping his *abaya* aside, he sat down.

Still holding his *abaya* back with a hand at his hip, he leaned forward to prop his right hand over his knee and struck a pose, a display of grandeur and entitlement that would be the standard for every king who came after him.

After he was satisfied everyone had enough photo and video documentation, he turned to her, his smile flaring again. "How about we feed all these enthusiastic people? They've yelled enough for their dinners, don't you think?"

Suddenly she was spluttering with laughter, then with surprise as she found herself plucked from her seat and up into his arms. He descended the steps, with her cradled against him as if she weighed nothing, and waded through the growing din of approval as people parted to let him pass.

The world spun with every thud of his powerful steps, with his feel and scent. Hoping she didn't mess her face or his clothes too much, she clung around his neck, burying her face in his chest, letting him take her wherever he wished.

Excitement swelled as he whisked her outside the citadel walls, where the gigantic wedding tent had been erected in the clearing overlooking Zahara, which was celebrating their new king and his wedding in the most delightful way.

Under a rising full moon, every dwelling in town had its windows open, and in each room blazed a light with a different color, turning the hills they were built over into a spread of glowing gemstones as far as the eye could see.

Then they came to the tent that looked like a fairy castle made of malleable materials, its whiteness silvered by moonbeams and gilded by the flickering flames of the thousand torches surrounding it at a safe distance. It was so big it would accommodate the three thousand people who were attending from the three kingdoms and the world.

The inside was adorned in the same color scheme of her bridal clothes, the rich tones giving everything a deep luxury bordering on decadence. Mohab carried her past hundreds of tables spread with satin tablecloths, lanterns, flowers, the finest local pottery and blown glass, all in vibrant, complementing colors. Then he was setting her down in their *kousha,* a gilded arabesque "marital cage," open on one side so they'd preside over the celebrations.

Right in front of them was the biggest dance floor she'd ever seen covered in hundreds of hand-woven *keleems*.

As soon as everyone took their places around the semi-circular tables, affording everyone the best view of the action, Mohab gestured for dinner to be served, and hundreds of waiters poured from every opening of the tent holding huge serving plates under brass domed covers. Her family and his were in the first row of tables across the dance floor. Her family looked so elated, it twisted the shard in her heart deeper. She brought it under control as she contemplated *his* family. Everyone, including that old goat King Hassan, looked happy with the whole thing. Everyone except Najeeb.

He hadn't talked to her again since the engagement, but his disapproval grated on her every nerve. Najeeb had long come to terms with what his father had done, yet another of his parent's ongoing transgressions that he'd had to put up with all his life. It was *Mohab* he couldn't forgive. Najeeb also couldn't understand why Jala was giving Mohab a second chance after everything that had happened.

As every hurt she'd ever suffered began rushing to her eyes, Mohab tugged at her. The music started to an overpowering rhythm and dozens of young men in flowing beige robes and red headdresses rushed in to form lines. Many women followed to face them, wearing beige-and-garnet dresses and head covers embroidered in cross-stitch designs. Then one of the most energetic folk dances she'd ever seen commenced, one she hadn't witnessed during all the entertainment they'd had in the past two weeks. It must be one reserved for big occasions.

As if reading her mind, Mohab shouted over the music. "That's a special dance for weddings. You haven't seen one before because they postponed all weddings to focus on ours."

As he talked he started clapping, urging her to clap,

too. She did and was soon swept up in the unbridled energy of the performance. Then her family and all of his, except Najeeb, were rushing to the middle of the dance floor, uninhibitedly imitating the steps and soon becoming one with the choreography.

Suddenly the dancers streamed toward her and Mohab, the women converging on her and the men on Mohab.

"You put them up to this!" she accused laughingly, as she was carried on their wave away from him.

He gestured to her, feigning innocence. Then the two waves of dancers rushed toward each other with them in the middle, met then receded, leaving only her and Mohab together, with their families forming a circle around them. Guffawing, he caught her by the waist and swung her round and round, then put her back on the ground and prodded her to dance with him. Recalling long-unpracticed dance steps from Judar, she was soon moving with him to the primal, blood-pounding beat, her heart booming exuberantly in her chest. Finding herself transported into another realm where nothing existed but him, she felt his eyes dominating her, luring her, inflaming her, as he moved *with* her. It felt as if he was connected to her on fundamental levels, as if it was his will that powered her body.

The dances went on and on, interspersed with brief pauses to snatch refreshments and bites of food, then resuming. At one point, the singers handed mikes to each of the celebrity dancers to sing part of the songs. Mohab, of course, sang his motherland's songs perfectly, but when she warbled through her own effort, the kind crowd still roared in approval.

At some point the music came to an end, and she couldn't tell how much time had passed, minutes or hours. It felt as though she was wading in a dream. Then hundreds of people were shaking her hands or kissing her, insisting they'd never enjoyed themselves like this before. Even her family said this rivaled the delight of their own weddings.

Then Mohab disappeared from her side.

Eleven

Before alarm could descend on Jala, her brothers swept her into a 4x4 and drove with her into the desert.

As Farooq drove and Shehab sat beside him, Kamal accompanied her in the back. She nestled into him, still stunned by everything that had happened, endorphins and adrenaline fogging her brain. She didn't even ask where they were taking her. It had to be to Mohab.

Then the car stopped and Kamal pulled her out, and there he was. Mohab. A dozen feet away, at the top of three-foot-wide stone steps leading to a columned patio that wrapped around a one-level adobe lodge. Fiery light glowed behind its closed windows.

His hair rustled around his head like silk, and his *abaya* billowed around his body like the wings of a preternatural bird of prey, with him in the middle of the enchantment, her every fantasy come to life.

Then he spoke, his voice as deep as the desert night enveloping them. "*Skokrunn ya asdeka'ee* for delivering your most valued treasure into my safekeeping. In return for this privilege and trust, I owe you everything."

"Oh, you certainly do," Farooq said, chuckling.

Shehab nodded. "And we have a lifetime to collect."

Kamal rounded it all up. "And don't think we won't."

Mohab bowed his head, his palm spread over his heart in pledge. "I'm counting on it."

With senses fixed on him, she barely registered her brothers kissing her one last time, then driving away.

As their vehicle receded, she forced wobbling legs to move toward Mohab. He wasn't smiling. Or moving. He stood there, his gaze roasting her alive, making her feel he was memorizing her down to her last cell.

"Is this another tradition in Jareer?" she whispered, her voice loud in her ears in the desert's pervasive silence. "Grooms here don't go to the trouble of sweeping their brides away but have their families provide delivery services?"

He smiled then. She didn't know how she remained on her feet with the eruption of arousal.

Ya Ullah...how was it possible to want that much?

He came down a step, then another, his movements tranquil, as if he was afraid she'd bolt if he moved too fast. He reached out a hand to her with the same care.

"Welcome to my sanctuary, *ya ajaml aroos fel kone*."

The way he said *the most beautiful bride in the universe* had her stumbling into his embrace. "One of your lairs?"

"Back to the predator motif?"

"I do feel I'm walking into a starving wolf's den," she confessed.

"That's perfectly true. I *will* gobble you up."

"I'm counting on it."

At her giving him back his words, a chuckle rumbled deep in his chest. "Everything you say or do rouses unprecedented reactions from me." His eyes suddenly sobered. "And after all these years, after I first laid eyes on you and wanted you—but thought I could never have you—here you are, my bride, in my sanctuary where I have never let another."

Shying away from dwelling on his declarations, she focused on his statement about this place. It was that vital and exclusive to him. That had to be why she felt as if her essence was flowing through the ground beneath her feet to forever mingle with this place. Why she felt she'd never belong anywhere else again but in this land, with this man.

She stared up at him, towering above her, swathed in moonlight, as one with the desert and the night, unattainable as the stars. But the universe was giving him to her for now. Sort of on loan. Not having him forever meant she only had to wring every minute with him of all it had of pleasure and intimacy.

Surging against him, she buried her face where his top was open, teeth pulling gently at the muscled power beneath, catching in the perfect cover of silky hair. "Here I am."

"And what you do to me…." Groaning, he swept her up in his arms, made her feel weightless.

She clung to him, burying her lips in any part of him she reached. "Show me, Mohab. Everything I do to you. Everything you need from me. Show me everything, do it all to me."

His growl was savage this time as he took her lips, making her nerves fire in unison.

He relinquished her lips only to stride into the lodge. Kicking the door closed behind them, he swept through a dimly lit corridor that made her feel as if he was taking her deeper into a wizard's den. Which he was. He'd always practiced magic on her. And for the next six months, she'd revel in surrendering to his spell—until the enchantment expired.

She now surrendered to the experience, every foot deeper making her realize for the first time what it meant to *have* a sanctuary. This place. Where he was.

It was as far as could be from the opulence of the palace of Judar or the ancient majesty of his citadel in Jareer. It was composed of elements of the desert, unpolished and unpretentious, and more evocative and atmospheric than those mind-boggling edifices for its starkness and simplicity.

He took her into a great room that seemed to comprise the whole place, apart from a kitchen and bathroom. It had stone walls and adobe floors, and was strewn with thick, hand-woven *keleems*. On one side was a settee with a long table in front of it spread with serving dishes on gentle flames. A fireplace presided over the area, its fires leaping in a hypnotic dance, with the other sources of illumination, brass lamps, on every surface. A mosaic incense burner emitting musk and amber was hanging by thick copper chains from the beamed ceiling.

On the other side of the room was the bed. A ten-by-ten-foot, two-foot-high concrete platform with a thick mattress on top of it was draped in the only luxurious touch around—solid dark gold satin sheets, pillows and covers.

He lowered her down on top of it, then mounted it and brooded down at her as he removed his *abaya* and top, muscles rippling beneath his polished skin, his face all noble planes and harsh slashes and grim hunger, all of him painfully male and beautiful. And hers. For now.

She scrambled to her knees, needing to be rid of her own shackles. She'd removed only the veil when he knelt in front of her, stopping her, his sure, deft hands replacing her clumsy ones. She moaned in protest. "You took *your* clothes off when I spent the whole night promising myself I'd do it."

"You can dress and undress me from now on. But I

spent the whole night having minor coronaries every time I looked at you in this getup, betting myself I'd get it off you in ten seconds flat."

And he did. He got the dress off as if by magic, his eyes on every part he exposed, making her feel purely feminine and utterly desirable. Then he moved around her so he was enveloping her from the back, his hard flesh plastered to her flaming back, his harder erection digging into her buttocks through his pants, making her feel contained… dominated.

His breath steamed down her neck as he whispered, "You want me to show you what I wanted to do to you during those three weeks of torture?"

Her nod was shamelessly frantic. "Yes, yes, show me. Do it all."

"I wanted to catch you, wherever I found you, and do this…." His hand cupped her breast, squeezing until she moaned and arched back, thrusting against his erection, making him growl and snap his teeth over her shoulder. "And this…." The other hand slid down over her abdomen to cup her mound, his fingers delving between her molten feminine lips, finding her entrance, slipping up her flowing readiness.

Her cry rang around the lodge.

His chuckle into her neck was unadulterated sensual devilry. His fingers twisted inside her, making her grind into him, desperate for assuagement. "I take only verbal requests. Graphic ones."

She'd give him graphic. "I want you buried all the way to my womb. I want you to ride me until you shatter me, until I wring your life essence from you."

He snatched his hand from her insides, the withdrawal as exquisite as the plunge. "I changed my mind. Be graphic later. Right now I might have a major coronary."

The sound of his zipper sliding down screeched through

her nerves. Moistness gushed from her eyes and core when his erection thudded against her back, hot and hard and heavy. Mohab. Here. With her. Her husband. For now.

He thrust against her, up and down, burning a furrow in her buttocks and back. "Here I am, everything you need. Take all of it inside you, take me whole, as I take you."

With what felt like the last heartbeat left in her, she turned, rose and sank on him. A cry of welcome rose from her center outward. His erection felt as big as a fist forging inside her. Filled beyond capacity, she writhed against him, pain and pleasure amalgamating into an indecipherable mass. She'd never get used to how he felt inside her, to the sensations his invasion wrung from her every nerve.

Delirious with the feeling of reclamation, she sobbed it all out to him. How he felt inside her, what he did to her, how he inundated her with exquisite pleasure. He only gave her more, thrusting up, harder, faster, forging new depths inside her, panting his own confessions.

The pressure built in her loins with each word, each abrading slide and thrust, spread from that elusive focus of madness he hit over and over. She rode him harder, each thrust layering sensation until she was buried, incoherent, insane for her release from the aching spiral of urgency.

Then it started, like shock waves heralding a detonation too far to be felt yet. Ripples spread from the outside in, pushing everything to her center, compacting it into a pinpoint of desperation. He plunged into her, taking her into one more perfect fusion…and it came. The spike of shearing pleasure, followed by slam after slam of satisfaction.

He pitched her forward, crammed a pillow beneath her stomach, angling her hips upward, then pounded into her wracking convulsions, pouring over her gushing pleasure with the long, hard bursts of his own release.

The next moments or hours, as pleasure raged, they strained against each other, shuddering all over, driving him deeper inside her than he'd ever been, until she felt they'd dissolved into each other.

Then the intensity broke, eased and everything receded, left her replete, complete, spiraling into oblivion....

It was morning when she came to. He had knocked her out for hours this time. And he was again propped beside her, watching her with a smile of supreme gratification.

She stretched luxuriously against him, rubbing her legs against his, delighting in finding him fully aroused. "Sorry I zonked out on you. Not what I planned at all."

"That was the best wedding night gift you could have given me. Lovemaking so explosive it pleasures us both into oblivion. *Aih,* I was knocked out right after you were."

Her lips spread, bliss humming in her bones. "You mean *I* knocked you out."

His indulgence deepened until she drowned in it. "That you surely did. I just woke up. I've never slept that well in...probably ever."

Her hands roamed his face, his head, shoulders, arms and back, reveling in every inch of him. "Anytime. And I want you to take that literally. I want you *any*time, all the time."

"Habibati." His growl went down her throat as he took her lips, pressed her under him and came fully over her.

And he took her up on her offer, plunging into her without preliminaries, knowing she'd be molten with need for him, would love his urgency, his ferocity. She more than loved it, she was mad for it, the fullness and the power and the domination of him. Just a few unbridled thrusts hurled her into ecstasy all over again. And he joined her in the abyss of pleasure, roaring his completion, jetting his seed inside her until he filled her.

He spoke as soon as she opened her eyes. "All these years, all I wanted was to have you again, have what we had, what kept me starving for you. Now I have you again, and it's not the same." Her heart thudded. Did he mean…? "It's way better. When I never thought there could be better."

Her heart filled with so much she couldn't reveal. But she could tell him at least one thing. "It *is* way better."

She didn't go on to say that she believed it would be that way only at first, with six years of frustration behind the initial explosiveness, before everything leveled then tapered off.

Needing to take them away from such disturbing discussions, she asked one thing that had been worrying her since she'd arrived here. "Why didn't you bring the kitties?"

His laugh revved beneath her ear. "Not even I would bring cats to my wedding night." He laughed again. "Though I might have considered it if the place had another room. They're good about staying in another room if I want to be alone…or with you, like that first night back in Judar. But they're in their favorite new place back in the citadel with all those places to explore."

Another worry struck her. "What if someone leaves a door to their quarters open? Or a window? Or if one zooms out when someone goes in to feed them or…"

Mohab swept her in a soothing caress from shoulder to buttock. "I've left as many paranoid instructions about keeping them safe as your heart can desire."

Still not satisfied, she said, "Can we check on them?"

"We certainly can. Mizar would even come to the phone. *Then* I will devour you again, and this time longer and harder, just for being so protective of my kitties."

She gasped as he turned her onto her back and reached over her for his pants on the ground. "Aren't they mine, too, now?"

"Oh, yes, they are. They are part of me, and I've already given you carte blanche to me and mine."

And as he called his people to fulfill her wish, she threaded her aching fingers through his silky hair, and wondered.

Did he mean everything he said to her the way it sounded? Did he really feel this way about her? The way she felt about him? Did she even want him to feel that way?

No. She didn't. She wanted to have this with him, let them enjoy each other as much as they wanted, as much as they could and nothing else. For six long—and way too short—months.

Twelve

"Can you believe six months have passed so fast?"

Jala felt the smile beginning to sink its claws into her flesh as she handed Sette to Ala'a, Kamal and Aliyah's five-year-old son. It gave her something to do so she wouldn't answer Aliyah's exclamation.

For what could she say? That there was nothing else she'd thought about every minute of these six months. That the days were passing so *horribly* fast? And now that the six months were up, she felt as if her very life was, too?

Aliyah threw herself beside Jala on the couch, grinning at her son's retreating back as he rushed to his sister in the other room with the last piece in his treasure, the tolerant Sette, having now collected all four cats.

"I thought once I got the kids four cats, too, they'd stop demanding to visit you to see yours every week, but no... your foursome are their first loves."

"One more thing to thank the cats for, then, making

me see you all much more frequently than I would have without them."

Aliyah laughed. "We all thought we loved cats, but you and Mohab put us to shame. Last time I saw Mohab he said you'll adopt dozens more as soon as you settle your schedules and make the citadel your base, because cats hate traveling."

Every word fell on her like a blow so that she almost gasped in relief when Aliyah's phone rang.

Thankful for the respite, she contemplated her sister-in-law. Aliyah was her very antithesis, glowing with health and happiness, her world built on the unshakable foundation of Kamal's love and of her certain future with him. While she… She'd been counting down the days she had left with Mohab and was withering inside. She'd taken to putting on makeup to prevent outward signs from showing.

Watching Aliyah melt with love as she talked to Kamal, she couldn't be happier for them, but at the same time, it made her own despondence deepen until it suffocated her.

With a last intimate whisper, Aliyah ended the call. "Kamal sends hugs and kisses. But insisted I tell you that your husband conned him."

Alarm burst inside her chest.

Aliyah went on. "He says Mohab said he doesn't know the first thing about dealing with the executive realities of running a kingdom, especially one that is growing and changing as much and as fast as Jareer. He now believes Mohab's protestations were just total pretense so he'd get him involved—not because he needs his help, but to get on his good side, so he'd help him have you, and now continues to rely on his input for your sake, too."

"I don't believe this is true…."

Aliyah waved her hand, her smile widening. "Kamal said you'd think that, but he knows a man who'd do anything for his woman when he sees one. And take it from me, that 'twin' of yours has…extensive experience and insight in that arena."

Any other woman would have considered this everything worth living for. Knowing the man she loved with all her being felt the same. But having someone corroborate the depth of Mohab's involvement, which she'd been becoming more certain of with each passing minute, only sank her deeper into despair.

"Kamal would have respected the hell out of Mohab for achieving what no one believed could be done around here, let alone in this time frame. But the fact that he has you at the top of his priorities makes Kamal feel progressively more smug that he pegged Mohab right from the first meeting, when he came proposing peace between our kingdoms…and offering it all as your *mahr*."

Time did keep proving that she and Kamal were identical. For it had substantiated that she'd pegged Mohab right, too, from that first second she'd laid eyes on him. That he was everything she would ever want in a man, everything she could—and did—love, respect and admire. And that everything that happened to make her believe otherwise had been just tragic mistakes and misunderstandings.

Contrary to what she'd tried to convince herself of in the years of alienation, that Mohab was unfeeling by necessity, he actually turned off his feelings on demand only in his work. In his personal life, with her, she'd never known anyone who was more in touch with his emotions and so generous with demonstrating them. And it had been killing her to realize how she'd misjudged him, what she'd done to him. What she'd have to do still.

Time had also proved she was a superlative actress. Not even Mohab, Kamal and now Aliyah, the people who loved her most, suspected there was a thing wrong with her.

Demonstrating her obliviousness, Aliyah went on, "I think you're making one hell of a queen, too. It's like you're made to rule this specific place beside your man, your every skill and quality just what it needs. I'm so impressed by the originality of your social and educational projects and the effects they're already having. I need you to teach me how to translate that to Judar."

And she could take no more. "Please, Aliyah, stop."

The pain in her voice had her sister-in-law sitting up in alarm. "What's wrong, Jala?"

Everything, she wanted to scream.

Up until Aliyah's visit today, she'd been escaping making a decision, thinking she could go on for a while more, maybe another month, maybe another six.

But after what Aliyah had told her earlier, so offhandedly, believing it would be nothing to concern her, she'd been feeling her world had already ended.

She swallowed past the burning coal that used to be her larynx. "I want to tell you something, Aliyah. And I need you to make Kamal understand that it is in no way Mohab's fault...."

"How are my darlings today?"

Mohab walked into their bedroom, taking off the band that held his hair in that severe ponytail, his smile flooding the soothingly lit chamber.

By the time he reached the bed where Jala was sitting with the four cats arranged all around her, he'd stripped off his jacket and shirt. Then he threw himself down beside her, grinning, spreading himself for his cats to climb all over him, stroking and kissing them. After a purring storm interlude, he turned his focus to her.

Before she succumbed and attacked him in her desperation for his feel and passion, he preempted her, dragged her down to him, surging up to take her lips as she tumbled across him.

Knowing, now that the kissing had started, neither

Mohab nor Jala would want them around, the cats jumped off the bed and prowled out to the quarters' farthest sitting room.

"Habibati, wahashteeni..." Mohab groaned into her lips as he swept her around and bore down on her.

I missed you, too, my love almost burst onto her lips. But as she'd done for the past six months, she swallowed back the endearments and the confessions until they'd scarred her forever with the intensity of their need for release, with the necessity of withholding them.

Mohab had them both naked in seconds, and she groped for him, opened herself for his possession as he cupped her buttocks and thrust inside her. This fever was a continuation of last night's conflagration, no need for buildup, just an instantaneous and ferocious plunge into delirium. He was soon pounding inside her, his force and momentum building along with her cries of abandon until it all exploded into a blaze of intensity. She remained conscious this time as he collapsed on top of her, his weight completing the magic and delivering the final injury.

When she couldn't take it anymore, she fidgeted beneath him. He rose off her, separating their bodies. For the last time. As she had to make it.

She took the plunge. "The six months are up tomorrow."

A slow smile spread on his heartbreakingly beautiful face. "So they are. How about extending for another six months?" He plucked her lips. "Then another?" Another pull, harder, deeper. "And so on and on?" His teeth sank into her trembling flesh, sending shards of pleasure and heartache splintering through her. Then he pulled back, grinning. "These constant extensions might be a great idea to renew the novelty and keep the fire raging...*if* we needed help in those departments. Which we don't. None what...so...ever."

"That won't be necessary."

"So you're going for the permanent version straight away. I approve."

"I am actually reinforcing the terms of our marriage. I agreed to six months, then it's over. As it is."

He stilled, the smile faltering on his lips, draining from his eyes. "What do you mean?"

And she smashed her own heart. "I mean I want a divorce."

The sense of suffocating déjà vu closed in on Mohab.

This couldn't be happening again. Not this time. This time he was certain of what she felt for him. Of what they had.

Numb, he sat up. "Joke about anything but that, Jala." When she made no response as she, too, sat up, he tried to find a sign of mischief in her eyes. There was none. "You can't be serious!"

"I am. *Ermi alai yameen al talaag.*"

The oath of divorce. She was asking him to "throw" it at her, ending their marriage.

Ya Ullah...she wasn't joking.

A bewildered groan escaped him. "Why? Why are you doing this? Again?"

"I'm only doing what we agreed on."

"But you can't want the same thing you did six months ago. Just last night, just *now*.... *Ya Ullah*...you've never been more incendiary in my arms."

"You know I could never resist my desire for you. But I have to now. It has to end."

"It wasn't only desire. You *love* me."

"I never said I did."

He opened his mouth to roar a contradiction, then it hit him. Skewered him right through the heart. She'd *never* said it. He'd only assumed she did. From her actions and desire.

He couldn't accept it. Wouldn't. "Even if you don't feel for me what I feel for you, if you want me that much, why leave me?" She only averted her eyes, and the expanding shock shredded his insides. "And if you'd already decided to leave me all along, what was last night and just now all about? Were you giving me one last ride before you walked away?"

She rose from the bed, so slowly, as if she was afraid she'd come apart if she moved any faster. "Let's not make this any worse than it has to be, Mohab."

Again. Just as she'd said almost seven years ago when she was leaving him the first time.

Paralyzed, he watched her reach for the dress he'd yanked off her half an hour ago. When she'd been his. She put it on now, no longer his, had said she'd never really been.

Then she was walking away.

At the door she turned. "I'll go to Judar until you conclude the procedures. Please, don't make any further personal contact. Goodbye, Mohab."

"Did you put her up to this?

Najeeb rose as Mohab burst into his office, placed both palms flat on his desk, his pose confrontational. "I assume you're talking about Jala."

"It won't take much to snap the last tethers of my sanity, Najeeb. Then I won't be responsible for what I do."

"King of Jareer or not, you're on my turf. Even if you weren't, you don't threaten me and walk away in one piece."

"I'm not threatening you, I'm promising you. If you're the reason why Jala left me…"

Najeeb straightened, a vicious smile of satisfaction spreading on his face. "So she finally did. Good for her. She should have never been with you in the first place."

"I swear, Najeeb…" Mohab's apoplectic surge drained. "You mean you had no idea she did, or *would?*"

"Do you have such a low opinion of the woman you married, you think someone can put her up to anything, let alone something like this?"

"*No.* But…" Anger deserted him, leaving him enervated with desperation and confusion, and he sank onto the nearest armchair and dropped his head in his hands, darkness closing in on him. "I don't know. I can't think anymore. I can't find a reason why she left me and I was groping for anything, even if it was insane or impossible. I just want to understand, so I can do something about it." He raised his eyes to Najeeb, who came to stand over him, his gaze pitiless. "I have to stop her, Najeeb. I can't live without her."

"*Ya Ullah,* if I didn't know better, I would have believed you without question, would have run out right now and tried everything I could to bring her back to you. But I *know,* Mohab. So stop your act right now. Now that Jala will no longer be your wife, it releases me from my promise to her."

"What promise?"

"Not to be your enemy. But now I will be, Mohab. I knew you were manipulating her when you announced your engagement out of the blue, but I couldn't object since I realized she was making a decision knowing full well that you were. Then it seemed as if your marriage was real, and happy, and I no longer knew what to think." He narrowed his eyes to dangerous slits. "But if she left you, then you must have dealt her another unspeakable injury. And for that alone, Mohab, no matter what it takes, I will destroy you."

"*B'Ellahi*…what are you talking about?"

"About how you set her up in the past. She made me promise never to confront you, wanted the ugly page turned and forgotten. I honored her request till this moment."

Mohab shook his head. "I know you found out and told her, and that was one of the reasons she left me then. She told me everything the very first night I saw her again. It's why I thought it might have been something you said to her that made her end it this time, too." He exhaled roughly. "This…and the dread that never went away—that I did come between you in the past, that your feelings for each other went beyond friendship…."

Najeeb wrenched his shoulder, his face contemptuous. "You think Jala could have had emotions for me and still came to your bed? Betraying us both?"

"I said it was a dread, not a suspicion. She's the most upstanding person I know, the most forthright."

"She is. I share a bond with her that was forged in the fire of our lives' worst experience and later nurtured by our kindred natures. There was never the least romantic involvement on either of our sides, as I told my foolish father. You should have both believed in *my* forthrightness and that if my emotions for her had been of that nature, I would never have denied them."

"That's why I'm going insane. Because I believe in *her*. And everything she did, said…indicated she'd forgiven me, proved she loved me now, even if she never truly did in the past."

"She did love you in the past. So completely your deception destroyed her."

He shook his head. "She told me what she felt for me wasn't strong enough to counterbalance her aversion to commitment and her fear that I was a threat to her independence. Her discovery of my deception was just the last straw."

"Then she told you a lie, so you wouldn't know the

depth of her past involvement and what your betrayal cost her."

Mohab gaped at Najeeb, a vice squeezing around his heart. If this was true, then he *had* hurt her more than he'd ever realized. Which made her being with him again at all a miracle. Was that her revenge? To make him fall as fully in love with her as she'd fallen for him once, then give him a taste of his own poison?

But…no. She *wouldn't* do that.

Najeeb went on, ending his confusion…and delivering a crippling blow. "When I told her the truth, she pretended that you hadn't succeeded in seducing her, that I saved her in time to salvage her dignity. But then I discovered the depth of your exploitation of her when I stumbled on her in a relief mission in Colombia…and found her pregnant."

By the time he arrived in Judar, Mohab felt he'd lost whatever remained of his sanity. On receiving him, Kamal had said he didn't care how this had happened, only that Mohab resolve it or have him as an enemy for life.

Mohab had told him to stand in line.

Now he entered Jala's quarters and found her standing at the French windows. She spoke as soon as he closed the door.

"I told you not to do this, Mohab, not to force another confrontation on me. I have nothing more to say to you."

And all his shock and anguish bled out of him. "I almost went insane all those months I couldn't find you after you left me. Now I know I couldn't because you did everything to disappear. So I wouldn't find out you were pregnant."

"You went to Najeeb." A ragged breath left her. "But you're wrong. I disappeared so I wouldn't cause my family a scandal. I didn't think you would bother with me again."

Every word made him realize he had dealt her an indelible injury.

But right now, there was one injury in particular that he needed to heal. "I want you to tell me what happened to our baby."

"What do you think happened? That I gave him away?"

Him. It had been a boy. The knife hacking his vitals twisted. "I think you lost him. I want you to tell me how."

"It was a landslide while driving up a mountain in Colombia. The jeep rolled over into the valley. One passenger died…and I lost the baby. I was seven months pregnant."

Her telegraphic account, condensing her horrific experience, felt like bullets. "And you hated me that much, you didn't think to tell me you were carrying my baby? Distrusted me so totally, you didn't even think it a possibility I'd want to be there for you after your ordeal?"

Another ragged exhalation. "I believed I didn't matter to you either way, so I assumed you wouldn't have cared if I carried your baby. And that you would have probably been relieved I lost it."

He squeezed his eyes. He'd hurt her even worse than his worst projections. "Is this why you're leaving me? Because you still don't believe I care?"

"I left because we had a deal."

And he stormed toward her, his every nerve firing as he grasped her shoulders, felt her again. "To hell with that deal. I never really meant it when I first proposed it, and I faced the truth of what I always wanted right before our engagement. *Ahwaaki, ya hayati, aashagek wa abghaki bekolli jawarehi.* I love you, and I worship and crave you with every spark of my being. You're not in my heart, you *are* my heart. And I can't live without my heart."

She wrenched herself free from his grasp, her features suddenly contorting out of control, her voice strangled with tears. "That's what you say now, what you think you mean. But you're not only a man, not only a prince, you're a king now. You will need an heir. An heir I *can't* give you."

He gaped at her, a cascade of mutilating suspicions crashing in his mind. Her next words ended them, solidifying them into terrible reality.

"My miscarriage was so traumatic, at such an advanced stage, the doctors told me I'd never have children again."

This was it. The dark secret that explained it all. All the pain he'd felt from her and could never account for.

When he'd learned she'd been pregnant, he'd thought losing their baby explained it. But it wasn't only the loss, the injury, but the permanent scar. She'd lost their baby, and any hope of having another.

He stared at her as her tears began to flow, as her shoulders began to shake, at a total loss.

What could he do to mitigate her anguish?

He heard his voice, choking on his own agony. "I don't *want* an heir, *ya hayati*. I didn't inherit my title, I was chosen for it based on merit, and when the time comes for me to step down, I will pass the throne to whomever deserves it."

A shaking hand wiped at her tears. "You do need an heir. Aliyah told me King Hassan is withholding signing any treaties until he knows the reason he blessed our marriage, the blood-mixing heir, is a reality. She wasn't worried, but only because she thinks we're postponing having children voluntarily."

And then he exploded. "To hell with my uncle and Saraya and the peace treaty. To hell with Judar and Jareer and everyone in them. I only care about you."

"You can't say that. Now that you're king, you owe it to your subjects to keep the peace in their kingdom. I'll be what stands in the way of your achieving it."

"I *will* keep the peace, and it won't be by bowing to any backward tribal demands. I only pretended to so it would give me a chance to approach you again."

She shook her head as she escaped his grasp, tears falling faster. "Even if you do, you *will* want a family...."

"We *already* have a family—me and you and our furry babies, and we'll have as many more as you want. And if you long for the human kind of kid, we'll try. The doctors' verdict doesn't have to be final...."

"It is. I didn't use protection, hoping they were wrong. They weren't. There is no hope."

"Maybe there will be with minimum intervention. If there isn't, or you don't want even that, I don't care."

"I can't, Mohab...I can't let you give up your right to have a child. I can't let you give *anything* up."

"But *I* want to give up *everything* for you, *ya habibat hayati*." She shook so hard, her tears splashed over his hands, burning him through to his marrow. He clamped her shaking head in trembling hands, tilted her face up toward his. He had to convince her, stop her from leaving him, destroying them both. "You carried my baby inside you, nourished and nurtured him in your body and with your essence. You wanted him and loved him, even when you thought I never wanted or loved you. And I wasn't there for you...."

A hiccup tore out of her. "I was the one who pushed you away, who made it impossible for you to find me. You looked for me, even thinking I never really loved you...."

"I should have looked more efficiently, not let my anxiety mess up my methods. You can't imagine how much it hacks at me to know you were pregnant, without me, and then had to go through the pain and desolation and loss... *Ya Ullah, ya rohi*...if I can't give you all my life in recompense, I would end it in penance."

"Don't say this.... *Ya Ullah*...don't...feel this way."

"I do feel this way. And as far as I am concerned, you *have* given me a son, and *we* lost him. And now I grieve with you as I should have at the time, and we cling to each other even more, and forever."

"No." Her shriek of agony pierced him as she stumbled around and staggered away.

He hurtled after her, caught her back and crushed her to him, out of his mind now with dread, begging her over and over. *"La tseebeeni tani, la tseebeeni tani abaddan."*

Don't leave me again, don't leave me ever again.

Mohab's litany sheared through her, and his tears—his *tears*—rained over her face, mingling with hers, singeing her soul. She never thought she'd ever see them. And now that she did, felt their agony rain down her flesh, she couldn't bear them, would do anything to never see them again.

But she had to do this for him. He would come to regret his emotional outburst when his head cleared and his passion cooled. He'd sooner or later long for a child of his flesh and blood. And she'd be what deprived him of fulfilling this need. He'd come to resent her for it. It was better for her to die, to leave him now than to live with him till this came to pass.

She pushed out of his arms, shaking apart, tears a stream draining her life force. "I never suspected you loved me as much as I love you, Mohab. That was why I agreed to marry you. I wanted to have some more time with you, give you the closure you said you needed, then disappear from your life again. If I suspected you felt the same, I wouldn't have done this to you." A sob tore out of her depths. "Please, believe me, I never thought I'd hurt you. But once I realized you had become emotionally involved, I knew it was better to hurt you temporarily than hurt you for the rest of your life. When I'm gone, in time, you will forget me."

He groaned as if she'd just stabbed him. "If I never

forgot you when I thought you didn't love me, when you weren't my wife, you think I'd ever forget you now?"

"You *have* to."

"Would *you* have left me? If you discovered I couldn't give you a child? Especially if you knew I couldn't on account of an injury you caused me?"

"You had nothing to do with my accident. I won't have you feeling guilty over this."

"I *am* guilty. Of injuring your belief in me and in your own self-worth. Anything that happened from that moment forward is my responsibility, my guilt."

She wiped furiously at her streaming eyes. "I once held you responsible, too, but I was wrong. If there was guilt, then I share it in full. I didn't give you a chance to defend yourself, intended to deprive you of your child. I deserve what happened to me...."

"*B'Ellahi*...you were a victim in all this, *my* victim."

At his desperate shout, her sobs ratcheted until they drove her down to the ground.

Jala gazed up at him as he stood over her, looking as if his heart had spilled on the ground, and she wailed, "If you love me, Mohab, let me set you free. I'm not leaving you. This time I'm begging you to let me go."

He let Jala go.

But only to set the plan to get her back in motion. Now that he knew she loved him, too, he was never letting her go.

He had called a summit of all the people who were players in this mess. His uncle, Najeeb and her family. They were all convened in Kamal's stateroom. Jala was there, too. This had been the last favor Kamal had said he'd ever do for him.

He walked in, swept them all in a careless gaze, before he focused on Jala. She looked pinched and drained, her beloved eyes extinguished. It nearly drove him to his knees, how much she suffered, how injured and scarred she was. He wanted to lay down his life so she'd be whole again, so she'd stop feeling any deficiency. But since he couldn't undo the damage, he could only move heaven and earth, dedicate his very life to making it up to her.

He started talking at once. He told them the truth about the past, what he'd done, what he'd cost Jala.

Feeling her brothers' rage boiling over, he went on, "I want you to know that I will accept, even encourage, any punishment you exact from me. But that isn't why I called you here. I did so to inform you that no matter what you do, no matter what happens, I'll part from Jala only when I die."

His uncle heaved up to his feet. "But you have to. I only agreed to the treaty, *and* the marriage…"

"Shut *up,* uncle." His roar made King Hassan sag back to his chair. "*You* didn't agree to anything, I was just humoring you, trying to save your face and avoid your folly. But if you make any more trouble, or if you don't sign the treaty, I will be the one to declare war on you."

"You don't even have an army," his uncle spluttered.

"I'll make one. Or I'll borrow one if it's faster. Jareer is far more important to so many powers today than Saraya, and they would do anything for me if I ask. I bet they'd help me depose you just to be rid of your nuisance. So *enough,* uncle. You've already cost us what your very life doesn't begin to make up for. Take my clemency and never let us hear from you again except as a voice corroborating peace."

His uncle looked shocked to his core. Najeeb, while looking at his father pityingly, seemed to wholly approve.

And he couldn't care less about either of them right now.

He turned to Jala's family. "My happiness, honor and all my hopes lie in whatever will make Jala happy, will honor her and fulfill her hopes. If she wants to try to have children, this is what we'll do. If she wants to adopt…"

"You can't adopt!" That was his uncle again. "It's prohibited by law in our region!"

"Uncle, you are now tampering with the gauge of your life. I won't warn you again. We will adopt as many children as she wishes, if she wishes it. I will give up my throne and two nationalities, and acquire one that will allow me to fulfill her every need." He walked up to Jala, knelt before her. Her whole frame was shaking, her tears like acid in his veins.

"Jala, you *are* my life. I want nothing but you, need nothing but your love. I would only have wanted a child as one more bond with you. I lost our baby, too, but my pain is over your loss. And the only loss that would finish me is if I lose you. Nothing is of any importance to me—not my throne, not my homelands, not my very life—if I don't have you."

Kamal suddenly heaved up to his feet. "This is not for our eyes or ears. Everybody, *out*."

Kamal's barked order had everyone rushing out, everyone except his bewildered uncle giving Mohab bolstering, approving glances. Kamal was the only one who stopped as he passed him, bent to squeeze his shoulder.

Then, dropping a kiss on Jala's shuddering cheek, he whispered to her, "I know when a man would die without his woman, *ya sugheerati*. You got yourself a prime specimen of that rare species. As only you deserve. So just take him back and keep him for life, if you don't want to kill him." He straightened, winked. "If you *do* want to kill him, then by all means, walk away."

Everything that had happened in the past years, everything Jala had suffered, everything she'd shared with Mohab in the past months, everything he'd just said and offered, built inside her until she felt herself overloading. Then Kamal winked teasingly at her, and everything snapped inside her.

And she howled. With laughter.

Mohab's jaw dropped. Kamal only bowed, as if he was taking applause for a job perfectly done, then with another wink, he walked out, too.

Recovering from the shock of her sudden transformation into a hyena, Mohab's smile broke out as he surged up, enveloping her in his arms.

"Ah, *ya habibati*...how I missed your laughter, feared I'd never hear it again."

A snort interrupted her howls. "You're that desperate for me...you call *this*...laughter?"

This drew a chuckle from him before her raucous glee escalated it into laughter, then guffawing.

It was only when she sagged in his arms, still gurgling and sobbing at once, that he stopped, too, storming kisses all over her face, murmuring extravagant endearments and professions of worship before stilling her gasping lips beneath his.

Breathing life and certainty into her once more, he managed to quiet her down. Then, holding her face in his palms, he withdrew, his heart in his still-beseeching eyes.

"I am that desperate and more. I'm also desperate in case you will keep thinking you'd be doing me a favor by walking away, that I can forget you 'in time.' When I wanted you for over ten years, had you only for just over ten months out of those, and couldn't forget you in between, that I never even thought of having anyone but you."

Everything stilled, inside and out. "You mean...?"

"I mean just as you never had anyone else but me, I never had anyone else but you. I'm yours, whether you take me…or leave me. So will you have mercy on both of us and take me, and this time never leave me?"

This was just too…enormous. He'd always been hers, just the way she'd always been his.

Everything inside her crumbling, she threw herself at him, hugged him with all her might, until her arms and heart ached. "I—I never wanted to leave you. I just want you to have everything you need and deserve."

He kissed one eye, then the other. "That's you, and you."

"Ah, *ya habibi*…I've loved you for so long."

He suddenly bombarded her with kisses. "And she says it at last."

Spluttering with laughter again, she gasped, "I made you wade in 'I love yous' in the past."

"Then forced a years-long drought on me in compensation."

"When I thought I would have to leave you, I didn't want to compound the mess with revealing my emotions. And then 'I love you' was no longer adequate to describe what I felt for you since I became your wife. *Ahwak wa abghak wa aashagak, ya roh galbi.*"

His eyes filled again as he heard her confess more than love and adoration and worship, *everything* anyone could feel with the whole of their hearts and minds and souls.

She surged to kiss his eyes, tasting his precious tears, which she swore she'd never cause again.

Withdrawing, she voiced her last lingering fear. "I'm just so scared…."

He wouldn't let her continue, enveloping her again. "That I don't know what I'm talking about? That I'd change my mind? If ten years don't prove to you that I was made to love you, that you are the one thing I need to be happy, I demand another test to prove that to you. The next fifty years."

And she surrendered. To his overwhelming love, to the unimaginable happiness of an inseparable life together… come what may. "If I have those, they're all yours. As I am. Always have been. Always will be."

* * * * *

And if you loved Mohab and Jala's story, check out all the novels in the
MARRIED BY ROYAL DECREE
series from
USA TODAY *bestselling author Olivia Gates*

TEMPORARILY HIS PRINCESS
CONVENIENTLY HIS PRINCESS

All available now!

Don't miss USA TODAY *bestselling author*
Olivia Gates's
THE SARANTOS BABY BARGAIN
a BILLIONAIRES AND BABIES *novel,*
available May 2014

"We need to talk."

Those four little words lay heavy with meaning, conjuring up a multitude of awkward scenarios from Kat's disastrous past. Ten weeks ago, they'd not only crossed that line between friends and lovers, they'd burned it to the ground, and part of her wanted to run home and hide under the bed covers.

"About?"

"We can talk on my boat."

She sighed. "Look, Marco, it's late and there's a cyclone approaching. Can't this wait another day?"

"You've been avoiding my calls, so no. And the storm's not due for hours yet."

He glanced up at the dark sky, narrowed his eyes at the barely discernible wind that had picked up.

"I'm tired."

He stared at her, irritated. "Phone calls. Avoiding."

She blinked slowly. "You're not going to give up until I agree, are you?"

"No."

"Dammit, you can be sooooo annoying!"

"Says the woman who still hasn't told me she's pregnant."

SUDDENLY
EXPECTING

BY
PAULA ROE

Published in Great Britain 2014
by Mills & Boon, an imprint of Harlequin (UK) Limited,
Eton House, 18-24 Paradise Road, Richmond, Surrey, TW9 1SR

© 2014 Paula Roe

ISBN: 978 0 263 91460 3

51-0314

Harlequin (UK) Limited's policy is to use papers that are natural, renewable and recyclable products and made from wood grown in sustainable forests. The logging and manufacturing processes conform to the legal environmental regulations of the country of origin.

Printed and bound in Spain
by Blackprint CPI, Barcelona

Despite wanting to be a vet, choreographer, card shark, hairdresser and an interior designer (although not simultaneously!), British-born, Aussie-bred **Paula Roe** ended up as a personal assistant, office manager, software trainer and aerobics instructor for thirteen interesting years.

Paula lives in western New South Wales, Australia, with her family, two opinionated cats and a garden full of dependent native birds. She still retains a deep love of filing systems, stationery and traveling, even though the latter doesn't happen nearly as often as she'd like. She loves to hear from her readers—you can visit her at her website, www.paularoe.com.

This story required an extra kick in the pants
and I truly appreciate kickers Shannon Curtis
and Kaz Delaney for doing that.
You know how much I love you girls xx
Huge cuddles to Helene Young for her wonderful
cyclone information, and Gabrielle Luthy for her
knowledge of all things French. And a special thanks
to Kaycie from the Football Federation of Australia
who went over and above to provide this soccer-
challenged writer with information regarding the sport.

I also need to mention some special characters in
Twitter Land who for one reason or another provided
either encouragement or sweet, hilarious distraction
throughout this particular story and kept this writer
sane: George IV, Will Shakespeare, Prince Henry, Jack
Sheppard, Philippe and Charles Brandon. Love you,
guys! Lastly, to the wonderful, gorgeous people behind
the epic French movie *Le Roi Danse*. Because period
dramas totally rock.

One

Ten weeks ago, Katerina Jackson had spent one night in bed with her best friend. And it had been absolutely amazing.

Now, as she drove down the Captain Cook Highway, just before she got into Cairns, she was confronted with an image of the man in question, naked and smiling seductively down at her.

Kat's foot instinctively tamped on the brake, and she only just managed to avoid the car in front as it stopped at the red light. The burn on her cheeks went all the way down her body, ending in her thighs, where it pooled annoyingly in her groin. She looked up at the familiar massive billboard featuring Marco Corelli, the golden boy of France's premier *futball* league and Marseille's highest goal scorer in the club's entire history.

Well, he wasn't exactly naked. The stacked Y-fronts

left little to the imagination, though, as did his splayed
hands across his low-riding waistband and the caption
"Come and Feel My Skins." But it wasn't his ridged abs,
popping biceps and the seductive Adonis line of muscle that disappeared into the low-riding underwear that
heated her blood. It was that familiar, tempting come-
here-so-I-can-have-my-way-with-you grin, the curve of
his overtly lush bottom lip and the forbidden promise
in those dark, sensual eyes. The way the camera had
captured his hypnotic charm as he looked up from behind artfully tousled, rakish black hair, one curl lying
teasingly across his forehead and cheek.

She'd had to pass that damn billboard every morning
for the past ten weeks, his perfect face staring know-
ingly down, as if he remembered every single thing he'd
done to her that night. How he'd made her sweat, how
he'd made her moan. How he'd made her pant.

She snapped her gaze back to the road, glaring at the
taillights as the traffic finally began to move.

"God, I am so stupid," she muttered in the air-
conditioned silence. It was Marco, her best friend
since high school. The arrogant former-soccer-star-
turned-sports-commentator, the underwear-endorsing
charmer, Mr. Flirt with a dozen different girlfriends.
She was his best mate, secret keeper, sounding board,
partner in crime. His plus one when he needed a date
to some swish function. He was also her boss's on-
again, off-again boyfriend.

She cast her mind back, sifting through her and
Grace's many conversations about Marco. Yeah, they'd
definitely been off for a while before that night, so there
was one less moral dilemma to worry about. Which just
left the main two.

Oh, she couldn't just have sex with her best friend, noooo. She had to end up pregnant, too.

If you could see me now, Mum. All your pretty, shiny dreams of your daughter having a perfect life, a perfect career. A perfect husband surrounded by perfect, healthy children.

The sliver of pain sliced through her, drawing blood, before she effectively sealed up the wound and pulled into Channel Five's parking lot. After flashing her ID to the guard, she parked, gathered her bag and strode into the studio. Then she tossed her bag in her office and checked her phone.

Four missed calls, one from her friend Connor, three from Marco, plus a text message. Back in town. We need to talk. Drinks on the boat? M x

She sighed then finally replied. Sorry, snowed under at work. Can't get away. Plus there's a cyclone warning, in case you haven't noticed. K x

After she sent it, she scrolled back to their texts from two months ago, a painful reminder that only rekindled her inner turmoil.

Have a good trip to France.

Hate to run and fly. We shouldn't leave last night without talking about it.

Nothing to say. Let's just blame it on booze and stupidity and forget it happened, okay?

Are you cool with that?

Totally. Erasing from my memory in three…two…one…

☺ Okaaaay. See you in a few weeks.

And that was it. Due to both their schedules, they had a mutual phone blackout during his assignments, although he always managed to send a few photos of the local scenery. But now he was back and wanted to do the usual drink-and-talk, and she had no idea what to tell him.

You can't avoid him forever.

"You can't avoid him forever," Connor confirmed five minutes later when she returned his call.

"What the hell, I'm gonna give it a shot."

"Don't be ridiculous. He deserves to know."

Kat slid her hip on the corner of her desk and sighed. "I can hear your disapproval all the way from Brisbane."

"Kat, I'm not disapproving. But I'm one of the few who know exactly what you've gone through these past few years. The guy deserves to know."

Trust Connor to tell it to her straight. Marco, Connor, Kat and Luke—the Awesome Foursome, they'd called themselves in high school. All so very different in personality and temperament, yet "perfectly awesome together," as Marco had put it. He'd been the cocky one, a skilled charmer, whereas his cousin Luke had had the whole bad-boy thing going on, always in trouble, always on detention. Connor was the devastatingly handsome silent-and-deep one, her unbiased sounding board who always told her the truth, uncolored by hyperbole or emotion. Sometimes it was scary how detached he could actually be, which was, ironically, what made him an exceptional businessman. He never let anyone into his private circle and she was always grateful she'd been allowed entry all those years ago.

"I...just can't tell him," she said now. "I'm already a wreck, and I can't deal with all the emotional baggage, too."

"That's unfair, sweetie. Marco would never do that to you."

She pinched the bridge of her nose and then glanced up as a runner gave her the wind-up signal, indicating she was due on set.

Kat nodded. "Look, I have to go. I'll talk to you later."

Connor sighed. "Stay safe during the storm."

"I will." She hung up, firmly pushed the conversation to one side and made her way to makeup just as her phone rang again.

It was Marco. "I do *not* want to talk to you," she muttered and slid the phone to Silent.

"Avoiding a call from the boyfriend?"

Kat slid a glance to Grace Callahan, the star of Queensland's number one breakfast chat show, *Morning Grace,* sitting in the makeup chair, getting her hair done. The woman was forty, only seven years older than Kat, but she had that polished, shiny look of someone who'd not only spent enormous amounts of time and money on her appearance, but was convinced it was the most important thing in her life. Her blond hair was curled into an artful tousle, her fake-tanned skin smooth, her body gym-honed. Yet for all her high-maintenance appearance, she had an addictive personality that attracted people by the bucket load. Which was probably why Marco kept coming back.

Kat glanced at her phone and nodded, unwilling to explain further. "No, just...a guy."

"Really?" Grace's wide eyes met hers in the mirror. "A real-life guy? Oh, my God, where's my phone? I want to take a picture of this moment."

Despite her mood, Kat smiled. "You make me sound like a nun."

"I was beginning to think you were, hon." She winced as the makeup girl pulled a lock of hair through the curler. "This is exciting—makes a change from all the Cyclone Rory news. Can I put it in the show?"

Kat snorted a laugh. "You know you can't, so stop asking. I'm not newsworthy."

"Are so." Grace waved the girl away and ripped the makeup cape from her shoulders. "You're a celebrity, and celebrities are always news."

"Please, don't remind me. I hate those people who're famous for just being famous."

"Sorry, hon, but your little scandals have fueled the gossip columns for ages. It only takes another to set it off again." She straightened her dress then walked to the door, Kat following.

Kat sighed. It was true. She was nothing particularly special: the daughter of a merchant investment banker and an events planner, a private school student. The gap year she'd spent between high school graduation and university had been twelve months of partying, but just as she was about to begin her journalism degree at Brisbane Uni, she'd been offered a job as society reporter for *The Tribune* instead. Then, she'd gone spectacularly off the rails a year later, after her mother's death.

"You never did set the record straight about everything, you know," Grace said over her shoulder as they continued down the corridor. "It'd make a fabulous feature." She swept her hands out, indicating a huge headline. "Former It Girl Katerina Jackson finally spills the dirt on her marriages, the seedy side of French football and *those* scandalous photos."

"Never going to happen, Grace."

"We could start at the beginning, make it a full show. We'd do background, talk about your childhood, your upbringing. How you beat up Marco when you were fourteen—"

"It was a shove, not a hit—"

"—and how you all ended up on detention like some modern-day *Breakfast Club* scenario—"

"I *knew* I shouldn't have told you that."

Grace laughed. "I'm not going to say anything, hon, unless you want me to. But I do find it fascinating that your closest friends are a soccer superstar, a billionaire merchant banker and the nephew of a rumored mobster. All hot alpha men. All completely different. And all newsworthy."

Marco, Connor and Luke. Her best friends since high school, since that awkwardly hilarious lunchtime detention had played out like some eighties teenage movie and they'd bonded over their hatred of school and their shared tastes in movies, music and computer games.

"What were you all there for again?" Grace casually asked as they walked to the studio.

"You know full well what."

"You'd decked Marco—"

"A *shove,* Grace. For showing off in front of his mates and getting all up in my face."

"Why? What did he say?"

"Honestly, I can't even remember." Yeah, she did —a stupid teenage comment about her lack of "womanly attributes" that, to Marco's credit, he'd apologized for later.

"Whatever. Luke had been caught defacing the toilets and… What was Connor's crime?"

"Correcting the economics teacher then threatening to bankrupt him."

"Wow, harsh."

"That was Southbank Private for you." She shrugged. "All the girls were too intimidated to talk to Luke and Connor. I wasn't. And from there we clicked. It just so happens they're guys."

"And you've never thought about…?" Grace waggled her eyebrows. *"You know."*

"What? No!"

"Not even with Marco?"

Kat threw her an exaggerated eye roll to cover up the warmth in her face. "No, Grace, I haven't," she replied as they walked onto the set. "And I have no intention of giving anyone an exclusive. I'm your research assistant now, that's it." Grace approached a raised yellow couch and coffee table surrounded by a cluster of cameras. The lights streamed down as the set director came over to go through the lineup. "The other stuff is old news. People don't want to hear about it."

"They do. But I'll just keep trying," Grace replied with a smile, taking the glass of water the runner offered.

"Of course you will." Kat accepted her usual green tea from the set assistant as Grace sat on the sofa and began to rearrange the strategically placed props on the table.

"Soooo…have you heard from Marco?" Grace asked casually.

"Not yet, no," Kat lied, fiddling with her phone. "He

was commentating the *Coupe de France,* and that was only three days ago."

"I heard he's supposed to be back today." She smoothed her dress down over her artfully crossed legs. "I'm arranging a surprise dinner for later in the week."

"Really?" Kat paused, her insides suddenly tight, and she took a sip of tea to cover up the weird feeling. "Are you two back on again, then?"

Grace laughed. "I don't think we've ever really been off. I've got plans." She took another sip of water. "Let's face it—my body clock's been ticking steadily for years. And now I have an established show and some serious credibility in this industry. It's time I started thinking about having a baby."

Kat choked, tea dribbling down her chin. She swiped at it then stared at Grace. "With *Marco?*"

"Of course with Marco!" Grace frowned slightly, eyeing the guy adjusting the lighting. "Is that a problem? I know you and he are close…"

"Oh, no. I mean, yes… I mean…" Kat took a breath, trying to steady her clenching gut. "We're close and share a lot, but we do have one rule—never butt into each other's love life."

"Really?" Grace looked intrigued. "So he's never commented on James or Ezio, not even in passing?"

"No."

"And you've never said anything to him about me?"

Kat gave her a look. "No. It's not my business. You want to have babies, it's fine with me." She gave a smile, one she'd learned to adopt out of necessity. A smile designed for intrusive cameras, when they'd been camped outside her door, trailing her on the way to work, shopping, to the gym, interrupting her family and friends and becoming so invasive she'd had to get a court order to put a stop to it.

"You sure?" Grace asked curiously as she gathered up her notes. "I always thought there was some subtle sexual tension going on with you guys, but—"

"Me and Marco? No. No way!" she denied, a little too forcefully. "I mean, he's a great-looking guy and he's my best friend, but he's..." She groped for a word. "A free spirit."

"I would've said a tart," Grace added with a smile. "And a world-class flirt. A good thing, too—he won't butt into my life and make demands on how I should be raising my child."

What could she say to that? Everything Grace said was true. Marco loved his life and lived it at break-neck speed. He had no room for a permanent partner, let alone a child.

Kat swallowed thickly, watching everyone fuss around Grace as the cameras got into position. For all her confusion, her crazy thoughts and outrageous scenarios she'd gone through these past few days, the choice was simple. He wouldn't want a baby. She most certainly didn't.

Kat adjusted her headset and sidestepped the studio camera as it wheeled toward her, watching Grace smiling into Camera One as she continued with her dialogue.

Grace could be snippy, snarky and demanding, but beneath the polished blond exterior she had a heart of gold. Kat sourced the hard-luck stories and Grace reported them, raising thousands for each charity they publicized. Grace was the public face, the ex-soapie star clawing her way back from alcohol and drugs to become the biggest-rating breakfast talk show in Queensland. Kat preferred it like that, preferred to work behind the scenes. It made a nice change, even though she still fielded a handful of interview requests every day.

No, she was content with her life. Work filled every waking moment, which meant no time for dating. Just as she'd told Connor during their regular "bon voyage, Marco" night out ten weeks ago in a Brisbane bar, she didn't do attachments or relationships anymore.

"Too much work, too difficult to navigate and way too painful when they inevitably end," she'd said, downing her drink and eyeing her friends across the table.

Marco and Luke had laughed, but Connor had had a weird look, a kind of sad-but-deadly-serious one that had annoyed her enough to order that last, fateful vodka and orange.

She swallowed an irritating lump in her throat. There was nothing wrong with her. As a teenager she'd never been obsessed with boyfriends, weddings or babies, which had set her apart from most girls in the elite Southbank Private School in Brisbane. Couple that with her preference for sport, pub bands and getting dirty over short skirts, makeup and gossip, and she'd naturally migrated toward the boys. And then there was "that incident"—as her father had called it—when she'd shoved Marco Corelli, the son of the now-notorious crime boss Gino Corelli. After the furor had died down and she'd done her counseling and detention stint, she'd realized she'd become a bit of a legend to her peers. Connor Blair, the moody silent one, had allowed her to sit with them at lunch. Luke—always so very angry—had bonded with her over obscure pub bands, and Marco... Well, he'd apologized and she'd scored a friend for life.

Complicated, complex Marco. The cocky, flirty teenager with an insane gift for soccer, who'd grown up into a gorgeous, talented, self-assured man. The guy knew her secrets, her childhood wishes, her family tragedies.

Especially her family tragedies. With her mother's death from motor neuron disease and the chances of Kat being a carrier, she'd never allowed that particular fantasy of becoming a mother take root. But now, faced with the bald-faced reality of actually being pregnant, she had absolutely no clue how to feel. After all those years of refusing the tests, of arguing with Marco that she preferred to spend her life living and not worrying, she'd actually gone and gotten tested. Now she had to wait for the results, which added extra stress to her already stressful situation.

Which was why she couldn't tell Marco. Ever.

With a sigh, she refocused on the here and now. By the time they'd finished filming the week's shows, it was eleven at night and Kat was dead on her feet. She said good-night to everyone and dragged herself to her car, fumbling with the keys as she went, her mind focused on takeout, a hot bath and double-checking her apartment for the impending storm.

Then she glanced at her car and stopped in her tracks.

Marco.

Her heart pounding, her gaze swept over him—his suit, his loosened tie, the dark hair flopping over his forehead and curling at the collar. The faint shadow of stubble dusting his firm jaw. The way he stood, all sexy and casual, hands buried in his pockets. And those wide, piercing brown eyes staring straight at her.

On another man, one with less confidence and overt sexuality, his features could almost be called pretty, if not for the overabundant aura of pure male surrounding him. His hair was a controlled crop of curls, perfectly framing those high cheekbones, lush mouth and come-to-bed eyes. And when he smiled…Lord, you could hear the knickers dropping for miles around. He reminded her of days gone by, of stocking-and-breech-clad heroes, flamboyant coats and huge romantic gestures full of wild symphonies and desperate, love-smitten poems.

And he'd been the best sex she'd had in her life.

Yes, he was adored by millions around the world. Everyone knew the story—only son of Italian immigrants, raised in Australia until a talent scout had recruited him for the French *futball* league at the tender age of sixteen. Marco, the dreamy Italian with romantic eyes and glorious touch-me hair. If that wasn't enough of an unfair advantage, he'd also acquired a hot French accent from his years living and working in Marseille and Paris. Marco, her best friend.

Her heart contracted then expanded again, and she wanted to die from the sudden ache of it all.

They'd known each other for nearly twenty years. Telling him would irrevocably change everything. Marco didn't do commitment. He loved his job, he loved women and he loved the freedom to enjoy both. And there was no way she'd lose him as her best friend after one foolish—*amazing*—night. She couldn't.

With a deep breath she continued, heading straight for her car. And the closer she got, the worse the weird feeling grew.

They'd done things—intimate things. Things she'd never imagined doing with him. They'd gotten naked, and he'd touched her and kissed her all over. Now he wanted to talk about it, and she'd rather swim with a pod of sharks than rehash her supreme stupidity that involved *that night*.

God, could it get any worse? With false bravado, she clicked off her car alarm and then crossed the last few meters to open the door.

"What are you doing here?" she asked, resisting the urge to lay a hand on her belly. Instead, she tossed her bag into the passenger seat.

"We need to talk." His unique voice—a sexy mix of French and faint Italian accents—never failed to make her shiver, but now she shoved her hair back behind her ear and steeled herself to face him. The bright security lights slashed across his face, revealing a serious expression that made her heart thump. But instead of giving in to the panic, she swallowed and crossed her arms, tilting her head.

"About?"

"We can talk on my boat."

She sighed. "Look, Marco, it's late and there's a cyclone approaching. Can't this wait another day?"

"You've been avoiding my calls, so no. And the storm's not due for hours yet."

He glanced up at the dark sky and narrowed his eyes at the barely discernible wind that had picked up.

"I'm tired."

He stared at her, irritated. "Phone calls. Avoiding."

She blinked slowly. "You're not going to give up until I agree, are you?"

"Non."

She sighed. "Fine. But be quick about it."

He eased off her car, moving into her personal space, and instinctively Kat took a step back, which only prompted him to frown. "You're not going to stand me up, are you?"

"No, I am not. Girl Guide's honor."

"Good." With a firm nod, he walked past her, got in his car and drove off.

She watched his taillights blink as he turned left out of the parking lot before she had time to fully comprehend what her acquiescence really meant.

We need to talk. Those four little words lay heavy with meaning, conjuring up a multitude of awkward scenarios from her disastrous past. Ten weeks ago, they'd not only crossed that line between friends and lovers, they'd burned it to the ground, and part of her wanted to run home and hide under the bedcovers. The other part wanted this awkward situation over and done with.

With a sigh she got in her car, fired up the engine and drove out of the car park. She couldn't run from him forever. It was time to suck it up and face whatever consequences that one night had wrought.

The marina was alive with activity, crowded with people securing their boats and belongings in preparation for the oncoming storm. Kat parked and headed down the wooden platform, eyeing the foreboding water as the dark waves lapped against the jetty. In a few hours' time, a category-four cyclone would sweep across the coast, and everyone knew all too well the devastation it would bring. The city had only just managed to recover after Cyclone Yasi had slammed into North Queensland some years before.

Marco's boat was moored at the end, a sleek, shiny thing he'd gone into great loving detail about when he'd first bought it. The only thing she remembered from that conversation was not the horsepower, the dimensions or the fuel consumption, but rather his little-kid excitement. It had made her heart flip then, as it did now when she recalled the three-year-old memories.

He stood on the deck and offered his hand as she stepped across the gangplank. Without thinking she took it.

It was weird—she'd held his hand a thousand times before, and yet right now this one simple gesture was making her jittery, as though her whole body had been put on alert and was awaiting the next eager move.

Which was stupid. Ridiculous. And highly inconvenient.

Dammit, that was what came with sleeping with your bestie. Because now she couldn't stop the memories of those same hands roaming all over her body and doing things that had gotten her all hot and panting.

As they walked aft, she managed to surreptitiously slip her hand from his, avoiding his sideways glance by determinedly staring straight ahead.

God, she hated this awkwardness. They'd gone and done the unthinkable and ruined everything, and for a second, she felt that indescribable pain slice into her heart, leaving a deep and wounding scar in its wake. Things would never be the same again. It was like one of her disastrous relationships all over again, like everything her father had blurted out that one awful time in the heat of argument.

For God's sake, Kat, can you just for once not *be front-page news? Stop with all the attention and drama and just be a normal person?*

The shame burned briefly as she recalled his expression, a bitter twist of anger and disappointment. Then her thoughts were interrupted by the familiar hum and throb of engines as they entered the cabin.

She stopped in her tracks. "Are you casting off?"

"*Oui*. We're going to the island."

She gaped. Annoyance quickly morphed into fury. "Are you out of your mind? No!" She strode outside but it was too late. Furious, she whirled, pinning him with dagger eyes. "I didn't agree to this! And there's a cyclone on its way, in case you haven't noticed." She threw an arm wide, indicating the dock rapidly disappearing. "The town's in lockdown. *And* my car is at the marina."

He crossed his arms and leaned back onto the rail, then absently pushed back a curl as the wind whipped his hair around his face. "First, my house on the island is designed to withstand weather extremes, cyclones included. It's probably safer than most places on the mainland. Second, I'll call someone to pick up your car. And third, the reports say the island will only catch the edge of it—the eye will hit Cairns after 3:00 a.m."

"And by that time, we won't be able to return for God knows how long. No. Go back, Marco."

"No."

She growled. "I hate it when you get pushy."

His mouth quirked briefly but he said nothing. She continued to glare, putting all her anger into it, but he merely held her gaze calmly.

"You've been avoiding my calls," he finally said.

With a frustrated growl she whirled, planting her hands wide apart on the railing. "Dammit, you can be sooooo annoying!"

"Says the woman who *still* hasn't told me she's pregnant."

A moment passed, a moment in which Kat's heart sped up, then slowed down again as she closed her eyes and dropped her gaze to the churning black water below. A moment in which those meager rehearsed words all crumbled to ashes in her mouth, and she was left with nothing but the sound of slapping water and rushing air.

"I'm going to kill Connor."

Marco raised one dark eyebrow. "Don't blame him. He thought I should know."

Finally she straightened, crossed her arms and faced him. "Turn the boat around. It's not safe to be out."

"I checked with the coast guard. We're fine for at least another hour, enough time to get to the island." He shook his head. "And we have things to discuss."

"There's nothing to discuss."

A dark scowl bloomed. "You're kidding, right? You're *pregnant,* Kat. It's not just about you. It's about me, too."

She knew that. But the bubbling frustration inside forced the words from her mouth. "My body, my decision."

He stilled, his expression a mix of shock and seriousness. "Are you saying you want an abortion?"

She blinked, shaking her head as her stomach pitched in time with the waves. "Marco, you know what I went through with my mother. She was dead within two years of diagnosis. I could be a carrier."

He dragged a hand through his hair. "So get tested. I've been telling you that for years."

"I did. Plus, I do not have one single mothering bone in my body. Babies hate me and—"

"Whoa, whoa, whoa. Back up." He frowned and held up a hand. "You actually went and got *tested?*"

"Yes. Last week."

"After all these years of 'I don't want to know' and 'I don't want that hanging over my head, directing my choices in life'? All the times we argued when I tried to convince you otherwise?"

She nodded.

She'd shocked him, if his gaping expression was any indicator. "When were you going to tell me?" he finally bit out.

"I just did!" she snapped back, inwardly wincing at his thinly concealed hurt. "And speaking of not telling, what about you and Grace?"

"What about me and Grace?"

"So there *is* a you and Grace!"

He scowled, confused. "What the hell are you talking about?"

"You and her, having a baby together?"

From the look on his face, she'd stunned him. "Since when?"

"She told me you were back together."

He sighed, hands going to his hips. "Well, it's news to me. We've been over since before the *Coup de France*."

"How long before?"

"Way before our night together, *chérie,*" he said softly.

She swallowed, refusing to allow herself a moment of remembrance. "So, you're saying Grace is lying?"

He shrugged. "Wishful thinking?"

She snapped her mouth shut, taking a deep, steady breath before mumbling, "This is a bloody disaster."

Was it her imagination, or did she see his mouth tighten? Then he sighed and dragged a hand through his hair and the moment was gone. "Kat, I can't stop you from making the final decision about what you do. If it were me, I'd be having the baby, regardless of those test results. But it's ultimately your choice."

"Then it's a good thing you're not me," she said quietly. "You weren't there. You didn't see what the disease did to my mother, every single day, for two years. I refuse to let that happen to my child."

His soft murmur sounded more like a groan. "Kat…"

The boat went over another wave, and suddenly the day's lunch didn't seem so secure in her stomach. She swallowed thickly then took a deep breath before meeting his eyes.

"I'll be here as much as you need me to be," he said, his gaze soft. "You're my best friend, *chérie,* and that's what friends do."

Friends. Her insides did another crazy swoop, just before the nausea surged again. This was no confession of love, no happily-ever-after, no I-can't-live-without-you. This was Marco offering his friendship and support, just as he'd always done throughout the tragedies of her embarrassingly public private life.

She swallowed a weird swell of abject disappointment. "Marco." She shook her head. "I don't know…. I haven't made any decision. Plus…" She took a breath. "I can't—I won't—have a baby just because you want it. And once this gets out—whatever my decision—there's going to be a media frenzy. Your career is more important than front-page gossip."

"Kat—"

"You know what the headlines were like last time. Do you honestly think I'd do that to you? I… Oh, God." She clutched her stomach.

He grabbed her arm, his face creased with alarm. "What's wrong? What—"

She turned to the railing but wasn't quick enough. In the next second, she threw up all over the deck, right on top of Marco's expensive Italian leather shoes.

Two

"Guess I should've seen that coming," Marco said drily as she rushed to the railing and continued to throw up over the side.

When he placed a gentle hand on her back, she shrugged it off with a groan. "Oh, God, don't."

His gaze darted from her to briefly stare up into the dark storm clouds. It was about to rain and rain hard, and if his captain, Larry, hurried, the crew could make it safely back to the mainland before it all came down. What he needed to discuss with Kat was between them alone; he certainly didn't need anyone else encroaching on their privacy.

He returned to Kat's doubled-up figure and shifted uncomfortably on the deck. He should've thought about seasickness. She wasn't a great sailor at the best of times, and with the added pregnancy, he wasn't surprised she'd thrown up.

"Can I get you anything?" he said now, frowning as her thick breath rattled in her throat. It tore little pieces from him, listening to her force down the nausea, willing herself not to throw up. She hated being sick, and he'd held her hair back on more than one occasion, watching helplessly as she went through the motions while he'd soothingly rubbed her back and made the appropriate sympathetic noises.

She stayed like that, bent over the railing, unfazed by the wind and ocean spray on her face until they finally docked at Sunset Island's small jetty twenty minutes later. As the boat edged slowly into position, Kat pulled herself upright, swiping at her mouth and swallowing thickly with a grimace.

"Bathroom," she muttered, and he silently watched her head into the cabin.

Five minutes later, as he was going over his choices in a long lineup of conversation starters, she emerged, her face pale and grim, a swipe of lip gloss on her mouth.

When she walked out onto the deck, that weird, tumultuous, out-of-control feeling had receded, only to be replaced with trepidation. This crazy situation was totally out of his hands, and that thought freaked the hell out of him. Yet she…she looked so cool and blank as she strode toward him that he felt the sudden urge to kiss her, to dislodge that perfect composure and make her as frustrated and confused as he felt.

Stupid idea. Because Kat had made it clear she wanted to forget what they'd done all those weeks ago. And if he looked at this logically, that was the sensible thing to do. They were best friends. Throughout all their sucky personal relationships, her mother's death, his one marriage and divorce, her two, plus the crazy media attention they always seemed to attract, their friendship endured. Sure, the papers always hinted at something more, but they'd both laughed and shrugged it off a long time ago.

Yet now, as his insides pitched with uncharacteristic uncertainty, she looked almost…calm. As if she'd already made a decision and was confident in making it.

She was so damn strong. Sometimes too strong. Just one of the things that both attracted and annoyed him.

"I don't know what more we have to discuss," she said now, watching his crew prepare to dock. "This is a waste of time. Plus, with the approaching cyclone, we need to let people know where we are."

"I called the authorities before we left, plus your father, my mother and Connor," he said calmly.

"Wow. You really planned ahead for this, didn't you?"

He ignored her sarcasm. "All bases are covered. We're perfectly safe."

Her face creased with such serious doubt that he had to smother a laugh.

Safe? No way, not when her expression became suddenly tight and he knew exactly where her thoughts were going. If they were anything like his, it was back to That Night, replaying every intimate second over and over, despite his determination to shove it to the back of his mind. She didn't want to be stuck anywhere with him, least of all in such an intimate personal space.

Her breath snapped in, eyes darkening just before she glanced away, and his groin tightened. It was incredibly arousing, knowing she was obviously remembering their crazy-hot lovemaking. Lovemaking that had, instead of quenching the hunger, only succeeded in stoking his desire for more.

His low groan was lost in the noisy preparations for docking, yet when he gently took her arm, she shot him a dark scowl and dug her heels in.

His eyebrows ratcheted up. "You're going to stay on the boat in protest?"

"I should."

"Well, that's a dumb idea. A storm's coming, in case you hadn't noticed."

"You're the one who dragged me out here."

He sighed. "Look, *chérie,* come to the house. If you want to yell at me, at least we'll be safe."

She paused, seeming to go through her limited options, until her chin went up and she shot him a glare. "Fine. But as soon as the storm's passed, you're taking me home."

He almost smiled. Almost. "Okay."

She gave him a final look then swept past him, down the gangplank and onto the rickety jetty, her heels echoing dully as he commanded his crew to take the spare vessel and return to the mainland.

They took a golf buggy to the house, efficiently moving along the road that edged the west side of Sunset Island. Just like all the times before, when the place came into sight, Kat held her breath and marveled at the architecture of the magnificent six-bedroom house. It was all glass and timber walls set in a lush tropical rain forest, with natural lines, arches and a sloping roof set on sturdy stilts, perfectly sheltered among the vegetation to avoid the fiercest storms yet taking spectacular advantage of the amazing Pacific Ocean sunsets.

This was Marco's haven, a place he could relax and be himself with his friends. The guy she knew so very well. The guy who was now intimate with her body, who had made her moan and climax.

As Kat ran her eyes over the house's familiar lines and tried not to think about *that,* the buggy wound its way along the driveway, until finally they stopped at the front door and Marco got out. Again, he offered his hand and she was forced to take it, although she quickly released him as soon as she stepped out.

"We need to secure the shutters before the storm hits," he said, eyeing the sky.

Kat nodded and followed him to the long path edged with a sturdy safety railing that ran all the way around the house. As the wind slowly picked up and the trees began to sway, they both worked in silence, cranking down the storm shutters covering the multitude of windows. With the last one firmly in place, they returned to the front.

"The birds and the bats flew off a few hours ago," Marco commented, frowning into the dark sky. "They know something's wrong."

A chill ran over her skin. "The Bureau of Meteorology said the main eye is bound for Cairns."

"Yeah, they're bracing for the worst—mobile phone towers down, power outages. The ports will be closed, too. So, not the best place to be right now. Let's get inside."

"I've got nothing to wear," she said suddenly as she stepped in the door.

"You've still got some stuff from last time. And you can borrow from me if you need to."

Walking around in Marco's clothes, smelling his scent, knowing the exact same garments had been right up next to his skin? Just. No.

Kat said nothing as she walked into the familiar coolness of the slate foyer, down the hall to the back of the house, past the amazing indoor pool with wet bar to her right, the elegant water feature bubbling away to her left.

Finally she reached the heart of the house—the huge combined kitchen and entertainment area with comfy sofas, a wide-screen plasma TV, dining table to the side, curved walls with floor-to-ceiling windows and a fully equipped kitchen. She and his guests always spent their time here, eating and talking current affairs, the state of the world, his second home in Marseille and the ever-present topic, European football.

She went straight to the fridge, grabbed a ginger beer and then walked to the barricaded windows that normally displayed an uninterrupted one-eighty view of the Pacific Ocean.

During the day the simple beauty of searing blue sky stretched forever until it eventually dipped to kiss the dark ocean in the far distance. At night, the absolute blackness enveloped everything, the only respite the tiny mainland lights on the horizon. Except this time she was more than acutely aware of the brewing storm playing out behind the shutters, matching her churning thoughts as she heard Marco's firm footfalls on the polished marble behind her. The vague scent of his aftershave brought back the uncomfortable memories from that one night, ten weeks ago.

"So we should be clear of the storm here," she began, her back still to him, the cold ginger-beer bottle cradled against her warm neckline.

"Yes." He reached for the patio door handle and swung it wide, walking out onto the lit deck. "But we've still got a warning and need to take all precautions."

"Your cellar," she said as he began to collect the deck chairs.

He nodded then grinned. "And you guys teased me for converting it."

She pulled a chair inside the back door. "Well, to be fair, the worst you'd ever seen was a tropical rainstorm, not a cyclone."

"Always a first time for everything."

Those words took on a whole new meaning tonight. She watched him carry the patio chairs inside, waiting for him to break the silence as she picked at the label on her ginger-beer bottle.

He finally closed and locked the door, and after a few minutes of him shoving the chairs into a corner and saying nothing, she was about ready to break.

"Marco—"

"Kat—"

They both turned and spoke at the same time, but it was Kat who paused for him to continue. When he sighed and ran a hand through his hair, she wanted to groan out loud. She knew exactly what that hair felt like in her fingers, how soft it was, how it curled and waved with a life of its own, and how with one gentle tug at the nape she could direct his mouth to a better place on her neck....

Oh, God, I have to stop thinking about that!

When she glanced up, he was looking at her with

those dark eyes, assessing her every word, movement and expression until she felt vaguely underdressed. Ridiculous, because the last thing on his mind right now was getting her naked and into bed.

What a vision that conjured up. *No. No! Stop it!*

Then he abruptly turned and the moment shattered.

"You need food," he said, striding over to the kitchen and opening the fridge door. "And we need to prepare for tonight."

Her stomach took that moment to remind her of her long-gone lunch, and with a sigh she followed him over, her mind on the immediate problem of her empty belly. "What do you have?"

He waved his hand inside the fridge. "You choose. I'm going to tape up the windows."

Kat prepared bread rolls, cheese, cold meats and potato salad while Marco placed thick tape across all the windows. After they ate, they sat on the sofa and had coffee, the muted TV spurting out nonstop cyclone updates.

It was a familiar scenario—the coffee, the silent television, their seating positions: she at one corner, sprawled across two spots and hugging a pillow, he in the opposite corner with ankles and arms crossed. Yet the unspoken tension in the air was smoke-thick and just as hard to ignore.

This time it was Kat who broke the silence. "You know, Grace was arranging a surprise dinner for your return."

His eyebrow went up. "Was she?"

"Yeah."

"Right." The slight grimace in his expression spoke volumes.

"What's that look for?"

"What look?"

"Don't give me that. You know the one."

He sighed. "I don't know why she keeps bothering. We broke up months ago."

"I see," Kat said slowly, pressing her lips together. Marco would never lie to her—so *was* it all wishful thinking on Grace's part? She frowned. Yeah, Grace liked to talk up all her relationships—that TV exec three months ago, the Russian writer, the ex-soapie star.

Then Marco abruptly turned on the couch, giving her his full attention, and she forgot all about Grace's love life.

"Kat, this is me here. We talk about pretty much everything—"

"Not *everything*."

He gave her a look. "Just stop avoiding the issue and talk to me now. Let's think this baby situation over logically."

She shook her head. "Were you not listening about the tests?"

"I didn't ask that. I asked if you wanted to have this baby."

"I am *not* turning this discussion into a pro-choice debate."

He scowled. "I'm not trying to. All I'm asking is for you to consider all your options."

Her insides ached. "That's *all* I've been doing since I found out. Marco, please don't do this. I can't get attached, knowing there's a possibility it will be carrying a fatal disease. Plus, I know women are supposed to have these ticking body clocks, supposed to be filled with a great burning need to be mothers, but I am telling you, I'm not one of them."

And yet…there'd been a few moments where she'd allowed her imagination to drift, where her thoughts had been occupied by something other than work, her swish Cairns apartment and all those solitary nights stretching before her. She'd imagined an unfamiliar future consisting of a house, a garden, a husband and babies. A scary, scary thought that had her breath catching and her heart racing every time she let her mind wander there.

No.

She sighed. "I…I don't know what to say. I really don't."

"Well, that's a start. At least it means you're not wedded to the idea of an abortion."

"I'm not making any decision until the tests come back. I'm not going to…" She swallowed and glanced away. "Not going to get attached to the idea if they come back positive. And anyway, what on earth am I going to do with a baby? This is *me* we're talking about here."

His scowl deepened. "Don't be ridiculous. You're a great person. You're funny and gorgeous and smart, and you have people in your life who love you."

She flushed under the unexpected praise. "But a *mother?*"

"Other women begin with a whole lot less."

"But it's a full-time job. A lifelong commitment." She worried the edge of the pillow, picking at the stitching. "You can't get a do-over with these things. What if I stuff it up?"

"Nobody's perfect at parenting—just look at Connor's family. I guarantee you'd do a lot better than them."

Kat nodded. It was impossible to avoid the Blairs, especially when her father and Connor's were business partners at Jackson & Blair. Unlike her relationship with Marco's parents, she'd never warmed to Stephen Blair, a ruthlessly ambitious man with a penchant for blondes, and his wife, Corinne, a cold gym-junkie socialite with a Botox habit. Connor's childhood was a perfect study in fractured family dynamics. A therapist's dream… more so than her own.

"My dad isn't much better," she said now. "He'd rather hold a grudge about old headlines than dole out any praise."

"At least they were happy, well, until…" He trailed off diplomatically.

Until her mother's diagnosis. Kat silently filled in the sentence. They had been strict but fair, even when she'd stretched the limits with the usual teenage smoking, drinking and sneaking out to parties. Certainly not overly demonstrative in their affections. But after her mother's diagnosis, her father had turned into an angry, bitter man, always judgmental, always unhappy. And Kat could never do anything right, from her decision to drop out of Brisbane University to her crazy, wild nights on the town that were her one respite from thinking about her mother's disease.

Until one particular night when she'd stumbled home at sunrise in a highly drunken state and her father had been waiting for her, scorn pouring from every tense muscle.

"You've had everything we could give you, and look

at you! Your mother is dying, so you throw in a perfectly good education to get drunk every weekend!"

"Maybe that's the point!" she'd stormed back. *"It's in my head every single waking moment. I need some time to clear it out, to just forget, otherwise I'll go crazy!"*

His fists had clenched, and for one awful moment she'd wondered whether he'd give in to the temptation and actually hit her. Instead he'd cut her with words, his particular specialty.

A month later her mother had died and Kat had run away to France, where Marco was the current darling of French football. Where she'd slowly come to realize there was more to her tiny little world than short skirts, wild parties and free drinks.

Kat swallowed, pushing the memory aside. God, no wonder the press had loved to hate her. She'd been such a spoiled little rich girl.

"But you've grown since then," Marco said now. "And he's still stuck in the past, rehashing old arguments. We don't have to be our parents. Not with our child."

Our child. Those two words were like a blow to the chest, leaving a shallow breath rattling in her throat.

"Look, Marco, let's be honest. You've worked incredibly hard to get where you are. You've got a great career and an amazing, wonderful life. No commitment, no ties—"

"Kat…"

"No, let me finish. You can jump on a plane at a moment's notice and be on the other side of the world. You have your pick of women—and there are a *lot* of women."

"Kat—"

She ignored the warning growl in his voice and kept going. "I'm not going to force you to change, and a baby does that, in ways you can't even imagine. The media frenzy will affect both our lives and careers."

"If you choose to keep the baby, then I'll do the right thing."

She blinked. "The right thing? What, are we living in the 1950s now? You don't have to marry me because I'm pregnant."

He paused, a second too long. "Who said anything about marriage? I'm talking about being here for you. As your friend."

She frowned, the unexpected sliver of disappointment stabbing hard. Oh, so now she wasn't good enough to marry, was that it? But just as she was about to open her mouth and say exactly that, she snapped it shut. That was manipulation of the worst kind, and she refused to do it. She couldn't put Marco in that position—she wouldn't. And marriage was the last thing she wanted.

"Good thing, too. I suck at relationships," she said lightly, her hand tight on the coffee cup. "I've tried too many times, but I just don't have that particular gene. They're messy, they're painful and they always end in disaster. I don't want to ruin our friendship."

"You don't suck. You didn't force James to cheat. You didn't hand the press those photos." Marco's brows took a dive, his expression dark. "And as for Ben…"

"Please do *not* remind me." If there was a Disastrous Relationship Museum, hers would take front and center as prime exhibit number one: her first marriage to Jackson & Blair's publicity manager, Ben Freeman, when she was twenty-two. He'd turned out to be a selfish, misogynistic bastard. Her second marriage five years later, a quickie Bali wedding to Marco's teammate, annulled after just seventy-two hours when she'd caught James screwing a waitress in their bridal suite. And then her engagement to Aussie Rules' wild child Ezio Cantoni barely a year ago. *He'd* taken nude shower shots of her then "accidentally" leaked them to the tabloids.

She was done with the scrutiny, the uncertainty, the angst. It was painful and humiliating and downright tiring. For her sanity and self-respect, it was just not worth the effort. And now she was bringing a child into that?

Kat sighed, shifting on the sofa. "And honestly, Marco, how are you going to be involved? Weren't you planning to move back to France after the Football Federation of Australia's awards in three weeks?"

"That was one option."

Her brow ratcheted up. "That's not how you talked about it a few months ago."

He sighed and cast an eye to the shuttered window. "I've got a lot of things going on—the coaching clinics, the sponsorship stuff. Plus my network contract is up for renegotiation next month. I haven't decided about France yet."

She paused for long, drawn-out seconds. "Oh, no. Don't you *dare* start to rethink anything. I won't allow it."

"You won't allow it?"

"No." She ignored his irritation with a wave of her hand. "We're not married. Hell, we're not even a couple. Just…best friends who may be having a baby."

He said nothing, just looked toward the shuttered windows and then the wall clock that read quarter past one. "It sounds to be getting worse outside." He stood. "We should go downstairs."

She paused, glancing toward the windows, then nodded. "Okay."

He offered his hand and she automatically took it, the sudden urgency of the moment pushing their discussion into the background. The innocent warmth of his fingers wrapped around hers created a frustratingly intimate sensation that she was loath to give up. He took her down the hall, to a door that led to the basement and his wine cellar, which he'd modified with this kind of situation in mind.

The wine was stacked neatly to the left of the small room, and to the right sat a couch, a fixed, fully stocked bar fridge and a small generator that powered the soft lamps that were now lit in preparation.

She hesitated at the door, scanning the room as reality flooded in.

"Don't worry, *chérie*," Marco said beside her, giving her fingers a reassuring squeeze. "We're perfectly safe."

Again, that word. The door was heavy but he closed it with ease, and when he turned to her, she swallowed the panic and offered a shaky smile.

They settled quickly in the room, Kat automatically going over to prepare coffee, Marco checking the small ventilation window high on the far wall and then the lights. After a few more minutes, they sat on the couch, Marco pulled out a pack of UNO cards and they settled in for the night.

"So how's working for Grace going? Still a pain in the butt?" Marco asked casually as he shuffled the pack.

"Oh, she's not that bad."

"Hmm." His expression was skeptical as he dealt them seven cards apiece.

She sighed. "Actually, I miss my old London job."

"What, the one you took up between Ben and James?"

"Ugh." She made a face. "My life's most significant moments reduced to a 'between exes' reference."

"Sorry." Marco's expression looked anything but. "Let me rephrase. The Oxfam job you took at the age of twenty-five when you spent a couple of years living and working in London in blissful anonymity."

She gave him a look, not entirely convinced he wasn't being sarcastic, before finally nodding. "It was only a year, but I felt better about that job than anything I've ever done. I felt like I should—" She cut herself off abruptly, her thumbnail going to her mouth, teeth worrying it.

"Like you should what?" He picked up his cards and fanned them expertly.

"Like I should do something more. Donate to charity or start up a foundation or something."

She waited for him to voice doubt, to echo her father's familiar refrain about giving up a perfectly good job for an uncertain dream when she'd casually mentioned the subject a few months ago. Instead he just looked at her and said, "You've never mentioned that before."

She shrugged and overturned the first card on the top of the deck. "I stopped thinking about it after I told my dad."

"Let me guess—he said you don't know a thing about running a charity, it's too expensive, why chuck in a perfectly stable job for a dubious flight of fancy in this economy when you'll lose interest in the first year?"

"All of the above."

He sighed and placed a yellow two on the pile. The

sudden silence sat heavy in the air now, until Marco finally spoke. "Have you done the figures? Worked out how much it would take to do something like that?"

"No."

"So work it out. Make a business plan. Talk to your old workmates. Call your accountant. Screw your father. I mean that in the nicest possible way," he added with a thin smile and placed the first card down on the table. "You're smart and clever and you have experience. You can work a crowd, raise funds and know how to handle the press. Whatever happens with those tests and the baby, you can still do this."

She stared at her hand, rearranging the cards by color as her mind worked furiously. Oh, she wanted to. In between the many fluff pieces and gossip segments *Morning Grace* aired, the human-interest stories drew her the most. The burning compulsion to do something herself, to help ease someone's burden, to bring a little joy into the lives of people who really needed it, got her every time. She always ended up donating to every cause she sourced. Every time.

"This'll be bigger than a ten-minute segment," Marco said now. "You'll be able to give things more media coverage, follow it through, devote more time. Really make a difference."

She put a Draw Two on the pile and murmured something noncommittal, signaling the end of the discussion.

Marco said no more and for the next half hour they played cards and pretended everything was fine, even though the faint sounds of the creaking house and the wind as it picked up forced their attention from the game a dozen times. Finally Marco turned on the small radio and the room was filled with a steady stream of weather updates.

When the lights suddenly went out, Kat jumped. Yet when the generator kicked in seconds later and the lights clicked back on, it did nothing to assuage her growing panic.

"What are we even doing here?" she muttered, flicking her thumb along the edge of her cards, eyeing the lights, then the generator. "We went out in a cyclone warning, for God's sake! This is stupid, not to mention dangerous."

"We're not in its direct path. Would I honestly do something to put us in danger? Trust me. We're safe."

When she shivered, he handed her the blanket from the couch, draping it around her shoulders, tucking it close. She half expected a tender forehead kiss to finish. Damn, she was actually wishing for it. He'd kissed her before, an I-love-you-you're-my-best-friend kiss on the cheek or the forehead. And they'd hugged more frequently than she could count. But tellingly, he'd never kissed her on the lips. Until That Night.

For the next twenty minutes they kept playing cards as the rain and howling wind picked up, the updates morphing into location reports and interviews of people in organized shelters and those who chose to stay in their homes and see the storm through.

Half an hour later, it hit.

Card game now forgotten, they sat in tense silence, hip to knee on the couch, glued to the radio. The wind screamed past the house, ripping through the trees and banging the shutters in their frames. From inside their refuge, they could hear the rush of air, the snap and crack of trees bending and breaking under the raw elements, debris being thrown around. The house remained firm but the wind and slashing rain was a constant, picking up in waves then petering out until the minutes stretched like hours.

The radio spat out crucial information as the cyclone careened across the coast, and as time crawled into an hour, then two, and the cyclone finally passed through Cairns and headed south before dying down a few miles out to sea, details began to trickle in. Details of devastating damage, heart-wrenchingly revealed via the mainland survivors.

"We're gonna have to start over. We've lost everything."

"We have family, friends, community. We'll survive this."

"I don't know whether we can rebuild. We weren't insured."

"Well, you just pick up and move on, don't you? You just get it done."

"Please, help us. Our house...everything. It's gone. We need help."

Kat's breath caught, the sob forming low in her throat as she listened to that last one, a woman and her family who'd been right in the storm's path. It ripped at her like claws, and she unashamedly let silent tears well as the extent of the damage was slowly and thoroughly detailed over the course of an hour.

When Marco's hand went to her knee, patting reassuringly, she jumped, eyes flying to his.

The look on his face undid her, a mix of sorrow and understanding that reflected everything she'd tried to keep inside. She watched him swallow, her gaze following his thumb as he leaned in to gently wipe away her tears.

"Don't cry," he said softly, knuckles and thumb resting firmly on her cheekbone. "It's okay."

Her breath jagged. "But all those people…"

"They'll rebuild. You know that. No fatalities have been reported, so that's one good thing. It'll be okay. We're safe."

She sniffed, unable to look away from his concerned gaze. "I was scared."

"I know." He cupped her face and leaned in, placing his warm mouth first on one cheek, then the other. Years ago, the familiar French-style greeting had amused her. But now, with his lips so very close to hers, and then as she watched him slowly pull back with a soft smile creasing those dreamy eyes, her heart leaped.

Keep calm, Kat. If you stop acting normal around him, he'll know something is wrong. But could she honestly do all those little things, the smiling, the hugs, the casual touching, and not be affected by what they'd done?

Her gaze darted to that mouth, that lovely, lush mouth that seemed like an evil conspiracy on a man already so beautiful.

Yes, *beautiful* was the only word to describe Marco Corelli. Outwardly he appeared cocky and confident, working the crowd, the camera, the press with smooth ease that trod a fine line between charming and practiced. He always got what he wanted, be it an interview, a prime restaurant table or a woman. But she also knew him better than anyone else and knew that public persona was only a small part of what made him tick. He was generous. Fiercely loyal. Fiery and passionate about the things and people he loved.

She could feel his eyes on her, taking in her expression, every single movement, and it was then that she realized she'd been staring at his mouth and daydreaming like some mooning soccer groupie.

With a suddenly dry throat, she darted her gaze to his.

And her breath stuttered all over again.

Three

Kat didn't know what happened because it was instantaneous, although in reality it probably took a little longer than that. All she knew was one second she was sitting there, heart pounding, his hand still cupping her face, the imprint of his warm mouth on her skin. Then his gaze slipped to her lips, she parted them, he made some choked sound and suddenly he swooped down and they were kissing.

Her arms went around his neck as if they belonged there. She groaned, opened up for him and was gone.

He dragged her to his chest, cradling her, almost as if inviting her to sink into him. So she did.

During the long, hot, unbelievable kiss, she felt his hands everywhere, tugging her clothing, sweeping over her skin, caressing and touching until she was all heated up and her heart throbbed hard against her ribs. Then he pushed her back, bunching her skirt around her waist, and she was grabbing his shirt, yanking it from his pants and fumbling with the waistband.

"Let me." He pushed her hands aside, quickly dragging down his pants, his urgency fueling her arousal as her mouth locked on his. Her blood raced as he jammed a knee between her legs, pushing them roughly apart then settling his hips against her before suddenly and swiftly entering her.

A harsh breath hissed from her lips, matching his as she stared into those dark eyes that bled black with passion, and she nearly lost it then and there. Then he uttered a low growl, hitched her leg around his waist, pinned her hands above her head and started to move.

She couldn't think, couldn't breathe, from the raw, animal sensation of being filled, fully and completely. He wasn't tender or slow. He didn't offer romantic words of love. He simply took, and when she got over the shock of the moment, she took, too, welcoming him, grinding her hips hard into his, her breath rushing out in a harsh groan, her teeth nipping the sensitive spot where his neck met shoulder. He cursed softly when she did that, upping the pace so she slammed into the sofa, the cushions grazing her skin. She gasped but kept moving, knowing full well she'd have wool burns come morning but totally beyond caring. Instead the moment took her, wiped away any reality until it was just them, their harsh breath coupling in the eerie silence and the air full of the familiar scent of sex and need.

Breathless and throbbing, she impatiently rocked her hips against his, eager for the final release. And when her climax came, it rushed in with little warning, and she was left floundering as the waves crashed, leaving her shaking and panting. Dimly she was aware that Marco still had her hands pinned, his deep murmur of release against her lips as he followed her, his body jerking into hers. She shook, his satisfaction heightening hers, and she tightened her leg around his waist, cradling his body, taking all of him with a groan that ripped from deep inside.

It was…he was… She groaned again and closed her eyes, willing reality to stay away for just a moment more so she could just enjoy this, them, here and now.

But of course, it wasn't possible. Reality always intruded.

The air cooled her naked flesh. His breath on her neck slowed. The shudders racking her body subsided. And soon, the angry wind against the house broke into their private moment. When he gently released her hands, blood rushed into her fingers once more. And slowly, so very slowly, she felt him slip from her body and then stand.

They'd done it again. After everything she'd told herself, every warning she'd mentally listed.

She opened her mouth to say something, closed it and then opened it again before giving up. Instead she sat up, yanked her skirt down and began to button up in the embarrassing silence, pointedly ignoring Marco as he did the same.

But when they were done and literally had nothing else to distract them, Kat sighed and finally looked up.

Marco had moved to the far end of the couch and was packing up their card game.

"Marco…" she began, her throat dry.

"Hmm?"

"I... We..." She paused, hands going to her lap as he continued to tidy. "Can you stop that and look at me?"

When he paused and finally met her gaze, she had to bite back a soft groan. He looked so serious, the raw curves of his face drawn into such a solemn expression that she was sorely tempted to trace her finger down his cheek to coax a smile from his full lips.

Lovely lips that she'd had the thorough pleasure of just moments before.

"What on earth are we doing?" she said now, acutely aware of the warm flush heating her skin. "How did we get to this?"

With a sigh, he flopped into the chair and crossed an ankle over one knee. "Well, the first time, alcohol was involved."

"And this time there's..." She waved a hand, indicating the storm outside that had eased into a dull rumble. "But that's not what I meant. I've never...thought of you in *that* way before."

"I see."

She couldn't meet his eyes without getting embarrassed, and that realization just flustered her further. Truth was, she'd thought about it more than once but every time refused to indulge for more than a few moments. Giving the fantasy more than that would've been weird, not to mention futile. He'd never seen her as more than a best friend, so what was the point? She'd been content with the tag for all those years.

Until now, apparently.

Dammit. She felt her entire body warm under his scrutiny, until the desperate need to move overwhelmed her. So she rose, went to the small bar fridge and fished out a bottle of water. With her back to him, she rolled the bottle over her neck then down, welcoming the icy shock on her hot skin.

She was exhausted, so tired of thinking. She had no idea where she stood. Her head was a mess, and she couldn't even blame this lapse on alcohol as she had last time.

The heat of the moment? Yeah, nah. She could have stopped if she'd really wanted to. She just didn't want to. She *wanted* to taste his mouth, have his body slide over hers. Wanted to feel his hot breath on her skin and have him fill her in the most primitive way possible.

He made her forget things, just for a while.

She twisted off the bottle cap and took a slow swig, her thoughts churning. She shouldn't be distracted, not now. She had other things to consider, important, life-changing events.

Swallowing the water, she stared at the small ventilation window that would herald a new morning, full of light and promise. A brand-new morning revealing the wild chaos of a passing cyclone. As the radio had revealed these past few hours, so many people had lost everything, and not only their homes. Personal effects, memories, things that meant so much to them, had been swept away by Mother Nature in the space of a few hours. It really was a miracle no one had died.

Relief surged, shaking her for one second before she swiftly got a handle on it. She was alive. So was Marco. They'd eventually return to the mainland, check over any damage to their homes, and she'd get the results of her test then make an informed decision based on those results.

Belatedly, she realized Grace would want her on the cyclone coverage, would need her expert digging to find that unique special-interest story that would spear-head the show's donation line. They'd done it for the Queensland floods, for the bushfires, even New Zealand's recent earthquake. Yet as she stood there with the cyclone's aftereffects thinning outside, punctuated by the constant radio chatter, all she could think about was…

Her test results.

Marco. A baby.

Their *baby*.

And her thoughts scrambled once more, rendering speech useless.

Marco kept his gaze firmly on her as she pointedly ignored his scrutiny. Her warm brown hair was sexily tousled, her neck flushed with faint stubble burn and the buttons on her shirt were crooked where she'd hastily tried to gather her composure.

"I guess," he finally said in answer to her previous question, "that we're giving in to some latent sexual tension, which is only heightened by the storm outside."

Startled, she flicked him a glance as she took another drink. "Sure."

He waited for more but she remained silent, all her attention firmly on her water bottle.

So of course, his eyes wandered, lingering on those long legs, the dip of her waist. The almost nonexistent curve of her stomach.

And suddenly an overwhelming bolt of emotion shot through him, a mixture of desire and fierce protection for both her and that unbelievable spark of life growing in her belly. No one except a handful of people knew the real Kat—the loving, fun woman who'd do anything for a friend, who'd wrestled with her parents' overprotective influence her entire life. Who'd been dragged through her own personal hell thanks to her mother's illness, front-page headlines and a bunch of loser men who frankly didn't deserve her.

She was intelligent, passionate…and stubborn. Way too stubborn. Once she made her mind up about something, there was no way she'd change it back.

Like that damn stupid decision not to get tested. It twisted like a splinter in his gut every time he allowed himself to think about it, every time he tried to convince her to just go and find out. And now she'd finally done it.

Even though she was avoiding his eyes, he knew she knew he was staring. The tension in her shoulders, the way her mouth tightened, all gave her away. And stubbornly he kept on staring.

After half a minute's standoff, he gave up and turned up the radio. Eventually she came over and sat in the chair opposite and they listened in silence, the weather updates and on-location reporters slowly charging the air with a sense of growing concern.

Finally she said, "Is it…? Do you…feel weird?"

He glanced up, but her eyes remained firmly on the radio. "What? The cyclone?"

"No, us."

He felt many things, but weird wasn't one of them. "No, actually. You?"

"Yes. No." Her gaze darted to a spot past his shoulder before returning to the radio. "I…don't know."

"Okay."

She sighed, her elbows on the table, her thumbnail going automatically to her mouth before she stopped halfway and dropped her hand. "This is…" She finally shook her head. "It's… We shouldn't have done this."

"A bit late now, *chérie*." He swallowed the small blow she dealt with no outward sign. "Although I totally expected that response."

Her eyes snapped to his. "Did you?"

"Mmm. You have a tendency to run when things get too…intimate."

"I do not!"

He lifted one eyebrow at her outrage. "You do."

Her eyes narrowed as she leaned back in the chair and slowly crossed her arms. "Ben was a selfish bastard who dumped me when he realized I was serious about not wanting kids."

"I wasn't talking about *him*." His hands involuntarily clenched at the memory. "And I still think you should've let me deck him."

"And have you charged with assault? No way."

He shook his head. "Anyway, I'm talking metaphorically as well as physically."

"James was screwing a woman in our hotel room. Ezio took naked photos of me and sold them to a gossip mag." She shoved a stray strand of hair back off her shoulder. "These are all deal breakers for me."

"And what about us, Kat? Is best-friend sex one of your deal breakers?"

"Sex *always* ruins things."

He frowned at her too-quick answer. Again, she was dancing around the question. But when she glanced away, hiding her expression from view in an uncharacteristically shy move, man, the sudden desire to kiss her pulled low and tight in his gut. Instead he swallowed the urge and remained where he was.

"So what are we going to do now?" he asked, deliberately casual.

She shrugged. "The media—"

"Screw the media," he growled, putting both palms flat on the table. "What do *you* want to do?"

"Marco…" His name came out as a groan, her fingers going to her temple, where she rubbed firmly. "I'm tired. I know it's your thing to talk things over ad nauseum, but can we just not right now? Please?"

He took in how she was reclining in the chair, her half-lidded eyes, the creases bracketing her mouth, and a sliver of guilt shot through his gut. "You should really get some sleep."

For once, she didn't argue. "So should you."

He shrugged. "I'm still on European time. Not that tired. Here." He stood and rearranged the pillows. "Sleep."

After a second's hesitation, she went to the couch and sat, then stretched out. He quickly dragged the blanket up over her.

"Thanks," she muttered, her eyes heavy as he covered her feet.

He moved to the single armchair and had just settled into it as her eyes closed. Moments later, her breath slowed and she was asleep.

With a small smile he got comfy, crossed his arms and ankles and let his mind drift.

He swept his gaze over her, from the dark lashes resting on the soft curve of her cheek and the soft hair streaming down her neck, to her long, lean body, which took up the entire couch. They'd been friends forever, ever since that embarrassing moment in Year Nine had changed everything. Fourteen was such a cocky, self-indulgent age, and he'd been the worst, so full of attitude and mouth. He'd made a stupid comment, showing off to his friends, and Kat had surprisingly struck back, shoving him so hard he'd fallen on his ass. He'd jokingly admitted that had been the start of his adoration, and their combined detention plus her innocent smile, offbeat humor and fierce loyalty had only cemented their relationship.

From then on they'd been a tight quartet—him, Luke, Connor and Kat—until he'd been offered the unbelievable opportunity to play European football and left Australia for France when he was sixteen. Then their individual lives had taken over—him with his soccer career, her with her mother's illness and her various tabloid exploits. He'd been shocked to see her three years later, barely a month after her mother's death, but he'd never questioned it, instead taking up right where they'd left their friendship. They'd traveled, she'd crashed at his house in Marseille for a few months and from there she'd bounced between Europe and Sydney for close to six years. It was like she'd been trying to find her place in the world, and until her stint in London, he wasn't sure she'd find it. But then, three years ago, she'd landed the *Morning Grace* job, and since then, she'd actually been happy. Sure, they'd both had relationship woes and she'd been his shoulder through the excruciating years his father had been dragged through the press, then an inquiry, before finally being cleared of money-laundering charges last year. She'd been his go-to girl when he'd been in between girlfriends and needed a date for some function or event. She was his wingman. His best friend. And now his lover.

She was having a baby. His baby. Theirs.

He swallowed thickly, a dozen emotions churning as he imagined her—his Kat—growing big with their child. Glowing, smiling. Happy.

But she isn't, is she?

His brows took a dive. *Don't think about that.*

For once, she wasn't talking. Odd, because they'd never had any problems talking about any topic, from exes to family to everything in between.

Well, almost everything. The ban on relationship talk was still in force, even though he'd wanted to overstep that boundary dozens of times. But for her, he'd bitten his lip and stayed frustratingly silent.

His speculative gaze ran over her sleeping form again. She might project a haughty, almost cool confidence to the world now, but to her closest friends she was just Kat Jackson, filled with doubt, frustration and a dozen dreams she worried she'd miss out on. She had a wicked sense of humor. She read literary fiction as well as popular crime novels. She was a *Star Wars* fanatic but adored the *Star Trek* reboots, had an insane collection of anime art and eighties retro music. She hated pickles on her burger, loved penguins and handbags, was funny, gorgeous, impatient, argumentative and incredibly intelligent.

And yet the press had first tagged her as ditzy and shallow, a party girl of the craziest kind with a penchant for bad boys. It didn't help that she'd gone overboard when she'd turned seventeen, bouncing from one publicity event to the next, dressed in designer heels and revealing clothing, getting snapped drunk by every single reporter eager to plaster Keith Jackson's spoiled baby girl all over the gossip pages. Not surprising that she'd taken up a position as society reporter, a job that had lasted until her mother's death.

He'd been living in France, where he'd quickly become Marseille's *Ligue 1* star forward on a million-dollar contract, treated like a rock star wherever he went. Ridiculous really, for a kid barely out of his teens to be suddenly thrust into celebrity life, rubbing shoulders with the rich and famous, dating supermodels and actresses, all while his best friend had been wrestling with life-changing events.

A low growl forced itself through clenched teeth before he bit it back. She'd turned up on his doorstep a week after Marseille had won the *Coupe de France* and broken down in his arms. Then they'd spent three months during his off-season backpacking through Europe, clearing their heads and getting their friendship back on track.

Those months had been a wake-up call for him, too. He'd stopped drinking, started making responsible choices, investing his money instead of blowing it all on thousand-dollar bottles of champagne, designer jewelry he'd never wear and vintage cars he'd never drive. And it had also been a turning point in their friendship. Now they were both thirty-three and had never gone longer than two days without a call or a text, except when he was traveling on business. And they told each other everything, no matter how private or painful. Well, except for that no-go relationship zone.

He still couldn't believe she'd actually gone and gotten tested. God, he still remembered that huge argument, a week after her mother's death, when they'd nearly ruined their friendship for good.

"How can you not want to know?" he'd demanded.

"Because I don't! I don't want a death sentence affecting how I live my life!"

She wasn't alone in thinking that, either. He'd done the research. He knew more people chose to remain in the dark about being a fatal-disease carrier. Yet it still didn't stop his heart from contracting every time he thought of her, his Kat, suffering the same fate as her mother. Dead within two years of diagnosis.

Marco released a long, slow breath, his eyes darting to the ventilation window at the far end of the cellar. The wind had downgraded to a strong breeze, the low hum of radio chatter white noise against it all. He grabbed a bottle of water and unscrewed the top, downing the contents in a few swallows, and then shoved a hand into his hair, dragging slow fingers through it.

This "let's not talk about it" attitude wasn't Kat. She always told him the truth, no matter how painful, and he did the same for her. And the only thing that had changed was the sex. Which meant it was already messing things up. She was awkward and self-conscious, holding things back, keeping her thoughts to herself. He didn't like this new Kat, not one bit.

With a scowl he shifted in the chair and tried to get comfy. Pretty soon, the wind outside lulled him and he managed to fall asleep.

Four

Marco was the first to wake. After glancing at the still-sleeping Kat, he quickly checked his phone—no signal—placed it back on the table and then cast an eye at the softly glowing lights, before to Kat, now yawning on the couch. She was rubbing her cheek where the cushion had imprinted, looking so adorably sleepy that for one crazy second, impossible thoughts of permanently waking up next to her rushed through his brain and his breath caught.

"What time is it?" she asked, voice hoarse with sleep.

"Seven a.m.," he replied, glancing away. Desperate for something to do, he grabbed his phone again, determined not to focus on the way her long legs swung from the couch to the floor, her normally straight hair all mussed up and her half-lidded eyes still languorous. And of course, his mind latched on to the one thing he'd been trying to avoid. *That* moment. That hot, amazing moment on the couch when she'd crumbled beneath him.

"Phones are still out," he said, then turned the radio up.

Pretty soon they were up-to-date with the full aftermath of Cyclone Rory.

"The ports are closed, then," Kat concluded, combing her fingers through her hair.

"And there's no planes going in or out, apart from emergency ones." Marco rose, stretched and cracked his back, working his knee firmly back and forth.

"You okay?"

"Mmm."

She studied him for a moment. "Does it still ache?"

"Only when I sit for too long."

"Must be weird having pins in your knee."

He smiled thinly. "You get used to it. Could have been worse."

She nodded, knowing exactly what he meant. The on-field injury had ended one stellar career but he was lucky—it could've left him unable to walk. The bitterness still burned sometimes but it was something he refused to dwell on, not when all the other amazing opportunities had opened up for him a few months later.

"There'll be debris in the water, so they'll have to clear that up first," he continued.

"So we're stuck here until further notice."

"Until they give water traffic the all clear in a few days." At her unexpected smile, he tilted his head. "What?"

"I could name at least a dozen women who'd give their left leg to be holed up on a private island with you."

He sighed. "Why do you do that, Kat?"

"Do what?" She looked confused.

"Always bring up the women."

"I…"

She looked so genuinely flustered that his irritation quickly dissolved, leaving only an odd frustration. He sighed. "Look, forget it. We should go and see if there's any damage to the boat."

"I was only teasing."

"I know." When he held out his hand, her brief hesitation before she firmly grasped it and stood was telling.

It only increased that vague sense of wrongness.

He walked down the hall, a half-formed scowl on his face until he swung open the front door and their attention was immediately commanded by the outside world.

The warm air was rife with the smell of rain and dirt. The blue sky was cloudless, the sun already streaming through the trees to heat everything up. The palm trees still stood, but many were leafless; downed branches and debris were strewn over every inch of wet ground. As they stood there, taking in the damage, the familiar screech of rainbow lorikeets as they returned to their nests echoed.

Marco waited until they were in the buggy, making their way carefully down to the dock, before he said softly, "You know it'll be different with your own child, right?"

Her gaze snapped to him but he kept his focus ahead, avoiding the fallen branches and clumped mountains of dirt the rain had swept across the road.

"Will it?"

"Sure it will. *Je vous le—*"

"So help me, Marco, if you say that stupid catch-phrase I will seriously do you damage."

He snapped his mouth shut but couldn't completely keep the amusement from his voice. "Still don't like it, huh?"

"*Je vous le garantis.* I can guarantee it? It's lame. No one can guarantee something."

"The press seems to think so. Everyone awaits my game predictions with bated breath."

"Full of yourself much?" She snorted. "And you *have* called it wrong before."

"Only you would remember that. Three times in two years," he reminded her, grinning as he saw her mouth quirk. "Uh—I saw that smile."

"Was not a smile."

"Sure it was." He glanced at her. "I hate seeing you so serious and angry, *chérie.*"

She crossed her arms and stared right ahead, her mouth twitching. "Keep your eye on the road. There's debris all over the place."

They finally reached the windswept dock, the trees familiarly bare, the water full of flotsam. But thankfully, his boat was still moored securely, bobbing in the water, jammed up against the jetty.

He cast an eye over the lines from bow to stern, then made his way on board to inspect further. Ten minutes later, satisfied there was no damage, they returned to the house.

It was only after they returned to the house, opened all the shutters and then went back outside to inspect the filthy pool that Kat's stomach began to rumble so violently the ache made her wince.

"I need food," she said as they walked in the patio door.

"Sure." Marco moved to the kitchen. "What do you feel like?"

"I can do it."

He huffed a sigh. "Seriously? What, you've had lessons since I was last home?"

"Don't be facetious," she sniffed.

"You haven't. Which means *I'll* cook. You—" he glanced over toward the bench "—do your usual and make the coffee."

"Fine." She opened the cupboard and grabbed the gourmet coffee beans, then the grinder. It felt so surreal, going through the motions of this familiar task when all around them everything had lost grip on reality. A cyclone had raged over the coast, devastating lives. A once-strong friendship had cracked from one impulsive night. And a baby would change their lives forever.

Stop. She stared at the grinder as it tossed the beans. She couldn't make that decision yet, not when the test results were still to come.

With that tiny mantra echoing in her head, they made breakfast then ate at the table, watching the TV reports outlining the damage, filling them in on every single detail, flashing up familiar scenes of devastation, until Kat's head buzzed with overload. She glanced at Marco and then away, focusing on her plate until the silence began to cloy and she was desperate to break it.

When it got unbearable, she finally said, "So, I hear you're up for a Hall of Fame award at the FFA dinner next month."

He nodded. "Yep."

"You taking anyone?" she asked casually.

When his gaze met hers, she winced. That totally

sounded as if she was fishing, when it was definitely not the case.

"You, if you want."

"Sure." Her response was automatic. The Football Federation of Australia's annual awards dinner, a three-course dinner in a five-star Sydney hotel, was always a good night. Ironically, in a nation where sport ruled supreme, soccer barely rated a mention on the national networks, and that included the biggest soccer awards event of the year. Which suited her low-key life down to the ground.

June. Three weeks away. *Three weeks plus ten weeks means...* She scowled. *No. Don't think about that.* "So you're staying in Australia until then?"

He nodded. "I have the coaching clinics to set up, plus a new shoot for Skins. And a guest appearance on *The Big Game* when the new season starts in October."

She smiled. "Still in demand. I knew that knee injury wouldn't slow you down."

His mouth curved. "Always right, aren't you?"

"Always."

As they finished their food, Kat asked, "So what else is news?" Marco took such a long time to answer that she glanced up from her empty plate with a frown.

"Ruby's on the cover of next month's *Playboy*," he finally said.

Oh. She waited for him to share, and eventually, with a clatter of fork on plate and a deep sigh, he did. "She's my ex-wife. I shouldn't care what she does."

Kat nodded. "True."

"We've been apart for four years, divorced for two."

"Yes."

He sighed, linking his fingers together on the table.

"Call me old-fashioned, but I draw the line at having my ex-wife's hoo-ha on display for every guy who's got ten bucks to spare. Those things are private."

She looked him straight in the eye. "I agree."

He picked up the fork and continued to toy with the remains of his food in silence for a few more moments. "She didn't even ask me. I don't care about the whole media thing. I just would've liked to be forewarned."

She nodded again, knowing that the situation cut deeper than he let on. It wasn't about the damage to his reputation, although the media attention had already started to swell following the sneak peek of Ruby's cover two days ago. It was more personal than that. It went to the core of who Marco was—a deeply honorable man who respected women, who valued manners and was known in the French *futball* league as a true gentleman, despite his multitude of girlfriends and on-field arrogance.

"You know, we should get married."

She stilled, the fork halfway to her mouth. "I'm sorry. Did you just say…we should get *married?*"

He nodded, his expression deadly serious as he leaned in. "Totally."

She gaped for one second. "Why?"

He stared at her, as if waiting for her to say something more. But when she just continued to gape at him in shocked silence, he shrugged and said, "Why not?"

Because you should be madly in love with me when you propose. Kat swallowed the words as her brow dipped. "Because we don't have to?"

"So you're *not* worried about your pregnancy hitting the papers?" He tipped his head.

"Of course I am. I'm worried about everything hitting the papers. But I can't live my life in a bubble because of it." She eyed him. "Anyway, what does that have to do with marriage?"

"Because we can lessen the damage. If we—"

She held up a hand. "I'm sorry, what?"

He sighed. "Look, just hear me out. For over twenty years you've not shown one symptom, so let's assume the results are negative until otherwise proven, okay? Like it or not, marriage is still a respectable option. You'll be pregnant with my child. Once the cyclone news dies down, the press will be on the lookout for the next big story, and they're going to love this. The attention they give it will be off the charts. They'll hound you, your family, and when they find out I'm the father, they'll come after me." He held up a hand, cutting her off. "The papers are going to rehash every romantic involvement, including our marriages and divorces. And you can bet they'll find a way to bring my father into it. Someone at my network is going to listen to all that crap, and there'll probably be repercussions because I do have a code-of-conduct clause in my contract. Grace will probably demand an exclusive. The attention will drag on and on. Even better, they'll bring the romantic 'holed up during a cyclone' angle into it."

"Marco—"

"Now think about the alternative. We get married in a private ceremony then put out a press statement. The deed is done. Everything's announced how we want it, when we want it. The media have their story for a week, two, max. We'd have to tell Grace, of course, but there'll be no backlash for me at the network, no comparisons to the past. And everyone returns to their normal lives."

She stared at him for a moment and then slowly placed her fork on the plate. "It's not that simple."

"Well, obviously not." He followed with a frown. "It won't stop the attention, but it will lessen the time we'll spend on the front page. Then they'll go back to real news."

She shook her head slowly. "You would seriously marry me?"

He shrugged. "Why not?"

She said nothing, just stared at him for the longest time. She'd be Marco's wife. Mrs. Corelli. For one second her heart swooped, an alarming response that sent her into a panic before she swallowed and it all crashed back down to reality. He wanted to marry her, but for all the wrong reasons. Duty. Respectability. To avoid publicity. Not because of love.

Wait, what?

This was Marco here. He didn't think of her in that way. Oh, she knew he loved her, but he wasn't *in* love with her, which was a huge difference.

Anyway, she didn't want him in love with her. Not at all.

"You know it makes sense," he said, chewing on the last piece of toast.

There were those annoying words again. *Sensible. Smart. Logical.* Everything she'd wished for after Ezio's betrayal. Everything Marco was offering.

She drew in a slow breath. "I don't want to get married."

"What, ever again?" His brow went up. "Or just to me?"

"I've done it twice already."

"I know, *chérie*. I was there to pick up the pieces, remember?"

Her heart squeezed. Yeah, he was. He was always there. Through the divorces, the horrific tabloid attention. Through the aftermath of her mother's illness. He was her rock, more dependable than any of her girlfriends or family. He'd dropped everything to listen to her rant, then cry, then get solidly drunk and make a complete fool of herself at some swanky French nightclub. Then he'd dragged her backpacking around Europe in blissful anonymity.

And now he was offering again, stepping up and taking on the responsibility for their one lapse in judgment.

"I can't marry you, Marco," she said now. "That would be selfish."

"Why? I suggested it. And it's not as if we have anyone else lined up."

"Oh, that makes me feel so special."

He laughed, much to her chagrin. "You are. You're my closest friend."

"What about Grace?"

He sighed. "What about her? We're over, I told you. It's all in her head."

She crossed her arms and leaned back in the chair, trying to get a grip on her jumbled thoughts. "Marco, this isn't the solution. I don't want to force you into something you'll come to resent. No, let me finish," she added when he opened his mouth. "You love your freedom. You love being able to pick up and go away on assignment. I totally get that. But I need someone constant, to really *be here*. Fly-by parenting doesn't work. I know that firsthand. A child can't just be an appointment in your schedule, someone you see whenever you have a spare few weeks."

He stared at her for the longest time, until he ran a hand through his hair in frustration, his eyes narrowing. "That's ridiculous."

"Which part?"

"Oh, just about all of it." He braced his hands wide apart on the table and pinned her with his dark gaze. "Don't tell me what I feel, Kat. Sure, I love my job, but it's just a job."

"Are you kidding me? Soccer is your life. It's a part of who you are. You would die if you couldn't do it."

"You say that like I'd be giving it up. Which I'm not."

She sighed. "And we're back to where we started. Being Marco Corelli takes you all over the world. You'll be away from your child for months on end." *Away from me.* She prudently swallowed those words.

"So what's stopping you from coming with me?"

She blinked. "I have a job, in case you've forgotten." Boy, he just didn't let up, did he? Her head whirled with all the scenarios, emotions running riot until she had to take a mental step back. It was all just speculation, pipe dreams. She couldn't make a decision based on that, not when she might not even have a future.

The black moment engulfed her, stealing her breath so suddenly she shoved to her feet.

It was too, too much.

"I can't think. I need some air." Without waiting for his response, she turned and walked down the hall to her room.

Thoughts still churning, she pulled open a drawer and rummaged through the clothes she'd left from her last visit. She took a denim skirt and white linen shirt from the chest of drawers, slathered on sunscreen and then swiftly changed. When she emerged fifteen minutes later, Marco was nowhere to be seen.

After digging out sunglasses from her handbag and picking up yesterday's newspaper, she stalked over to the patio doors and slid them open, thankful Marco was not around.

That was good, wasn't it? It meant a respite from the questions she had no answers to. A break from thinking for once. And a reprieve from those annoying emotional responses that kept hijacking her thoughts whenever he smiled, shoved back his hair or touched her...or...

Simply breathed, it seemed.

With a deep sigh, she stepped outside. The tiles that ringed the eternity lap pool warmed her feet and the morning air teased over her bare arms, making her hairs stand on end.

Blinding sun speared across the deep blue ocean, the sky unmarred by clouds. She shoved on her sunglasses and assessed the now-familiar storm debris scattered over the deck and tiles, the leaves and filth floating in the pool, and then padded over to the small storage room, removed a broom and pool skimmer and set to work.

It was good to have something to do, and she set to her cleaning task with singular concentration. The sun shone brightly down, making her sweat through her shirt as she first swept the deck and surrounding tiles, then took up the skimmer and went to the pool. By the end of the repetitive skim-and-tip, her shoulders pleasantly ached and her brow was damp. Finally, she walked over to a lounge chair and settled back with the paper.

Five minutes, that was all it took, and her mind

began to drift back to what she'd effectively avoided the past hour.

With a sigh she closed the newspaper, folded it and stuck it under her leg.

"Test results aside, do you want a baby?" she asked herself aloud now, as if by voicing the question, she was giving it the proper gravitas.

"I don't know. Maybe." Pause. "Kat," she added, her voice dipping lower as if she was conducting a self-interview, "are you thinking about what others think again, and not what *you* think?"

Yeah, she was. Her father would be livid when he found out she was pregnant. The press would have a field day with this seemingly unsurprising return to form. Grace would... Well, she wasn't exactly sure what her boss would do.

On the flip side, Connor and Luke would offer support and be happy if she was, and honestly, their opinion meant more to her than all the others put together.

"Just forget about the test results for a second and think. Would having a child make you happy?"

With a sigh she recalled that odd thought from a few weeks back, the one where she'd allowed her mind free rein and had imagined a home and husband and a family.

Oh, Lord. Her breath hitched as her chest tightened, sending her emotions haywire. Maybe it was the aftermath from the storm. Maybe it was because she'd suppressed so many urges for so long. Or maybe it was because deep down inside, she didn't want to be that woman whom everyone pitied, who projected a fierce "I don't care" attitude, but inside died every time someone made a joke about her staunch opposition to having kids.

She'd thrown herself into researching motor neuron when her mother was first diagnosed with the debilitating disease that attacked the muscles but left the mind clear. The statistics, the chances of survival, the death rate... It broke her heart piece by tiny piece with every detail she'd uncovered. So after a few weeks of agony, she'd bundled up the research papers, untagged all the bookmarks and cleared her computer history, then solemnly made the choice not to get tested.

She'd come to terms with that decision, even made her peace with it. Outwardly, she'd projected that capable-career-woman persona, had brushed off any discussions about family and babies. Of course, her mother's illness wasn't a huge secret, but she'd refused to let that be a reason for people's pity. To the outside world, she'd made a conscious decision to remain childless. If everyone wanted to pour scorn on her because of that, that was their choice. Her skin was tough—she could handle it.

But now...

A baby. A family.

"Emotional stuff is scary," she said to herself now and then paused.

She sat back on the lounge, blinking out over the ocean view. There. She'd said it. It was *scary*. Opening herself up meant she'd be vulnerable. She'd done it so many times with relationships, and it was getting harder and harder to get over it when they inevitably ended. Most often badly, too.

She'd opened up once before, when she'd revealed to Ben why she didn't want kids, and he'd asked her for a divorce via text the next day.

Hang on. This is Marco we're talking about. Marco would never hurt her. He got her as no other guy did. He understood her offbeat pop-culture references, and he sang along to the music she played in her car. He let her choose the movie more often than not, and he discussed, argued and laughed with her.

He was her perfect partner.

She sat up abruptly, alarm tightening her muscles. No. Definitely not. She would *not* go there, not with him. He was her friend, not a future ex. She was supposed to be thinking about this baby, not romanticizing a one-way attraction.

"Right," she huffed, shoving her hair off her sweaty neck. "The baby. Think about the baby."

She paused. Okay, since when had she started thinking about it as an actual baby?

With a soft groan she tipped her head back. "You're going to keep it, then?"

She let that question hang in the midmorning air, the wind picking up around her, rustling the trees. The parrots squawked, the only sound punctuating the silence, and she placed a hand over her stomach and closed her eyes, cautiously giving her imagination free rein.

A baby. A miniature of her and Marco—a gorgeous child with wild curls, a beautiful mouth and high cheekbones. Marco's dreamy brown eyes…or maybe hers— sharp blue to contrast with masses of black hair. A fierce, adventurous child with charm and attitude. A combination of both, but also entirely unique, not a black-and-white copy but one that had been enhanced with color and shape and form.

She felt the catch in her throat and was helpless to stop it, until it came out as a gasping sob.

She wanted this baby. She *actually* wanted it.

Wow.

After all those years of not caring, not wanting. She wanted. It was like an epiphany, a shiny new revelation that actually made perfect sense the more she thought about it.

Marco was right: things would be different with her child. Yes, the prospect of becoming a mother was scary, different and way out of her comfort zone.

She'd never allowed herself the luxury of thinking about a family. She was Katerina Jackson. She'd handled paparazzi, the crème de la crème of society, weird celebrities and total-jerk boyfriends. She'd come through two divorces a stronger person. She was fortunate enough to have money, friends and support. And when the blood tests from the geneticist came back negative, the only obstacle remaining would be gone.

"A mother," she said softly, skimming a hand over her still-flat belly. "Me. That's…incredible."

She had to tell Marco.

Five

Kat swiveled her feet to the tiles and stood, then padded across the courtyard and back into the house.

"Marco?"

Loud in the silence, her voice echoed off the walls. She tilted her head and paused, her brow furrowing in concentration as she listened.

Was that…music? Violin, to be exact.

Her frown deepened. Marco liked a collection of hard rock, Europop and Top 40, but he'd never professed a great love of classical. She slowly followed the thread down the corridor to the closed doors that led to the indoor pool and paused, her hand resting lightly on the sliding door's handle.

He was obviously in a private moment. The verticals were drawn, door closed, music cranked up.

And yet this had to be done.

Before she could talk herself out of it, she clicked the handle and walked in.

Just like all the times before, this room stole her breath away. The low whitewashed arches, the concrete floor with Grecian tiles leading to a kidney-shaped heated pool, the fully stocked wet bar in the middle. And to the right, an intimate entertaining alcove that always made her think dirty thoughts.

Dirty thoughts that suddenly morphed into reality when she spotted Marco lying shirtless, listening to music.

Oh, God. She sucked in a silent breath, frozen in her tracks. He was facing her, his eyes shut tight, expression creased in concentrated passion and his hand moving through the air as he focused on the piece—a beautiful, haunting piece that made her heart swell and thump, a soft groan sticking in her throat as it echoed off the walls.

She ran her gaze hungrily over his figure, from those jet-black curls, noble nose and defined jaw, to shoulders of corded muscle, broad chest, ridged abdomen and lean waist. By the time she'd reached his firm thighs, encased in pants, she'd become more than a little hot. Who would've guessed that watching him as he listened to the music—his expression moving in rhythm, his hand conducting as the notes went through the dips and troughs—would be so arousing?

But damn, it was. It was as if her insides had suddenly been set on slow burn, and coupled with the hot music as an erotic sound track, everything began to slowly melt, making her steadily damp the longer she stood there and stared.

And stare she did. It was as though the music possessed him, commanded him. Touched him. And she couldn't look away from his expression as it moved and morphed, his hand swaying in time.

She'd never been turned on so much in her life.

Then the song abruptly finished, his eyes springing open on the very last note, and she was caught standing there gawping like some weird, obsessive stalker.

He noticed her almost immediately, so she couldn't even preserve their dignity by retreating. His dark eyes fixed on her, his expression blank as he stared for long moments, a light sheen of sweat glistening under the soft overhead lights. Slowly, he wiped his brow, shoving his hair off his forehead, and Kat's mouth went dry.

Marco was her best friend. He infuriated her. He made her laugh, made her yell. He was her rock, her shoulder to cry on. And she was his plus one whenever he needed her, his sometimes clothing consultant, drinking buddy, confidante. Of course she loved him, just as she loved Connor and Luke.

But now, as he sat there and stared right back at her, residual emotion slowly bleeding from his expression, all she could think about was how much she wanted him.

He was glorious. A perfect example of passion and beauty, all wrapped up in dark Botticelli curls and a classic European profile that had women swooning even before he opened his mouth and that dreamy French accent came out.

She twisted her fingers in the ties of her shirt and said faintly, "Since when have you been interested in classical music?"

He slowly stood. "Since last year."

"And you didn't tell me?"

He shrugged.

Odd. "What was that piece called?" She forged on with a small frown.

"*Idylle sur la Paix* by Jean-Baptiste Lully." He absently plucked at the hem of his trouser leg.

"Never heard of him."

"Seventeenth-century French dancer and musician. He invented baroque music."

"Oh." She smiled. "No one important, then."

His mouth quirked. "He was King Louis XIV's court composer—a musical genius who also knew how to get what he wanted. Best friends with playwright Molière. A fascinating character, but unfortunately there's not a lot about him, unlike Mozart or Beethoven."

"That's a shame."

"I've got a couple of books and a French movie, but not much else." He slowly reached for the stereo remote and clicked it off. "You should see the movie—you'd like it." He smiled. "Especially the costumes. Historically inaccurate but still flamboyant."

"You'd have to translate for me."

"I could do that." He dragged a hand across his chin then put both hands on his hips, and Kat couldn't help but linger on all that casually exposed skin—the taut shoulders, the defined ridges of his abdomen, that tempting Adonis belt disappearing beneath his waistband.

Her heart began to canter and her mouth was dry when she finally met his gaze. His expression was unreadable, but his eyes darkened in an oh-so-familiar way as he leisurely took in her warm face and neck, then farther down to her torso partially exposed by her shirt. He finally finished his perusal at her legs before returning to her face, and her fingers involuntarily clenched hard into fists.

"Kat..."

Her name tripped so deliciously off his tongue in that beautiful accent, and she was gone. He must have realized it, too, because all he had to do was hold out a hand and crook his finger in a "come here" gesture and she leaped to do his bidding.

She walked, slowly and purposefully, around the edge of the pool, her bare feet on the cool tiles a welcome relief compared with the warmth curling in her belly.

When she finally stood before him, her lungs emptied on a shaky breath. *Lush:* that was the perfect word to describe Marco Corelli. Lush and romantic, especially with those dark curls and perfect lips.

He'd be a hit, of that she was sure.

She held her breath as he slowly reached out and curled a lock of her hair around his finger, tugging gently on it for a moment before pushing it behind her ear.

Then he leaned in, inch by agonizing inch, until his mouth was a whisper away from hers and she could feel his warm breath feather across her skin.

"Kat," he murmured, his dark hooded eyes dropping to her mouth, then back up to her eyes.

She swayed, every single cell in her body tingling from anticipation, breath rattling low in her throat. "Yes?"

"Kiss me."

With a soft groan she jerked forward, demolishing the divide between them and bringing her lips to his.

His mouth was warm and tasted faintly of peppermint. As she pressed her lips urgently against his, she heard a moan low in his throat a second before his hands were on her shoulders, dragging her to his chest.

Yes. She felt the excited flush sweep her from head to toe and, with another groan, put her arms around his neck and deepened the kiss.

Breath mingling. Hearts racing. Skin heating. It all happened in an instant, as if her body had been waiting for this exact moment to spark to life. When his tongue expertly parted her mouth, diving inside to tangle with hers, she gasped, legs wobbling, and immediately his arms tightened, taking all of her weight as her insides melted. They stood like that for ages, tasting each other, the room echoing with soft moans and heavy breathing. And finally, after she'd been thoroughly and skillfully aroused just short of the point of frustration, he began backing her up to the daybed.

She went willingly, clinging to him while his mouth continued to make her breathless. He took her bottom lip between his and gently sucked, his hands sliding down her lower back to firmly cup her bottom then press her urgently into him.

She gasped, feeling the hardness of his arousal against her clothes. The sudden urgent desire to be naked, to have him cover her, have him inside her, flamed.

"Marco," she groaned as her legs hit the edge of the bed.

"Hmm?" His lips were trailing over her jaw, then down her neck, and when they hit her most sensitive spot where her neck met her shoulder, she sucked in a gasp.

"Take your pants off."

She felt his mouth curve on her neck just before his hands went to his waistband, quickly unsnapping his pants and dragging them down, and she barely had time for the reality to sink in—*Marco is getting naked!*—before he went for her clothes.

Soon she was shirtless, and he was pressed up against her, his mouth returning to hers for a deep, breathless kiss before he slowly made his way down her neck.

She swallowed thickly, the heat from his lips trailing small shudders across her skin. Dimly she was aware of her bra being removed, and then he was pushing her gently down onto the bed, his hand cupping one breast. Her back curved, arching into his touch, and with a soft murmur he obliged, his thumb sweeping over one peaking nipple before he took it in his mouth and sucked.

She shuddered, which was unbelievable considering the amount of control she normally had over every single waking moment of the day. But with Marco it was different. He had suddenly become chaos in her ordered world, and she was experiencing all sorts of things for the first time. As his mouth and tongue worked magic on her skin, coaxing her nipple into an achingly hard peak, she shoved any doubts she had into the back of her mind and just let the moment take her.

Her hands went to his boxers, hooking her thumbs in the waistband then slowly taking them off. And when she reached for him, his soft exclamation in her ear only fueled her desire.

Then he leaned back and her eyes flew open to stare into his dark depths.

"Kat…" he groaned, expression twisting. "Do you want to…? Should I…?"

Her breath came out slowly, heavily, as she cupped

his face with one hand, emotion and desire and need roiling in her stomach in one heated mass.

"Yes." She placed a soft kiss on his mouth. "I need you." Her teeth gently captured his bottom lip. "Deep." She sucked on his lip, her breath ragged, matching his. "Slow." Darting her tongue out, she licked the curve of his mouth. "Please."

His eyes closed on a thick gasp, and she watched his throat work, swallowing slowly. Then his knee was nudging her thighs apart. When his hand went between her legs, her body jerked.

His long, skillful fingers teased and tempted, his thumb coaxing the swelling nub of her arousal over and over as she trembled with every stroke, rocking her hips into his hand, grinding firmly as she whimpered beneath his mouth. With a low chuckle he continued, sliding first one finger inside, then another, working her with a steady, sensual glide that swiftly reduced her to a quivering mass of need.

"Marco!" She was beyond caring how desperate she sounded, how much she needed him, how damp he made her. Because right now, all that existed was his mouth, his hand...and suddenly, his throbbing manhood as he swiftly positioned himself and pushed inside with one hard thrust.

Oh...! Everything shorted out, until all that was left was thick heat and a hard pounding heartbeat echoing inside every single nerve. And when he slowly shifted his hips and inched deeper, she gasped, eyes flying open to meet his.

His face, that beautiful face, was so close to hers she could smell the arousal rolling off him. Her entire body pulsed from it, hot and breathless. How could she withstand these sensations, this glorious heat, the tightness, the pure friction of taking him deep inside her? Then he moved again and she knew she'd do more than withstand it. She'd revel in it, enjoy the pure moment of claiming him in the most primitive way possible.

She groaned, rocking back to meet his thrusts, the friction of him steadily flaming her arousal. Her thickened heartbeat throbbed wildly in her head, and she pushed back into him, hard, squeezing her eyes shut, groaning. "Marco…"

"Hmm?"

Instead of answering, she grabbed his hand, sliding it to where they were intimately joined. "There. Touch me there."

He did as she asked, moving his fingers over the hot, sensitive nub of her arousal. "Oh, yes…" She bit down on her lip, her hand still on his, losing herself in the sensation of his fingers, his mouth on her nipple and him hard inside her as he slowly and firmly moved.

They remained that way for excruciating minutes, rocking together, his finger flicking her intimately over and over, until she was sure she'd explode from it all. And then he surprised her by suddenly flipping her onto her stomach, looping a hand under her hips and pulling her up onto all fours. Before her brain could register the interruption, his hand swept over her butt. He nudged her legs apart and entered her from behind.

Her breath came out in a harsh gasp, and she had to brace her hands wide on the mattress to accommodate all of him. He paused, a palm gently sweeping over the curve of one butt cheek.

"Kat? Are you okay?"

Was she okay? Hell, no. She was about to die from

every single piece of her exploding in joy. Instead, she managed to get out, "Yes...yes."

"You sure?" His hand stroked her back, her hip, before slowly easing around her waist to cup one breast.

"I won't be if you don't keep going."

His chuckle—partly amused, partly dirty—nearly did her in. Instead she pushed back into him and felt no small satisfaction in hearing his harsh intake before he gripped her hips and began to rock.

She gasped as sensation took over; she felt his mouth as he leaned over and bit gently on her shoulder, his hands firmly cupping her breasts, and the hot, sweet sensation of him deep inside, filling her completely, creating such an arousing, intimate friction that a whimper welled deep in her throat.

Then it hit and she went down to her elbows, unable to hold back as the shuddering release swept her entire body, and she heaved in great gulping breaths, welcoming his weight as everything pulsed in pleasure.

"Marco..." For the third time, his name ripped from her mouth, like a mantra, and she felt the stinging sensation of his teeth grazing her neck, then her name echoed and the room filled with their harsh cries of release.

Dimly, she was aware that she'd collapsed on the bed, and Marco's body was flush on hers, damp and heavy in the aftermath of passion.

"That was... You are..." She groaned into the mattress, chest heaving.

His hand went to her face, gently turning her to him, his mouth seeking hers. "Kiss me."

She did, sweetly and softly, and a groan escaped his lips when he finally broke away, lifting his body off hers. "Sorry. I'm way too heavy to be lying on you, especially when…"

He petered off, letting her fill in the blank, which she did way too quickly.

It was a definite mood killer.

She sighed, watching him move around the shadowed room, picking up his boxers and pulling them on. With a flush she glanced away from his perfect form—long, corded thighs; strong, muscular back; and perfectly shaped behind.

"Marco, we need to talk."

He finally turned to her, hands on hips, and she couldn't help steal a brief glance at his chest before quickly forcing her gaze to his eyes.

She didn't know what she expected—amusement over her perusal, a sarcastic eye roll over the clichéd relationship line they both hated. Even residual lust wouldn't have been unusual. But there was none of that, only a carefully blank countenance that accompanied the vague sense of anticipation in the air.

"I think we should."

Right. So far, so good. She gathered the sheet around her, covering her breasts, before continuing. "Okay, so I don't want to make any major decisions without the test results, but I do know one thing. If the tests turn out to be negative, I want to keep the baby."

The silence fell like a blanket, and yet he still said nothing, just waited for her to elaborate. The simple fact that he knew there *was* more was as unnerving as it was disturbing.

"And here's the thing, Marco," she continued. "I don't want this child to have a part-time parent. You're either totally in this or not at all."

He frowned. "What makes you think I'm not in this?"

She sighed. "I don't want you making major decisions based on what *I* want. You want to go back to France, you go."

The frustrated growl was low in his throat. "You can't throw out something like that and then tell me *not* to think about what you want. That's not the way I operate."

"I know. But you have to. I'm giving you permission to walk away from all the craziness now."

"You're not making any kind of sense." He raked her with such a look that she felt her cheeks flush. "First you say I should be in this totally or not at all. Then you say I should do what I like." His hands went to his hips, his expression darkening. "Let me ask you this—knowing me so well, do you actually think I'd walk away?"

"That's not what I'm saying."

"Oh, that's exactly what you're saying." His expression remained tight, almost too tight. "That's pretty low, Kat. Thanks. Thanks a lot."

She blinked. Had she hurt him? His face said no, yet the brief flash in his eyes said the opposite. "I just…" She swallowed when she saw his scowling countenance. "I don't want you to feel trapped."

"How long have we known each other?"

She paused, calculated. "Nineteen years."

"Right. And in all that time, have you known me to do something I didn't want to do?"

She hesitated. "No."

"There you go." He yanked on his pants, slid up the zipper.

"But—"

"Dear Lord, Kat, can you stop? Just…stop." He finished dressing, then gave her a frustrated look. "If all you're going to do is lump me in with past boyfriends, then I'm going for a shower."

She opened her mouth for a second and then closed it. "Great. Fine. Go."

He narrowed his eyes. "So we're done here? You've said everything you need to?"

"Looks like it." She scooted to the edge of the bed with as much dignity as possible, anger welling up inside. But when he stalked out in long, ground-eating strides, she collapsed back on the mattress. Could it be more uncomfortable? From best friends to arguing lovers in the space of a day.

Must be some kind of record for her.

This wasn't what she wanted. Not at all. But how in the hell could she fix it?

Good Lord, Kat was so stubborn.

Marco was in the kitchen, gathering up food and utensils for lunch with more noise than necessary, his thoughts dark, before moving onto the patio, to the huge four-burner barbecue.

She was so determined to make her own decisions, to not even consider a different opinion unless she'd thought of it first.

Sure, his long absences from home were sometimes inconvenient, and there were times when he felt he was playing catch-up with people's lives. But after his knee injury had forced him into early retirement and the network had offered him this prime job, he'd jumped at the opportunity. And from that choice, a whole new bunch of opportunities had opened up—his Skins contract, the football clinics. He couldn't afford to regret any of it, not when things were as pretty close to perfect as he could get.

But right now, at this moment? A flame of frustration had flickered to life, refusing to be quenched.

Damn, he missed everyone, missed being able to drop everything and catch up with a meal and a beer. But with Luke and Connor in Brisbane and he and Kat up here in Cairns, plus their work commitments, it was a logistical nightmare trying to sync their schedules.

With an irritated flick he threw the steaks onto the hot plate, his bad mood momentarily rewarded by the satisfying hiss.

For example, if they were all together right now, they'd have this issue picked apart and solved within an hour. Instead of what had really happened—his making a lame marriage proposal, her getting all offended for some reason and now this weird standoff.

After a few minutes of grilling the hell out of the steaks, a movement through the glass caught his eye. He turned to see Kat standing in the middle of the living room, her attention commanded by the TV.

The sight hit him low and hard. She was barefoot and wide-eyed, looking sexily rumpled in nothing but short-shorts and an old gray T-shirt that skimmed her thighs. Magnificent thighs.

His head flashed back to what they'd done in the pool room. Then, further, to the larger issues they were both determined to avoid until hard evidence left them no choice.

He scowled. He'd never craved—yet dreaded—the outcome of a test so much in his life. The knowledge would change their lives forever, for the better or the absolute worst, and it wasn't until this moment that he understood why Kat had deliberately chosen the path of not knowing. It took a strong person to fight, but it also took someone equally strong to choose the other path, to live their lives with impunity when somewhere, in the back of their minds, they would always be wondering, thinking, considering.

Kat was way stronger than he even thought possible.

Humbled and angry, he turned his attention back to the grill and waited for her to approach him.

He hadn't long to wait—a few minutes was all it took.

"Can I do anything?" she asked, standing in the open door.

He glanced up briefly then back to the grill. "We need drinks."

"Sure."

He watched her pad to the kitchen, his eyes skimming over her long legs. He took in the way her back remained firm and straight, and he swallowed the lump in his throat.

Quickly he served up the steaks then went inside.

When she took the plate he offered, a whiff of scent hit him, tightening his gut. "What are you wearing?"

She glanced down and plucked at the T-shirt. "This? It's a sleeping shirt."

"No. Your perfume."

"Oh." She looked disconcerted for a second then said faintly, "Lemongrass and cloves. I keep it in my underwear…drawer…"

Her words trailed off at the exact same moment he grinned. He could practically read her thoughts—*Great,*

Kat, just talk about your knickers, why don't you?—and his mouth curved wider.

"Is that enough?" Marco said.

"Hmm?"

He nodded at her steak. "Do you have enough?"

She swallowed. "Yes, thanks."

He watched her take a seat at the table, her gaze darting up to his before she steadfastly focused on the food, and the brief moment of amusement was gone.

What the hell was wrong with…?

Riiiiight. He sat in his chair, his eyes going anywhere but to her. She was nervous. But why? He'd teased her a hundred times before, and about things a lot more personal.

Yeah, but that was Marco-the-best-friend, not Marco-the-lover. Like it or not, things had changed. It was almost as if…she was uncomfortable now.

He swallowed a curse. What the hell was he supposed to do with that?

"Kat," he said in a low voice.

"Hmm?" Her attention remained firmly on her plate.

"This is weird for me, too."

Her eyes darted to his. "What, specifically?"

"You and me."

She blinked. "Is—?" He watched her swallow. "There isn't a you and me."

Isn't there? The unspoken question just hung in the air, the seconds gathering, until he realized he was frowning, and she'd darted her gaze back to her plate.

"So we're just occasional bed partners, then."

The sarcasm was lost on her. "I don't think that's a good idea."

He stared at the top of her head in silence, and finally, reluctantly, she brought her eyes up to his and he stifled a groan. Soft skin. The indent of her waist, the curve of her butt cheek. Her damp body shaking as he took her, desire raging hard and fast. And her moans of pleasure as they both reached their climax.

His thoughts raced, nostrils flaring with remembrance, but he let the silence drag, until her eyes widened and she swept her gaze back to her plate. "You're my best friend, Marco. I don't want to ruin our friendship."

"It's not ruined. Just…" He searched for a word and finally settled on "Different."

"Different," she repeated with a small scowl.

He nodded. "Of course. We've slept together. We're having a baby. How can those things not make it different?"

"I don't *want* it different."

"You've made that perfectly clear," he snapped back and then took a breath. "But denial is stupid."

Her head jerked up. "Are you calling me stupid?"

"No! Jeez, Kat…!" His breath was sharp on the intake as he tried for calm. "I'm not calling you stupid," he said deliberately, rising from the table with his plate. "But wishing the past was different is a waste of time. You know that."

When she said nothing, just slid her gaze away and refused to meet his eyes, he swallowed a groan. It was her infuriating you're-right-but-I'm-not-going-to-admit-it look. God, that annoyed the hell out of him!

"It was fine the way it was," she said now, her gaze now on her plate.

The blow hit him like a stray free shot. She didn't want him.

No, that wasn't right—she didn't want *anyone*. She'd made that clear. He shouldn't take it personally. Yet how could he not, when they'd been together three times now and every time she'd indicated she'd rather be friends?

He knew exactly what she was doing. Things were getting emotional and she was pushing him away. She'd done it with everyone when her mother had started getting sick, and she was doing it now. Only this time, she had to deal with not only pregnancy hormones but the mental effort of waiting for those damn test results.

If this was what she really wanted, he'd let her have it…for now. He'd keep his thoughts and hands to himself, support her and stand by her as a best friend, and only that. But eventually, after they got off this island and went back to their reality, things would change. They had to. Because they'd stepped over that line and he was damned if he'd remain on the sidelines, where she was so determined to push him.

Six

The next morning Kat lay in her bed, staring at the ceiling as the sun slowly crept through the blinds.

They'd spent the evening in uncomfortable silence. Even the constant TV chatter did nothing to ease the awkwardness. She'd finally excused herself and went to bed, then lay for ages staring at the window and listening to the sounds of the night creatures rustling around outside.

Marco as her lover? Ridiculous.

Yet every time she'd lost her head, forgot who he was and just let the moment take her. It was crazy. Exciting.

Dammit, she couldn't stop those hot memories from filling her thoughts at the most inopportune moments. The way he kissed her, as if he couldn't get enough. The way he touched her, his fingers making her shiver in anticipation. And the way he took her, hard and possessive.

Yeah, and you've given him the "just friends" talk. Which he accepted without argument. She'd told him he was the father of her child, nothing more.

The question was, did she want him as more? Did she want to start something that could end in disaster? Or worse, drag him into an emotional mess when she had no clue what those damn tests would reveal?

You can't.

With a hitched breath, she rolled over in bed and hugged her pillow. This was Marco Corelli, a guy she knew better than anyone. Yet in this one thing, she had absolutely no clue.

And then there was the matter of Grace.

She groaned and gave the pillow a vicious thump. Everything was such a mess, and on top of that, she had to figure out something to tell Grace. Oh, she'd contemplated not saying a thing, but experience had taught her it was better to be honest. And anyway, she liked and respected her boss. She deserved to know.

Sorry, Grace. The guy you wanted a baby with? He's having it with me.

She winced.

Grace, I know you had plans for Marco—

Urgh. Terrible.

Grace. I need to tell you about something that happened....

She rolled her eyes. It sounded so much better in her head. Come to think of it, lots of things sounded better in her head. Truthfully, she had no idea why she was practicing—she worked much better off-the-cuff. And it was something she should really think about *after* the test results came through.

"I can't wait to get off this bloody island," she muttered.

When she walked into the living room half an hour later, the breakfast things were already laid out on the table. Marco was dressed in a white shirt and jeans and was flicking through the TV channels.

"What's the situation with the cyclone?" she asked as she sat and reached for the cereal.

"They're saying the phone towers may be up and running in a few hours," he said as he moved into the kitchen and pushed down the toaster.

"Good."

"Eager to escape, *chérie?*"

His smile lacked warmth, which only made her feel bad. "I'm eager to know the results of my tests," she said slowly as she poured the milk then grabbed her spoon.

He nodded, his attention riveted to the toaster.

"Marco…"

"Hmm?" He remained focused on his task and she bit her lip, her gaze sweeping over him before darting away.

"Nothing," she mumbled and shoved a spoonful of cereal in. "We should watch that DVD you were telling me about. After breakfast, maybe."

He glanced over at her, his expression unreadable, and then back to the toaster as it pinged. "Sure."

Just as they did yesterday, they ate in silence, their attention focused on the TV. *It's still happening,* she realized, her eyes determinedly fixed on the news updates. She hated this awkwardness, as if they were waiting for the other to address the elephant in the room.

It was excruciating.

When he got up with his plate, she couldn't help but lift her gaze to follow. He had a way of walking, a kind of fluid motion that had earned him many women admirers when he'd played for Marseille.

Actually, he still had a few.

She sighed and rose. Three times now they'd ended up in bed, and every time it still amazed her. But to voice her need, her wish to have him as a friend *and* a lover…that was too damn scary. She'd be a fool to start something, only to have it implode if the test results came back positive. Because then she'd have to deal with that on top of everything else, and she was damn sure she didn't want to put Marco through even a millionth of what she'd suffered, watching someone she loved slowly wither away.

She walked over to the sink to rinse her bowl and unthinkingly settled her soft fingers on the warm flesh of his waist to nudge him out of her way.

He jumped like a scalded cat, which in turn made her jump.

"Sorry," she said when he shot her a look. Her face was a hairbreadth away from his shoulder—within kissing distance, she realized dazedly. Yet his small shiver had her frowning as he slowly moved to her right.

"Your hair," he murmured, removing his plate from the sink. "Tickles."

"Sorry," she said again unconvincingly, leaning down to open the dishwasher. Her breath caught when her arm skimmed his chest; she knew she'd gotten to him when she heard the snag in his throat.

The heady feeling of power winded her. "You should put a jumper on."

"Huh?"

She nodded at his bare arms, now littered with goose bumps. "If you're cold you should put a jumper on."

He sent her a closed, indecipherable look that confused as much as aroused. How on earth had she been able to look at that face, into those dark eyes, without feeling her pulse spike before? But she had. She'd hugged, laughed and touched with impunity, secure in their platonic-friend zone. But now…now all she wanted to do was touch him. Kiss him.

Get him into bed again.

With a thick swallow, she called on her thinly shredded control and turned away.

"Let's watch that movie."

From the very first minute, the very first strike of classical music booming through the speakers, she was hooked.

Of course, it was all in French and Marco had to translate. Her breath caught every time he leaned in, his deep voice soft over the lilting on-screen French. The music was rich and powerful, the costumes beautifully flamboyant, and she could feel her senses spike in response. And of course, there was Marco sitting close, his body heat and faint cologne a frustrating accompaniment to the period drama. She had to stop herself from squirming after one intimate scene, to firmly focus on the screen and not turn and kiss him as he bent in to translate a particularly hot piece of dialogue.

She swallowed, suppressed a shudder and made a move to rise. "I need a drink. Do you want a drink?"

She squeaked when his arm went around her, pulling her back down. "No. Wait until after this scene. It's awesome."

"Just let it play. I won't be a second."

He groaned and clicked Pause. "You always do that. I hate it!"

"It's only a few seconds," she said, grabbing his fingers and pulling. "Let me go."

"No. Louis is about to confront his mother. You'll miss something important."

She worked at his fingers but he held her fast, and she couldn't help but stifle a giggle. A giggle that rushed out in a gasp as he yanked and she ended up sprawled in his lap. "The drink can wait."

"But—"

"Quiet, woman. I'm trying to watch the movie and you're ruining the mood."

With an exaggerated sigh she settled her head on his thigh and watched the scene.

When Marco casually draped his arm over her waist, an involuntary shiver coursed down her back. She was suddenly very much aware that his hand was curled at her hip, his hard thigh beneath her cheek and the back of her head in his lap.

Oh, dear.

She tried to focus on the movie, but it was no good. Amid the powerful scene, full of heightened tension, coupled with Marco's soft translation, she could feel her body heat up.

Her breath hitched. She couldn't take her eyes off the screen, and she couldn't switch off her senses because Marco was everywhere—his hand resting lightly on her hip. His scent, all male and clean. And that voice, so achingly intimate that her insides just seemed to shudder every time he opened his mouth.

When she stirred, she felt his thigh beneath her cheek shift and tighten, and she had to clench her fists to stop herself from involuntarily stroking that hard muscle.

She closed her eyes, swallowing thickly as his hand suddenly left her hip to gently toy with her hair.

So soft. Marco heard her faint sigh, barely discernible against the rich baroque sound track. Yet his senses went on high alert at the sudden tension riding her back as he continued to stroke her hair, the silky chocolate strands twining around his fingers. The sudden urge to bury his face in that hair, breathe deep and never come up for air winded him.

"Marco?"

His name, warm and whispery on her lips, sent a bolt of heat to his groin.

"Yes?"

"You should stop."

He didn't pretend to fake ignorance. "I don't think I can."

She turned her head in his lap and he groaned under his breath. Her wide blue eyes stared up at him, and he couldn't help himself. He needed to kiss her. Now.

So he did.

She had ample time to protest or move away, but she did neither, just watched him get closer and closer until his lips gently brushed over hers, tentative at first, then with more urgency.

Her sigh ended on a groan and told him everything he needed to know.

They spent long moments that way, just exploring

each other's mouths with lips, tongue and breath until Marco finally pulled back with a soft curse.

"What the hell is this, Kat?"

She stared up at him, eyes wide. "I have no clue. But…can we just…not talk about it?"

"Kat—"

"Please, Marco. With everything else going on, let's just not…not analyze this."

His hand skimmed over her jaw then down her neck to finally rest across her collarbone, a frankly possessive gesture that she ignored. "We're going to have to at some point."

She sighed. "I know. Just not now, okay?"

When she tentatively leaned up, lips seeking his, he pulled back, and for one brief second he saw her tense, as if preparing herself for rejection, and it just about killed him then and there. With a groan, he cupped her head and captured her lips in a deep kiss.

They kissed for ages, the rich music and French dialogue a sensual background that only flamed his need, urging him to do more, to touch, to possess.

He abruptly pulled back. "We should…"

She swallowed. "Stop?"

"Are you asking me or telling me?"

He heard her breath rattle as he studied her, taking in the curve of her lips, the mix of emotion in her darkened eyes. Did she…? Would he…?

Impossible.

Or was it?

"You're right."

He gently eased off the couch and moved away to the kitchen, leaving her in silence. She'd surely stop him, say something, if she thought any different, right?

But as he went through the motions of getting a drink, the silence was loud and obvious.

He hadn't mistaken that look—a mix of want and trepidation. He'd seen it so often in other women.

But this was Kat. His Kat.

No, not his.

Annoyed, he lingered in the kitchen as she sat on the couch, until the unmistakable ping of his phone broke the silence.

He paused. "Did you hear that?"

"What?"

"My phone pinged."

"That means the towers are working," she said.

He frowned and then quickly strode over to his phone, flicking it on. She picked up hers and did the same, hurriedly scanning through the messages.

Disappointment curled in his belly as he read. Ridiculous. They couldn't stay here forever. They needed to get back to their lives, to reality. Which meant work, test results. Press coverage.

He groaned softly, dragging a hand over his face. God, they'd have a field day with this trapped-alone-in-a-cyclone scenario. And Grace, she'd definitely want in on that story. Then there were Kat's test results that frankly scared the crap out of him.

He glanced over and saw her staring intently at her phone and frowning. They'd all want a piece of her. She could skillfully avoid the press, but Grace… Yeah, Kat's boss was demanding and challenging. It took a special person to work for her, and he knew she bugged Kat for an exclusive at least once a week. So far she'd held out, but after the past few days he wasn't entirely sure Grace would keep taking no for an answer.

The sudden urge to escape, to take Kat somewhere where they could relax in blissful anonymity and just ignore the realities of the outside world, swept over him, and his grip tightened on the phone. Japan, maybe? The Himalayas? Alaska. Alaska was nice....

Or they could just stay here.

Her soft exclamation broke through his thoughts and he quickly busied himself with the cups.

"The geneticist called. They have my results."

He spun around, but she'd already pulled open the patio doors and stepped outside. The soft click of the door was as final as any slam.

She'd shut him out.

Damn. He busied himself with coffee, refusing to look further into it. As always, she'd tell him in her own time, and as always, he'd be there for her, whatever the result.

He paused, and damn, the panic he thought he'd managed to ignore these past few days just swept right back in, leaving him floundering in a pool of helplessness.

He couldn't lose her. Not his Kat. Not the woman he'd just realized he was totally and completely in love with.

Wait, what?

Before he had a chance to let that realization take bloom, she'd reopened the door and was standing, pale and still, in the middle of the room.

"Kat?"

"I know they're not supposed to tell you over the phone," she said slowly. "But Dr. Hardy and my mother go back a long way, and I wasn't sure when we'd return to the mainland and—" She stopped, took a deep breath and looked him in the eye. "Sorry, I'm rambling.

I just…" She dragged a hand through her hair with a sigh as he just stood there, his heart lumping in his throat, blood pounding way too loud.

"Kat, you're killing me here," he said softly. "What did he say?"

"They're doing another test, to double-check the results," she began. "But…"

"Yes?"

"Preliminary tests were…" Her eyes rounded, disbelieving. "Positive." She swallowed, her voice cracking. "They were positive."

Oh, dear God.

For one second the world stopped spinning. He realized he'd gotten out a thick "What?" but the shock quickly drowned everything else out. She was… She had…

No. Just no.

NO.

He realized he was staring, silent and disbelieving, until he saw her tears spilling, slowly coursing down her cheeks, and his heart just shattered into a million tiny pieces.

Nonononono—

He surged forward just as she let out a gut-wrenching sob. In a few strides he'd crossed the room, and then he was crushing her against his chest.

She collapsed into him, and when he felt her begin to shake, he just held on tighter.

Impotent fury surged because he couldn't help her, couldn't stop her tears, couldn't do a damn thing but hold her, muttering totally useless sentiments while she cried and cried and broke his heart over and over.

He swallowed thick gulps of air, tightening his embrace as she trembled in his arms. She was so damn strong all the time, and it killed him to see her so broken now. After her mother's death, she'd never allowed herself to think about this possibility. She'd been determined to live her life without a death sentence tainting every moment. But now…now…

He held on tight, feeling her body shake, her tears dampening his shoulder, and he swallowed again and again, sucked it all up and bit back all his pain even as he felt his own tears spill on his cheeks. She needed him to be the strong one here. He'd be useless to her any other way.

Yet how could he when everything inside him throbbed with pain and fury and the injustice of it all?

That anger took flame, growing with each second, until thankfully he managed to force back the tears. "We'll get another test," he muttered against her hair. "And then another. They could've made a mistake—it happens all the time."

She muttered something unintelligible, and when she finally lifted her face to his, her expression so broken and torn, he couldn't help himself.

He leaned down and kissed her, hard.

She kissed him back just as fiercely, her small whimper warm in his mouth, her cheeks wet against his. When he angled her head and thrust his tongue between her lips, she groaned, welcoming him, her hands fisting in his shirt to pull him closer.

His brain shorted out as lust instantly exploded. He grabbed her arms and kept kissing her, her gasps of pleasure feathering over his lips, her hands grappling with his shirt, yanking it from his pants.

And then she was backing him up, and suddenly they

were sprawled on the couch with her on top, mouths still locked.

He couldn't think, couldn't speak. The emotion of the moment had completely hijacked any thought of common sense. With frantic hands they worked his pants open then off, then attacked her shirt, ripping it with their urgency. This was lust at its highest, the kind of clothes-ripping, skin-biting rush that left no room for soft words of love. It was just about the physical coming together of two people in desperate emotional need to connect, to prove they were still alive and were far from done yet.

He yanked up her skirt then dragged down her knickers, briefly reveling in her soft skin, in the warm, throbbing life of her, before she was bracing her hands on each side of his head. With mouths still locked in a desperate kiss, he grasped her hips, shifting her slightly, before plunging her straight down onto his aching manhood.

Her gasp rent the air and he groaned against her hot mouth, feeling the hard pulse of his arousal buried deep inside her. For a dozen breathtaking moments they remained still, intimately joined but unmoving as their eyes locked and they shared one breath.

It was…she was…incredible. Amazing.

With shaky hands, he swept his thumbs over her cheeks, sweeping away the last of her tears, before placing a slow, agonizing kiss first over one eyelid then the other.

"Kat…"

Her expression crumbled. "Please, Marco. Don't talk." Then she swooped down for a kiss, silencing him, and began to slowly, sensuously rock.

Instinctively he gripped her hips, taking charge of
the rhythm, commanding her body. His heart pounded
thickly, blood racing. He may have heard her whimper;
he wasn't sure because his heart was beating so damn
fast it felt as if the whole room echoed with it. And past
that, there was the faint, sensuous sound of flesh on
flesh coupled with their heavy breathing.

She rolled into him, biting her lip. "Marco…"

"Yeah?" His gaze met hers, and the raw need etched
on her face blew him away.

"Touch me…"

He did as she asked, and her eyes closed in pleasure, her hands covering his as he skimmed over the
velvet flesh of her stomach, her waist, then up over
her ribs to finally cup her breasts. His thumbs teased
her already sensitive nipples and she hissed, grinding
harder into him.

She leaned down and he took her mouth in breathless kisses over and over, until he was about to explode,
until the friction and heat where their bodies joined escalated to the point where they were both on the brink.

He felt her tighten around him and he groaned,
gripping her hips and thrusting hard, until she panted
against his mouth, her eyes squeezed shut. Then, with a
soft cry and a ragged breath, he felt her go over the edge.

He shuddered, a deep, satisfied groan wrenching
from his lips as he followed her. She collapsed on his
chest as he murmured her name, his breath against her
cheek, arms tight, holding her close. He felt her response against his neck, her body damp and shaking
as she wrapped her arms around him, legs tightening
with a sigh. "Don't move. Stay right here."

"I'm not going anywhere, *chérie*." His fingers went

into her hair, stroking her nape as the tight throb in his body began to slowly ease.

He blinked.

He loved her.

Just when the hell had that happened? And how? He searched his memory, going over each moment with determined concentration. Had it happened since that night ten weeks ago? Or sooner?

A frown furrowed his brow. It really didn't matter when, just that it *was*. He loved her as a best friend, as a lover. As a smart, amazing, funny, gorgeous and incredibly vulnerable woman. He loved that fourteen-year-old girl with the perfect hair and bright blue eyes, who'd stood up to his teasing. He loved that vulnerable, crazy nineteen-year-old, the one who'd needed him so desperately, the one who'd leaned on his shoulder, who'd needed *him* in her moment of grief. The woman who'd made mistakes in love and life and still continued to get back up, to forge her way and give the finger to all her critics.

The woman who had just received the worst possible news you could ever get.

No. He couldn't stop reality from intruding, but damn, he gave it his best shot. He knew the moment she felt it, too; her breath shook just a little on the intake and her arms tightened around him.

"No, don't," he said softly.

Too late.

She slowly slid off him in silence. As she fiddled with her underwear and pulled her skirt down, he took the moment to quickly adjust his pants. When he swung his feet to the floor, his breath snagged at her expression. How much effort was she exerting now, just to remain so calm, so in control? She was trying to hold it all together so he wouldn't see her at her absolute worst.

When she turned her back to him to do up her buttons, the curse he swallowed hurt like jagged glass. *Don't you dare lose it. Not when she's managing to keep it all together.*

"We should find out when we can go back to the mainland," he said softly, her back still to him. He had a few seconds to admire the smooth skin of her thighs, the gentle curve of her hip, the strong shoulders as she squared them and finally turned to face him, pushing back that mane of hair.

"Yes. I'll need to make some more calls, too."

"Kat." He leaned forward, looped an arm around her waist and pulled her to him. Surprisingly she offered no protest, just went into his arms silently. He held her, without passion and without subterfuge, just two friends sharing an embrace.

Finally he said, "Let's not jump to any conclusions here. They want to retest you. We should wait until that happens before we start making decisions."

He felt her nod against his chest, knew without confirmation that she was already thinking, planning. Making decisions. Her brain never stopped working, and now, of all days, she needed to make logical, sensible choices.

With a sigh she finally pulled away from him, and reluctantly he let her go. She went over to the table and grabbed her phone. "I have to make a few calls."

Seven

After Marco confirmed that the port at Cairns would reopen in a few hours, Kat used all her negotiation skills—and a few pleas—to wrangle an appointment with the geneticist for the very next day. Then they made a number of calls to let people know they were alive and well.

From what they gathered, Cairns was a disaster area. Parts of the city still had no water and electricity, and phone coverage was spotty. With the tropical climate, it was crucial those services be up and running again as soon as possible. It would be an arduous task, one that required a coordinated effort of all rescue services, plus private contractors. At least when the ports were clear and operating, supplies could be shipped in, and the massive cleanup could begin.

Armed with that information, they set about doing

physical tasks around the house—ripping the tape off the windows they hadn't already gotten to, and clearing more of the debris that would probably take a few weeks to get into some semblance of order, because all services would give priority to the mainland.

It was good to keep busy, to just focus on the pure physicality of lifting, clearing, moving. She'd assumed there'd be no time to think about tests, babies, Grace or the situation with Marco, but as they worked and sweat quickly soaked Kat's shirt, she found her mind was not so easily swayed.

You can't have this baby. She couldn't. It was the exact reason she'd vowed not to have kids. Her heart squeezed painfully and she scowled, putting more force than necessary into her raking task.

What her mother had gone through, what *she'd* gone through, watching her slowly wither and die from that death sentence… It was a pain so unfathomable that she'd willingly shift a mountain to prevent it from happening. It was one thing to cope with having the disease, to know exactly what she'd be facing every single day for the rest of her short life. But to willingly bring a child into that equation? No. Never.

Her eyes flicked briefly to Marco, then away. Yes, the pain of termination would cut deep, but it was preferable to a lifetime of anguish, of knowing she could have prevented it but selfishly did nothing. She would not put a child nor Marco through that.

Ah. No. Don't think about it. But she couldn't help it—her thoughts were already there, crowding her head with every single possible scenario until it was the only thing she could think about.

She gritted her teeth, wielding the rake with such

force that she heard the handle creak. *Damn. Something else. Think of...the cyclone. Work. Yes, work.* Grace would want her on top of this, sourcing stories, digging up information. She'd be so busy she wouldn't have a second to scratch herself, let alone think about...*that*.

She winced. And so it would begin again—Grace would choose the stories worthy of their effort and attention, the appropriate donation lines would be set up and a dozen other untold issues would remain just a couple of sentences in her notes.

The futility frustrated her.

And so she spent the next half hour focused on cleaning up, and eventually, with her arm and thigh muscles aching from the effort, they managed to clear a good part of the mess surrounding the house.

Finally Marco straightened, grabbed a bottle of water from beneath the tree and took a swig, then picked up his phone. "We should finish up."

Kat paused, scratching at a thin bead of sweat running down her neck as he handed her another bottle. "Okay."

"We'll probably make the mainland by three."

She nodded, one hand on her hip as she took a long swallow.

When he fell silent, she could feel his eyes on her. "Kat..."

Her gaze snapped to his as she finished the water, and the look in his eyes had her insides crumbling all over again. "Marco," she breathed. "Don't."

"But I have to say—"

"No," she said, a little too forcefully. "Don't say a thing. We did that already and look where that's gotten us. I don't want to say anything more until I have those

follow-up tests in my hands. Until I know for sure."
She studied him for a moment, taking in the tightness
bracketing his mouth, his slightly clenched fist. "Promise me. No talk until we know."

As the seconds stretched, she held her breath, willing him with her mind. She'd coped with her mother's
illness by not discussing, by not talking. She couldn't
recall having one single deep and meaningful conversation with her father about what was going on, how she
was coping, what he was feeling. He wasn't a talker at
the best of times, but in this his lips had been perfectly
sealed. Not talking was the only way she knew—that
and partying until the nights had all just become one
big, glitzy blur.

If Marco made her discuss just one more thing about
this mind-boggling situation, she was sure she'd dissolve into a bawling mess on the floor.

"Fine."

Her breath whooshed out, relief flooding in. "Thank
you. Now—" she attempted a smile but it fell way flat
"—I don't know about you but I definitely need a
shower before we head back to civilization."

How she managed to keep everything together for the
entire day, Marco would never know. It was a testament
to her inner strength, to her willpower, that she went
through the motions of the boat trip strong and silently,
pale-faced but determinedly swallowing her nausea.

And slowly, as the mainland came closer and closer,
their attention was commanded by the shocking result
of Cyclone Rory against the mainland of Cairns.

The radio reports had done nothing to prepare them
for the devastation. It looked as if someone had stomped

through in giant boots and created total havoc. A dozen private boats were all bunched up and shoved against the harbor wall like toys. The majestic palm trees were flattened, some crushing houses, some merely uprooted. Debris, sand, trees, glass, broken buildings and belongings… Everything had been displaced and reorganized into odd clusters, like the small speedboat half-buried in a luxury beach house. The kid's bike hanging from a lone palm tree. A cracked plasma TV lying in the middle of a now-sand-covered Esplanade pool. There were ripped roofs and scattered belongings and broken dreams left bare and torn.

Everywhere they looked, the cyclone had transformed the coastline into something neither of them recognized. In solemn silence they managed to dock, even though flotsam still floated in the water, then picked their way across the amazing wreck that was The Esplanade, to the next street, where Marco had arranged for a car to pick them up.

The drive north through town was made in similar silence as they were guided through the traffic snarl and stared out at the damage, trying to wrap their heads around the utter devastation the storm had wrought.

Physical devastation to accompany the emotional.

Marco swallowed, his gaze going briefly to Kat in the passenger seat, then back to the litter-strewn road, his eyes firmly on the police and rescue workers directing traffic and controlling the dozen news cars competing with business owners and volunteers eager to start the cleanup.

No, he had to stop those thoughts right now. They didn't know. Not until—as she said—she had the hard evidence in her hand. Then they would deal with whatever needed to be dealt with. So he bundled all those horrible thoughts, the possible future scenarios, and locked them up tight.

Her ringing phone provided some respite. After a brief conversation that mostly involved her listening to the caller, she hung up and said, "Grace needs me." He simply nodded.

"I'll drop you off."

When they pulled up outside the studio, Kat swung from the car and then glanced back.

"Thanks. I'll let you know how I go."

"You sure you don't want me there?" he asked for the third time, studying her face carefully as she leaned in.

She nodded. "Grace confided in me. I should be the one to tell her. And the sooner she knows the better." Her ironic smile was brief. "Preempt that press statement I just know she's been working on."

He snorted but said nothing more, so she gave him a smile, said "Thanks" again and left.

But as she strode into the studio, her mind was still on the island, far from the Grace situation. It was as if the time they'd spent there had been their own personal bubble. Now it was back to reality.

She sighed as she dug out her ID and then swept into the building. Time to focus on what she needed to tell Grace.

"Just say whatever comes into your head" had been Marco's advice on the boat. And he was right. Some of her best stuff for *The Tribune* had been spontaneous and off-the-cuff. Too much rehearsing had felt overedited and scripted. This was one time where she didn't want things to sound forced.

With a pounding heart, she clipped down the corridor straight to her office, grabbing a runner on the way to determine Grace's whereabouts. She eventually ended up at the canteen, pausing in the doorway to scan the room, her eyes eventually landing on the TV star at a corner table with their executive producer.

Right. This was it. She took a deep breath and strode over, a smile on her face.

Grace spotted her a few feet away, and a second later she gasped and shot to her feet, commanding everyone's attention.

"Kat! Oh, my God, it's great to see you! How've you been?"

She was quickly enveloped in a warm Estee Lauder–scented hug, and then firmly cheek kissed. "You were so vague on the phone—you were with Marco on the island, right? Did the cyclone hit there or pass by? Was there much damage? Did you take photos? Sit and tell me everything!"

Acutely aware of the sudden attention, Kat went through the motions of nodding and smiling, accepting hugs and arm pats then thanking everyone for their good wishes until her face started to ache from the smiling. Finally, when the minor fuss had settled and everyone moved back to their tables, she leaned in to Grace.

"I need to talk to you. Privately."

Grace's unlined brow went up. "Sure. Let's go into my office."

It took a few minutes to get out of the canteen and then down the corridor. But finally they were in Grace's vibrant yellow-and-blue office, the air smelling faintly of Estee Lauder's Beautiful, her signature scent.

"So, what's up, Kat?" Grace smiled curiously, closing the door behind her. "Did you want to run a new story idea past me?"

"No." Kat eased onto the edge of the sofa, her insides churning. "It's about Marco."

"Oh?"

"Yes." Boy, this was awkward, way more awkward than she'd thought. It was because it was Grace, someone she cared about. Someone who'd be hurt, no matter how skillful or pretty or unscripted her words were. It was personal this time, and she hated every single minute of it.

Still, she had to put on her big-girl knickers and get it done. So she took a breath and plunged right in.

"Grace. Marco and me…me and him… Well, we're kind of…" Kind of what? *Together? Bed partners? Having a baby?* "Involved," she finished lamely.

Oh, way to go. Put those media skills to great use there.

Silence reigned, somehow made thicker by the soft fragrance permeating the air, as the expression on Grace's perfectly made-up face went through the emotions in a matter of seconds—amused surprise, confusion, disbelief—until she settled on a dark frown. "I'm sorry…what?"

"Marco and I are…involved."

Grace slowly crossed her arms. "Yes, you said that. But what does that actually mean? You guys are always involved in one way or another."

"We slept together."

Grace's eyes rounded. "What? When?"

Kat swallowed, her gaze firm. "Ten weeks ago, just before he left for France." *And these past few days…* Although she didn't need to spell that out, because judging from the look on Grace's face, she'd already assumed that.

Grace's slow blink and sudden laden silence said everything and yet nothing at all. So instead of elaborating, instead of trying to justify an action that had obviously cut deep, Kat waited.

Grace slowly sat down behind her desk then leaned back on the plush office chair, her face carefully blank. "I see. A little farewell private party, was it?"

"Grace…" Kat's chest tightened. God, this was hard! "You two weren't together at the time—"

"Oh, thanks for checking on that." The brief grimace slashing Grace's features twisted a little knife in Kat's belly. "It makes me feel so much better."

"I meant, I didn't plan on—"

Grace held up a hand. "Stop. I really don't need to know the details." She paused, raking her gaze over Kat until the burn of humiliation and betrayal had formed a small pool of sweat at the base of her spine.

"You knew when I mentioned wanting a baby," Grace finally said.

Kat nodded.

"And you said nothing."

Kat nodded again. "And I'm really sorry about that. I didn't know what to say. At that point, the thing with me and Marco was just a…a…one-time thing. We'd both decided to just ignore it and move on. But now, after these last few days, we've talked and it's all become a bit more…um…complicated."

"How?"

Kat flushed. "Just…complicated."

Grace's eyes narrowed. "You're not pregnant, are you?"

The shock of having it put right out there made Kat gasp, and she had to scramble for a breath. "Wh— what?"

"Are you pregnant?" Grace repeated, her expression tight.

Because it was Grace, a person she admired and respected, a person she'd come to trust with parts of her personal life, Kat hesitated over her automatic denial. But it was the small hesitation that gave it away, gave Grace clear and direct confirmation. And when the older woman's face creased into a small smile, Kat's conflict grew a thousandfold.

Please don't ask. I can barely wrap my head around it all myself...and the test results just totally screw everything up.

Kat bit her lip and slid her gaze away. "No comment."

Silence descended for a few moments, silence in which Kat firmly swallowed every emotion she'd been battling the past day. Damn, she couldn't lose it again. She *wouldn't* lose it again. She'd had her moment of weakness with Marco, had let the overwhelming feelings command her, make her vulnerable. She couldn't do it every single time someone mentioned it. Otherwise she'd just be a blubbering wreck on the floor.

Grace finally sighed and said, "I can't deny I'm hurt, Kat."

She grimaced. "I know. And I am really, really sorry about that. But it wasn't planned. If there's anything I can do to make it right for you..."

"An interview."

Kat blinked, her brow furrowed. "What?"

"You can give me that interview we were talking

about." Grace stood swiftly, hands wide on her desk, a gleam in her eye.

Oh, wow. That was a bit... Kat's head spun a little. "That's...uh. No."

"You're still saying no?" Grace lifted her brow. "After what you've just told me? Knowing nothing in this business is kept a secret for long?" At Kat's look of alarm, she waved a hand in the air. "Oh, honey, you should know by now it won't be me leaking details to the press. But once others get involved, it's inevitable."

Kat remained silent as Grace gave her a long look, then fished out a makeup bag from her desk and went through the motions of reapplying lipstick. It was true. A secret was kept only by one person, and over the next few days more and more people would be involved, like it or not.

"The offer is still there," Grace finally said, unplugging her phone and scrolling through her messages. "We'd do it your way, with your final approval. And you know I don't often say that."

Kat paused, trying to get everything straight in her head. "So you're okay with the Marco thing?"

"No." Grace smiled thinly.

She swallowed. "Grace...is this going to be awkward between us?"

"Most likely." The older woman eyed her, her expression still tight. "You denied it too much, you know. I always knew you had a thing—one that predates my claim—so I shouldn't be that surprised."

Kat swallowed her guilt, glancing away. "That's not what—"

"Oh, please." Grace rolled her eyes theatrically as she

walked to the door and pulled it open. "Give me some credit here. You and Marco have *always* been a thing."

Kat followed her out the door then down the corridor in silence, until Grace finally turned and eyed her. "So when are you going public?"

"*If,* Grace," Kat said. "If we go public."

Grace threw her a knowing look over her shoulder. "Oh, it's a 'when,' hon. Trust me."

Kat frowned. "That's not something we've thought about."

"Really?" Grace kept walking. "Well, you'd better start. Gossip has a way of getting out, you know."

Kat stared at her back. Was that a threat? That definitely sounded like one. And to be honest, she couldn't deny Grace her bitterness. If she could make this right with her, she'd gladly do it.

Even giving her an exclusive?

Ugh. That thought lay heavy in her gut for the rest of the afternoon, until she finally made her way home, barely made it through a shower and finally collapsed into a blissful sleep coma on her bed.

Eight

The next day Marco and Kat sat in Dr. Hardy's waiting room, nervously waiting for her name to be called. Most structures in North Cairns had survived cyclone damage and it was still a surreal sight to see: half the town had been flattened while the other half stood tall and proud as if everything was normal.

Instead of offering empty it'll-be-okays and you'll-be-all-rights, he remained silent, loosely holding her hand, occasionally brushing her knuckles with his thumb as the minutes ticked by.

One minute.

Five.

Ten.

He glanced at the clock then scanned the pristine waiting room for the umpteenth time. Life still went on, despite the destruction outside. People still needed results, still needed diagnosing, needed to know what was wrong and how to fix it. Only a few people waited with them—a young couple, an elderly man, a woman with two small children—and briefly he wondered what each of their stories was, how they'd come to be here, right now. How they would cope with bad news, what they had vowed to change if the prognosis was good.

He watched the young mother settle her toddler with a book, and he smiled at her as their eyes met over the child's head.

That could be Kat in a few years' time.

Or not.

"Thank you for coming with me," she said now with a small smile.

"I wouldn't be anywhere else, *chérie*." He squeezed her hand, careful to keep his worry firmly under wraps as he met her gaze. She needed him to be strong, whatever the result. He was there as her best friend, not the man who loved her so much he'd willingly sell his soul to trade places if he could.

Her finger softly traced his frown lines with a half smile. "Don't," she said softly.

He captured her hand, kissed it gently before his gaze slid away. "Sorry."

"Please, Marco. I really couldn't cope if you fell apart on me now."

He nodded, breath catching for a moment before he slowly huffed it out.

You need to tell her.

He grimaced, his gaze firmly on the floor. *No.* She had told him quite firmly they were friends. Nothing more. He had no doubt if he did tell her, that it would be the end of their friendship. And fighting about that now, proving to her that they should be together when she had so much more on her mind, would take everything he had. Waiting was not something he did well, but he wanted her in his life. He'd damn well have to wait for now, regardless of how it frustrated him.

Just not for long.

The door suddenly opened and all eyes went to Dr. Hardy as he walked purposefully over to them with a pleasant smile.

His heart thudded, hard.

"Good afternoon, Kat. Thanks for coming in." He said it softly, but still the people closest to them heard. A gentle murmur of recognition rippled, followed by all eyes swiveling to her as she stood with a flush. To her credit she ignored it all, just tightened her hand in Marco's and followed the doctor down the hall.

"Have you seen the town?" Dr. Hardy began as they settled in his office, his elderly face creased into concerned lines.

"Yes. It's unbelievable."

"Not quite as bad as Yasi but pretty grim."

She nodded, her expression neutral. Yeah, she was impatient, though. Marco could tell by the small muscles bracketing her mouth, the slight dip of her eyebrows.

"So," Marco said. "The tests. You ran them again?"

"We did." Dr. Hardy coughed then slowly removed his glasses, tossing them on the file.

"And?"

He spent interminable seconds shuffling through the file, then finally pulled out a piece of paper and read, pausing way too long.

Kat leaned in with a frown. "What?"

Dr. Hardy flushed. "First, I want to offer you my heartfelt sympathies for what you've been going through. We do have strict protocols, and regretfully I broke from that because of the history I had with your mother." He coughed. "But right now I can confirm that…" He stared at the paper before returning to her. "There was a mix-up at the lab. Some samples were mislabeled. And as a result, you have tested negative for motor neuron disease."

It was like taking a football to the chest, meted out by the world's best striker. Marco's gasp mingled with Kat's softer, higher one. Her hand went still in his as she froze, eyes wide. Her voice, when it came, wavered as if she'd just raced up a flight of stairs. "I'm sorry…what?"

"Your blood-test results have tested negative for motor neuron disease. You are clear and healthy, and—"

Marco's pounding heart drowned out the rest. She was healthy. The tests were clear.

The relief was unlike anything he'd ever known in his life. Nothing compared—not national selection, not the not-guilty verdict from his father's trial. Not even the positive results after his knee surgery telling him that yes, he would be able to walk. This…oh, this…

Joy, pure unadulterated joy choked his breath, and he felt the crazy laugh well inside, just before he choked it down.

She's going to have a child. Our child.

His expletive came out like a shot, and then he was turning to her and dragging her into a hug that was way too tight, way too emotional, but damn, she was clear, and the joy that swelled was too hard to contain.

She was going to live to see their child grow up. Take its first steps. Go to school, go on dates, get married.

Damn, she was going to *live*.

Eventually he pulled back enough to cup her teary face, knowing his smile stretched from ear to ear, because hers matched it.

"Clear," she whispered, her joyful expression a watery mess.

"Clear," he repeated, then slowly added, "We're going to have a baby."

Her eyes widened for a second, and then a small nod followed. "Oh, we so are."

Kat swallowed. She had tested negative. She was having a baby.

She couldn't even begin to quantify these two life-changing statements. She'd done enough survivor stories to know the emotion involved in processing this kind of information. The mix of elation and sheer panic running through her mind right now was…overwhelming. Overpowering. It choked her breath, snagged a laugh in her throat, forced tears to her eyes.

She stared at Marco as he brushed her damp cheeks with a shaky hand. How many times had she nodded sympathetically when all those survivors had tried to verbalize their feelings, tried to compose their thoughts into some semblance of control yet let everyone know of the emotion behind it? But she didn't know, not really.

Until now.

The adrenaline rush was amazing. She wanted to cry and laugh and dance and take on the world. She wanted to do reckless things just for the hell of it. She wanted to fulfill all those silly, crazy dreams she and Marco had laughingly thought up in ninth grade, trying to outdo each other on the ridiculous scale. Bungee jumping off the Eiffel Tower. Hiring Disneyland for the day. Biking down Everest. Flying a fighter jet.

She wanted to *live*.

After all these years of steadfastly refusing to get tested, pushing the worry and doubt to the back of her mind, then those agonizing hours of unbelievable anguish, she had finally been cut a break.

Everything seemed surreal, as if she was walking through a dream where nothing and no one could touch her. And couple that with Marco's gentle kiss, his obvious joy at her results, and there was no better moment than this, right here.

It was… Well, she couldn't even find the words to describe it. *Amazing* and *unbelievable* were way too tame for such a life-changing occasion.

She wasn't sick.

Dr. Hardy's discreet cough, when it came, had them both turning in surprise. He sat in the same position, leaning forward on the desk, arms bent, his expression professional.

"Thanks, Doctor," Kat got out, the smile stretching her face until it ached. "That's the best news I could've had."

"You're welcome." He leaned back in his chair, a hand brushing over his sparse gray hair. "There is, however, one more issue."

"Yes?"

He cleared his throat and focused his gaze on her. "Your mother's blood group is O, correct?"

She nodded. "Yes, it was in the hospital documents."

"And you are AB."

"Yes."

"Well, here's our problem."

She shook her head. "Sorry, I'm not getting it."

"Kat, normally I'd recommend further blood tests, make the standard speech about getting more results, seeing your doctor, etc., etc. But I knew your mother for a long time and I owe you this." He sighed. "I'm saying an O parent cannot have an AB child."

She blinked then shook her head with a snort. "Well, obviously there's been a mistake. We need to test it again."

He fixed her with a look, part sympathy, part concern. "I'm sorry. It's been done three times already. There's no mistake."

What?

Kat stilled, her thoughts all crammed in tight as she tried to decipher what this meant.

Okay, so her mother was O. She was AB. And O and AB couldn't be related. Which meant…

Her hand suddenly tightened in Marco's. "Hang on, you're saying it's impossible for my mother to be my *mother?*"

Dr. Hardy nodded.

"No," she croaked, and then more firmly said, "No, the tests are wrong. Just…just…" she stammered, her head whirling. "Just like with my first results! An accident. Human error."

"No, it's quite correct. We were very careful this time around. Everything was done properly." He paused, taking in her pale face and thinning mouth. "Kat, look, I can put you in touch with someone who—"

She stood so quickly, the blood rushed to her head. "I can't…I can't…" She didn't finish that sentence, just strode over to the door and stalked out.

Impossible. Ridiculous. It had to be a mistake.

She made it out the waiting room, then down the corridor, oblivious to Marco calling her. The elevators gave her pause, and she viciously punched an elevator button as her mind tried to make sense of these past few days, put them in neat little boxes and bring her some order and peace.

She couldn't. She was as far from peace as she could possibly be right now. She'd had a life-threatening disease for a day and everything involved in that—the feelings, the worry, the entire universe of emotion that came with the ordeal—had drained her. Yes, she'd managed to wrap her head around it, even though part of her deep down had refused to accept it. And now here she was, her greatest wish come true. She was disease-free....

But she had no clue who she was.

Who was her real mother? Was her father even her father? Did she have brothers, sisters out there somewhere? Where was she born? Did she look like anyone in her family?

Had someone given her up and then turned around and walked away without another thought? Was she stolen? Or had her parents loved her and been involved in some horrible accident?

A sob caught in her throat and she lifted a shaky hand to her mouth, determinedly glaring at the elevator doors as she felt the tears form.

It was as if someone had just suddenly erased her entire past, every single moment and memory effectively wiped and replaced with...what?

A million questions.

She sensed rather than saw Marco standing beside her, a silent presence that did little to calm her chaotic insides.

Was her real name Katerina, or was that another lie? Did her father know? Did *anyone* know?

Just who the *hell* was she?

She choked back a sob just when the elevator doors swung open, and she silently entered, hand still on her mouth as if to hold in all those raw, spilling emotions.

Marco pressed the basement-floor button and finally broke the silence. "What are you going to do?"

Her eyes remained firmly on the doors as she desperately tried to gain control, swallowing thickly and blinking over and over. She would not break down here, not now.

Later, yes. Not here.

"I'm going to see my dad."

A pause. "Flights will be limited until the airport's given the all clear."

"I know. I'll take the next available to Brisbane."

"I'll come with you."

Desperate for something else to focus on, she pulled out her phone and tapped on the travel app. "You don't have to do that."

"I want to."

"Can you take time off work?"

"I'll make time," he said firmly. "This is important."

She chanced a glance at his determined expression and then quickly looked away. *Of course you want him there*.

Just as during every other emotional time in her life, his presence would give her the necessary strength to get through this. He was her first and last choice.

"Okay. I'll let you know." The elevator opened and she walked out the foyer, then through the automatic doors. "Can you drop me off home?"

"Sure."

They walked across the car park to the vehicle in silence, and when she finally slid onto the soft leather seat with a groan, she closed her eyes. She was physically and emotionally drained. Thank God Marco said nothing, just drove in silence.

They finally reached her apartment block, and still not a word had been said.

What could she possibly say? She'd been through the emotional wringer and her brain was desperate to focus on something else. Yet when she crawled out of the car and glanced back at him, the small frown furrowing his brow and the look on his face crumbled her composure. "Kat, are you okay?"

She gave him a shaky smile. "No, actually. But I will be."

"Do you want me to come up?"

She pulled back, shaking her head. "No. No, thanks. I just need some time alone. Time to sort some things out."

"Okay." His blatant skepticism almost had her smiling. Almost.

"I'll call you." With that she turned and walked off, her disappointment echoing with every click of her heels on concrete.

What was she expecting? She'd said no, and he'd taken her at her word. End of discussion.

Except her reality had been ripped from her in the space of one afternoon, and she had no idea what to think or feel anymore. So instead of focusing on the whole messed-up bag of her parentage—the sensible thing when she had no clear answers—she latched on to the other issue she'd been avoiding.

Her and Marco.

Marco's reality was being absent six months out of the year. And the truth was, she didn't want him 30, 50, even 80 percent of his time. She needed his 100 percent commitment. But she also knew she couldn't ask that of him.

She unlocked the door to her third-floor apartment and went in, tossing her bag onto the kitchen counter and yanking open the fridge.

Honestly, it'd be easier for both of them if she raised this child by herself.

She could do that. She'd take time off work, hire a nanny. Women did it all the time, and she was in the fortunate position of having a healthy bank account to ease the burden.

And yet…

Hadn't she always resented her parents' piecemeal approach to parenting? Oh, her mother had been there when she could, but she'd been so involved in her work as an exclusive events planner she'd missed the bulk of Kat's high school activities. And her father… Well, she had as much chance of flying the starship *Enterprise* as she had of seeing him there for her. It would've been a shock to actually have her father attend something.

Their long and pointed absences had hurt the most, the overwhelming feeling that they'd just simply lost interest, gotten bored or had something more important to focus on shaping her insecurity all the way through high school. The familiar thread of instability still made her gut tighten even now.

Except she wasn't her mother's daughter, was she? Maybe they hadn't been totally committed because the blood bond that tied normal families together wasn't there. Maybe she was a disappointment, someone they'd not come to expect much of. And when her mother had become sick—

A sudden sickening realization swept over her, and she grabbed the bench for support.

If Nina wasn't her biological mother, and they'd known all along…

Then they'd know she wasn't a carrier or infected.

They had *known*. And not told her. For nearly fourteen years, her father had had so many opportunities to reveal this information, to put her mind at rest. But he hadn't. He'd let her go on believing every single day that her body was a ticking time bomb and that she could fall sick at any time.

The cry that erupted from her throat was almost primeval. She actually felt physically sick.

How on earth could the secret of her birth be more important than her physical and mental health?

Her hand shook as she poured a glass of juice and then quickly placed the carton on the bench. Her head hurt just trying to sort through everything. She could either make herself crazy going around in circles about it, or she could do something. Except until she saw her father, there was nothing *to* do.

Wrong. She could start to preempt the damage.

She grabbed her phone from the bench and scrolled through the contacts, finally calling a Brisbane number she'd never thought she'd need again—the publicist who'd skillfully navigated her around her last disastrous divorce, then those awful photos.

"Emma?" she said when the woman picked up. "It's Kat Jackson. I need to hire you."

Nine

Three days later, after Kat had begged off early on Friday afternoon, she and Marco managed to get a flight into Brisbane, and Kat arranged to meet her father at work during his lunch hour. Not that he actually took one, she thought, as they both rode the elevator up to the executive offices of Jackson & Blair International Investments. She'd grown up on the stories of how her father and Stephen Blair had overcome the odds of humble family beginnings to develop their business. How they'd used their trademark determination and ruthlessness to throw every penny and waking moment into what was now one of Australia's top-ten investment companies.

And with such a sacrifice came a price. She barely remembered her father during her childhood. Instead he stood out by his lengthy absences—the times her mother had brought her to the offices for their "quality time," the weekends vying for his attention when he'd been on the phone, in his office or hunched over some important papers. In that, she and Connor had bonded, recognizing similar upbringings but rarely needing words to confirm it.

If Keith Jackson had intimidated her growing up, Stephen Blair had done so tenfold. Even now, passing by his office on their way to her father's, catching a bare glimpse of his towering, expensively suited presence in heavy discussion with similarly suited men, was enough to set her nerves on edge. He was a man who silently judged, for whom perfection meant everything, and nothing was good enough unless it was his way.

What a nightmare for Connor to have a father like that.

Five minutes later, Kat left Marco in the waiting room and strode into her father's office, a mix of anger, intimidation and frustration congealing in her belly.

Calm. Stay calm. She had the truth on her side, and she had the courage to confront him because what he did was wrong.

"Katerina," Keith Jackson said with a thin smile as she walked into his office then closed the door behind her. "I'm surprised the network let you go amidst all the cyclone coverage."

"It's only one afternoon." Not to Grace it wasn't, and she had the feeling her boss would be calling in the favor fairly soon.

"So, what's so urgent you had to fly down to Brisbane to talk to me?"

She took a seat opposite him, saying nothing. On

the two-hour flight south, she'd rehearsed this over and over, until her head spun and she'd exhausted herself.

It simply wasn't possible for her father *not* to know. Which meant beyond a shadow of a doubt that he also knew the chances of her having her mother's disease were low to none.

He could have told her anytime. They both could have told her. Instead they'd said absolutely nothing, letting her go through the pain, the anguish, then the ultimate decision to not get tested. Anger had surged every time she thought about that, so she'd vowed to not think about it until she had confirmation. Then she could silently go to pieces.

"I need to ask you something and I need you to tell me the truth, okay?"

His eyebrows went up, mouth in an impatient "okay" expression, as if she'd just told him she was buying a new handbag or going to the Gold Coast for the weekend.

"Dad," she said without preamble, her gaze direct. "Am I adopted?"

His expression froze, a perfect display of shock and confusion all rolled into one. She waited calmly as he leaned back in his chair with a dark frown, his face faintly flushed.

"What kind of question is that?" he said tightly.

"A perfectly legitimate one, considering it's impossible for Mum's blood type, O, to produce a child of my AB type."

His long pause was telling. "And why on earth are you getting blood tests? I thought you didn't want to know."

"I'm pregnant, Dad." Wow, that came out way smoother

than she'd practiced. It felt liberating, actually. "And I wanted to know if I had the disease. I don't, by the way. But then, you probably already knew that, considering Mum isn't really my mother."

She'd never seen him so still. Wow, she'd actually robbed him of speech—an ironic first. Swallowing the hysterical little laugh, she just slowly folded her arms and stared at him. And yet, he said nothing.

Great. It was up to her, then.

"Did you have an affair? Did the woman leave you with the baby?"

"No!" He flushed again, this time deeper. "That's ridiculous."

"So I'm adopted."

His nod, when it came, was frustratingly short.

She clamped down hard on her anger, but it still ended up bubbling over. "Oh, my God, Dad! I've had that disease hanging over my head for *years,* sitting there in the back of my mind, a death sentence." She sprung to her feet, fury flushing her face hot. "How the *hell* can you justify not telling me? Why on earth would you let me go through all those years of worry, of thinking…of thinking…" She couldn't stand there and finish the sentence, not with her father's face twisted into such uncharacteristic lines of pain that it hurt her heart just to look at him.

It was like the night of her mother's death, the only time she'd ever seen him weak and vulnerable, a man without power, without control. Just a man.

It had scared the hell out of her. Just as it did now.

She slowly sat, hands gripped on the armrests. "So why adopt? And why keep it a secret?" Her gaze softened. "Dad, if Mum couldn't have kids, it's nothing to be ashamed of. Why didn't you just tell me?"

He sighed, leaning back in his chair. "Because we made a promise."

"To whom?"

When he shook his head, her irritation spiked again. "Dad, tell me!"

He scowled. "Why bring this up now, Kat? Don't you have other things to worry about—like how the press is going to react to you being pregnant?"

She blinked and bit back a curse. *That* was what he was worried about? "I'm handling that."

His expression was borderline skeptical. "Right."

Dark, hot anger surged, making her skin tingle with the power of it, but her voice was calm, unwavering. "We're talking about my blood tests, Dad."

Oh, she desperately wanted to spill the entire story of the past few days, throw the false positive in his face and reveal her anguish, anger and every other single emotion that had accompanied it. She even choked on a sob as the words caught in her throat, but at the very last minute she clenched her fists and bit her tongue.

He lapsed into silence again, and she just stared at him. She knew her face reflected all the thoughts and emotions bubbling to the surface, every single one of them. When he broke eye contact first, she took just a little joy in that.

"Your mother wanted to tell you, you know," he said, carefully moving his coffee cup from the corner of the desk to the middle. "Many times."

"Why didn't she?"

He sighed. "The timing was never quite right. Because she knew you'd start asking questions, and she couldn't answer any of them." He slid her a glance. "That was why we never pushed you to get tested. The likelihood of you being positive was practically non-existent."

She swallowed, dragged in a shaky breath as the past few days crashed over her. *You're negative. The test was negative, remember?* "Who are my birth parents?"

He paused a moment. "I can't tell you. I gave my word."

"Who on earth would make you promise something like that? Who would hold either so much power or so much loyalty…that…that…" She petered out, her mind clicking through the possibilities until she finally latched on to something crazy, something so far-fetched that she realized it fit perfectly.

No. It couldn't be *him*.

And yet…

It so totally could.

But that would mean…

Her back straightened in the chair. "It's Stephen Blair, isn't it?"

"No," he snapped quickly, the tight lines bracketing his mouth deepening.

It was so quick she barely had time to register it— the tiny twitch of a muscle near his eye, the clench of his hand. The almost imperceptible thinning of his lips. All signs of guilt.

"It so is." She stood, head spinning. "And I'm going to ask him."

"You will not!"

Her father's harsh command stopped her midturn. Slowly she turned back to face him, and his expression—

a mix of fury, tension and…yes, fear—was enough to temper her anger.

"Tell me, Dad," she said softly. "Please."

He paused, pursing his lips. She could practically see his brain working through the different outcomes of telling versus silence.

Thankfully, he made his decision quickly. "You can't say anything. Not even to Connor."

She blinked, gripping the chair back for support as the implication suddenly sank in. *Oh, God. Connor was…*

Connor was her *brother*. This was…

She couldn't even wrap her head around this. Connor. Her brother. Stephen. Her father. So…

"Who's my mother?"

He sighed then nodded to the chair. "Sit."

Marco sat in the waiting room, flicking through his phone and resisting the urge to get up and pace. For the fifth time he glanced up at the receptionist, and just as she had those five times before, she quickly dropped her gaze and hurriedly pretended to be doing something else.

Finally he strode over to the huge twentieth-floor window, to the panoramic view of Brisbane spread before him.

He sighed. When Kat was growing up, Keith Jackson had been the quintessential workaholic, but where he was gruff, terse and had little time for people other than his social circle, Kat's mother, Nina, had been his polar opposite. Whenever Kat talked about her mother, her face lit up, her eyes alight with love, even though she hadn't been a perfect parent herself. Marco had lost count of how many times he'd watched Kat swallow disappointment over her mother's prior commitments and broken promises. Yet all of that had become unimportant in the wake of her illness. And boy, he clearly remembered the time Kat had turned up on his doorstep in France, barely a few weeks after her mother had died. It was as if something essential had been stolen, something he wasn't sure she'd get back. But slowly, over time, she'd found her way back to who she was— his Kat. Changed, with added maturity, yes. But still Kat, deep down.

"I'm sorry, but aren't you Marco Corelli?"

His thoughts scattered, and as he glanced up at the receptionist, he quickly put on an automatic polite smile. "I am."

Her grin widened. "I knew it! My little brother plays local league and watches the European games religiously on cable. He's so excited for the World Cup selection next year, I can't tell you." She laughed. "He'll be so jealous I got to meet you."

Marco couldn't help but return her smile. "Thanks. We're all pretty excited about the selection, too."

"So will you be calling the match again? Our whole neighborhood stops to watch, you know," she added, rising from her seat, clutching pen and paper.

"That's the plan." When he held out his hand, she shook it in silent awe, and for the next few minutes, he answered her breathless questions, signed an autograph and smiled for a photo.

"Congratulations on the FFA award, by the way," she said, finally returning to her seat as the phone began to ring. "My cousins in Sydney will be stalking the red carpet on the night." She paused and picked up the handset with a smirk. "I'll have to text them that photo and make them jealous. Good morning, Jackson & Blair. How may I help you?"

"Marco?"

His soft laugh abruptly cut off and he whirled at the sound of Kat's voice, her pale face choking off the last of his amusement. He said nothing, just pushed the doors open for her, sent the receptionist a smile and a wave and followed Kat to the elevators.

"Well?" he asked as they rode down to the ground floor. "What did he say?"

She opened her mouth once, then closed it, then just stared at him, a dumbfounded expression on her face.

He gently took her shoulders. "Kat?"

"I am…" She shook her head, as if she couldn't believe it. "My father is…"

"Yes?"

She dragged in a harsh breath. "My birth father is Stephen Blair. Connor is my half brother."

His soft expletive bounced off the walls, but she barely winced, just turned back to the elevator doors, staring as the descending floor numbers lit up.

"Apparently Stephen had an affair with his housekeeper's daughter and I was the result." Her mouth thinned. "This was after my mum discovered she had motor neuron and decided not to have kids."

"And where's the housekeeper now?"

"They paid her off and she moved back to New Zealand. She died a few years ago."

He scowled.

"So they adopted you? Why keep it a secret? And how?"

"They went to the States for a year to hide the fact

my mother couldn't get pregnant." She sighed. "Stephen begged my father not to say anything—gave him the whole 'my wife will divorce me, my life will be ruined, the company will suffer' spiel. Dad agreed."

"And your dad just told you this voluntarily."

"Well, not at first." Her mouth thinned.

He paused, digesting that information.

"So are you going to tell Connor?"

The doors slid open and they walked through the elegant marble and crystal ground floor. "If you were him, would you want to know?"

He nodded. "Yes, I would. What about Stephen? Are you going to tell him you know?"

She remained silent as they pushed through the turnstile doors out onto George Street.

"I don't know." Her expression tightened. "I think it's a fair bet to say he won't care."

"Yeah." He glanced around then leaned in. "Whatever you decide, if you tell Connor—things always have a way of getting out." At her look, he added, "I'm not saying any of us would deliberately say anything. But the more people who know, the higher the chances."

She nodded then cast a casual glance up then down the busy Brisbane street, scanning the people going about their day. He noticed one or two do a double take as they passed, and he knew it was Kat they recognized and not him. The pull of her celebrity still amazed him, even after nearly a year of absence from the headlines.

Except that would soon end, and in spectacular fashion. His network had already fielded a handful of calls about his whereabouts during the cyclone, and he knew Kat had hired a publicist to issue a statement. Plus there was that thing with Grace, who was still on her case about an exclusive. After she announced her pregnancy, the press would start to piece things together, and then the nightmare would really start.

He suppressed a groan, remembering what it had been like the last time for her. All that stress, all that anxiety. Outwardly she'd handled it with aplomb, but he knew firsthand how much damage it had caused on the inside to her confidence, her self-esteem.

Not good for the baby.

They walked into the parking station, paid for the ticket and then made their way to his car, both wrapped up in their own thoughts until he glanced at his watch. Three hours before their flight.

With a frown he turned to face her, leaning against the door.

"Kat."

"Marco," she said in the same serious tone. God, he'd missed her humor. These past few days had drained him to the point that he wondered if things would ever get back to normal again.

He just wanted to see her smile again. Was that too much to ask?

"You don't have to do this, you know. You could just issue a statement then move into my place for a few weeks, until it blows over."

She stared at him for a moment and then slowly shook her head. "I have a job, Marco."

"One that Grace is making very difficult, so you said."

"She's angry. I understand that."

He let out a breath. "So if you're not going to take my suggestion or give Grace her exclusive, then tell me again why getting married would be a bad thing?"

Her expression twisted, telling him it was precisely the wrong thing to say. "Marco, please…"

He sighed. "Look, I'm trying to wrap my head around this and work out the best way to deal with everything."

"And you think I'm not?" She scowled. "My head is a mess. My life is…crazy. And my past, everything I just assumed was real? Gone. All thirty-three years of it." She slashed her eyes away from him, her frustration palpable. "Asking me to marry you is—"

An audible gasp interrupted her, and they both whirled to find two girls, shopping bags forgotten at their feet, busily clicking away with their cell phones.

One of them jiggled on the spot, a wide grin on her face. "Ohmygod, are you guys getting *married?* That is so awesome!"

Click, click, click.

Marco flushed, his hand instinctively going up to shield his face as he glanced to Kat, but she'd already moved and was yanking open the car door. She scrambled inside a moment later, and after he quickly joined her, he fired up the engine and they pulled out of the car park.

Her soft curse in the still air said it all, as did her glare in the rearview mirror. "That was—"

"Probably nothing," he said, taking the next turn to get them onto the highway. "A couple of fans."

"A couple of fans with cell phones and social media at their disposal," she muttered, glaring out the window, her face tight with emotion. Just as during the times before, he knew exactly what she was thinking.

Here we go again.

The phone calls, the questions, the borderline stalking. Her family getting hassled. Photographers camped on her doorstep, at work, at the gym. TV and radio dissecting and analyzing their every move, offering expert damage control.

And there wasn't a damn thing he could do about it.

"Kat…" he said now, but she quickly held up a hand and made a call.

"The press statement will be out today, for whatever good that'll do me," she said when she hung up.

"Maybe it's not that bad."

She gave him an "Oh, really?" look. "Trust me, something will show up."

He couldn't argue with that.

They drove another twenty minutes in silence, until they finally pulled into the airport parking station and Marco turned to her.

"I have to be in Darwin tomorrow," he said.

She glanced from the window to meet his eyes. "Oh?"

He nodded. "One of the remote coaching clinics I set up. We're doing a grand opening with the mayor."

"When are you back?"

"In a few days. I fly in Monday."

She nodded. "Okay."

"Listen, Kat, I don't want to leave you in the middle of this, but I also have a thing in Melbourne, then Sydney. I won't be back until the day before the FFA awards."

She shrugged. "It's okay."

"No, it's not." Her cavalier attitude irritated him—as if she expected his absence.

"I have an appointment for an ultrasound next week," she added.

Damn. He scowled. "Why didn't you tell me?"

"I'm telling you now."

He frowned. "I could've rescheduled."

She gave him a look. "Not when you're booked months in advance. And anyway, it's only an ultra-sound."

He dragged a hand through his hair. "I'm not abandoning you, Kat."

"I know. But until I make a public announcement, I think we should keep you out of it, don't you?"

He gritted his teeth and grabbed the handle, swinging the door wide. "No, I bloody well don't. Honestly, this is getting ridiculous. There comes a time when you just have to say, 'What the hell,' ignore what everyone says about you and live your life."

He got out of the car, slammed the door and, with long-legged strides, headed into the airport terminal, Kat following. And thanks to that little encounter earlier, he spent the whole time surreptitiously glancing around at the crowd, wondering if someone somewhere was taking photos, eavesdropping on their conversation. It was bloody unnerving.

Finally they made it through departures, past the check-in counter and into Qantas's private VIP lounge, which consisted of a bar, dining area, plush lounges and a communications center. They settled in and ordered drinks and food, but otherwise the silence stretched out between them. Marco checked his phone. Kat opened her iPad for her mail. Still not a word.

Was this how a friendship ended? he thought as he stared at his phone screen. Not with a spectacular all-out screaming match, but in a forced silence so uncomfortable she couldn't even bring herself to look at him.

It wasn't an argument. They didn't hate each other. He just… She just…

She didn't want to marry him. And he wanted her to.

He scowled at his phone. They had nineteen years between them, and he was damned if he'd let her push him out of her life. Once they dealt with this current situation, they'd have a serious talk about everything—including marriage.

It must've been some kind of record. Barely a day later, their "marriage proposal" hit social media, then the national papers, spreading out what could have just been a one-off article into a planned series on celebrity weddings and divorces, which were advertised with annoying regularity on TV. Marco and Kat were, of course, given plenty of airtime through the media, and, with the tabloid press, including the TV networks, setting up camp at her home, she'd had to hire a driver to take her to and from work.

Some photos still managed to leak out—one of her getting out of the car at the station. One when she'd not quite closed her curtains all the way. And some old cringe-worthy celebrity shots of her in full party mode.

That last one had been published two days ago, and she hadn't heard from Marco since. A dozen times she'd picked up the phone, ready to call, but stopped herself every time. It was something they needed to talk about face-to-face, not get into over the phone.

Of course, Grace had been mega-pissed about the attention, and the pressure at work had been high, compounding her stress about her family issues. After each day of her Job from Hell, she'd come home and collapsed on the sofa, finally allowing herself to think about the whole adoption thing, not to mention where to start finding out if her biological mother had had family, which in turn would be *her* family.

How did you tell someone you were his sister? Granted, it was Connor, one of her closest friends, but still. She wanted to do it right.

Armed with a laptop and a bowl of cereal, she crawled into bed and started on some research. Thanks to a bunch of online forums and chat rooms, she'd gathered heaps of information, read about people in similar situations and how they'd gone about connecting with their biological family.

That evening, after she'd bookmarked the last site and closed down the laptop for the night, her mind swung back to the physical part of her reality. In less than seven months, she'd be having a baby. The appointment she'd scheduled for next week loomed on the horizon, and suddenly her body went prickly with nervous tension.

She curled up in the bed, gently sweeping a hand over her belly. An official appointment. In writing. Out there.

It was really happening.

And Marco would be away for it.

She squeezed her eyes shut, refusing to let the guilt get to her. There was nothing she could do, right? He couldn't reschedule everything for her. It was as she'd said—just an ultrasound. There'd be plenty more opportunities for him to be involved.

Except she'd told him she didn't want him to be.

Did she even know what she wanted anymore?

Unable to answer that question, Kat buried herself in her work the next day, in the frantic energy of detailing Cyclone Rory's tragic path and sourcing stories that were all too depressingly bountiful now. Yet during their regular staff meeting when they argued the merits of each story and rearranged and reworked them for maximum viewer impact, she couldn't help but refocus on Marco's suggestion to follow her own dream.

A charity. A foundation where she would be in control, raise money and see each case through to completion from beginning to end.

So she began drafting a list, slowly filling in more details until she had two pages of handwritten notes. That night, during her usual hour on the treadmill, she reorganized it all in her head, until she finally had a semblance of a game plan. And the more she thought about it, the more excited she became. She'd even reached for her phone, eager to discuss it with Marco, but ended up balking at the last minute.

He was obviously busy, which was why he hadn't called.

She pressed the end button on the treadmill and grabbed her bottle, downing half the water as she cooled down. As amazing as it had been, the stupid sex thing had ruined it. She was thinking like a woman in a relationship, not as a best friend. Best friends didn't care who called whom first—they just *called*. They didn't stress about how many days, hours, minutes had passed since they'd spoken. And they certainly didn't let the other person get away with such a lengthy silence.

Just as she finally stepped off the treadmill and picked up her phone, it rang.

It was Connor. "Hey, stranger," she answered, way too cheerfully, as she grabbed her towel and walked into the kitchen.

"What are you doing tomorrow?" he asked.

"Saturday?" She jammed her phone under her chin then flicked on the hot water jug. "Oh, the usual. Watching TV. Eating by myself. Hiding from the hundreds of paparazzi camped on my doorstep."

"Where's Marco?"

"Swanning around in Darwin, I believe."

There was a pause as he picked up on her tone. "Did you guys have a fight?"

Kat sighed. "No, we are having…a difference of opinion."

"Anything to do with this engagement thing the press is going crazy with?"

She walked slowly back to her lounge room, clicked on the TV and muted the sound. "Partly. I just…" She sighed. "It's complicated. The baby. This press thing. Work. And I feel guilty that his appearances have been overshadowed by the media craving a sound bite. Did you know someone actually asked him about us during a ribbon cutting yesterday?"

"The press is full of idiots. Which is why I'm coming to see you."

She perched on the edge of her lounge. "If that were the real reason, you'd have come to see me way earlier than this."

His chuckle brightened her mood. "We'll lounge around and ignore the press together, eat pizza and watch *The X-Files*."

She couldn't help but smile. "Sounds divine."

"Or, you know, we could just go to Marco's island. Plenty of privacy there."

"God, don't you start. Next they'll be hooking you and me up instead of Marco."

He laughed again. "I dunno—I do like the sound of 'Kitco.' Much better than 'Markat.'"

"Shut up." When he laughed, she reluctantly joined him. "You're an idiot, Connor."

"Shh, don't tell anyone. You'll ruin my reputation."

She was still grinning when she hung up. Yes, her emotions were all over the place, and she had too many questions to ask and no idea how to approach Stephen... if she even wanted to. Frankly, the man scared the hell out of her and always had. But the one thing she had no issue with was accepting Connor as her brother. She loved him like a brother. More, actually, because she'd had years to appreciate him as a friend without any pressure or family obligation. As she walked down the corridor to the bathroom, she had to admit that she was looking forward to telling him. She had no idea how he'd react, but hopefully he'd feel the same way.

The next night, barely thirty minutes after she made it through her door with a relieved sigh, her intercom beeped.

"Chez Jackson?"

"I heard someone's having a pizza party."

She grinned at Connor's commanding voice. "Yep. With beer and juggling monkeys."

"I'm so there."

She buzzed him up and then unlocked the door. He stepped through the door five minutes later with an overnight bag, a steaming-hot Crust pizza and a huge grin.

"You are my savior." She hugged him then took the pizza and stepped back to allow him entry. He strode in with his usual lanky gait, his broad frame filling her space.

He dumped his bag near the couch. "Midnight must be a bit late for the paparazzi. I didn't see anyone about."

She shoved the pizza on the coffee table. "Oh, they're there—you just can't see them. Like cockroaches."

His laughter followed her as she went into the kitchen to get drinks and plates. When she emerged, he was scowling at his phone.

"What's up?" she asked.

"Everyone's got marriage on the brain." Connor slowly placed his phone on the table and sprawled on her couch. "My mother's been bugging me about it. Apparently a successful thirty-three-year-old guy needs a wife to appear more stable to our conservative European investors."

Kat patted his hand sympathetically. "Well, between Marco and me, I can honestly say it's not what it's cracked up to be."

Connor snorted. "Yeah. Two apiece, right?"

"I'm two. Marco is one and a half."

Connor centered a coaster on the table and placed his beer bottle on it. "So is there any truth to the rumors?"

"Which ones?" She flopped down on the single-couch chair.

"The marriage ones. Because everyone's waiting for the real press statement, you know, not the lame 'no comment' one."

"I know." She fixed him with a look. "Yes," she said at length.

"Yes, what? Marco actually asked you to marry him?"

"A few times, yes."

His breath came out in a whoosh. "Wow. And?"

Kat shook her head. "He only offered to avoid the nightmare PR—which is ironic, considering we're in the middle of it anyway. I haven't even announced I'm pregnant yet, so imagine what that'll do," she said as she flipped open the pizza lid and inhaled deeply. "Anyway, enough about that. I've got something more important to talk to you about. I need to—"

"Hang on, reverse." He leaned in. "More important than you being happy?"

"What?"

He sighed. "Can you not see it?"

"See what?"

He thumped a palm on the table. "You and Marco. You're perfect for each other."

Kat felt the tingle of embarrassment all the way down her spine, her eyes quickly darting away. "It's not like that, Connor. He's my—"

"Best friend, yeah, yeah, I know." Connor rolled his eyes. "You've both been preaching that old chestnut for so long, I'm ready to strangle someone. Why don't you guys just admit you love each other and put yourselves out of your misery?"

"I do love him, Connor. I love you, too."

He grinned. "Ditto, sweetheart. But you're not *in love* with me."

She frowned, the denial on her tongue, but instead she just pressed her lips together. "Look, forget that for a moment. I need to talk to you about something." She leaned in, hands tucked between her knees. "You know how I went for that blood test last month?"

Connor paused, midchew. "Yeah?" At her look he slowly placed the pizza on the plate, wiped his hands on a napkin and gave her his full attention. "Ah, Kat, don't tell me they got it wrong again...."

"No, nothing like that," she said quickly. "Okay, so the reason why my test was clear was...because... well..." It was still unbelievable, no matter how many times she tried to process it. Saying it aloud only made it more real. "Keith and Nina aren't my biological parents."

A deathly silence permeated her apartment.

Connor's brow dipped. "What?"

"I had a blood test. Nina and Keith are not my biological parents," she repeated patiently.

Connor's jaw dropped, eyes rounding. "No way."

Kat nodded. "It's true. My blood type and Mum's aren't compatible. Then we flew down to see my dad and he confirmed it."

"We? Marco went with you?"

She nodded. "And there's more."

He huffed out a breath. "Jeez, what?"

Kat smiled. "Connor..." She held his gaze unwaveringly. "My father is Stephen Blair."

Everything was still for a few seconds, maybe more, until Connor's loud bark of laughter split the air like a shot and she jumped. Frowning, she watched in silence as he sat there, chuckling and shaking his head. What did that mean? Was he...upset? Happy? Freaked out?

"Are you okay?" she finally said after a few moments.

He shot to his feet. "No, actually. Give me a moment."

She watched him pace, with one hand running through his hair, the other on his hip. It was worrying, not knowing if he'd taken the news as a good thing or not.

Finally, after a few interminable minutes, he turned to her. "You know, I just knew it was something like this. I *knew* it."

"What?"

He paused, taking in her expression, and shook his head. "About ten years ago, I caught the tail end of an argument. Couldn't hear much but I did eventually work out Mum and Dad were talking about a child. Oh, I didn't realize at the time that it was you," he hastened to add. "I never would've worked that one out."

She blinked. "What did they say?"

"Well, Mum was pretty pissed off—that was clear. Dad didn't want to talk about it, as usual. Then after, Mum ended up with a new Prada handbag and a necklace from Paspaley, and everything just seemed like normal."

Kat sat back in her chair, processing that information. "You didn't say anything about it to us."

Connor gave her a look. "I don't tell you guys everything."

True. Connor was extremely private when it came to his family—it had taken years for him to share even the most basic of details. It was only because they'd witnessed his parents' arguments firsthand that they knew about them at all. It was a deep source of embarrassment for him.

"Mum's always going on about Dad's affairs. You know that," he said now, picking absently at the label on his beer bottle.

Kat nodded, her expression solemn.

"So I overheard a bit more than usual. Apparently my mother still hasn't forgiven him for being in bed with another woman the day I was born."

Kat's mouth thinned. Connor projected such a hard and capable facade that people refused to believe there was a heart of gold under that swish Armani suit and classically handsome face. She knew that mask was to protect him from feeling too deeply, but she'd known him long enough to realize that he sometimes felt more than any of them put together.

"My sister, huh?" he said now, taking another swig of beer with a smile. "How do you feel about that?"

She was his sister. She had a *brother*. With everything else going on in her life, she'd pushed the impact of that detail to the back of her mind, but now, faced with a grinning Connor and the familiar way his eyes creased, the easily recognizable sweep of his nose, it was unmistakable.

She felt her mouth stretch into an answering grin. "Do we need to hug to mark this momentous occasion?"

"Hell, yeah." When he opened his arms, she got up, moved toward him and was enveloped in his embrace. The relief, the utter joy she felt at this moment, when it had just been bad news after bad news, was like a weight off her shoulders. She leaned into the hug, into his solid, hard warmth, and felt the tears well up. She couldn't believe how happy this actually made her.

Damn pregnancy hormones.

"Are you going to tell your dad that you know?" she asked, muffled against his shoulder.

He pulled back with a grimace. "I have no idea. After all these years of keeping the secret, do you think he'd want us to know? Plus, it could create a backlash with yours."

She nodded. "And it doesn't really change anything, him knowing, does it? I mean, I'm not going to demand in on the will or anything."

Connor laughed. "But it would be fun to call him Grandad in seven months' time." He glanced pointedly at her belly.

"You're terrible."

He laughed again, and again she felt the burden of the past few weeks shift.

Finally, something was going right. If only she could fix things with Marco.

Her expression must've given something away, because Connor's brow suddenly creased.

"Problem?"

"Oh, besides the gossip, pregnancy hormones and the fact Marco won't speak to me?"

"Well, you're not exactly speaking to *him,* are you?"

She opened her mouth to deny it but wisely closed it instead. "Plus his network contract's up for negotiation, so naturally they're speculating on that, too."

"They won't drop him. He's too much of a draw." Connor leaned back, cradling his beer with a small smile.

"What's that look for?"

"It's awesome you two are finally a couple. I always knew there was something, despite your denials."

"Connor, we're not. We're not speaking."

"Only because he's not here. Wait until you guys see each other again…next week, right?"

"Yes. At the awards thing."

"There you go. You'll be in Sydney, in a hotel. A

perfect opportunity to talk alone." When Kat remained silent, he impatiently tapped a finger against his bottle. "Listen. Is moping around with a head full of what-ifs better? No. Just say you love him, then kiss and make up."

"But I don't—"

"Sure you do."

"No…" *Yeah. You do.*

It was like a revelation. As if something fundamental had changed deep inside her. The false positive, the adoption, the baby had all added bit by bit to this moment, forcing her to see what was truly important in her life. To reassess again, to work out what was of true value to her.

The answer was so blindingly simple she gasped from the impact.

Marco. He was the one.

She sighed. "I told him we're just friends a few times, Connor," she said softly, voicing the doubt that had plagued her the past few days. "Surely there comes a time when he actually takes me at my word."

"You're talking about Marco here," Connor said. "And anyway, you're his best friend and you're having a baby together. He can't cut you out of his life permanently."

Kat nodded, saying nothing. Three times she'd pushed him back into the friends zone, and three times he'd not put up a fight.

Surely that said something?

She sighed, leaning back into the sofa. Either way, she'd have her answer next week.

She took a shaky breath. This was scary, so much scarier than anything she'd ever done in her life. Because in laying everything out there, there was a real possibility of rejection.

He could reject her. Say he just wanted to remain friends. And the question was, would she be satisfied with that?

Ten

The next five days were a crazy, breathless mess of activity. Kat was flat out at work, working on the Cyclone Rory stories, the follow-ups, the charity lines, but the overwhelming media attention on her personal life had started to impact on her work, with some sponsors severing their partnership at the last minute, leaving her frustrated and angry. Outwardly, Grace didn't seem overly concerned, but Kat knew she was furious. Couple that with their already cool tension, and work was not a pleasant place to be.

Marco had managed to call her once, the day of her ultrasound, but other than that, their texts had been short and sweet. And it broke Kat's heart, knowing their friendship was showing those irreversible cracks.

Finally something had to give. So the day before she

was due to fly to Sydney, she walked into Grace's office and firmly closed the door.

"I'll do it."

"Do what?" Grace asked, glancing up from stirring her morning coffee.

"The interview. An exclusive." She quickly put up a hand as Grace started to speak. "But everything—and I mean *everything*—has to go past me first."

Grace blinked slowly, then her face broke out into a huge grin as she shot to her feet. "Kat, this is brilliant! Wonderful! Oooooh…" She rounded the desk and embraced her in a cloud of perfume. "This has made my week…my month—hell, possibly my entire year!" Kat slowly pulled away, smiling thinly as her boss perched on the corner of her desk, beaming. "Can I ask you why now?"

Kat shrugged. "Timing. It's the right time."

Grace paused, watching her closely. "Really."

"Yep. Time to set the record straight once and for all. About everything." She met her boss's gaze unwaveringly, and in that small pause, an understanding passed between them, one that needed no words. This was Grace's moment and Kat was giving it to her. They both knew there'd never be another opportunity, just as they both knew things had fundamentally changed between them these past few weeks.

She knew it and Grace knew it.

"When?" Grace finally asked.

"Next week. After Sydney."

After another moment's pause, her boss nodded. "I'll set it up and let you know."

"Okay. And can you wait until after the awards before you start publicizing? The night should be about the players, not me," she added with a thin smile.

To her surprise, Grace nodded. "Sure."

"Thanks." Kat moved toward the door, unprepared for the wave of sadness that engulfed her. They both knew it wasn't just an interview date they were setting: it was Kat's quitting date, too.

Even knowing she was moving on to something bigger and better, something that really made her heart sing, didn't make leaving hurt any less. Despite the stress, the imperfections and the recent personal issues, this job had come at a perfect time, when she'd needed it the most. She'd always be grateful for that.

"Grace," she said now. "I want to thank you for—"

"No." The older woman shook her head, smiling softly as she reached for her ringing phone. "I thank *you*. It's been a pleasure working with you, Katerina Jackson."

Their gazes held for a moment, then Grace answered her call and it was Kat's cue to leave.

Kat flew into Sydney on Saturday and spent all day getting massaged, primped and fussed over, satisfied she'd gained at least some control over the spiraling situation. Meanwhile, Marco spent hours under harsh studio lights dressed in nothing but his underwear, fulfilling his Skins contract, so the first time they actually saw each other was half an hour before the limo picked them up for the FFA awards ceremony.

When she heard the knock at her hotel door, she nervously smoothed down her pale blue satin dress and pushed her hair behind her ears. All the half sentences she'd barely had time to practice crumbled on her tongue when she opened the door and saw him standing there, looking incredible and perfect in a designer suit and tie, his hair casually tousled and a familiar this'll-be-fun smile on his generous mouth.

His eyes swept over her thoroughly, taking in every last detail from her tight elaborate updo, to the dangling earrings and the strappy floor-length ice-blue ball gown with a respectable amount of ever-growing cleavage on show.

Then he held out his arm, said softly, "You look beautiful," and her heart just melted.

Twenty minutes later, stepping out of the limo onto the red carpet together, Kat took a moment to note the familiar players currently in European competition, now all returned for this special night that honored Australian-born sportsmen and women. As usual a smattering of die-hard and local fans stood behind the roped barriers, taking photos, and she felt her mouth curve, her expression calm.

She was ready to face the crowd.

She spent minutes gaining more confidence, her tension relaxing as she mingled with people she knew, chatting casually to old acquaintances.

This was going to be a good night, she thought as they made their way slowly down the carpet. No intrusive press, no focus on her. Just dinner and the awards. Yet as she turned, midsmile, and saw a familiar figure stride across the carpet, she faltered.

James Carter. James Bloody Carter.

Marco's former Marseille teammate, the Irish-born center who'd charmed her for over a year then convinced her to get married in a quickie Bali wedding. Then had promptly shagged some woman in their bridal suite seventy-two hours later.

It was too much to expect that he'd gotten fat and ugly in the years since she'd last seen him. If anything he was more handsome, more toned. Broader in the shoulders, leaner at the waist. His flashy suit set off a healthy physique so discreetly that to the untrained eye it might have seemed effortless. Kat knew better.

"What?" Marco was squeezing her arm, and she glanced up to see the concern in his face.

"James is here."

His mouth twisted briefly. "Really?"

She frowned, ignoring the fact they were on a red carpet with cameras within recording distance. "Wasn't he supposed to be in Italy or something?"

"Yeah." He took a step forward and they kept on walking. "Look, he's just a presenter. He'll be onstage most of the time, not at our table. He won't come over, and if he does, just say nothing."

"Easy for you to say. He's not the one who cheated on you."

Marco sighed. "Just...be cool, okay?"

She snorted. "I am *always* cool."

"Uh-huh."

He squeezed her hand, she grinned at him, and suddenly it was just as it was before, where they'd been so familiar, so close. So comfortable.

Damn, she missed that. It'd been three weeks since she'd seen him, and boy, she hadn't realized how much she'd missed him until he'd turned up at her door dressed in a formal suit and one of his expensive silk ties. And when he'd smiled...it had taken a massive effort not to tackle him then and there.

Now, with the heat rising in her belly, she glanced around at the smattering of people who'd stopped to rubberneck, the long red carpet that led into the plush foyer and the familiar faces of Sydney's football community. With a deep breath, she put on a smile and firmly shoved everything else from her mind. This was Marco's night, and she should just enjoy it. There was time enough for stress and worry later.

The ballroom easily seated two hundred and was elegantly decorated, with tiny blue downlights in the ceiling casting a cool glow over the round banquet tables. The tables themselves featured art deco–style centerpieces. People hovered around the bar, and a slide show above the stage was playing highlights of the past season backed by a classic-rock sound track.

Surprisingly, despite the presence of cameras and James, Kat was less tense than she thought she'd be. For one, the evening was about the awards and the players, not her. There were no intrusive questions or random photos or the usual stares-and-whispers from complete strangers. Sure, there were cameras, but she could smile nicely and handle a few shots. And as long as James kept his distance like he'd been doing for the past hour, she'd make it through the night unscathed.

She smoothed her gown down, thankful for the flowing empire style that hid her growing belly, only just managing to stop herself before placing a telling hand on the thirteen-week-old bump as she walked over to the bar. Even though this was a private function and she was fairly relaxed, everyone was still equipped with a camera and a Twitter account.

After she reached the bar and ordered drinks, she casually scanned the room, a small smile on her lips. A smile that immediately fell when she felt a guy standing way too close behind her. She frowned, preparing to say something, but when she glanced back, all the words just stuck in her throat.

"Hi there, Kitty."

James Carter was standing there, all casual as you please, hands in his pockets, face creased into a charming grin. After darting her gaze around to see who was watching—and seeing the coast was clear—she sent him a withering look.

"What do you want?"

James's smile was perfect—too perfect. "What—no hello? No 'how've you been these last few years?'" His faint Irish accent oozed over her like thick molasses, bringing with it a wealth of conflicting memories.

"I have nothing to say to you, James," she snapped.

His mouth quirked. "Is that any way to greet a long-lost—"

"A long-lost what? A friend?" She snorted. "Let's call it like it is. You're my cheating ex—a drinking and gambling ex with a serious money-management problem."

"Kitty, darlin'…" His expression was pained. "Don't be like that. I didn't come over here to rehash old wounds."

"Don't call me that." She frowned. "So why? You want to give people *more* to talk about?"

"No." He drew a slow hand over his eyes. "But you're kind of a one-woman pap magnet—the magazines and papers are all over you. I flew in for the awards and—"

"I'm not interested in your life," Kat interrupted, turning back to the bar.

As she waited for her order, she could feel his scrutiny. *Dammit, don't take the bait. Just ignore him, and then go back to Marco. Ignore it, ignore it. Ignore—*

With a sigh, she turned to him. "Fine. What do you want, James?"

"Forgiveness."

Kat blinked. "Sorry. Fresh out of that."

James took a step closer, and instinctively she stepped back against the bar. He winced. "Believe me, Ki-Kat. I'm truly sorry."

"Are you."

"Yes."

Kat flushed. "Well, 'sorry' doesn't cut it."

"What do you want me to say?"

"Nothing. Absolutely nothing." She nodded to the barman and then took the drinks.

"You know, after the divorce I spent a year working my way down to rock bottom," he began stiffly, following her as she made her way across the room. "I got into a car accident, spent forever in rehab. I'm a completely different person now."

She stopped. "I know. I read all about it." Briefly she recalled the headlines, the shock then relief she'd felt at reading about his struggles. "But I don't see what this has to do with me."

"I told you. I want to make amends."

"Fine. You've apologized. Now I'm going."

"Wait." His hand shot out, grabbing her elbow, and she stilled, staring at him.

Slowly he withdrew then self-consciously looked around at the clusters of noisy people milling about the room.

"You can't expect absolution just because you ask for it. This is so typical of you, James." She scowled.

"So selfish. I was your trophy girlfriend and then you cheated on me. There's no forgiving that."

"I know." His expression dropped, and for a second he looked genuinely contrite. "I can't excuse my past behavior."

"No, you can't."

She moved off, hoping he'd get the hint, but still he followed, until she got to her table and she finally put the drinks down.

James's mouth thinned in frustration. "You never let me explain. I wanted to talk on our honeymoon, but you stormed off. And anyway, you weren't such a saint yourself."

"What?"

"Yeah. You had this chip on your shoulder the size of Alaska. You carried around your toughness as if it were some goddamn bravery badge, instead of the defense it really was. And I always had to compete with Marco. The perfect, do-no-wrong, everybody-loves-me Marco Corelli."

"He is my *best friend!*"

"Really. Can you swear, right here and right now, that you never thought of him as more?"

"Of course not!" But she'd hesitated a second too long, and the look on James's face said it all.

"Did you sleep with him?"

She sucked in a sharp breath, gaze darting to the people around them. "Oh, my God, James, I am so not doing this with you. This is ridiculous!"

He glared at her, his handsome face twisted into angry lines, until he finally let out a breath, hand going to the back of his neck. "Look," he muttered, his gaze firmly on the floor. "I didn't come here to argue. I just wanted to—"

"You okay, Kat?"

Kat whirled, the words dying on her lips as her eyes collided with the steel of Marco's at the same time his arm looped loosely around her waist.

She was so stunned by the suddenly intimate gesture that she totally forgot to step away, to create a more platonic space between them. And Marco… Well, it was as if someone had cast a spell and turned him to stone, he was so still. Yet beneath that stillness, that cold expression, Kat could sense his body coiled as if he was ready to spring into action any second.

Dangerous.

"James," Marco finally said, his voice low and painfully polite.

James looked startled but swiftly recovered, holding out his hand. "Hi, Marco."

Marco slowly and pointedly looked at it and remained where he was. "Congratulations on your award. Player of the Year is quite an achievement."

James shot Kat a look of part frustration, part wariness. "Thank you."

She had to hand it to him—her ex was smooth. From the top of his expensively shaggy haircut to the soles of his shiny black dress shoes, the man had all the right props. He was someone who used charm and looks to get what he wanted.

When he flashed a perfect let's-all-be-friends-now smile, she couldn't suppress one of her own. *Oh, you're good, aren't you? So smooth. And Marco can see right through that.*

"So, Kat," James was saying, "we need to talk some more. I'm in room fourteen-oh-five."

"She won't be coming," Marco cut in smoothly before she could reply.

She gave him an irritated look then turned to James. "We've got nothing to discuss, James. End of story."

James scowled, his eyes going from Marco back to her. "Whatever you might think, Kat, I'd like to smooth out our differences. Start a clean slate."

A pause. Then, "Do you have a hearing problem?" Marco asked coolly.

"Butt out, Marco," James snapped. "This is between me and my wife."

"Ex-wife. She's my fiancée now. Oh, please, be my guest," he murmured as the other man clenched his fists.

"Fiancée? So you guys *are* getting married?" James's eyes widened, his gaze darting from Marco to her. "Huh. Guess that confirms things, then." As Marco bristled, he pulled himself up to his full six foot five and glared back.

Oh, for heaven's sake. It was like watching two dogs snarl and growl over a bone.

"No, we're not." She couldn't believe Marco had said the *F* word.

With a snort she moved out of Marco's embrace. "Okay, you need to leave now, James."

James sighed. "Look—" he stuck his hands on his hips "—I didn't want to do this here, but you leave me no choice. I've been asked to write my biography, a kind of inspirational, overcoming-the-odds thing. And I can't do it without mentioning you."

She sucked in a breath. "No."

James eyed Marco then came back to her. "Like it

or not, Kat, you were a part of my life. I'd like your approval on the chapter, but I can still publish it without your consent."

"James…" She took a deep breath, waiting for her brain to catch up. She could sue him, but that would take money and time, plus attract more attention to the book than it was worth. Or…

"If I don't like what I read, can I change it?"

"It depends what it is. But sure." He nodded. "I'm open to amendments."

That didn't mean a thing, but it was all he was offering. With a short nod, she said, "Fine. Email me the chapter when you have it."

James nodded and his mouth tweaked, a hint of what she used to think was the most devastating smile in the French soccer league.

She watched him leave in silence, her mind still halfway in the past. But at the last minute, as he was walking by the video tripod that had been filming the night, he abruptly turned.

"Congratulations on getting engaged," he called loudly, causing a few conversations to halt. "I knew that press release was a smoke screen—very clever. I hope you'll be happy. For what it's worth, I could totally see it coming."

A dozen people in earshot quickly turned to first James, then to Marco and Kat, and all of a sudden a chorus of cheery woo-hoos erupted.

No. Oh, no.

Kat's stomach bottomed out yet she refused to let it show. She simply shook her head at the closest group of well-wishers. "We're not… No, we haven't…"

Too late. The damage was done.

Embarrassment leached into a low, slow burn, one

that tightened her back, then her neck. She gritted her teeth, smilingly denied everything and stalked through the crowd, straight for the doors leading outside.

A handful of curses ran through her mind as she went. Damn James. Grace's exclusive was supposed to set everything straight, but now he'd gone and ruined it. Which meant they'd have to bring the interview forward.

Just as she dug out her phone and was about to reach the balcony doors, Marco grabbed her arm. "Kat. Stop."

"Marco…" She was barely holding it together, and his concern only tipped the scales.

She turned slowly to him with a dark frown. "Your fiancée?"

Marco shrugged, eyeing the people passing them by and giving them a casual nod. "I thought he needed a little encouragement to leave."

"With a lie?"

Marco studied her for a heartbeat. Then he said, "What upsets you more—the unwanted attention or me staking a claim?"

"You've no right to claim anything."

"Not even when you're having our baby?" he murmured.

Kat put a hand to the wall for support. Now that she was alone with Marco, she could no longer hold the memories at bay. They all came rushing back, making her skin heat and her head spin with remembrance. His lips and what they'd done to her. His warm breath, teasing her skin. And his wonderful hands, hands he now shoved aggressively in his pants pockets.

"Do you have any idea what this is going to do?" she said tightly. "How people are going to—"

"Going to what? Gossip?" A hand dived into his hair. "Christ, Kat, I'm really sick of hearing about it. I'm trying to help but you keep saying no. Stop complaining when you know you could fix it with one simple yes."

"Marco, this, on top of everything else…I just can't deal—"

"I know that." He leaned in, his face tight with anger. "I'm only guessing how things are for you because you haven't called, haven't wanted to discuss anything. It's like trying to get information from a goalpost."

She blinked, frowning. "Marco, I…"

"Look, this isn't the right place to talk," he said, curling his fingers around her wrist. "Let's go."

The automatic refusal was there, but she quickly swallowed it, giving him a brief nod. And when he turned and began to lead her firmly through the crowd, her breath quickened in anticipation.

This was it. They'd finally put it all out there. It would either be the end of their relationship or the beginning of one.

God, she was praying for the latter. Because the former would be like cutting a vital piece of her heart out.

There was no way she could do that. Ever.

Eleven

They stood in the middle of her hotel room barely ten minutes later, and as Kat watched him work his tie loose and slowly peel it off, everything just flew out of her mind.

It was incredible how her heart reacted to his presence. Her body just went all tingly, her blood heating as her eyes hungrily took in his broad frame, his strong cheekbones, his hair.

Everything.

When his gaze met hers, his expression was deadly serious. Not good.

He gestured. "You first."

She swallowed thickly. Could she honestly lay everything out in the open, finally? How on earth was she supposed to do that? Her nerves shook at the very thought.

And yet what was her alternative? Live with this painful ache, always wondering if things would have worked if she'd just had more courage to voice her feelings?

She barely had time to sort through her thoughts before he was right there, next to her, his expression unreadable.

She shoved her clutch onto the table and then threaded her fingers together, trepidation suddenly engulfing her. And all of a sudden she was left just staring at him, the words stuck in her throat. And that made her incredibly, annoyingly nervous.

"I'm waiting."

"I'm thinking."

"Okay." He crossed his arms and studied her, which made it that much worse.

"Stop looking at me!"

His eyes suddenly creased. "Sorry. Where would you like me to look?"

"Just... I don't know. Anywhere. The view." She waved to the window displaying a magnificent night panorama of Sydney Harbour. "You're making me nervous."

"That is not my intent, *chérie.*"

She sighed. "I know. Look, there are a lot of things I have to get through and I wanted to tell you face-to-face, so you might want to take a seat, okay?"

"Is it the baby? Is everything all right?"

"Yes, it's fine. Everything is fine there." She took a deep breath, one that shook on the exhalation. "I was just reading about your contract negotiations."

He shrugged. "You know how the press likes to beat things up."

"So you're not going to move back to France, then?"

"It's one of many options on the table right now," he said cautiously.

"Right."

She let the silence fall, chewing on the inside of her lip as she tried to gather the right words.

He crossed his arms with a frown. "Kat, this isn't you, always second-guessing your words. Just come out and say it."

He was right. She'd handled more than her fair share of difficult situations. She could do this now. However she'd planned to do this, whatever preparations she'd made, this was it. She had to tell him.

And yet…her determination just seemed to crumble, making everything ache from the gaping hole it left. She may want to, so very badly. But it wouldn't be right. Or fair. Not when she was desperately in love with him but he just saw her as his best friend and marriage as a way to handle her PR nightmare.

She didn't want to marry him when he wasn't in love with her. That wasn't selfish, right? It was noble. It was good. It meant she cared for him way too much to see him unhappy.

Even if it killed her inside.

God, she was killing him! Marco's control had gone from torn to shredded in the space of a few moments as he sat there, waiting for her to say something, until he'd finally had enough.

"Kat." When he got abruptly to his feet, her surprised gaze followed him, and for another few seconds he chewed over the words, discarding a dozen imperfect ones, until he finally came up with everything he needed to say. "I love you."

She stilled, eyes wide, expression frozen for one horrible second. Then she shot out a soft breath and her small smile ripped at his heart. "I love you, too."

"No," he repeated, dragging in a breath. *Suck it up and just finish it already.* "No, I really love you."

"And I—"

"Kat, you are not getting it." He shook his head, heart thudding. "I am *in love* with you. I want to marry you, but not because of some press stunt, or out of any moral obligation. I want to marry you because I am desperately and hopelessly in love with you. I want to be with you, but only if you want that, too."

Shock didn't begin to describe the look on her face. She just stood there, silent and gaping, and for one horrible moment every terrible rejection he'd ever faced came bubbling up to the surface.

Her soft groan, the twisted expression, cut him swift and deep, but he could do nothing but stand there, waiting with his heart laid bare, waiting for her to let him down gently.

"I…" She floundered, frowning, then took a ragged breath.

"Kat…" he said, hating the way his voice came out all husky. "Say something. Anything."

Her eyes closed briefly, then opened again, and in that gaze he saw the truth. "These last few months— hell, these last few weeks—have been crazy for me. A baby, a pregnancy, this whole adoption thing. My head's been in ten different places, and I'm sick of it. Nothing is perfect, Marco, and I've just realized it doesn't have to be."

He remained silent, giving her nothing until she finished saying what she needed to say. He didn't have long to wait.

"It's taken all of this to make me see what is truly important," she said slowly, as if it was a revelation to herself, too. And when she reached out and took his hand, he offered no resistance, just let her link her fingers through his, the intimate glide of skin on skin sending his heart racing.

"And that's you. I don't want to spend the rest of my life wishing I'd had enough courage to tell you how I really feel, and I don't want to spend another day without being with you, talking with you. Loving you. If that means I only get you six months of every year, then, by God, I want those six months to count."

He closed his eyes as if her words had somehow cut, and Kat held her breath, waiting, waiting as the seconds ticked over.

"Dieu."

When he finally opened his eyes, the expression there had her going weak at the knees.

And suddenly, he was dragging her in for a kiss, a deep, hungry kiss full of emotion and feeling and heat. She squeaked in surprise then opened up for him, her arms going around his neck.

"Kat," he finally murmured against her mouth, hands slowly stroking her hair. "God, do you know how much I missed you these last few weeks?" Then he groaned, capturing her mouth for another kiss, and she was sure she was going to die from the joy of it all.

When he finally broke away, the look on his face was unmistakable. *"Je t'adore, chérie."* He cupped her cheek in his hand, placing his mouth softly on the corner of hers. "I've loved you for such a long time, but you've been so damn stubborn and I—" His breath caught in a growl and he kissed her again, a little more desperate, a little more hungry.

She whimpered against his mouth, her body pressed hard against his, every single inch of her skin tingling with awareness.

He loved her. How was that even possible? After everything she'd been through, how on earth had she managed to score this amazing, wonderful guy—her best friend—as her lover, as well?

"Come here."

She led him into her bedroom then closed the door, her entire body beating out a loud pulse as her blood rushed to every corner. With a trembling hand she shoved her fingers under his shirt and swept the outline of his ribs. After she lifted his shirt, she followed with her lips, kissing softly.

She took a deep breath, trying to calm her nerves, but it only succeeded in filling her lungs with his unique scent. "You smell amazing."

His chuckle did crazy things to her gut. "Thanks. You don't smell so bad yourself."

She grinned against his skin, her lips grazing across his hip, her hand curling around the other. "Is that a murmur of appreciation I hear?"

"Yeah." His guttural response made her flush and smile. "Kat…"

"Yes?"

"Stop talking."

When she began to mouth her way slowly across to his navel, he groaned and relaxed back on the couch, her kisses flaming a path while she stroked his hip and he muttered in Italian. He had the most perfect voice. Perfect hands. Perfect everything.

"You're perfect," she muttered against his skin.

"No..." he ground out.

"Yes," she countered. "And this part, right here—" her hand skimmed over the defined muscular V-line flanking his hips, the Adonis belt "—is such a temptation."

"Yeah?" His breath came out in a rush as she continued to stroke.

"Yes. Just above your waistband. Drives me crazy every time."

"How crazy?"

"Like this." Quickly she unsnapped his jeans and placed her mouth on the spot, softly trailing her lips over the muscle, before heading back to the center, tracing the thin line of hair downward.

His sharp breath as she finally eased his jeans down fueled her already stoked fire. He raised his hips a little to help, and when she'd tossed his pants aside, she couldn't help but swallow thickly at the sight of him lying there.

Wanting *her*.

"Kat..." It was only one word, yet the raw vulnerability behind it made her heart contract.

She slid her hands up along his corded thighs, gripping his hips, and then took him in her mouth with firm command. When his hips bucked, she placed a steady hand on his stomach.

"Shh." She continued to pleasure him, reveling in the heady power and the wonderful hard-velvet feeling of having him in her mouth.

And when she felt his body finally tense, she stopped.

His gasp and obscene curse echoed loudly. "Kat? What the hell?"

She slid up, her naked body gliding against him, and she stopped to nibble on his bottom lip briefly before straddling him.

"Impatient," she muttered against his mouth.

"Tease."

"No way." Eyes locked on his, she positioned her hips then swiftly eased down on him with a sharp breath.

They moved together in perfect time, two people in love, experiencing joy in each other, reveling in the pure physical moment. And when everything just became too much, her emotions so overwhelming she couldn't take any more, her release crashed in a wave of pure ecstasy, leaving her trembling and spent. With a soft groan, Marco followed her, his arms wrapped tight, holding her in place as their damp bodies slid together as one.

The minutes ticked by, the thick air punctuated by their ragged breathing. Kat lay there, soaking up his heat, a thousand words on the tip of her tongue but reluctant to say a thing because she didn't want to shatter this most perfect moment.

But finally, as their bodies cooled and their heartbeats returned to normal, Marco glanced over at the clock on the bedside table and said, "Maybe we should be getting back to the ceremony…"

Kat followed his gaze. "I guess."

He chuckled. "So enthusiastic."

"Well, given the choice, I know where I'd rather be."

"I know how you feel."

They remained perfectly still, as the moment stretched.

"Marco…" Kat finally said. "I'm quitting my job."

A pause. "Really?"

She nodded, glancing up at him. "I'm going to start up a charity. Not sure what, yet. I'll think about it while I'm busy with being pregnant." She smiled faintly.

When his hand slid to her stomach, palm moving possessively over the gentle swell, her breath caught. Then he smiled and leaned down to kiss her, and everything just choked her up all over again.

"I don't want you to overdo things," he murmured softly against her mouth.

"I can hire people. Delegate."

He spent a few moments lazily kissing her. "So you really want to do it?"

"Do you think I *can* do it?"

"*Chérie,* you can do anything you want."

She basked in the warmth of his smile, until seconds passed and realization began to seep in.

"Sooooo…" she said softly. "About that marriage thing—"

"Yes?"

"Is the offer still on the table?"

He blinked. "No."

"What?" She frowned.

He cupped her face, brought her to his mouth in a gentle kiss. "It's not a business offer. I am asking you to be my wife. To be with me for the rest of our lives. To have my children, to make me happy and to let me make you happy. It's a marriage proposal made with love."

Oh. Breathless, all she could do was stare at him, at the tender look in his dark eyes, at the curve of his mouth. And she fell in love with him all over again.

That was…absolutely perfect. More than perfect.

It was Marco.

She felt the tears well a second before he reached

out and caught one on the tip of his finger, his smile gently warming her.

"Tears, *chérie?*"

She sucked in a breath. "It's the hormones."

"Sure. Not tears of happiness?"

She sniffed, blinking furiously. "Maybe." At his look, she laughed, a weird watery sound. "Probably."

"I know." His kiss was tender, soft and everything she could have wanted to mark this moment. "So," he breathed against her lips, "will you marry me?"

"Of course I will," she replied without hesitation. "You're my best friend. My Marco. I love you."

"And I love you. My Kat."

* * * * *

*Don't miss these other stories from
Paula Roe:
THE PREGNANCY PLOT
BED OF LIES
PROMOTED TO WIFE?
THE BILLIONAIRE BABY BOMBSHELL*

All available now!

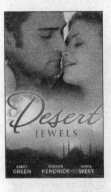
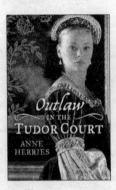

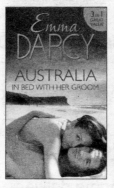

The World of Mills & Boon®

There's a Mills & Boon® series that's perfect for you. We publish ten series and, with new titles every month, you never have to wait long for your favourite to come along.

By Request
Relive the romance with the best of the best
12 stories every month

Cherish™
Experience the ultimate rush of falling in love
12 new stories every month

Desire™
Passionate and dramatic love stories
6 new stories every month

Nocturne™
An exhilarating underworld of dark desires
Up to 3 new stories every month